IS IT SEX? OR IS IT ASSAULT?

Consent is ambiguous when a sexual encounter
between two teenagers, Micah and Penelope, escalates.
Their mothers, Zoe and Amelia, who are neighbors
and best friends, are pitted against each other as they
seek to protect their children from the social and legal
consequences of that night. As the case steamrolls
toward trial, lifelong friendships and family bonds are
tested as everyone struggles to reconcile the past with
their search for the truth.

Early Praise

Dondlinger drops her readers into a palpably, terrifyingly
real world from the first paragraphs. She weaves a
complex pattern of perspectives and assumptions, daring the
reader to assume they've sorted the tangled knot of guilt
and innocence. But there are no simple solutions to the
cat's-cradle web of this he-said-she-said. Unnerving and
provocative to the last, I couldn't put *Gray Lines* down.—
Angela Bier, author of The Accidental Archivist

Absorbing and gripping until the final page, *Gray Lines*
examines the complexities of human relationships – parents,
children, siblings, and best friends – and skillfully explores
the love, the pain and the insecurities of families as well as
the ongoing struggle to ever fully know even those we care
about the most. With beautifully drawn characters, this is
one emotionally satisfying read.—*Alice Benson, author of
Her Life is Showing and A Year in Her Life*

Dondlinger's *Gray Lines* pushes us firmly onto the testiest path and sends us into the shadows where we're not sure who is right and who is wrong. The parents? The boy? The girl? Prepare to find yourself immersed in the push and pull between the characters and situations.—***Kathie Giorgio, author of All Told and If You Tame Me***

His eyelashes tickled her cheeks as he brushed her with kisses. His elbows pressed against the curves of her shoulders, a glove, squeezing her in. Fingers splayed in her wet, tangled hair. Pulling back an inch or so, he took her in. His brown eyes were a polygraph of red. "I love you—" His voice sounded gritty, parched, aching, his breath labored. "—Penelope Mae Swanson."

Before she could process his words—Did he say he loved her???—he fused their bodies together. A hot, searing pain plunged through the depths of her core, as if someone lit a firecracker. It fizzled inside before exploding, sending shock waves down every nerve pathway.

Too late, she understood. She was having sex. SEX! With Micah. In her bed. Right. This. Minute.

She lay paralyzed as he moved above her, a shadow of himself. How did this happen? How did she let this happen? How did they go from kissing and touching to this? So quickly?

How could she stop him?

GRAY LINES

Marisa Rae Dondlinger

Moonshine Cove Publishing, LLC

Abbeville, South Carolina U.S.A.

First Moonshine Cove Edition NOV 2022

ISBN: 9781952439445

Library of Congress LCCN: 2022918927

Copyright 2022 by Marisa Rae Dondlinger

Front cover image provided by the author; cover and interior design by Moonshine Cove staff.

About the Author

Marisa Rae Dondlinger lives in Wisconsin with her husband and two young daughters. A graduate of the University of Wisconsin  Law School, Marisa practiced law for several years before devoting herself to writing fiction. She's also the author of *Scenes From a Bar* and *Open*. When not writing, she enjoys reading, going for walks, margaritas with friends, and watching her daughters play sports.

Acknowledgement

Writing a book is a mental and emotional journey, filled with exhilarating highs and time-to-send-out-my-resume lows. That is where the love, support, and belief of my "team" keep me going. Without those listed below, this book wouldn't be possible.

Thanks to the publishers and editors at Moonshine Cove Publishing. For their enthusiasm about publishing *Gray Lines*, for believing in the strength of my storytelling, and for being receptive during the publishing process.

Kathie Giorgio at AllWriters' Workplace and Workshop, LLC for being my mentor. Your generosity with your time to always answer questions regarding craft, the publishing process, and publicity does not go unnoticed or unappreciated. To my Tuesday night writing group. Thanks for always providing insightful critiques and encouragement.

Kaitlyn Lewis for answering my many questions on juvenile sexual assault and the juvenile justice system. To Kathleen Eull at Pyxis Creative Solutions LCC for her stellar marketing job. Julie Boglisch for designing an amazing, eye-catching cover.

To my parents. Always inspiring me to dream bigger and live brighter.

Lolita and Harlow. My lovely, smart, funny, enigmatic girls. You two are the greatest teachers in my life, always reminding me to slow down, laugh, and enjoy the moment. Watching you two grow is an absolute joy.

Andy. Thanks for always letting me bounce ideas off of you, being my "first reader," my cheerleader when I feel discouraged, and, best of all, knowing exactly when I need a hug.

Marisaraedondlinger.com

Dedication

To Mom, my biggest fan. And Dad, who reads everything I write even though there are no spies, aliens, or superheroes.

GRAY LINES

CHAPTER ONE
PENELOPE

After wrapping a white towel around her body, Penelope opened the bathroom door and shrieked. Someone—an intruder? A ghost?—stood leaning against the wall directly opposite the bathroom. The dark hallway, lit only by the streetlight coming in through a nearby window, tripped her up for a second before the person stepped closer and she realized it was Micah. Her best friend of eleven years. More recently, her first boyfriend. Her secret.

"You scared me!" she said, swatting his shoulder.

He caught her hand, kissing her knuckles. When he touched her, smiled at her, looked at her, the rest of her world shrank. But right now, she felt hyperaware that she wore only a bath towel and they were alone. Mom was working late and her twin brother Ollie was in the basement.

"Did you win?" he asked, referring to the tennis match she played tonight.

"Six-one, six-three." She let go of his hand, tugging down the hem of the towel, which covered her to mid-thigh.

"You gave up four games?" Micah held a hand to his heart, feigning shock. His knees buckled—was that part of the act? He laughed as he reached for the wall to steady himself.

"I lost focus," she said, her anger like a switchblade, cutting through her confusion about Micah waiting for her outside the bathroom, putting her back in the match. Bianca was seventeen to Penelope's fourteen, a top player from Chicago—and Penelope beat her. Outplayed her, really. But serving for the second set at five-two, Penelope was broken, a case of nerves she couldn't afford against a better opponent.

"Busy thinking about me." Micah ran his fingertips from her shoulder to her wrist. She shivered involuntarily, her breath catching. "Admit it. You're crazy 'bout me."

He kissed her, sweet and slow, his tongue gently flicking hers, zapping her taste buds awake, filling her mouth with the taste of lemons.

"You can't be up here," she said between kisses. His kisses drove all common sense from her mind, but the thought of Ollie catching them broke through. Ollie, who had no idea that his best friend and sister had been hanging out without him all summer. Ollie, who was too shy and sensitive to talk to girls, would feel left behind, extra, if he knew the truth. Unlike Micah, who had a new girlfriend every week since sixth grade—until kissing Penelope. "We'll get caught."

Micah's breath was hot against her lips. "There's no one here to catch us."

"Where's Ollie?"

"Don't worry, he's cool," Micah said, planting kisses on her neck.

"Meaning what?" Penelope jerked away and looked up at Micah. It was still an adjustment, looking up. She'd always been taller, but Micah shot up several inches this past year, over six-feet, all wiry muscles. "You promised not to tell him—"

"Chill," Micah said. "Just meant we'd hear him if he came upstairs."

Something else was at play, but, like finding Micah waiting outside the bathroom, Penelope couldn't pinpoint it. That was what being a teenager felt like, infinite feelings with infinite interpretations. No one to tell you which one was right. "I have to get dressed," she said, walking to her bedroom and pushing the door closed behind her.

Micah caught it. She turned around. "Go downstairs. I'll come down when I'm done." She laughed, crossing her arms and blocking his way. Mom had a strict rule—no boys in the bedroom. Then again, Mom had strict rules about everything.

"I wanna congratulate you on the win," he said. He laced his hands around her hips, backing her into the bedroom, inch by inch, a dance of sorts. He kissed her again, deeper this time, massaging his tongue with hers. Blood soared though her limbs, giving her a feeling of weightlessness. Possibility. Bliss. Kissing Micah felt like diving underwater. A forehand scorched down the line. The first bite of chocolate cake. How had she ever lived without it?

Mid-kiss, Micah tripped, sending her stumbling backwards onto the bed. He fell on top of her. They both giggled.

"Damn, girl," he said, lips fluttering against hers. "Don't you ever clean your room?"

"Can't you look where you're walking?"

He kissed her again. His penis, which amazed and terrified and baffled her, pressed hard against her hip. A flutter of panic tightened her chest. Constricted her breath. She tilted her head back, disentangling her lips, needing oxygen. A great, heaping mouthful to clear her thoughts, slow him down.

"We should stop. Ollie might come up," she said, afraid to tell Micah the truth. That she was panicking. Throughout the summer, kissing replaced eating, talking, *being*, but he never saw her naked. She wasn't ready. Instead, they used their hands to explore each other's bodies over their clothes, a mental jigsaw puzzle she put together in bed at night.

"He won't bother us," Micah said.

How could Micah be sure? Before she could ask, Micah pressed up on an elbow, guiding her hand down to his penis, stroking it with her over his gym shorts. This, she could do. Clothes on? Okay. Soon, it would be over. And he'd go back to kissing her. Whispering. Cuddling. The part *she* loved.

He let go of her hand, hovering above her in a modified plank, his breath painting a line between her lips and eyebrows as he thrust. She continued the way he taught her, fast and tight. The smooth texture, the way it grew in her hand, his groans—she felt embarrassed, turned on, afraid, but most of all, powerful. Making him shake and shudder felt like a special talent. Along with painting the lines with her groundstrokes. Making her opponents run corner to corner.

11

Give up. She could make Micah lose himself. Just her. She was his girl. The high fell short of winning a match, but not by much.

"I. Like. That," Micah grunted, but instead of moving with her hand, letting the moment culminate, he reached down, tugging his shorts and boxers beneath his hips. His penis sprang forward, rocking against her thigh, skin on skin, soft and hard. Where once three layers separated them, now there was only one, her towel. A flimsy piece of cloth that jacked higher up her thigh each time he thrust.

"Micah." A plea for him to look at her, realize she didn't want to do this.

"Uh-huh." His eyes stayed closed. His lips were pressed with tension.

He didn't stop.

Tears of frustration sprung to her eyes. Why did he take his clothes off? That wasn't the deal. Was she supposed to like this? Was she a freak for wanting to stop? "Can we..." She didn't finish the sentence. Didn't know how to.

"I got you," he said, between breaths. He arched her hands over her head, running his tongue along her lips. "Just you wait." He moved down her body, his head dipping between her thighs. She sprung backwards, her head smashing against the headboard, the surprise making her want to cry more than the pain. Why was he acting like this? Pushing her? He made varsity football a few weeks ago. Was it the older guys? Giving him ideas? Some sick hazing ritual?

"I don't like that," she said. A nervous pit formed in her stomach the moment she saw Micah waiting outside the bathroom. A pit that now felt like an oil spill—dark, heavy, toxic.

"Relax." He reached up and rested one hand against her cheek. "Have I ever led you wrong?"

Before she could answer—*Yes! Dozens of times. Not on purpose, but still*—he pulled her knees apart, resuming his pursuit. She shut her eyes, bit her lip. Her muscles became rigid, her mouth dry. The certainty that this was wrong, that he shouldn't be here, that they shouldn't be doing this, made leaving her only option.

"I need to pee," she said.

Micah crawled up her body until his face was inches from hers, his lips hovering, a smile playing on the corners. "That's because it feels good. You need to let go. Enjoy it."

Relieved he was finally listening, she said, "I can't."

His eyelashes tickled her cheeks as he brushed her with kisses. His elbows pressed against the curves of her shoulders, a glove, squeezing her in. Fingers splayed in her wet, tangled hair. Pulling back an inch or so, he took her in. His brown eyes were a polygraph of red. "I love you—" His voice sounded gritty, parched, aching, his breath labored. "—Penelope Mae Swanson."

Before she could process his words—Did he say he loved her???— he fused their bodies together. A hot, searing pain plunged through the depths of her core, as if someone lit a firecracker. It fizzled inside before exploding, sending shock waves down every nerve pathway.

Too late, she understood. She was having sex. SEX! With Micah. In her bed. Right. This. Minute.

She lay paralyzed as he moved above her, a shadow of himself. How did this happen? How did she *let* this happen? How did they go from kissing and touching to this? So quickly?

How could she stop him?

Before her mind could solve this riddle, Micah moaned, pressing his face against Penelope's neck. He wasn't looking at her. This summer had been about the two of them, the secret they kept, communicating their feelings through their eyes. *Kiss me. Meet me after everyone's asleep. I miss you.* And now? He wasn't looking at her. He was inside her, but she could be anyone. Nameless. Faceless. Nobody. Nothing.

"That was amazing." He grinned, once again the boy she knew.

"Ye-ah." Her voice broke on the word, elongating both syllables. Tears spilled from her eyes and she hated herself. Hated that she let this happen. High school started in three days. If this got out, her life would be ruined. She was a tennis prodigy. A future champion. Not the school slut. That was *not* her story.

"Overwhelming, I know." He pulled out of her, a knife drawn from a wound. No longer fused together, pain started in her center and radiated outwards, evicting all thoughts of school from her mind. "You bled some. Think that's normal though."

She turned on her side, letting the pillow catch her tears, breathing in and out, wondering if she was screaming. Or whether the high-pitched keening was inside her head.

Micah lay down next to her, wrapping his arm around her waist. "Being close with you felt perfect."

She couldn't feel his touch. She looked at her hands, spreading her fingers, noting there were ten, but she couldn't feel the softness of her sheets. The warmth of his body. The air in her lungs. What was happening to her?

"Me too," she said, trying, desperately, to act normal.

"You're my perfect world. My perfect girl." His words sounded like low-grade static. A few minutes later, he added, "I wish I didn't have to leave, but I'll be thinking about you. About tonight..."

After he left, she didn't move. She couldn't. Instead, she dove into the pit of nothingness inside her, letting it seal away the pain.

CHAPTER TWO
AMELIA

Amelia clicked the key fob for her Nissan Murano, opening the trunk to load her twelve-gallon storage crate filled with pens, laundry sticks, chargers, and mini sewing kits that she brought to every event she worked, regardless of how fancy or casual. Then she sat on the bumper, exchanging her three-inch heels for a pair of flip-flops, before walking around and lowering herself into the driver's seat with a heavy sigh. The Driscoll's engagement party was a success, but she felt her fifteen-hour day in every muscle, particularly the nerve in her neck that flared up when wearing heels.

As the sole owner of Elevated, an event planning company, Amelia worked long days. Summer was her busiest season, filled with weddings, family reunions, and birthday parties. June, July, and August made up for January, February, and March when everyone hibernated in a post-holiday stupor. Amelia consoled herself that after the McCallister-Bishop wedding tomorrow, she would have the long Labor Day weekend, two days, to recover. Recharge her batteries. Spend time with her twins, Penelope and Ollie, before they started high school on Tuesday.

She checked her phone, reading a text from her own twin brother, Austin, updating her on Penelope's match. Another win, though Austin warned her Penelope was upset after blowing her first two match points. Moments like this, Amelia felt deep gratitude for her brother. He knew how to reach Penelope, talk her down from a tirade. As a former tour pro, Austin knew what it took to make it, and Penelope hung on his every word. Unlike anything Amelia said.

No text from Ollie or Penelope. A bit unusual. But, apparently, Penelope was angry. And Ollie and Micah were just hanging at the house tonight. So, maybe not. Besides, they're fourteen now, she reminded herself. She needed to give them some independence.

Amelia started the car and weaved her way out of the fancy sub-division, the vintage carriage house lampposts at the end of each driveway guiding her way. Once she hit the main road, she called Zoe, Micah's mother and her best friend. Both single moms, they ran a tag-team on the kids, ensuring nothing seeped through the cracks.

"Tell me you're coming over with a bottle of wine," Zoe answered.

"I wish." Amelia kept her hands at ten and two, conditioned to model good driving behavior for the twins, who, scarily enough, would be driving in a couple years. "I have to be up for work in eight hours, and surprisingly, it's bad form to show up drunk."

"It's also bad form to drink alone and that's not stopping me."

Amelia laughed, feeling the stress loosen in her neck just from hearing Zoe's voice. She met Zoe eleven years ago, when she moved in across the street and their kids entered preschool together. It was a time when Amelia's late husband, Derek, worked from sun up to sun down. Zoe answered Amelia's calls. Was available for playdates. Or to split a bottle of wine. Amelia felt like a kid again, having her best friend within walking distance. But it wasn't until Derek died six years ago that Zoe became irreplaceable. Austin too. In *Grey's Anatomy* terms, they were "her people."

"I'll join you for a drink on Sunday." Amelia, Austin, Zoe, and the kids had a standing Sunday date. TV, food, games; always fun. "Maybe even two."

"You're wild," Zoe said.

"Cut me off if I start dancing on the kitchen island."

"Now that could get interesting."

"Ha-ha. Listen, I'm home," Amelia said, relieved to be pulling onto her street, that much closer to bed. Less swanky than the Driscoll's neighborhood, hers boasted tree-lined streets, actual sidewalks, and neighbors that shared baked goods. Derek thought of

16

it as their "starter home," but Amelia loved the charm. The reading nook beneath the stairs, the archways separating the rooms, the farmer's porch. And with Derek gone, she'd never sell. Derek lived in each room, his spirit in each fixture. "I'll check on the kids, tell Micah you say hi."

Silence. "Micah's here. He said Ollie wasn't feeling well so he came home."

She pulled into her garage. "Weird. I didn't get a text."

"I'm sure it's nothing," Zoe said quickly.

Zoe knew Amelia worried. And how could she not? After Derek collapsed during a steamy summer run, dying from an undiagnosed hypertrophic obstructive cardiomyopathy, and her mom succumbed to breast cancer three years ago, she didn't take risks when it came to health. "All right," Amelia said. "Talk tomorrow."

The house was unusually quiet when Amelia stepped inside. She set down her bag, charged her phone, and loaded the dishes the boys were kind enough to leave in the sink. Then she ventured downstairs.

Ollie was sprawled on the sofa, arms and legs askew. Amelia smiled as she took in the rhythmic inhale and exhale of Ollie's narrow chest, the legs growing longer each day, the peach-fuzz on his cheeks—not quite boy, not yet man. Ollie was easy to love. From the warm blue eyes, to the crooked, bashful smile, to his kindness first approach to life. A gift.

Penelope, on the other hand, came out screaming, her temperament intensifying with age. While Amelia admired her drive, ambition, and work ethic, Penelope was exhausting in her demand for perfection. Always needing to hit one more shot, hire a trainer, physio, nutritionist...anything to be the best. With Penelope, the demands never stopped, especially on herself.

Amelia crouched down next to Ollie, gently rubbing his shoulder. "How do you feel, sweetie?"

He groaned in response, grabbing his stomach.

"Did you eat something bad?" she asked. "Have you tried going to the bathroom?"

He sat up, rubbing his face with both hands. "Mom, stop."

Amelia put her hand against his forehead. It was sweaty. "Come on." She flicked off the TV. "Let's get you in bed."

He stood up and teetered backwards, catching himself on the arm of the couch. "I'm fine," he muttered.

They walked upstairs, Ollie first, so Amelia could catch him if he felt dizzy again. Two flights of stairs later, he collapsed on the bed, his head tucked between two pillows. "Do you need anything?" she asked. "Water? A bucket? Tylenol?"

"No."

She watched him, but he didn't move. His breath was steady. Maybe he did eat something weird. Or perhaps nerves about starting high school? He was sensitive.

Resigned, she closed his bedroom door and walked across the hall to Penelope's room, knocking lightly before pushing the door open. Penelope lay on her bed, a towel covering the lower half of her body. Her breasts, tiny buds really, were on display, nipples erect and pointed at the ceiling. Instinct made Amelia turn away, a rote response from a thousand cries for "privacy" ever since Penelope started puberty last year. But then Amelia noticed that her beautiful blue eyes were open, staring blankly at the ceiling.

Breath locked inside her throat, Amelia ran toward her, fearing Penelope might be dead. That's how still, lifeless, desolate, her body appeared.

"Penelope!" Amelia sat on the edge of the bed, grabbing Penelope's cold wrist, feeling for a pulse. She counted the beats, repeating Penelope's name. Penelope's heartrate was in the low fifties, a number which brought to mind her latest doctor's appointment. *The nurse said I had the heartrate of an elite athlete,* Penelope bragged to an indifferent Ollie.

"Penelope!" Amelia gripped the sides of Penelope's head. Penelope blinked, slowly. *Finally.* "What's wrong, P? Talk to me!"

18

Penelope shivered, an uncontrollable shaking that started in her shoulders and spread throughout her body until her teeth were chattering.

"Clothes," Amelia said to herself, grabbing Penelope's favorite Orange Bowl sweatshirt from the dresser, as well as some underwear and flannel pajama pants. "Sit up, babe." Amelia tugged Penelope until she was upright, her body trembling, eyes unfocused, as Amelia pulled the sweatshirt over her head.

The towel was damp, wrapped haphazardly around Penelope's lower body. Amelia unfolded each end, taking care to avert her eyes, but got caught on a flash of red. Blood. On the towel. And near her vulva, giving the hair an almost glossy finish. She had her period. Amelia turned away, knowing Penelope would be embarrassed whenever she snapped out of this fugue state, but the smell of salt and seaweed invaded her nostrils. Amelia looked back, seeing now that the shiny substance wasn't just blood but—

Amelia recoiled, falling backwards, as the knowledge bulldozed her.

"Did you—" Amelia couldn't think the words, let alone say them to her fourteen-year old daughter. Her daughter that, as far as she knew, never kissed a boy.

Amelia pulled Penelope's pants up, feeling terrified. Confused. Unsure what to say or do next. But whatever happened tonight, Penelope needed to know Amelia was there for her. She sat next to Penelope and held her close. "You can talk to me. Always."

Maybe it was the infusion of warmth, the comfort of being held, the reassurance that Amelia would listen. Because Penelope said something. Too soft for Amelia to hear.

"Micah," Penelope repeated, crawling toward her pillow and lying back down. She pulled her legs to her chest.

Amelia lay next to Penelope, stroking her long, damp hair. Tears leaked from the creases of Penelope's closed eyes. "What about Micah?"

19

"After my shower, He—he—he kissed me....and then he followed me..." Amelia felt the tension in Penelope's hip as she squeezed her thighs together. A shuddering moan escaped her lips. And in that one small gesture, Amelia's suspicion was confirmed. The kids had sex.

Micah. Whom Amelia loved. Adored. From the slick-talking, rambunctious three-year old to the magnanimous fourteen-year old with big plans and an even bigger smile. They shared family vacations, celebrated holidays, birthdays. Amelia loved him as her own.

Until now. Because if Penelope was saying what Amelia feared, Amelia would excise him from her heart with a scalpel and use it to destroy him.

"Did you want to have sex?" Amelia kept her voice soft, soothing, even as the question felt like a grenade exploding inside her soul.

Penelope squeezed her eyes tighter and shook her head. Small, but perceptible.

"Are you hurt?" Amelia asked, wondering whether she should take Penelope to the hospital. Get her checked out. The blood. The sperm. A possible pregnancy?

"I don't know," Penelope said.

"Where does it hurt?"

Penelope let out the slightest breath. "Everywhere."

Everywhere. That sounded more emotional than physical, but Amelia wasn't a doctor. She needed help. Zoe, who she always turned to in times of crisis, was no longer an option. The thought chilled Amelia. A gulf of loneliness she quickly skirted. Now was not the time.

Amelia held Penelope, humming "Lullaby, (Goodnight my Angel)," as she had every bedtime until Penelope turned six. Meanwhile, her mind continued the game of twenty questions. Why would Micah do this? What set him off? And should Amelia take Penelope to the hospital? Get a rape kit? Should she call the police? Traumatize Penelope further by allowing a stranger to question her, look for inconsistences, reasons to justify Micah's behavior? Because women were never believed. Teenage girls less so.

When Penelope fell asleep, Amelia tucked a blanket around her shoulders, turned off the light, and slipped out of the room. Closing the door behind her, she slumped against the wall and slipped to the floor, allowing herself to wallow for a brief moment in the fear. The devastation. The knowledge that Penelope's life would never be the same.

On shaky legs, she stood. Walked down the stairs. Tugged her phone from the charger and called Austin. As twins, Amelia and Austin had been to hell and back. Nothing and no one would ever drive them apart. If she called, he would come. Her only hope? That she caught him *before* he left the bar with tonight's lucky lady.

CHAPTER THREE
MICAH

Micah lay in his bed, heels resting against the ledge of the window, the warm late summer breeze drifting over his body. His eyes were closed, but he was nowhere near sleep. He felt alive. Jacked. Giggly—though he'd never admit that out loud. His body buzzed with a hum of pleasure. Was it losing his virginity? Being in love? The vodka he drank? Whatever the reason, he wanted this feeling to last forever.

It still amazed him that bossy, driven Penelope, with her swinging ponytails and Nike gear, could drive him wild. It switched in an instant. For eleven years, Penelope, Ollie, and Micah were inseparable. As twins, they could've made him feel extra, but it was the opposite. He was the glue, the bridge, the secret sauce. He made Ollie adventurous, encouraged Penelope to slow down. They gave him a home. Around Penelope and Ollie, he never had to pretend.

But this summer, three dwindled to two. For him, everything orbited around Penelope. It started with a game of hide-and-seek at the block party in June. Running through the O'Leary's dark yard, he heard his name. He slowed, looking around. Penelope parted the plastic windows of the kid playhouse and poked her head through, telling him to hide with her. He crawled inside and sat next to her, the grass cool against his butt, and BAM! Like a sixteen-wheeler flattening a squirrel, ending everything that animal ever knew, his past with Penelope was gone. The blinders were off.

He saw Penelope. *Saw. Her.* Wisps of reddish-blond hair escaped from her ponytail, framing her face, setting off her blue eyes. Puckered cherry lips. Nipples poking through her tank-top. Long, toned, smooth legs, that she stroked lightly with her fingertips. She smelled of apples, fresh and sweet, and he longed to taste her.

22

He played it cool, assuming he was undergoing this metamorphosis alone. But when the game ended, she said, *Let's stay here.* Relief penetrated deep, paralyzing him with terror. The terror that one day, he might not have her, that some other guy might grab her attention.

Two months of Penelope—kissing, touching, talking—culminating in tonight. When Penelope stepped out of the bathroom, she looked like a Greek goddess, white towel draped around her fine body. Her hair was wet and mussed. Drips of water ran down her face, catching on her bottom lip. He stood entranced, one-hundred- and fifty pounds pulsating with desire.

The vodka he and Ollie found stashed in the freezer made the room spin, warmed him from the inside, a smile lighting up the outside. Somehow, Penelope stayed his center, his focus. Touching the silky smoothness of her skin, feeding the hunger of her kisses, feeling her hands wrapped around his dick, running his tongue between her legs—his brain took a siesta and emotion took over. Their bodies vibrated with need, aching to be closer, one. Their eyes met, each posing a question, and they answered it. Love.

They were in love! Period. Were they young? Sure. But how do you put an age cap on love? Real love. Timeless love. They were like Romeo and Juliet—without all the family baggage.

He held her afterwards, naked, both too overwhelmed to say much. Never before had he felt so relaxed. He wished he could have slept there, but a bomb ticked away in the corner, counting the seconds until Ollie woke up or her mom got home.

P trippin' over keeping them a secret was the one hitch to their relationship. Micah didn't understand. Maybe Ollie would feel left out for a good minute, but he'd come around. And their moms? Come on. Ms. Swanson wouldn't care unless it interfered with P's tennis or school. And Ma? She'd tease him against sweating some girl, but she'd be smiling, because the girl was Penelope. And she loved Penelope.

Missing Penelope something fierce, Micah grabbed his phone and opened Snapchat. Normally, he'd feel stupid, gushin' his feelings, but, tonight, he wasn't worried. She said being close to him felt perfect. She loved him too.

He blew a kiss. *Dreaming of you, pretty girl.*

After sending the message, he fell asleep, smiling. Life didn't get better than this.

CHAPTER FOUR
AMELIA

Amelia sat in darkness on her front porch, waiting for Austin to arrive. She didn't trust her legs to stand, walk, pace. She felt shaky, unbalanced, keenly aware of the pull of gravity, drawing her toward the ground, wanting her to collapse in a fit of hysteria.

Instead, she sat broomstick straight, jaw locked tight, fingers stabbing her phone as she texted her sole associate, Whitney. Amelia told her truthfully, yet vaguely, that she had a family emergency, needing her to cover the McCallister-Bishop wedding tomorrow. It was less than eight-hour notice, but Amelia had little choice. She couldn't leave Penelope.

YES!!! Whitney texted back immediately. One problem solved.

Amelia began emailing the pertinent documents. When she finished, she scanned the street, finding nothing. The moon cast shadows on the neighboring houses, making them look sinister and uninviting. Haunted houses. Silent witnesses to this nightmare. The silence, once a draw of this neighborhood, punished Amelia, putting the questions inside her head on a megaphone. One question after another. Relentless.

Finally, she heard the soft rumble of a motor. Looked up and saw headlights. The fist in her stomach relaxed a degree. When she called Austin, he was out at a bar. No surprise there. He answered with a laugh in his voice, his smile beaming across the satellites, warming her ear—a subtle sign he had a woman on the wire. *I need you*, she said. It was a testament to brotherly love that he came—twenty agonizing minutes later.

He slammed his car door and jogged toward the stairs. "What? What is it?" he asked, taking the steps by two. "You look..." He ran a hand over his dark stubble. "Terrified."

Amelia burst into tears, covering her face with her hands. Her shoulders shook with the pressure of each sob, as waves of relief pummeled her body. Relief that someone else was here. Someone who loved Penelope. That would share Amelia's horror.

Austin sat next to Amelia. "It's okay." He rubbed her back with his knuckles, his touch reminding her that the worst hadn't happened. No one died tonight. "Whatever it is, we'll fix it."

Amelia took a deep breath, holding her hands out in front of her, as if she could hold the news at bay. Erase the last hour. Before tonight, she'd have said life was pretty good. Penelope's tennis game was improving at an explosive rate, making her dream of going professional tangible. Ollie finally found his niche performing on the stage. Work was insanely busy, but lucrative. "Penelope said Micah came into her room tonight, after she got out of the shower, and forced her to have sex."

"What?" Austin barked a laugh, hand stilling on her back. "Micah? Forced Penelope?"

She cut him with her eyes. Austin was easygoing, rarely serious outside the tennis court. But sometimes, his chill vibe made him an insensitive prick. Like right now.

"They're practically brother and sister," Austin said, the vein in his forehead swelling.

Amelia tugged her jersey dress, which clung to her skin with sweat. Confusion, pain, anger, leaking from her pores. "But they're not. That's a fiction we've been living under. You've seen the way Penelope's changed. The breasts. The hips. She's filling out."

He looked down, running both hands through his shaggy, curly hair, unwilling to comment on the burgeoning womanhood of his niece. "I can't believe Micah would do this. There has to be an explanation—"

"Like what?" Amelia reeled on him. "He happened to walk into her room when she was naked? Happened to pull his dick out? Fall into her? Become blind and deaf?"

"I don't know! But that's my point. Neither of us does." Crickets chirped, wanting to get in their two cents. "You must have questions."

"Of course!" Amelia said. "But I believe Penelope." This argument reminded Amelia of the Kavanaugh hearings. Austin considered the accuser's confusion, forgetfulness, omitting details as evidence she was lying, while Amelia understood that no woman would expose themselves to such ridicule unless telling the truth. But this wasn't theoretical anymore. This was her daughter. His niece.

"I believe her," Austin said, A patch of curly brown hair fell into his eyes. "Don't ever doubt that..."

"But...?"

He softened his voice. "I want to believe in Micah, too. It feels wrong to turn on him so...abruptly."

Amelia had no room for Micah. Somewhere down the line, perhaps. But right now, Penelope filled her heart and brain to capacity. "Should I wake her? Take her to the hospital? Or wait until morning? I mean, if she's sleeping, she can't be hurt that bad, right?" Amelia felt herself spiraling, questions coming machine-gun style, leaving her mouth before she processed the thought. "But why risk it, right? And what about the morning-after pill? I assume it works the morning after, hence the name, but it's probably more effective right away. We should go." Amelia nodded. Penelope couldn't have a baby. *She still was a baby! My baby!* "Right now. I never should've waited for you."

"Slow down." Austin mimed taking a deep breath. "Why do you think she's hurt?"

"There was blood—"

"She's bleeding?" he yelled, a fight appearing in his eyes that reflected hers.

"Yes. And there's sperm between her legs." She heard the hiss of his breath as he ingested that fact. "Obviously, he didn't use a condom."

"Idiot. *Idiot*," he muttered. "Go. We can't risk this. Besides..." He glanced at his phone. "It's eleven. You'll probably get in right away."

"Ollie's sleeping." She walked briskly inside the house. Armed with a plan, she wanted to leave. "He's not feeling well." Questions nagged her—Where was Ollie when this happened? Did he hear anything? If so, why wouldn't he say anything when she got home?—but she didn't have time to delve deeper. "If he wakes up, maybe see if he knows anything?"

Austin lifted his hand halfway, in a bid to salute her, as he always did when Amelia got bossy. But he thought better of it, letting his hand fall limply to his side. She paused at the bottom of the stairs. "And Austin? Thanks for coming."

"It's going to be okay," he said, infusing confidence into his words. "I promise."

"I don't know how." Her voice broke on the word *know*. Because Austin was right, there was so much they didn't know. Never had she felt so powerless, unprepared, incapable, as a mother. How could she help Penelope, protect her, when she didn't understand what happened?

But there was no time to dwell. She needed to get Penelope to the hospital. Then, she would figure out what to do next.

CHAPTER FIVE
PENELOPE

Penelope lay in bed with her eyes closed, painting the walls black in her mind. She imagined holding the brush, dripping with thick, oily paint, watching as it ran down her arms, stained her clothes, the floor. Watching as it darkened the pristine white walls. Wall after wall after wall. Endless black. If she concentrated on the blackness, the nothingness, perhaps her mind would erase the memory of tonight.

But flashes, like a movie trailer, kept playing. Micah waiting outside the bathroom, his face buried between her legs, the searing pain when he pushed inside her.

A knock at the door startled her. Mom came in and sat on the edge of her bed, flicking on her bedside lamp. Their eyes met and Penelope looked away, unable to stomach the pity.

"We need to go to the hospital," Mom said. "You're bleeding and I, I want to make sure you're okay."

Bleeding. Down there. Penelope pressed her fingers against her eyes, a second shield. Black paint. Black walls. Nothing.

"I know you're scared." Mom leaned over, wrapping her arms around Penelope, whispering in her ear. "But I'll be there with you."

Too soon, Mom let go. Reluctantly, Penelope followed her down the stairs and into the car, feeling neither the footfall of her steps or the air leave her lungs. On the way to the hospital, Penelope studied her Nike slides. She remembered getting them at the beginning of summer, ecstatic that they came in neon pink—her favorite color. She wished she could go back. Do everything different. Not invite Micah to hide with her. Not give into her crazy, complicated feelings.

Once they arrived, Mom checked them in while Penelope sat in the waiting room. She pulled the hoodie over her head, tugging the

29

tassels tight. Only her nose poked through. Blackness. Penelope didn't want to know what Mom was saying, how she would explain what happened. How would Penelope explain tonight? To Ollie? Their friends? They'd find out. And then what? They'd think she was a slut. Judge her.

Unless, unless...what if Penelope pretended like nothing happened? Told Micah to stay quiet. He'd keep the secret, right? He kept their dating a secret.

In tennis, Uncle Austin taught her to focus on each point, regardless of the score line. Leave her mistakes behind. Gone. Done. Finished. She tried to summon that mindset now. Tonight was a mistake. She *would* forget it. No one would ever find out—

"Sweetie, they're ready," Mom said, squatting in front of Penelope, resting her hands on Penelope's knees. Penelope followed Mom and a nurse through two sets of doors and into a private room.

The nurse gestured toward the exam table. "Take a seat. I'll grab some vitals."

She took Penelope's blood pressure, temperature, asked her to rate her pain.

"Five," Penelope guessed. Through tennis, she learned to read her body. Nagging, niggling pain? Forget about it. Burning pain? Play through it. Sharp? Stop immediately. But the pain she felt right now was different. It was all-encompassing and yet indiscernible. Her heart hurt. With every beat, it blasted a relentless ache to every muscle, tendon, bone.

"Dr. Bilson will be in soon," the nurse said before leaving.

Penelope lay back on the table, staring at the ceiling, the florescent lights piercing her eyes. Everything cut a little too close. Mom sat in the seat perpendicular to her, tapping her toes. Click-click-click. Without looking, Penelope knew Mom was playing a game of ping-pong with the clock and the door, impatient to know what was wrong with Penelope. Impatient to fix her.

But what if she couldn't be fixed? What if she never felt normal again?

Black paint. Black walls. Nothing.

"What's that, honey?" Mom asked.

Without realizing it, Penelope was talking out loud. She did this during matches, reminding herself to move her feet or swing through the ball. Before she could respond, the door opened.

"Hello, I'm Dr. Bilson." Penelope sat up, relieved to see a woman. The doctor was pale with red hair pulled back in a ponytail. "Let's talk first and then I'll do a physical exam." She gave Penelope a sad smile. "Can you tell me what happened tonight?"

Being put on the spot made Penelope feel guilty. Like she was ill-prepared for a pop quiz.

"She had tennis tonight," Mom said, rescuing Penelope. "Her brother Ollie and their friend Micah were home..."

Penelope stopped listening, thinking about Ollie. She needed him something fierce. Ollie made her a stronger, braver, *better* version of herself. If he was here, she'd have the courage to talk—

Or maybe not. Because then he'd find out that she lied. Would he still be on her side, support her, if he knew the truth about her and Micah?

"I'd really like to hear from Penelope," Dr. Bilson said.

An audience of two sat patiently, ready to listen, but to Penelope, it felt like thousands. She often dreamed about thousands of eyes on her, but in the dream, she was playing center court at Wimbledon. Not sitting in a hospital room.

"Tell her what you told me," Mom encouraged.

What did I tell you? Penelope couldn't remember.

She closed her eyes and dug her nails into the plastic matting of the exam table. She had to find a way to go deeper, succumb to the darkness, while talking. They were just words. They had nothing to do with her. "I came home after my tennis match and took a shower. When I got out, Micah was waiting in the hall. We talked and then I went into my room to change."

She opened her eyes and glanced at Mom. Her stomach coiled into a tight knot, wondering how she would avoid talking about this summer. Mom would wonder why Micah kissed her tonight. Came into her room. Her only option? Doubling down on the lies.

"Would you like to talk privately?" Dr. Bilson asked. "Without your mom?"

Mom sat up, eyes, like the Grinch's heart, growing three sizes. "No!" Penelope felt the same fear pulse through her. "No," Penelope repeated. "I want her to stay." Much as she hated lying to Mom, the thought of being away from her was unbearable.

"Micah came in and he kissed me. I told him to leave, but he..." Penelope trailed off, afraid that if she admitted she liked kissing him, that they messed around before, the doctor would never believe her about what happened next. She'd probably think Penelope encouraged him, that she brought him to the point of no return when she touched his penis. That was a thing, right? And he tried to do stuff to her, to make her feel good. Stuff she didn't want. But he wouldn't have done that if he just wanted to have sex, right? He cared about her. But then why didn't he listen when she said she didn't like it?

"Take your time," Dr. Bilson encouraged. "You're safe here. No one can hurt you."

Dr. Bilson didn't realize that the mere act of remembering hurt. "We were on the bed and he—" Heat rose to her cheeks. The knot in her stomach cinched several inches tighter. She feared that a stream of bile would emerge from her mouth *Exorcist*-style. "He did some stuff—I didn't like it—he didn't listen—"

Black paint. Black walls. Nothing.

"I can't." She hung her head as tears streamed down her face. She was a wreck. A hot mess. A disaster.

But she wasn't alone. Mom rushed over, enveloping Penelope in her arms. Penelope could never tell Mom the truth, risk losing this, risk disappointing her.

CHAPTER SIX
AMELIA

After Penelope's physical exam, Amelia stepped into the hallway with Dr. Bilson. Amelia declined having a rape kit done on Penelope's behalf. They already knew the culprit, but more so, once Dr. Bilson told her what was involved—a two-to-four-hour exam, where she would comb through Penelope's pubic hair, swab her genitalia, both internally and externally, photograph the injuries—Amelia refused to put Penelope through that. While no longer catatonic, answering questions had her sputtering erratically, succumbing to crying jags.

"She has some fissures, cuts, in her vagina," Dr. Bilson said in a hushed voice. The hallway was empty, but Amelia appreciated her discretion. "Which explains some of the blood. The rest was probably from her hymen tearing. I'm going to prescribe some antibiotics to prevent an infection. The fissures should heal on their own within a week, but if they open back up, she has unusual discharge, or is in excessive pain, bring her back in."

"The cuts." Amelia hesitated. "Did that happen because he forced his way in?"

"I can't say for certain, although vaginal fissures are one sign of sexual assault. The vaginal tissue is thin and sensitive, and if there's no lubrication, there's a chance of tearing. For some women, this can happen during consensual sex." Dr. Bilson rested her hand on Amelia's arm. "Penelope told you she didn't consent and I believe her. Her demeanor aligns with most victims I treat. And while physically, she will heal, the more important healing has to take place emotionally." Dr. Bilson handed her a list of websites and therapists, pointing at the third name down. "Suzanne's excellent. She's worked with many survivors."

Survivor. Amelia used many adjectives to describe Penelope, but never that one. "And the morning after pill, it will take care of any chance of pregnancy?"

"No method of contraception is one-hundred percent, but we're talking about a matter of hours, which is as effective as you can get. You do need to watch her, though. The pill makes some people nauseous, and she's already traumatized. If she gets sick, vomiting or diarrhea, within three hours of taking the pill, she needs to have another dose."

"Percentage-wise," Amelia pressed. "How effective?"

"Ninety-eight to ninety-nine percent effective." A nurse pushing a cart walked down the hallway and Dr. Bilson waited for her to pass. "Don't go looking for worries, okay?"

Amelia thanked her, eager to get Penelope home, hold her while she slept. It wasn't much, not nearly enough, but it was the only place she knew to start.

"One more thing," Dr. Bilson said as Amelia turned away. "Because she's a minor, and says the sex was nonconsensual, I'm obligated to report it to the police."

Mostly, it was a relief. It took the decision out of Amelia's hands. The police would decide whether to pursue Micah. She could focus on healing Penelope. But there was no way Penelope was up to talking to the police tonight.

"Can you wait until morning to report it?" Amelia asked. "She's not strong enough to answer their questions right now. It might retraumatize her, make her feel like *she* did something wrong."

"I'll request they wait until morning. I'm sorry, I wish I could do more. This situation is unfortunately all too common."

Dr. Bilson left Amelia alone in the hallway, wondering how they would get through this. The "they" being collective. Because Penelope wasn't the only one who would suffer. Micah's actions created a tidal wave, sweeping everyone along. Ollie would lose his best friend. In many ways, his only friend other than Penelope.

And Zoe? Amelia pressed her hand against the wall, needing stability. How would Zoe react when she found out what Micah did? Zoe wasn't much a disciplinarian; more of a free-range, meet adversity with love and kindness. Her hands-off approach drove Amelia nuts at times, but Amelia never doubted her love and commitment to Micah. Any of the kids. Surely, Zoe would react appropriately? But what was the appropriate response? An apology from Micah wouldn't cut it.

She and Zoe would grow apart. What choice did they have? Amelia doubted she would ever forgive Micah, and Zoe, as his mother, would have to find a path to forgiveness.

Stop, she thought, squaring her shoulders and stepping back inside the exam room. Seeing Penelope curled up in a ball, hugging her knees to her chest, all but sucking her thumb, steeled Amelia's nerve. Penelope wouldn't just survive, she would thrive. This would not be the defining moment in her life.

CHAPTER SEVEN
ZOE

Zoe lay in bed, scrolling through Pinterest, checking out bathroom remodels, the next project she wanted to tackle in her never-ending list to make her three-bedroom, one-and-a-half bath craftsman her dream house. When the doorbell rang, she thought it was a prank. A game of ding-dong-ditch. Nearly midnight; way too late for visitors.

Then, the doorbell rang three times in succession. She swung her legs off the bed and pulled on a lightweight sweatshirt. She padded down the stairs—steel cables, bamboo treads, which thrilled her during each trip—peeking through the window above the front door.

Austin.

She jumped back, her heart and mind accelerating. What was he doing here? Could it be possible...? Zoe's attraction toward Austin ebbed and flowed over the years. Six years to be exact since he quit the tennis tour to move home and help Amelia with the kids. But she was the only one counting. Some days, she needed a fidget toy to keep her hands and mind occupied around him. Others, the proximity to him felt like a low-grade stomach-ache, wanting what she couldn't have. Even if Austin was interested, a premise without evidence, Zoe couldn't risk losing her friendship with Amelia, the makeshift family they made for the kids. The only family Micah knew.

With a sweaty hand, she opened the door and smiled.

"I need to talk to Micah," Austin said.

These were not the words or tone Zoe imagined Austin using in her middle-of-the-night fantasies. "He's sleeping. What's going on?"

Austin ran both hands through his hair. He had great hair—curly, thick, shiny—the shade of rich chocolate fudge. She should know.

She cut it every six weeks, relishing their rare one-on-one time together.

"I'm sorry...I know it's late," he said, stepping inside. "But it's important."

"You're freaking me out." Zoe pressed her hands against Austin's muscled chest to stop him from going any further. The undercurrent of sexual tension was a live wire, but worry cut through any excitement. "Are the kids okay? Amelia?"

"Can you get Micah?" He rested his hands on hers, burning her skin. "Please. Then we'll talk."

Zoe jogged up the stairs, springing between each step with a youthfulness her thirty-five years was unaccustomed to. It was nerves. Being alone with Austin always put her on edge. And he was upset. Clearly. His warm, easygoing manner, one that rarely slipped to darkness, was gone now.

She knocked on Micah's door. Hearing nothing, she walked inside, smelling sweat, sleep, and high-octane hormones native to teenage boys. Micah lay on his back, snoring softly. She hated to wake him. What could Austin want? Austin and Micah always got on. Check that, Micah got along with everyone. Happy from the moment he arrived on earth. She was lucky. Twenty-one, pregnant, Duante long gone—a colicky baby would've been a disaster. Micah, his sparkle, *made* her life instead of complicating it. *Duante missed out*, she thought for the millionth time. But his loss was her gain.

"Wake up," she said, gently shaking Micah. "Austin's here. He needs to talk to you."

Micah rubbed his eyes. "Headache," he mumbled.

"Grab some ibuprofen and come down." She left him to get dressed and walked back downstairs. As Zoe stepped off the bottom step, she saw Austin standing at the kitchen sink through the open living-dining-kitchen space. His back was to her, arms crossed, staring into her backyard.

"What's going on?" she asked when she reached him, close enough to get a whiff of his woodsy cologne. "You look stressed."

"It's been a horrible night—" He shook his head, cutting himself off. "How was Micah when he got home? Did he say anything?"

Zoe thought back. "Not really. Just that Ollie got sick. Wait. Is Ollie okay?"

"Ollie's fine—"

Micah walked into the kitchen wearing a too-small T-shirt and a pair of joggers. His eyes were bleary, a tad bloodshot, as he gave a half-awake "what up" nod to Austin. Then he opened the fridge, grabbed the milk and drank directly from the container, his Adam's apple bobbing with each swallow.

"Okay." Zoe clapped her hands. "What's going on, Austin?"

Austin cleared his throat. "Micah, what happened tonight between you and Penelope?"

Micah stopped drinking, rivulets of milk dribbling down his chin. He missed the shelf on his first try as he put the carton away. "What're you talking about?"

Zoe wanted to give Micah the benefit of the doubt, but she saw how the question worked as an alarm clock, waking up his brain, scrambling to find an appropriate response.

"Penelope says you came into her room tonight, after she took a shower," Austin said.

Micah wiped his mouth with the back of his hand. "We talked. No biggie."

Zoe ran a hand over her face, stifling a sigh. That's what this was about? Amelia and her many, many rules. One of them being, no boys allowed in Penelope's bedroom—even Micah. She loved Amelia, but she needed to lighten up.

"Micah shouldn't have been in her room," Zoe said. "He knows the rules." She shot Micah a look as he carried a box of Captain Crunch to the peninsula. Micah rolled his eyes. They joked about Amelia's rules, but she always stressed, Amelia's house, Amelia's rules. Respect. "But is it worth a middle of the night conversation?"

"She says they did more than talk," Austin said. "So, I came here, man-to-man, to hear your side of the story." He walked to the peninsula and rested his elbows on the counter, interweaving his hands. His voice was soft, friendly, reasonable. His "coaching" voice. "Because you're family. Because I trust you. So, come on, man, this is your chance. Tell the truth."

All this talk about truth had her mom radar firing. She positioned herself between them at the end of the peninsula. "What am I missing?"

"That's what I'm trying to find out," Austin said.

Micah shoved some cereal in his mouth. "We-messed-around-a-bit," he mumbled while chewing, condensing the sentence into a single word.

Zoe released the sigh she'd been suppressing. Okay, they messed around. Got curious. They were fourteen! Not a shock. Not for Zoe, anyway. She'd been talking to Micah about sex, love, race, religion, since he started asking questions at four. Even now, no topic was off-limits. But Amelia would definitely get worked up about it.

"A bit?" Austin's tone was as impenetrable as cement. "She says you forced her to have sex."

Zoe gasped, each cell of her body filling with cold dread. Sex. Fine. Fourteen was young but not unheard of. But forcing Penelope? How could Amelia think this of Micah?

"Wh-what?" Micah's brown eyes widened and his mouth hung open, exposing golden mush. "Uh-uh. No way. I didn't. I mean, we had sex. Yes. Okay. But we're...in love."

"Stop," Zoe said, holding up her hands. Time both slowed and sped up. Micah was having sex. With Penelope. They were in love. Each thought smacked harder. Thankfully, she talked to him about having safe sex. She didn't necessarily condone him having sex, but understood that ignoring, forbidding, and demonizing it, as her parents had done, would backfire. "Everyone. Just. Stop."

"Don't lie to me," Austin said, ignoring her directive.

"I'm not lying." Micah shook his head rapidly, a bobble head on its last screw. "She wanted to. I swear."

Sex. Truth. Love. Lies. Each word contained gray lines. Held moral opaqueness. Even for adults. But teenagers navigating these issues? Christ. Schools gave talks on "ambiguous consent situations." And Zoe did her part, telling Micah how the girl always had the final say. But nothing about sex was straightforward or painless, especially the first time.

"I understand you're upset," Zoe said, placing a hand on Austin's wrist. "Penelope's your girl. But Austin, look at me." He turned slowly, his eyes a mix of fear and anger. "Micah would never do that. He would never hurt Penelope."

"Did you?" Austin asked, turning back to Micah, almost pleading. "Did you hurt her?"

"No! Never!"

"Teenagers have *sex*, Austin," Zoe said, emphasizing that this was, in fact, sex. Nothing else. She feared this day might come. When you grow up Black in America, being falsely accused of a crime was the cost of living. But she never expected the attack would come from inside. Her best friend. "Don't guilt him in some misguided protection of Penelope's virginity."

"Man, this is *cra-zy*." Micah pushed off the chair with a loud screech. "I'm going over there. There's no way P said this."

"Micah, go upstairs." Zoe grabbed his elbow. "You're not going anywhere. Understand?" His jaw tightened. His skin was hot. She knew he was fighting himself not to snatch his arm away and run out the door. Thankfully, he listened, rushing up the stairs. His bedroom door slammed a second later. She turned back to Austin. "Obviously, Penelope and Micah got in over their heads. I'm sure she's overwhelmed, maybe lied to Amelia to avoid her wrath. It's hard, the first time—"

Austin brushed past her. "This was a mistake, coming here."

"Austin!" She ran after him, catching up as he stepped outside. The coolness of the cement was a stark contrast to her boiling blood. "Please."

He turned around, closing the gap on the too small cement ledge. "Penelope's in the hospital." His voice was low, gritty, his breath a light breeze. "She's hurt."

Zoe desperately searched his face for an explanation. "The hospital? What? Why?"

"I can't—fuck!" His yell echoed down the empty street. "I can't get into details. Look, call me if he wants to talk. If he's ready to be honest. Otherwise..." Austin tossed his hands up and walked across the street.

Zoe went inside to call Amelia. She told herself it was concern for Penelope that made Amelia her first stop before Micah, but, deep down, she knew, there was more at play. Miles lay between Micah's and Penelope's version. Micah was in love and Penelope said he forced her? And it wasn't just the truth she sought to remedy. A Black boy and a white girl? Having sex? Accusations of rape? That was a story as old as time. And it never turned out well for the Black boy. She had to get Amelia to see reason before she did something rash.

CHAPTER EIGHT
AUSTIN

Walking back across the street to Amelia's house, Austin had so much adrenaline pumping through his blood that he briefly considered changing his clothes and going for a run. Anger, frustration, boredom—exercise was his cure-all. But then he remembered Ollie. Amelia wouldn't be happy if Austin left when Ollie was sick and Penelope was...what? Christ, what the hell happened tonight?

Austin liked Micah. Fun, athletic, smart—he was Penelope's equal, both competition junkies. But the two of them hooking up? Having sex? In love? It was hard to imagine.

Austin remembered being a teenager, hanging out with a girl you liked. The surge of hormones came on like a freight train, eyes playing connect the dots between their lips, breasts, ass; ears piqued to hear the starting pistol; cock straining against your pants, always in need of an adjustment, camouflage, release. Was it possible Micah misread Penelope? Got overeager? Sure. Was it equally possible Penelope got caught up in the moment? Possible, but less likely for her to jump to sex. Sexist? Maybe. Paternal? Probably that, too. At fourteen, Austin wanted to believe girls wanted sex as much as he did. At thirty-eight, spending dozens of hours on court each week with P, Austin doubted it. The truth likely lay in the middle.

With nothing to do but wait, Austin microwaved leftover pepperoni pizza. Greasy, but digestible. He ate it over a paper towel at the kitchen island, scrolling through Tinder, too distracted and disinterested to swipe right on anyone. Lately, all the women he dated felt like clones—same style, conversations, goals. Mady, his most serious girlfriend, moved on since their breakup last year. Engaged. Likely pregnant soon. Austin never met anyone that made him want to take those next steps. He was beginning to doubt he ever would.

The hinges in the garage snapped to action, alerting Austin that Amelia and Penelope were home. A little after one a.m. The brevity of the visit a good sign.

Amelia opened the door with Penelope trailing behind. Penelope's shoulders were curled in, arms hanging like two loose noodles, her head bowed, her steps light, almost imperceptible.

Austin walked around the kitchen island and tried pulling Penelope into a hug. She flinched, stepping backwards. Could she be scared of him? He said nothing, not wanting to upset her further.

"I'm going to shower, but can I...sleep in your bed tonight?" Penelope asked Amelia, her voice small.

"Of course."

Once Penelope disappeared upstairs, Amelia drank some water at the sink before crumpling into a heap on the floor. She pulled her knees to her chest, resting her head against the cabinets. Tears slipped from her eyes.

Austin flipped off the overhead lights before joining her on the floor, knowing Amelia hated crying for an audience. "How'd it go?"

Amelia filled him in on the vaginal tears; the morning-after pill; the therapy Penelope would need. "Do you think Penelope and Micah were..." Amelia hesitated. "More than friends? I know she talks to you."

"She didn't say anything." A strike against believing Micah. Austin spent too much time with Penelope, practicing, meals, travelling to tournaments, for her to stay quiet. He didn't have kids, but he had something better with Penelope. Not quite the stress of a daughter, but the closeness of it. "Why?"

"The way she brushed over kissing, like it wasn't a big deal, made me think something might've already happened. Before tonight." Amelia bit her thumbnail. "I don't know. Am I reading too much into that?"

"Micah said they're in love," Austin said.

She fell silent. "And that's what he thinks you do to people you love? Assault them?"

Austin held up his hands. "Hey, I'm just telling you what he said."

"He's an idiot."

"He's a kid. A teenage boy. A walking hormone. They're not exactly known for their decision-making skills."

"Don't use that 'boys will be boys' shit on me. He knows the difference between right and—" Amelia's eyes widened. "Wait. When did you talk to Micah?"

Austin cleared his throat, wishing he could avoid this part. "Don't get mad."

"I *hate* when you say that."

"I went over to Zoe's when you were at the hospital."

"Why?"

"Let me ask you this," Austin said, speaking slowly and deliberately, trying to appeal to Amelia's rational side. Amelia ran hot, particularly when her kids were involved, but his calmness in the face of stress was the x-factor that helped him become a professional athlete. He wanted to be the voice of reason here, see if anything was salvageable. "If some other girl accused Micah of assaulting her, what would you think?"

"Don't do that. Don't defend him. Not tonight." Amelia released a heavy breath. "I know you think I need to lighten up, stop being so over-protective, but this is a situation where there's no grace to extend." She shuddered as tears fell. "He forced her, Austin. And that alone..."

Austin wrapped his arm around Amelia. "I'm sorry. I'm on your side, okay? Whatever you and Penelope need."

An apology, as always, mollified Amelia. "Did Ollie wake up? Say anything?"

"Nope."

Amelia's phone vibrated, Zoe's name lighting up the screen. "She keeps calling."

"Maybe hear her out?"

Tears made Amelia's eyes glassy. She pressed her fingers against the lids. "Not tonight. I can't even say Micah's name without—" She let her hand drop to her thigh. "What did Zoe say?"

"She thinks it's a misunderstanding. The kids got in over their heads—"

Amelia's calm vanished like a puff of air on a cold day. "Zoe assumed Penelope was lying?"

"Well..."

"Unbelievable!"

"Come on. It's almost two," he said, standing. "Rehashing this all night won't help. Let's go to bed."

"You're staying?" He heard relief in her voice. He didn't stay over often anymore—he owned a beautiful loft downtown—but he could suffer the living room pull-out tonight.

"You have your hands full with Penelope." He stretched his arms above his head and yawned. "I'll take care of Ollie if he needs something."

She stood up and hugged him, holding on longer than usual. "I'll get you some sheets." She returned a few minutes later, sheets and a pillow in her arms. After making up the bed, they said goodnight.

Austin opened the living room window and lay down in bed, listening to the crickets, grass rustling in the wind, an occasional car pass. The sounds of suburbia, summer, his childhood.

As he closed his eyes, his mind turned to Zoe, remembering how her face lit up when she opened the door. And later, the shock and fear, the way she bit her lower lip, not quite trusting herself to speak, when Austin confronted Micah. He felt guilty, knowing he put that fear there, that less than a hundred yards away, she was likely wide awake, contemplating a world of problems she couldn't fathom existed an hour ago.

CHAPTER NINE
MICAH

Micah stood by his bedroom window, hands sweaty as he texted, called, Snapchatted, trying to reach Penelope. Ollie, too. With each dead end, he grew more frustrated.

"Pick up!" he hissed, gripping his phone. "Pick up!"

Ma knocked on the door, poking her head inside. "You want to talk now or in the morning?"

"You can't possibly believe Austin!" Yelling didn't help his headache. It pounded behind his temples something fierce. His first hangover. Awesome. "I didn't do anything wrong."

She sat on his bed. "I believe you."

"She would never say I forced her." He ground his teeth, embarrassed by his emotions. He was too old to cry to Ma. "Or, if she did, she didn't mean it. Probably wanted to get Amelia off her back."

"Babe, it's also possible she felt guilty afterwards," Ma said. "Or regretted doing it. Girls, particularly perfectionists like Penelope, are pressured to stay virgins—"

"We both wanted this," he replied, adamant. Penelope *was* nervous, though. But so was he! First-time nerves. They'd never done it before. Once they started kissing, feeling on each other, excitement, *love*, replaced the nerves.

Not that he had much experience to compare. He kissed six girls; three of them let him touch their tits, and one, the magical Evie Gates, gave him a blow job during *Spiderman*. He still got chills thinking about it. But Penelope? She was next level. With her, he was happy just being close to her.

That's why having sex tonight was such a surprise. The happiest surprise—until Austin ruined the best night of his life.

"In that case, give her some time," Ma said.

"How much time? I mean, she has to tell the truth, Ma. She can't—" Micah punched the speed bag hanging in the corner of his room. "What if our friends find out? What if people think this is true? You've got to talk to Amelia."

Ma frowned. "I'll take care it." She came up behind him and rested her hands on his shoulders, pressing her forehead between his shoulder blades. "Get some rest."

After Ma left, resting proved impossible. He waited a half-hour, until one-thirty, ensuring Ma was asleep before he crept out of his room. Their house was old. He walked barefoot on his tip-toes down the stairs, carrying his shoes. Still, the floorboards creaked, screaming his rebellion.

Once outside, he slipped his shoes on. The moon was a perfect disc, lighting the way to Penelope's house. Maybe this was due to the full moon. Didn't crazy things happen on those nights? Girls and their cycles or something?

He looked both ways before crossing the street, not expecting traffic, but wary of prying eyes. Much as his neighbors liked him, they wouldn't hesitate to call the cops if they saw a Black boy out this late.

Approaching Penelope's darkened house, he crept past Austin's Audi TT to the side yard, crouching by the bushes outside Penelope's bedroom. He tried texting her. Calling. No answer. He reached down and grabbed a fistful of mulch, throwing it against her second-floor window. It sprayed against the dark window, falling to his feet, but the curtain remained undisturbed.

"Goddamn it, Penelope," Micah hissed. He planned to try Ollie's room when he heard his name. He turned around.

"You shouldn't be here," Austin said, walking toward Micah.

"I need to talk to P. You can't—you can't come over, accuse me of that, and then leave."

"I wanted to hear your side of the story." Austin sighed. "Believe it or not, I'm trying to help."

"Prove it, man," Micah said. "Give me two minutes with her, you'll see. I would never force her to do anything." His voice cracked, and he was embarrassed to find himself close to tears. He felt misunderstood. Helpless. Overwhelmed. "She loves me."

"Micah." Austin's voice cut through him. "You're too young to know that both propositions can be true. She can love you and still say you sexually assaulted her—"

"We had *sex*, man. Sex."

Austin rested a hand on Micah's elbow. "Let's go."

Hope flushed through Micah. "To see P?"

"No," Austin said. "Home. You can't be here. If Amelia found you—"

Micah backed up, his butt hitting a bush. "So, that's it? I'm family until I'm not?"

"Micah." Austin pressed his thumb and index finger to his temple, just as Ma did when losing her patience. "Let's talk tomorrow."

Reluctantly, Micah followed. He'd always liked Austin, considered him a solid dude. But after tonight? After he accused Micah of sexual assault? Austin was dead to him.

When they reached Micah's house, Austin headed up the front stairs, pressing the doorbell.

"Don't!" Micah said. "Ma is sleeping!"

"If I let you sneak back in, you'll be outside P's window as soon as I leave. Not happening." Austin pressed the doorbell again. "Not on my watch."

When Ma opened the door, Micah marched past her, going to his room and locking the door. He flopped on his bed, pressing the pillow to his face, wanting to scream, but tears spilled instead. They were family. That's what Amelia always said. But one lie—one insane, fucking lie—and they locked their doors, shut off their phones, cut him off.

He needed to talk to Penelope. Fix this before—no. He couldn't even think what might happen if people found out.

CHAPTER TEN
AMELIA

Amelia slept in fits, waking every time Penelope wept. Which was often. Penelope dampened her pillow with tears, while Amelia held her, whispering words of comfort. That she loved Penelope. That she was safe. It was all over now.

Around eight, Amelia went downstairs for coffee. She expected to find Austin sleeping, but the sheets sat folded on the couch, pillow on top, with a note explaining he had to teach an early tennis lesson. Disappointed, she flipped on the coffee maker and propped open the window behind the sink, letting in the warm air. The white cabinets in the kitchen shone with rays of golden sunlight. Any other day, she would've enjoyed the peacefulness of this early hour alone.

Not today. With a cup of coffee in one hand and her phone in the other, she sat at the kitchen table. Zoe called five times last night, leaving one message. Amelia pressed play.

"I'm worried about Penelope. Austin said you took her to the hospital. You don't want to talk, fine. But will you update me? Let me know she's okay." Here, Zoe took a deep breath, likely searching for the perfect words.

Problem was, Hallmark didn't make an "I'm sorry my son sexually assaulted your daughter" card.

"Micah loves Penelope," Zoe continued. "You know he'd never hurt her. Anyway, call, text. *Please.*"

Amelia pressed the phone against her heart. Was Zoe right? Admittedly, Penelope's story had gaps. Questions needed to be answered. But Penelope wasn't talking. There was an unsettling emptiness to her. Amelia didn't know how to draw her out. She didn't know if she *should* draw her out when she was so fragile.

She needs time and space to recover, Amelia texted Zoe as Ollie staggered down the stairs, his fair hair mussy. He shaved the sides recently, a fohawk, creating a new image—punk, apparently—for high school.

"Morning," Amelia said, setting her phone face-down. "Feeling better?" Ollie getting sick irked her. Mom intuition said it was related to Penelope. But how?

"Twelve hours of sleep and I'm golden." Ollie slathered three pieces of bread with peanut butter before sitting across from her. He shoved a slice in his mouth, eating it whole.

She sipped her coffee. "We need to talk about last night."

"What—" He stopped chewing. "What about it?"

She felt another ping of unease; why was he defensive? "Did you know Micah went up to Penelope's room?"

"No." He licked crumbs from his lips. "I got sick and he left."

"He didn't leave. Micah went into Penelope's room and..." The words tasted bitter. Poisonous. "He forced her to have sex."

Ollie stared, uncomprehending. "No...no...he'd never—" He stopped abruptly, his blue eyes skittering around the room. "Wait. Where's P? Is she okay?" His voice rose, sounding like her little boy, needing her to reassure him there were no monsters under the bed.

"No." They both turned to see Penelope sitting on the stairs, arm wrapped around the baluster, head resting against it. Dressed in a sweatshirt, leggings, and socks, she was overdressed for the humid day. Only her face exposed.

"Penelope, honey—"The doorbell rang. Amelia regretted texting Zoe. What did Zoe not understand about needing time and space? "Be right back."

But when Amelia opened the door, she found two cops standing on her porch. A woman, early forties with dark eyes and dark hair slicked back in a severe bun. The other officer was a man; young, probably straight out of the academy, with a starched uniform, and a buzz cut.

"Ms. Swanson?" the female officer asked. "I'm Officer Avery and this is my partner, Officer Mullins. We'd like to speak to your daughter, Penelope."

Amelia wiped her hands against the back of her shorts. Doctor Bilson said she'd wait until morning to inform the police, but she sure didn't give any extra time. Time Amelia would've liked to prep Penelope for this possibility. "Come in." She held open the door and got them settled in the living room. "I'll get Penelope."

Back off the kitchen, Ollie sat next to Penelope on the stairs, neither talking. Amelia looked at Penelope and said, "The police need to ask you a few questions about last night."

Penelope's head hung as if connected to her spine by fish wire. "I can't even..."

"It's important, honey," Amelia said. "If it gets too hard, we'll stop."

Penelope rose, her eyes swollen, face blotchy, and walked with Ollie to the couch. Amelia followed, too antsy to sit. Officer Avery angled the upholstered chair to face Penelope and introduced herself. Office Mullins stood behind, taking notes on a small pad.

"Some questions might seem too personal or invasive, but I'm trying to understand exactly what happened last night," Officer Avery explained. "What time did you get home?"

"Around nine. I went upstairs to shower," Penelope said, hands squeezed between her knees, staring at the floor. Amelia noticed this phenomenon last night. The way Penelope's body tensed and closed in on itself when answering questions, as if she was belatedly trying to protect herself. "When I got out, Micah was waiting."

"Where?"

"In the hall."

"Was anyone else around?"

"No."

"I was sleeping," Ollie said, his voice cracking on *sleeping*. "In the basement."

"What happened?" Officer Avery asked.

"We talked. And then he—" Penelope pressed her fingers to her lips. "He kissed me."

"Did you want him to kiss you?"

"I—maybe?"

Ollie jerked his head toward Penelope, eyebrows furrowed. If Amelia's instincts were right, that something had been going on between Penelope and Micah, Ollie didn't know about it.

"I don't know," Penelope amended. "I told him he couldn't be up there, that we might get caught."

"Did he leave?"

Penelope shook her head. "I had to change so I told him I'd meet him downstairs." Penelope shifted, almost imperceptibly, her shoulder blocking Ollie from her peripheral sightline. "He came into my bedroom and kissed me again. He sort of tripped and we fell onto the bed. He was on top of me—" Penelope glanced quickly back at Ollie. "And he..."

"Perhaps we should talk about this privately," Officer Avery said, picking up on Penelope's obvious discomfort with having Ollie hear these details.

"I agree," Amelia said. As close as the twins were, it was still weird to talk about sex at that age, with anyone. But the awkwardness increased exponentially with family. Add in that Ollie, Micah, and Penelope were usually a trio, it was no wonder that Ollie looked dazed, Penelope traumatized. "Do you want to go upstairs, Ol? Maybe prepare for your audition?"

Ollie flinched, realizing belatedly, that he was being kicked out. "All right." He looked at Penelope, but she kept her head down.

Officer Avery waited until Ollie turned the corner for the stairs. Then she prompted Penelope. "You said Micah tripped and you both fell onto the bed. What happened then?"

Penelope closed her eyes, her eyelashes a dark fan across her cheeks. "He pulled down his pants. He put my hand on his..."

"Penis?"

"Um-hmm."

"Did you want to touch his penis?"

"Not like that." Tears fell from Penelope's eyes like a leaky faucet. "I told him that we should stop, that Ollie might come up..."

Amelia took Ollie's vacant seat next to Penelope. "It's okay." Amelia pressed her lips against Penelope's hair, inhaling the rich scent of Aveda. "You didn't do anything wrong."

"What happened next?" Officer Avery asked.

Amelia was ready to end the interview, but Penelope said, "He put his head between my legs."

Amelia's breath left her lungs in one fell swoop. New details. Horrifying details. How had this escalated so fast? What gave Micah the right?

"He performed cunnilingus?" Officer Avery asked.

"Cunn-a-what?"

Cunnilingus. Who used that term? And why, the first time her daughter learned it, did she have an audience?

"Did he put his mouth on your vulva and clitoris?" Officer Avery asked.

"Uh, yeah," Penelope muttered. Everyone leaned forward, struggling to hear Penelope. "I jumped away from him and told him that I didn't like it. That I had to pee."

"Did he stop?"

Penelope nodded. "He came back up and just looked at me. Then he said he loved me and he—" She squeezed her eyes shut. "He pushed inside me."

"He put his penis in your vagina?" Officer Avery asked.

Penelope's body was taut as a piece of wood. "Yes."

"What did you do?"

Penelope whimpered. "I-I-I froze. I didn't know what was happening at first."

"Did you tell him to stop?"

She put her hands over her face, while Amelia rubbed her back. "It happened so fast."

"Were you afraid that if you told him to stop, he would hurt you?"

Penelope looked up, scrunching her nose. "But he was hurting me," she said slowly. Penelope didn't understand the nuance in the question, because the entire encounter hurt, body and soul. Amelia felt her loss of innocence viscerally.

"Did he ejaculate?" Officer Avery continued.

"I think so..."

"Yes," Amelia said. Thank God Penelope didn't get sick last night. The morning after pill should've done its magic, leaving one less worry.

Officer Avery cleared her throat. "Penelope, have there been any previous sexual encounters between you and Micah?"

"I'm a virgin." Penelope's face cracked open with fresh tears. "*Was* a virgin."

"Any reason he thought you might be interested—?"

Amelia's guard went up. "You mean did she encourage him?"

"No," Officer Avery said. "I'm wondering if anything changed in their friendship—"

"Amazing. He hurts her and you're defending him."

"Ma'am. Please." Officer Avery narrowed her eyes at Amelia. "I'll ask again. Was there a previous sexual relationship between you and Micah?"

A motorcycle rumbled on the street outside. "No," Penelope whispered.

Amelia couldn't sit silently while the police came up with excuses to justify Micah's behavior. If they were investigating, she would make sure they did it right. "Can we get back to last night? I thought consent only mattered in the moment."

As Officer Avery asked more questions, Amelia watched Penelope struggle to answer. It wasn't revictimizing her per se, but it also wasn't helping.

"That's enough," Amelia said. "Penelope needs to rest."

Amelia led the officers outside, while Penelope retreated upstairs. "What happens next?"

"We'll talk to Micah and write a report," Officer Avery said. "Our supervisor will then decide whether to arrest him."

Amelia swallowed down the fear expanding in her chest. This was moving quickly, and she couldn't catch up. Couldn't catch her breath. What would Zoe say when the cops showed up? Should she call her? No. She couldn't. Micah's actions drew a line between them, their families. Penelope had to be her only concern.

"And if he gets arrested?" Amelia asked.

"Then the DA will decide whether to press charges."

This was no longer in Amelia's control. What little control she had, she spent last night the moment she took Penelope to the hospital. "The DA decides, not us?"

Officer Avery gave Amelia a sympathetic smile. "The DA will talk to you first. It's unlikely he would pursue this without Penelope's support."

After saying goodbye, Amelia walked inside, finding Ollie back on the couch. "Did you actually go upstairs or were you listening from the stairs?"

"Listening." He rubbed both hands against his face, leaving red marks.

She didn't have energy to reprimand him. He was worried, curious, confused. She understood. "Are you okay?"

Silence. Then, "How could I be?"

They both stared at the chairs the cops occupied minutes ago. None of them were okay. They were at the starting line of an emotional marathon and Amelia's job was to support them. Penelope especially. Get her the best possible care.

CHAPTER ELEVEN
ZOE

Zoe pulled into her driveway Saturday afternoon with a trunk full of groceries. It was a sleepless night, patrolling Micah's room, followed by back-to-back appointments at the salon this morning. She wanted nothing more than to binge HGTV and stress-eat red velvet cupcakes.

Stepping inside her house, grocery bag handles digging like thumbtacks into her palms, she breathed a sigh of relief. Her house was her sanctuary. It was cramped and outdated when she bought it—three bedrooms, one-and-a-half bath—but it was all hers. And, most importantly, it got Micah into a college-prep school district. Over the past decade, she went about renovations piece-meal. The kitchen, formerly a boxy room with sea-foam green appliances, now had an open gray-blue-white color palette that evoked a Caribbean beach.

That calming vibe vanished in the middle of unpacking groceries when the doorbell rang and she found two cops on her front stoop.

"Good afternoon, ma'am," the female officer said. The title "ma'am" drilled into Zoe's teeth, putting her on edge. "I'm Officer Avery and this is my partner, Officer Mullins. We're looking for Micah Gray. Are you his mother?"

While she wanted nothing more than to slam and lock the door, Zoe knew that would make matters worse. "Yes, I'm Zoe Gray. How can I help?"

"We'd like to question Micah about his involvement with Penelope Swanson last night."

The officer wasn't asking. Clutching the railing, Zoe forced her feet up the stairs. Shock soon gave way to fury. How dare Amelia call the police! They parented differently—Amelia helicoptered, while Zoe gave Micah freedom to make mistakes, find himself, talk to her without worrying about consequences. But, like a de facto married couple, they always discussed issues involving all the kids first before distributing punishments. Why didn't Amelia take a beat? Call Zoe? Instead, she staged a coup, plunging the knife in Zoe's back with no warning.

Micah lay on his bed, wearing his Beats by Dre headphones, thumbs snaking across his iPhone. Exactly where he was when she left for work this morning. He looked up and pulled off his headphones.

"The police are downstairs," she said, sitting on the bed. "They want to talk about last night. Be honest, but—" But what? She warned her son that cops weren't his friends. To always be polite. Keep his hands visible. Never run. But she struggled to find advice for when the cops showed up at home, falsely accusing you of a crime. "But don't elaborate. Stay calm and, most of all, no attitude."

Several emotions slid across Micah's face—surprise, fear, guilt. "Ma?"

"It's fine, baby." She squeezed his hand. "They want to clear things up. That's all."

Back downstairs, Zoe invited the officers into the kitchen. Micah slid onto one of the peninsula stools. Zoe sat next to him, while Officer Avery and Officer Mullins stood opposite, the peninsula a barrier.

Officer Avery introduced herself and launched into questions. "Did Penelope invite you over last night?"

"I was with Ollie and he got sick," Micah said, "so I went upstairs to find her."

"And what was she doing?"

"She just got out of the shower."

"What was she wearing?" Officer Avery asked.

Micah flicked his eyes toward Zoe. "A towel."

New details. Not favorable. Not horrible either.

"Did she ask you to leave so she could change?"

Micah slid his hands against one another, making a faint rustling sound. "Look, I know why you're here, so I'll be one-hundred with ya. We messed around last night. Okay?"

Officer Avery tilted her head. "Messed around. What does that mean?"

Zoe felt the rumble of Micah's foot tapping the hardwood floor. She wanted to reach out a hand, press it against his thigh, steady his nerves. Instead, she got up and filled a glass of water at the sink and handed it to him. She looked into his eyes—a beautiful mix of cinnamon, nutmeg and chocolate—reminding him that he did nothing wrong.

"We had sex," Micah said quietly. "We're in love, okay?"

"Penelope says she never consented to sex." Officer Avery's eyes bored into Micah. "We're talking sexual assault, Micah."

"I didn't force her. I would never. *Never*," Micah repeated, the slightest tremor in his voice giving away his anxiety. "Ma raised me to respect girls."

She squeezed his shoulder while her mind rallied for a solution, a way to walk this accusation back. "Look," Zoe said. "The kids got overexcited and maybe moved too fast. Everyone knows teenagers are prone to acting first, thinking later." Zoe raised her right hand and pressed it against her heart. "But I can tell you, truly, that Micah would never hurt anyone, especially Penelope and Ollie. They're family."

Officer Avery pursed her lips. "Are you saying Penelope's lying? Because that's the rub, Ms. Gray." Officer Avery gestured toward Micah. "Someone is lying."

"I'm saying there's two interpretations to a single event," Zoe said. "Maybe Penelope thought she would get in trouble if she admitted she wanted to have sex." Zoe's stomach wrenched as she realized she was going to, if not push, nudge, Penelope under the bus. A girl she loved. A girl she thought of as her daughter. But what choice did she have? Micah *was* her son. He needed help. Now. "She lives in a gilded cage. Perfect grades. Perfect tennis player. Perfect Penelope. She's not allowed to mess up."

"Back up, Micah," Officer Avery said, ignoring Zoe.

Zoe bit her tongue. The dismissal stung. Made her feel invisible, less-than. It brought up memories of teachers, bosses, clerks, letting their eyes slide past her when she spoke.

"Where did you two have sex?" Officer Avery asked.

Micah exhaled. "In her bed."

"And she was wearing a towel. What about you?"

"Shorts and a tee."

"Did those come off?"

"I, sort of, pulled down my shorts and boxers; she touched me—"

"Your penis?"

Micah's dark skin shone. "Um-hmm."

"Did she choose to touch you or did you put her hand on your penis?"

"I don't know." Micah looked up. "But she kept her hand there, rubbing and stuff."

"Were you on top of her or lying down?"

"On top," Micah said.

"What are you, six-foot? One-seventy-five?"

"Six-one, one-fifty."

Panic seized Zoe as she watched Officer Avery size up Micah, peg him as a stereotypical Black boy—large, dangerous, hyper-sexual. Zoe felt in her pocket for her phone. Perhaps she should get help. A lawyer. But wouldn't that make Micah look guilty? Didn't cooperating prove he had nothing to hide?

She didn't know!

"Did you perform cunnilingus on Penelope?" Officer Avery neither blushed nor stuttered. She looked poised to talk about the kids' sex lives all afternoon.

"I, ah..." Micah looked at Zoe, his brow furrowed.

"Did you go down on her?" Zoe filled in, aiming for blasé, refusing to be embarrassed either. She wasn't going to let Officer Avery shame Micah.

Micah coughed and looked down. "Yeah."

"Did she ask you to?"

"I just did it," Micah mumbled. "Girls like it."

Zoe suppressed a groan; his knowledge likely came from porn, not personal experience. Her confident, curious, clueless boy.

"Did she ask you to stop?" Officer Avery asked.

Micah hesitated. "Not really."

"What do you mean, 'not really'?" Officer Avery used air quotes.

"At first she said she didn't like it, but then she said she needed to pee." Micah sighed. "Like Ma said, Penelope's sheltered. She'd never kissed anyone before me. So, I gotta, like, help her along." He made a circular motion with his hand. "She didn't understand that feeling was her getting turned on."

"You decided that her wanting to stop was really an indication she was turned on."

"You're twisting my words." Micah shook his head. "And just so you know, I did stop. I wasn't trying to force her to do anything she didn't want."

"Okay," Zoe cut in. They were twisting his words, but he was also wrong to assume how Penelope felt. She'd deal with that later. "What happened after you stopped going down on her?"

"I'll ask the questions, Ms. Gray," Officer Avery said, raising her voice even though Zoe was done talking. "What happened next?"

"We had sex," Micah said.

"You put your penis in her vagina?"

Micah nodded.

"Did she ask you to?"

Zoe squeezed his hand, a warning. They were looking for something to make him look guilty. He needed to stay strong, stay calm.

"We were in the moment," Micah said through gritted teeth.

"What about the moment indicated she was consenting to sex?" Officer Avery asked.

Zoe squeezed harder, her knuckles turning white. Micah's hand was hot, his anger fit to burst. *Please, please*, she willed him.

"I don't know." He shrugged off her hand. "Because she kissed me. Because she was grinding against me. Because we're in love. This isn't new. We've been together all summer—"

"Exactly when did this start?"

"June. This is going to sound bad—"

Zoe's heart started pumping blood overtime. If he thought something sounded bad, it must be horrific, because the rest didn't sound great.

"—but we kept our relationship on the DL. She thought her mom would freak if she found out." Micah sat back, crossing his arms. "I guess she was right."

Zoe focused on her breathing, stilling her body, ensuring she didn't react. Zoe and Micah didn't keep secrets. Or so she thought. But here he was, evidently lying all summer. Was it true? Honestly, she had a hard time imagining Penelope being duplicitous. Even interested in boys. Tennis was her life. But then Zoe thought about herself as a teenager. Hormones had her exploring her body at night, falling for any boy that gave her attention. Girls could create a façade of innocence much easier than boys—if they wanted.

But none of this excused Micah's lying.

"You're saying you two are together? Boyfriend, girlfriend?" Officer Avery clarified.

Micah clapped his hands. "Yes!"

Officer Avery looked back at Officer Mullins, then asked, "Was this the first time you had sex?"

"Yes."

"Did you use a condom?"

"No. It was..." Micah's tongue pressed up against the inside of his cheek. "Spontaneous."

He wouldn't look at Zoe. And for good reason. She never yelled. But this, *this*, was worth losing her temper. How many times had they talked about safe sex? Using condoms? Hell, he asked her to buy some earlier this year. She laughed at his bravado, but if carrying a condom made him feel like a man, she wasn't going to discourage him. But now, he didn't even use it?

Was Amelia afraid Penelope got pregnant? Was that why she took Penelope to the hospital? But Austin said she was hurt. Questions had Zoe's head spinning. Worst of all, Amelia wasn't taking Zoe's calls.

"What happened afterwards?" Officer Avery asked.

Micah shrugged. "We cuddled and then I kissed her goodbye. She said it was perfect. Everything was great."

After a few more questions, the officers left, saying they'd be in touch. An ominous ending. But Zoe wasn't going to catastrophize. There was so much truth to this story, teenage recklessness, stupidity, first love, for it not to be accepted. The police were investigating because Amelia reported it. It was their job. Nothing more, nothing less.

Zoe watched the cops drive away, her gaze settling on Amelia's house. Even if the cops dropped this, as they should, Zoe would never forgive Amelia for betraying her.

CHAPTER TWELVE
MICAH

Seconds after the cops left, Micah ran out the back door, his sport pack banging against his back. He couldn't run fast enough or far enough to let out his rage. Frustration at the way the cops twisted his answers. Disbelieved, ignored, belittled him. He was telling the truth!

The high school track was a half-mile from his house, which hardly left him winded when he arrived. Football practice didn't start for an hour, but he'd run sprints. He tossed his bag on the grass without stopping, pushing himself to go faster with every lap, feet kicking his butt, chest striding forward.

"Trying to show everyone up?" Micah turned to see Xavier Lyons. Micah felt like a boy next to Xavier, in awe of his talent. At six-foot-five, two-hundred pounds of muscle, Xavier was an all-state quarterback, team captain, and had a full scholarship to UW next fall.

"Burning off some steam," Micah said, slowing to a walk. Sweat ran into his eyes, making them sting.

"Something happen?"

For reasons Micah didn't understand, Xavier had Micah's back, ensuring Micah had enough reps on the field. Off the field, he told Micah which football camps helped to gain traction with colleges. Maybe he'd know what to do now. "Last night, my girlfriend and I—" Micah clenched his fists, frustrated that he felt shame now where last night he felt love. Wonder. Luck. "We had sex."

"Whoa!" Xavier raised his hand for a high-five. "Big man."

Micah didn't meet his hand. "This afternoon, the cops questioned me. Accused me of sexually assaulting her."

Xavier stopped walking. He crossed his arms, biceps bulging. "Tell me exactly what happened."

"They twisted my words, made it seem like I forced her." Micah's voice shook, panic stealing his breath, some sort of delayed reaction. "But I swear, Xavier, Penelope wanted this as much as me. She said being with me felt perfect."

A girl ran past them on the track, her footfalls heavy, breath labored. Xavier didn't speak until she rounded the corner.

"I have a cousin whose girlfriend accused him of stepping out. He told her nothing happened. Didn't matter. She was crazy." Xavier twirled his index finger by his head. "She started telling her friends that he liked rough sex, choking her and shit. One night, at a bar, she picks a fight, makes sure everyone sees them arguing. Later that night, she calls her friend, saying my cousin raped her. He's doing five, man."

His eyes were two black coals imparting knowledge Micah never wanted to hear. Choking? Rough sex? What he and P had was nothing like that.

"Oh, and did I mention she's white?" Xavier added.

Mic drop.

"You think the cops showed up because Penelope is white?"

"I don't think, I *know*. This is racism, plain and simple, bruh," Xavier said. "It's why I don't mess with white girls."

This news felt like a kick to the balls. Micah felt discrimination in small doses—the only Black kid in kindergarten, teachers overly enthusiastic with praise when finding out he was smart and hardworking, store clerks stalking him with their eyes—but he never felt singled out so blatantly, so unfairly. Until now.

"What should I do?" Micah felt dumb, playing family with Ollie and Penelope, never thinking his Blackness mattered.

"You got any pictures?" Xavier asked. "Texts to back you up?"

Micah walked over to his bag and pulled up a secret file on his phone. He handed it to Xavier, watching as he scanned texts, pictures, and videos.

"Post this." Xavier indicated a selfie of Micah kissing Penelope on her cheek, her smile wide, eyes shining. Their arms wrapped around each other like licorice strands. "And screenshot this text."

We need to stop, Penelope texted a couple days ago. *But I can't. Can't say no to you.*

"Write this," Xavier said, dictating. "Today the cops accused me of raping—what's her name?"

Micah stopped typing. "I'm not calling her out."

"Nah, man. You gotta at least say she's your girlfriend. It's important. It's not just any girl, it's *your* girl."

Xavier was right. The most ridiculous part of the police's accusation was that it was Penelope. Micah would never hurt her. He always had her back. And vice-versa. All of their friends knew that. Micah was nervous Penelope would be upset that he was outing their relationship, but he had no choice. He had to fight. Prove his innocence. Penelope would understand. Eventually. She was a fighter, too. "Okay. I'll say girlfriend."

"Type, 'Today the cops accused me of raping my girlfriend. Say what???? She said being with me felt perfect. Cops be criminalizing interracial love. Pegging Black boys as trouble. Stand with me. Make the police accountable. Acknowledge the disparities.'"

Micah's thumb hesitated for a second. The text sounded too sophisticated for Micah, but he trusted Xavier. Fury at Amelia, the police, for ruining the greatest night of his life, fear at what might happen if he did nothing, gave him courage. He hit post on Insta, sending it out to his five-hundred-seventy-eight followers.

CHAPTER THIRTEEN
OLLIE

Ollie stood against the wall outside the high school auditorium, rehearsing lines as he waited for his turn to audition for *Almost, Maine.* Kids paced the hallway, a few sat on benches, nobody able to sit still for long. Much as Ollie tried to focus, the words on the page looked like computerized code, a bunch of random numbers, letters, and symbols. He didn't feel well. Feverish. Nauseous. Sore. And it wasn't just the hangover. Or the fact that it was sweltering, too much body odor circulating, in the un-air-conditioned hall. He woke this morning with a familiar ache in his bones, the same feeling he had the morning Dad died. Something was wrong. He wasn't an empath; more that he was in tune with the rhythms of the world.

Then again, maybe not. He hadn't picked up any vibe from Micah that he liked Penelope.

Ollie rubbed his sore head, wanting to scream. Penelope and Micah? No, no, no. NO! Why would Micah go up to Penelope's room? Kiss her? Have sex? The thought hit somewhere inside Ollie's ribs, just below his heart, a knockout punch.

When Micah found the vodka in the freezer last night, Ollie laughed. *Come on,* Micah said. *Let's get drunk.* Micah was Ollie's kryptonite, brought out an incurable weakness, a neediness, a delusional hopefulness. He took any scraps of attention Micah offered, lapped them up, regardless of the self-loathing that followed. *Weak bitch energy,* as Micah would say. That's what Ollie was, a weak bitch.

Any way Ollie twisted it, Penelope got hurt last night because of him. Because he didn't tell Micah no. Two letters. One syllable. N-O. Because he got drunk. Sick. Passed out cold.

Ollie wasn't sure whether it was the alcohol or the way it made his desire for Micah transparent that made him sick. Ollie caught himself staring at Micah instead of playing Madden, turned on by Micah biting his lower lip. He wanted to kiss Micah. And he could! After months of wondering, fantasying, jerking off, it suddenly felt within reach. One kiss and he'd have the answer. Whether Micah wanted him back.

Quit lookin' at me, Micah grumbled, obviously freaked out. The realization of how close Ollie came to imploding his life, losing Micah forever, made his stomach contract. Ollie ran for the bathroom. On his knees, head hovering over the toilet, sweat dotting his hairline, Ollie puked and puked, terrified that Micah knew.

And while Ollie succumbed to the darkness, where was Micah? Not by his side. Not checking on him. Nope. He left Ollie all alone. Chose Penelope over him.

Not anymore. Micah blew up his phone last night and this morning, but Ollie refused to answer. Micah finally went too far.

Ollie had to tell someone that Micah was drunk. That was the only explanation for why Micah did something so crazy. But who? Mom would flip. Uncle Austin? Possibly.

"Kid posted on Insta that the cops are trying to bang him up for having sex with his girlfriend. All cuz she's white," Ollie heard someone say. Ollie saw two guys dressed in gym shorts and tanks walking toward him.

"Penelope Swanson." The guy held his phone up. "Ever heard of her?"

Ollie's heart thudded, each beat reverberating throughout his body. School had yet to start and he didn't know anyone here, but did they know him? That Penelope was his sister?

"Damn." The second guy whistled. "She's a snacc and a half."

"I love when a fresh crop comes in," the first guy said as they passed Ollie.

They turned the corner, their conversation drifting away. Ollie fumbled pulling his phone out of his bag, his fingers clumsy. And he wasn't the only one. Ollie looked around, finding that everyone else set their scripts aside for their phones too.

He clicked on Micah's Insta, horrified by the image of Micah kissing Penelope. Why would Micah play like he and Penelope were boyfriend and girlfriend? Tell everyone they had sex? What was up with this text Penelope sent? When was this picture taken? She told the cops Micah had never kissed her before. Did a kiss on the cheek count?

Already, over a hundred comments poured in. Several tagging Penelope. Many congratulating Micah. Asking for details. Others called Micah a rapist. This was going viral faster than a thirsty Kardashian pic.

"Oliver Swanson?" A girl with a shock of red hair stood at the auditorium door, calling his name. He looked around, self-conscious. Had anyone made the connection that he was related to Penelope?

"That's me." Ollie walked toward her, debating whether to leave. He was in no state to audition. But Ollie spent the last few weeks rehearsing, watching MasterClasses of his favorite actors. And the idea of being someone else, leaving this morning behind, even for a few minutes, appealed. Ollie relished stepping inside someone else's world. Having the opportunity to do and say wild, interesting, *normal* things, without facing any backlash. He'd never experienced that freedom, being comfortable in his skin, before.

After entering the dark auditorium, Ollie followed the girl down the long aisle.

She gestured toward the stage stairs. "Good luck."

He walked up the three steps and onto the brightly lit stage. Mr. Richards, the drama teacher, sat in the fifth row, flanked by two women. Ollie's fingertips stuck to his script, sweat making the pages damp. He opened his mouth, but nothing came out.

"Breathe," Mr. Richards said in the same calm voice that praised Ollie during drama camp this past summer. "The stage is your home."

Did Mr. Richards know? He never said anything. Why would he? That'd be weird. And probably illegal. But Ollie's intuition flared, and he knew, *knew*, that Mr. Richards was on the last leg of a journey that Ollie was just starting. Encouraging Ollie to audition was a way of waving Ollie onto a different path.

Ollie closed his eyes. Amazingly enough, when he opened them, he was no longer stuck inside his body. No longer the object of Micah's rejection, the butt of the joke, the irremediable brother, the outcast. Yet these emotions—regret, anger, sadness, confusion—piled up in his mind like apples, there for the taking.

A few minutes later, he walked off the stage, praying silently. He wanted this part. Bad. Needed something to break the hold Micah had over him. Needed Mr. Richards' belief to prove true. He needed a home away from home, away from Penelope and Micah. Somewhere he could just be.

CHAPTER FOURTEEN
PENELOPE

Penelope sat on the cement ledge of her front porch late Saturday afternoon, seething as she alternated between looking at Micah's Instagram post and across the street at his front door. Why would Micah post a private picture? Her text? Was the entire summer a sham? She couldn't imagine any reason he would out their relationship, expose her as a slut, unless he never really loved her.

How was she going to start high school on Tuesday? Hundreds of kids staring, judging, gossiping. Already, she had dozens of texts and DM's, asking what happened. She deleted them. She couldn't explain what happened to herself, how would she explain it to anyone else?

Micah hurt her last night. Didn't listen. Didn't care. Seemed different, a world away. But he didn't rape her. Rape? Rape was like when a guy held you down, threatened you, became violent. Horrible stuff Penelope didn't want to imagine. No. Micah didn't rape her.

Why would the cops jump to that conclusion? She never said that. Could it really be because he was Black? The thought made her head hurt. What did race have to do with it?

She imagined running over to Micah's house, yelling at him until he cried, sobbed through an apology. But what if he didn't apologize? Judging by his Insta post, he didn't think he did anything wrong.

Not that an apology would help. Nothing could. He took something from her last night, something intangible and priceless. No amount of crying, yelling, begging would bring it back.

It wasn't her virginity. Everyone—Mom, the doctor, cops—focused on sex. She couldn't go there. Not yet.

No. Micah stole her trust. The way he pushed inside her. Closed his eyes—she could've been anyone! Shut his ears. Ignored her pain, when he promised to never hurt her.

Stop thinking about it!

She was eight when Dad died after going out for a run one morning and never returning. His sudden death left her anxious. Tennis became her refuge, blocked out her fears, allowed her to focus only on hitting the ball perfectly. But tennis couldn't fix this. Breathing took all her energy.

Penelope saw Ollie walking on the sidewalk toward their house. His gaze was fixed on Micah's house, not even noticing Penelope until he turned into their driveway. She held up her phone, Micah's post highlighted. "Did you know about this?"

He plopped down on the porch swing and scratched the wood with his thumbnail, asking for a sliver. "I saw it."

"How could he do this?" she asked. "Now everyone knows we had sex."

Ollie's hands covered his face. "If I hadn't fallen asleep, none of this would've happened."

"You were sick."

"I wasn't really sick," Ollie said. "Micah and I—"

"Ollie, can we not?" She pressed the pads of her fingers into her burning eyes. Ollie wanted her words, her feelings, forgiveness, but she couldn't soothe him. She was depleted. Operating on fumes, but unable to sleep. Turn off her thoughts. After recounting what happened at the hospital and with the police, Micah dealt the knockout punch when he outed her to the entire school.

Ollie didn't stay silent for long. "Why did you let him kiss you?"

Penelope's anxiety skyrocketed. *Fuck. Fuck. Fuck.* She should've ended it! But being with Micah felt so good! She couldn't think straight. His kisses addicting.

"It just happened," Penelope said, choking on her lies. When the cops asked whether this was the first time she and Micah hooked up, she panicked. She couldn't risk Mom not believing her, judging her along with everyone else. Then Mom interrupted, arguing that the past wasn't relevant. Penelope never loved her more.

"Do you like him?" Ollie asked.

"I did." True.

"What was up with that text you sent?"

She feigned a sudden interest in her nails. His blue eyes, usually so caring, felt like daggers. Knives sinking deep into her muscles, torturing her to come clean. "It's hard to explain—I started having feelings..."

"Why didn't you tell me?"

"We never talk about, like, crushes, and stuff." Also true. His ambivalence toward girls was part of the reason she lied. Unlike Micah, whose favorite topic was girls, who's hot, who's not, Ollie never mentioned anyone. Which led to her other reason. She feared he'd feel excluded. Never leave her and Micah alone together if he knew the truth. "You don't seem..." She hesitated. "Interested."

"I've liked people before," he responded, sounding defensive.

Who? she wanted to ask. *When?*

But he had another question lined up. "Was this the first time he kissed you?"

"Yes." False. So very false. All summer, the lies grew like vines around the three of them, twisting and strengthening its hold, binding Micah and Penelope together. Leaving Ollie on the outside.

"That pic he posted looked like it wasn't the first time," Ollie pressed.

"He was joking around." It hurt to downplay their relationship. But she had no choice. "Maybe...maybe he had a crush on me too."

Ollie quickly swiped a tear from his eye. "Maybe."

"I'm sorry I ruined everything for you," she said, hating to see him cry. Hating that he lost his best friend because of her.

"It's just hard to believe, that he'd do this."

Her heart thudded, terrified, but needing to ask this question. She wished there was someone else, someone more experienced, but there was only Ollie. The blind leading the blind. "Do you think

72

Micah couldn't stop once we started kissing? Like, we'd gone too far for him to pull back?"

A blush grew from Ollie's neck to his cheeks. He looked over at Micah's house. "It aches if you stop. But he could, P. Definitely."

Grief swallowed her whole. Fact, Micah could've stopped. Fact, she told him she didn't like it. Conclusion, he didn't care. His decision to post their relationship on Insta, when she begged him to keep it secret, hammered home the point.

CHAPTER FIFTEEN
AMELIA

Sunday night. Quiet house. Kids upstairs. Any other Sunday, Amelia, Zoe, and Austin would've spent it laughing and cooking in the kitchen or out back on the deck with a drink, while the kids hung out in the basement.

Instead, Amelia sat on the couch in the living room, laptop propped on her knees, reading articles about how to support teenage sexual assault victims. Problem was, she hadn't made any headway on step one. *Encourage your teen to express themselves.* Despite Amelia's efforts, Penelope remained silent, her emotions locked away. She hadn't eaten. Refused to sleep, let alone step inside, her room. There were no outbursts, slammed doors, eye rolls. Nothing to suggest her live-wire girl was still in there.

Was she expecting too much, too soon? The articles didn't really give a timeline. Amelia liked concrete data, identifiable goals. And nothing about this situation fit inside a box. It involved shades of gray Amelia never encountered before.

She heard footfalls coming down the stairs and closed her laptop halfway, preparing for Penelope. But Austin appeared. He'd been here most the day, first trying and failing to appeal to Penelope to play tennis, then playing video games with Ollie.

"How's he doing?" she asked. Ollie wasn't talking either. He seemed withdrawn, depressed, moping from his bedroom to the kitchen and back.

"He's..." Austin took a seat next to her. "Grappling with the facts. He can't believe they kissed, let alone—" He stopped, not labeling what happened. Probably trying to avoid an argument. "He's pretty cut up about not seeing him."

"At least he's talking to you."

Austin laughed. "This was over hours of video games. It's not like we broke bread and had a tete-a-tete."

Amelia glanced down at her hands; hands that held her babies, bandaged their cuts, wiped their tears, hugged them. Hands that failed her now. "I don't know how to help them," she said softly. "They won't talk to me."

Austin rubbed the stubble on his jaw, which sounded like sandpaper. "It's been two days. One for Ollie. Give 'em time."

"I'm afraid she'll get worse."

Not even he could summon false reassurance. "Have you talked to Zoe?" Austin asked.

The dishwasher hummed in the kitchen. Someone upstairs flushed the toilet. "No," she said finally. The thought made her wistful. Amelia ached for Zoe—their easy conversations, the intimacy of being known, motherly support—feeling her absence like a phantom limb. But then she thought about Micah on top of Penelope, forcing his way inside her, tearing her apart. Ice from her heart filled the limb.

"So, that's it?" He cut his hand through the air. "Eleven years of friendship gone?"

Tension mounted in her muscles. "What would you have me do?"

"Try and separate her from your feelings about Micah. She's an innocent bystander, too."

"She didn't apologize," Amelia said, rubbing the sore spot on the back of her neck. "She texted, saying Micah would never hurt P. She doesn't think he did anything wrong."

He pressed his hands to his knees, pushed himself out of the chair with a sigh. "I'm going. Let me know if you need anything."

She waited by the bay window until she saw his headlights pull out of the driveway before locking up for the night and turning off the lights. Then she made her way upstairs. She stopped in Ollie's bedroom first, peeking her head inside the doorway to find him sleeping. She bypassed Penelope's darkened room to find her lying in Amelia's bed, staring at some indiscriminate point on the wall.

"How are you, sweetie?" Amelia asked, sitting on the edge of the bed, gently pressing her hand to Penelope's forehead. She wasn't sick, but Amelia felt a visceral need to tend to her.

"I'm not going to school." Penelope said it matter-of-factly, without emotion, as if she held the decision-making power. And maybe she did.

"Okay. Talk to me. What's going through your head?" Nothing. "Penelope, look at me. Please." Slowly, Penelope turned her head. Her face was unusually pale, with two banana shaped bruises beneath her eyes. "Are you afraid of seeing Micah? Because I'm planning to call school. Explain everything. He won't go near—"

"No. You can't—I can't—" Penelope stuttered. "I would be...mortified."

Amelia didn't dare breathe. This was the most Penelope talked since the police interview. "This isn't your fault," Amelia tried, repeating another phrase the article suggested. "You did everything you could."

Silence followed. "How about some dinner?" Amelia hadn't seen Penelope eat anything since Friday. *Honor her boundaries*, the article said. Did that include letting her daughter starve? How long should she let this go on? "You'd be amazed how a good meal—"

"Food?" Penelope gaped at Amelia. "You think food will fix this?"

"No. But it might help."

Penelope turned away. Tears ran down her cheek. "You don't get it."

Amelia brushed the tears away from Penelope's cheek with her thumb, but they fell faster than she could issue cleanup. "Help me understand. Please."

Penelope pressed her hands to her eyes, not so subtly flicking Amelia's hand away. "Tomorrow. I'll eat tomorrow."

Extend invitations, another article said. *Don't let them isolate themselves.* "Let's go for a walk in the morning," Amelia said. "Get some fresh air."

"No."

All right then. "Well, we have your first therapy appointment Wednesday; maybe that will help."

Penelope closed her eyes. "I'm not going."

"Sorry, sweetie." Given Penelope's reluctance to go to therapy, Amelia guessed now was not the time to broach calling a survivor support line. "Therapy's not up for debate."

Amelia watched Penelope, the way her eyes darted beneath the lids. Cleary awake but wanting to pretend she spontaneously fell asleep. A dismissal. Again.

After a minute, Amelia went in the bathroom to wash up. As she lathered on face lotion, she nodded to herself in the mirror. She could concede on school—Penelope wasn't ready. But not on therapy. Penelope needed help. From someone skilled in navigating these treacherous and confusing waters. Clearly, since Penelope refused to string more than three words together, Amelia wasn't cutting it. She couldn't let Penelope keep her pain inside. It would drain her personality, outlook on love and life.

That was no way to live. Amelia, who had been living with a ghost for a husband the past six years, understood this best.

CHAPTER SIXTEEN
MICAH

When Micah arrived for his first day of school Tuesday morning, his nerves jangled. He always imagined taking this step with Penelope and Ollie, but he hadn't seen or talked to either since Friday night. Neither returned his Snapchats, DM's, calls. The silence hurt. Didn't eleven years of friendship earn Micah a conversation?

While his best friends ghosted him, thanks to Xander, he received over a thousand comments on his Insta post. Many strangers, saying justice would prevail. That you couldn't prosecute love. There were the usual miserable trolls, spitting racist shit, but he scrolled right past those.

Walking through the high school halls, however, he couldn't scroll past the way people treated him. Kids he'd known since kindergarten. Staring. Gossiping. Laughing. Girls shied away. A few guys gave fist bumps, but many walked right past him. He was used to being popular, standing out, but this was something else. He felt uncomfortable in his own skin, an outsider.

What's worse, he didn't see Penelope. All weekend, with each unanswered message, Micah counted on being able to talk to her today. He looked around every corner, inside every classroom, and down every hallway. He saw bouncing ponytails, waterfalls of strawberry blond hair, but never Penelope. She was avoiding him. Fine. He got it. She was pissed that he outed their relationship on Insta, but he had no choice. If she would listen for five minutes, he could explain how the cops trapped him, twisted his words. His Instagram post wasn't meant to hurt her, but his only means of fighting back, clearing his name. It killed him that people tagged her, threw shade, blamed her, but what else was he supposed to do? Let people spread lies about him?

By fifth period, Algebra One, Micah's body ached from holding his emotions inside, absorbing the prying eyes, insults without flinching. Before he could take a seat, the teacher pulled him aside. Micah was needed in the principal's office. Second floor. Immediately.

Micah backed out of the classroom, alarmed. Was this about his Instagram post? Why would the school care? He wiped sweat from his brow. Maybe it was nothing. He'd been sent to the principal's office a few times in middle school, unafraid to speak his mind. Perhaps his reputation preceded him? But on the first day of school? Nah.

Micah came to abrupt halt, something golden flashing in the corner of his eye. Could it be? His stomach flipped. But it wasn't Penelope. It was Ollie, sitting in the last row of a classroom. Ollie sensed Micah's presence and looked. Micah waved. Ollie stared for a moment, his cheeks reddening, before turning away.

What in the actual fuck? Micah could understand being pissed that he and Penelope lied all summer. But was that all this was? Ollie throwing a fit? Or could he...was it possible that Ollie thought he forced Penelope?

Whatever, Micah thought, taking the stairs to the second floor. If Ollie wanted to trip, fine. Micah didn't need him, either. His football crew had his back.

Inside the school office, Micah handed the note to the secretary. She directed him to a closed door behind her and told him to go in. When he opened the door, the two officers that interviewed him stood there. Along with an old guy with white hair and a paunch. Micah glanced backwards. *Run!* Ma told him to never run from cops—great advice in theory, ignorant of the adrenaline rush of reality.

"I'm Principal Weinstein," the old man said, closing the door behind Micah. Weinstein kept his back to the officers and his voice low. "Bad news is the police are here to arrest you. The good news is we've called your mom. She'll meet you at the station."

Micah felt lightheaded. Arrested? He reached out to the wall for balance. The lady-cop reintroduced herself as Officer Avery and told Micah to turn around and put his hands behind his back. What choice did he have? They had guns. The cold metal of the handcuffs clicked tightly against his wrists. The stretch pulled on his neck like a leash.

"You're under arrest for the sexual assault of Penelope Swanson. You have the right to remain silent..." His thoughts drowned the cop's words. Sexual assault? He told the cops the truth. How could they believe Amelia, who wasn't even there, over him? In what world was that fair?

The cops marched him down the hall, one on each side, making him feel as conspicuous as an elephant breaking out of the zoo. Class was in session, but stragglers remained in the halls. They gawked. One followed him outside, videoing his walk of shame.

Riding in the backseat of the police car, he felt close to tears. From fear. What would happen now? Would he spend the night in jail? But pain, too. The cuffs cut off circulation to his fingers, his balled-up fists made it impossible to sit back. He bit the inside of his cheek until he tasted blood.

Ten agonizing minutes later, they arrived at the police station. It was nothing like he imagined. Instead of cops yelling into phones, perps swearing, the station was clean, vacant, and eerily quiet. The quietness terrified him more. These blood-thirsty cops needed an outlet for their aggression. With no one else in sight, they'd come at him hard.

A different cop—balding, white, humorless—uncuffed him and took his fingerprints, mug shot, and info. Each step was belittling, surreal, a made-for-TV movie where he won the starring role, but never auditioned.

Officer Avery reappeared, leading him to a small, windowless room. A square table, bolted to the floor, with two chairs, tan walls, one mirrored. Micah was exhausted and thirsty, but most of all, scared. Arrested. On the first day of high school.

"Where's my mom?" he asked. "She's supposed to be here."

"She will be. But first, we have paperwork. This is a DRAI exam." Officer Avery handed him a sheaf of papers and a pen. "It stands for Detention Risk Assessment Instrument. It'll help the court decide placement at your hearing—whether you'll go to a secure detention facility or whether you can function at home with moderate supervision."

A pop quiz! They were setting him up to fail. Nevertheless, he worked his way through it, answering questions about home, school, extracurricular activities, and alcohol and drug use.

"Thanks," she said when he finished, turning to nod at the mirror. A moment later, her partner came in, wearing plastic gloves and carrying a small bag. "Officer Mullins is going to take your DNA—don't worry, it doesn't hurt. But I need you to sign here first." She pushed another paper to him, tapping her pen on the signature line.

"What's this?" Micah's eyes skimmed the words.

"Basically, it says you consent to giving DNA. Standard procedure."

Micah signed, because, again, what choice did he have? Officer Mullins told Micah to open wide and then scraped the inside of his cheek with what felt like a Q-tip. It didn't hurt, but it was insulting.

"Let's go back to the night of September second," Officer Avery said after her partner left. "I want to iron out some details."

He sighed. "I already told you everything. I don't get it. How can you arrest someone without evidence?"

She opened a folder, flipping it so he could see the papers inside. Criminal complaint. Four words swam before him: third degree sexual assault.

"See here." She pointed. "We talked to the emergency room doctor. Turns out Penelope had vaginal lacerations—tears," she clarified. "Do you still think this was something she wanted, something she was enjoying?"

81

He stood, feeling hot and dizzy, the room a cave, its walls bearing down on him. The sex he thought was hot and beautiful and the best damn thing that ever happened to him hurt Penelope?

He thought bleeding was normal the first time. She must have been so scared. He needed to talk to her! Make things right. Not let these cops poison her mind with lies.

"Micah, sit down," Officer Avery said. "Let's talk."

"No, no." He shook his head, pacing from one cinderblock wall to the other. Why talk? They heard only what they wanted, anything to make him sound guilty. "I'm done talking."

After baiting him, without success, Officer Avery pulled out another paper. "This is the Temporary Physical Custody Order. It lays out the conditions you must abide by upon release."

Micah grabbed the back of his chair, relief making his knees buckle. "You're letting me go?"

"For now," she said. "Provided you sign this document."

Micah sat down and started reading, each sentence vacuuming the air from his lungs. No contact with victim. No unsupervised contact with children under twelve. No unsupervised social media. No R-rated movies. No porn. Absolute sobriety. No other criminal charges. Compliance with curfew. No sexual contact.

He looked up. "Is this for real? I can't talk to Penelope?" His voice cracked. How would he fix this if he couldn't talk to her?

"Absolutely not," she said, her steely eyes issuing a threat. "If you break any of these conditions, you could end up at the Juvenile Justice Center until your case is resolved."

His head spun. He couldn't watch movies? Be around children? The sobriety one tripped him up, too. Did they know Micah drank that night? Nah, if they did, they'd charge him with underage drinking.

"Judith Kenley is your social worker." Officer Avery highlighted the name at the top of the page. "She'll check in with you soon; monitor your compliance with the TPCO."

Without any real choices, he signed the paper.

Officer Avery stood and walked behind him, handcuffing him again. Then she led him out of the room, down the hall, through two locked doors, and into the lobby. Ma stood there, fingers flying across her phone. Only then, did the officer uncuff him and leave.

"Ma!" He fell into her embrace. The warmth of Ma's body, the tightness of her hug, the smells of vanilla and jasmine, made him feel safe.

The feeling didn't last long. Once inside Ma's car, the tears he kept bottled up all afternoon were on the cusp on release. He dug his palms into his eyes. Why arrest him? Plenty of teenagers had sex. Could Xavier be right? Did this really come down to being Black? Was society that fucked up? "Why did this happen?"

Ma cupped his cheeks with both hands and that was it. He was gone. Done. The tears came out violently.

"I got us a lawyer," she said, kissing his forehead. "And she's going to take care of everything. But right now, I need you to be brave. You're a smart, kind, capable young Black man. You have nothing, *nothing*, to be ashamed of. Okay?"

The weight of the afternoon rested heavy on his shoulders. He looked down, where the ink smudged onto the palm of his hand. A visual reminder that he was now a criminal. A word he thought would never apply to him.

CHAPTER SEVENTEEN
PENELOPE

Penelope lay atop foam padding in the garage loft, their "secret clubhouse" as kids, surrounded by pillows, blankets, and books. She buried her face in the pillows, trying to resurrect Micah's scent, but all she smelled was mothballs and dust. There was probably a nest of mice nearby, but she refused to move. She felt close to Micah here. They met here a few times during the summer, kissing and talking in hushed voices. If she closed her eyes and delicately ran a finger across her lips, she could pretend it was his lips.

This was what she was doing when Ollie climbed up the ladder. School must be over. She missed her first day of high school.

"Why don't you have your phone?" he asked. "I was looking for you."

"Forgot it." Truthfully, she didn't want to be found. Everyone wanted her to talk, reassure them she was okay. But she wasn't and couldn't pretend otherwise.

"It's hot up here." Ollie sat next to her, crisscross-applesauce, using the frayed edge of his T-shirt to wipe his forehead.

"I'm cold." She couldn't get warm. Chills rattled her body like an oncoming train. It didn't make sense. Then again, nothing did right now.

"Something happened today," Ollie said, chewing on his lower lip. The skin around it was red—a sign he'd been stressing. "Micah got arrested."

"Arrested? How—"

"Handcuffed—"

"Handcuffed?" Penelope repeated, incredulous.

"—and marched out of school."

Penelope felt sick. She leaned over the edge of the loft, ready to purge her complicity. But nothing happened. Too little food, or maybe not enough guilt. Somehow, she blocked out the possibility of Micah's arrest during the police interview. Her goal had been to get through it. Get back to bed. Even after reading Micah's Insta post, she did nothing, too pissed about being outed.

God, she was selfish.

"This is all Mom's fault. She made me talk to the cops," Penelope said, creeping back from the edge of the loft, suddenly afraid she might fall. That she might *let* herself fall. "How could she do this to him?"

"Mom's freaking—"

"I'm sure." Penelope rolled her eyes. "Give me your phone. I want to see if he DM'd me."

Ollie pulled out his phone, both of their heads bent over it as Penelope logged Ollie out of Instagram and checked her account. She had a slew of DM's from Micah the past few days, ramping up in hysteria as she remained mute, all questioning why Mom called the cops.

She didn't respond because he never apologized. Never said he went too far.

Was *she* the problem? Had she misinterpreted everything? Why was she alone struggling?

He must have known, based on her silence, that she was upset. Shouldn't he be trying to figure out why? Why did only his feelings matter? These thoughts felt like falling through a trap door, some laced with anger, others confusion, most with regret. She fell for his act, fell in love—ugh!

A new DM popped up. Micah must have seen she was active. She tapped it. *R you hurt???* Micah wrote. *That's the line the police r feeding me. What happened after I left? Quit playing and tell the TRUTH. Ur Mom is fucking with my life.*

"Tell the truth?" Penelope screeched. Yes, she was hurt! Why would she make this up? To what end? "He thinks I'm lying?"

"Honestly, P, he probably doesn't remember what happened."

She turned to Ollie. "How could he not remember? We had sex!"

Ollie cleared his throat. Wouldn't meet her eyes. "Micah and I were drinking. That's why I got sick and passed out. He was drunk when he went upstairs."

Penelope's shoulders dropped. That's why Micah didn't listen. Didn't look at her. Did he know what he was doing? Did he realize he was hurting her? Tears made the familiar path to her eyes. She was so sick of crying. Sick of being weak. Damaged. Missing Micah one second, hating him the next, guilt a second skin. "Why would you do something so stupid?" she asked.

"He found the bottle in the freezer and he—" Ollie gnawed on his lip. "You know how he gets. I couldn't say no."

Penelope closed her eyes. Micah had some hold over Ollie that she didn't understand. Then again, he had a hold over her too. What would their lives be like without him? "Why didn't you tell me?"

"I tried," Ollie said. "I'm...I'm sorry."

She opened her eyes and saw that Ollie navigated to Micah's page. Micah posted a shirtless pic (shirtless pics became his thing this summer as his muscles popped), in a black and white filter. His 'fro looked like a halo in the shadowed light, his abs slashed, his hand reaching out toward the camera. The caption, posted ten minutes ago, said, *Officially a statistic. #speakup #blacklivesmatter*

Ollie scanned down to the comments and abruptly shut off his phone.

"Let me see," Penelope said.

"No."

She held out her hand. "Give it."

He put the phone behind his back, out of her reach. "It's junk."

She tried to snatch it. "You're so annoying!"

"Why won't you let me protect you?"

"You're too late." It was a cheap shot, given her lies, but she didn't care.

"Whatever." He tossed her the phone and started down the ladder. "You'll just feel worse."

"Nothing can make this worse." A minute later, she regretted those words. Each comment more toxic than the last.

LOL. Now it's rape when you have sex with your girlfriend? What's next ladies?

Regret doesn't equal rape. Sorry, Penelope. Turns out you're just a closeted slut.

She gasped, covering her mouth with her hand. *Penelope Swanson is a two-faced white biatch who needs some deep dicking to get that stick outa her vag.*

Penelope choked on her sobs. Everyone hated her. Blamed her. Accused her of ruining Micah's life. Didn't they realize hers was ruined too?

CHAPTER EIGHTEEN
AMELIA

Between learning about Micah's arrest last night and then a morning spent on the phone with florists, caterers, and one bride who wanted Amelia to look through dozens of bridesmaids' dresses to ensure a flattering style for all body types, she was eager to pick up Penelope for therapy. Start her on the path of healing.

Penelope sat on the top step of their front porch, dressed in a black hoodie, black joggers, and oversized sunglasses, looking like a forlorn Audrey Hepburn. She walked to the car with her head down, getting in without acknowledging Amelia.

They drove silently through the residential streets, surrounded by cars, buses, and bikes. Normalcy. "I was thinking we could grab lunch after," Amelia said, still concerned by how little Penelope was eating.

"Not hungry."

"How about we hit some balls at the club first and work up an appetite?" Amelia's tennis game was rusty, but she played college tennis for UW and could still spar with Penelope.

"Don't you have work?"

"I can take the afternoon off." Amelia lightened her voice, tried to sound upbeat. "Come on! Let's work up a sweat, release some endorphins!"

"Probably shouldn't," Penelope said. "Life isn't free, you know." All sarcasm now. "We need money for the house, food, my tennis lessons—"

Amelia interrupted her by squeezing her thigh. "Okay, okay. I just want to talk, make sure you're okay."

Penelope jerked away. "God, stop already."

Penelope's soliloquy on work and money caused the guilt in Amelia's heart to metastasize. It wasn't guilt that she could've prevented Micah from assaulting Penelope—no one could have predicted that. Rather, guilt that she was too busy running her company to give the kids the attention they needed. She envisioned having heart-to-heart talks with her children as they grew; cooing over first loves, mending broken hearts, commiserating about impossible college standards. They'd tackle it all.

Instead, Amelia drove to the appointment, processing the disturbing truth that her children believed work was more important than them. That they didn't feel they *could* interrupt her, confide in her. It started with taking calls in the car, then Saturday events where she'd miss Penelope's tennis meets, late nights working instead of joining them to watch TV. While Amelia knew her children were everything, her actions didn't always show it. Amelia could defend herself—Derek was gone and they needed money, security, a future—but nothing was more important to a child than time. And lately, she'd put hers elsewhere.

"I've heard Suzanne's quite good," Amelia said, unable to quell the relentless desire to help Penelope. Somehow. Someway. "But it's important you feel comfortable—"

"I don't want to talk to anyone. Is that an option?"

"I wouldn't make you do this unless I believed it would help."

"Nothing will help," Penelope muttered as they pulled to a stoplight next to the high school. Kids ran around the track. Amelia glanced at Penelope, wondering how she felt, knowing that, but for last weekend, she'd be with them. Her mouth remained fixed in a line though, the sunglasses masking her eyes.

"It might seem pointless—"

"Can we go five minutes without talking?" Penelope reached over and turned up the music, loud enough to shake the car. Amelia turned it down, but took the hint.

Penelope added a side of surliness to her nothingness yesterday after finding out about Micah's arrest. Amelia tried to think positive;

any emotion was better than nothing, right? But Ollie hinted that she blamed Amelia. *Just a feeling*, he said when Amelia pressed him. But with twins, a feeling was as good as a verdict.

Did she get Micah arrested? Inadvertently, she supposed. She took Penelope to the hospital, which alerted the police. But the police wouldn't have arrested him unless they thought a crime was committed. And for that, Micah had himself to blame. Actions had consequences. And seeing the consequences Penelope suffered didn't make Amelia regret that Micah was enduring his own difficulties.

Penelope's attitude evaporated by the time they were ushered inside Suzanne's office, an aesthetically calming room with sky-blue walls, nautical decorations, and deep, plush chairs covered with pillows that enveloped you like a snuggly blanket.

After Suzanne introduced herself, Amelia updated her on what happened since they talked on Saturday—Penelope's refusal to go to school, play tennis, Micah's arrest. The old Penelope never would've let Amelia speak for her. But this Penelope sat next to Amelia with her sunglasses on, her gaze settled out the window, as if the conversation had nothing to do with her.

When Amelia repeated how worried she was about Penelope's silence, Suzanne interrupted, asking if she could talk to Penelope alone. "But before you go," Suzanne said, "I want both of you to know that whatever Penelope and I talk about in here is confidential. Short of any concern of self-harm, I won't tell your mom anything you say, okay?"

Penelope turned to Amelia, her voice panicked, "Please don't go."

Evidently, Penelope was listening. "I'm right outside," Amelia said. "Just try, okay? You might surprise yourself and feel better." Amelia rubbed Penelope's shoulders, pulling her into a hug, not loving having to go either. And the news that she wouldn't know anything Penelope said? Brutal. She understood wanting to give Penelope privacy, create trust with her therapist, but she could help

Penelope progress if she knew the exact nature of the issues she faced.

Suzanne met Amelia's eyes and nodded. "We'll be fine."

Out in the hallway, Amelia pressed her fist against her lips to hold in the tears. Leaving now reminded her of when she dropped the twins off for their first day of nursery school. Except, back then, Ollie, always the sensitive one, gripped her thigh like a rattlesnake while Penelope ran away. That was also the day she met Zoe and Micah. Micah, already a ball of adorable energy, asked Ollie to use the foam blocks to build a spaceship together. Amelia introduced herself to Zoe, complimenting Micah's kindness.

He was born with a glow, Zoe said. *When he shines it on you, you can't help but smile.* They ended up grabbing coffee together, discussing motherhood. Turned out, Zoe was under contract to buy the house across the street. Amelia didn't realize how lonely she'd been until Zoe moved in. Having the twins at twenty-four, barely a year into her marriage, Amelia was at home, changing diapers, doing laundry, feeling like an express-milk cow, while her college friends were starting their careers, partying, hooking up. Derek worked crazy hours, not understanding why she felt so frazzled. But Zoe did. Despite their differences—Amelia married and a stay-at home mom, while Zoe was single and worked—there was an immediate connection as young mothers, surviving the trenches together.

Amelia sat in the waiting room and picked up *People*, forcing herself to read celebrity nonsense. Evict these memories. Because if she gave them air time, she couldn't accept that Micah assaulted Penelope. It didn't add up. No one graduates from charisma to sexual assault.

But the alternative, that Penelope was lying, was also unthinkable. Something horrible happened and Micah was at the center. Why should Amelia punish herself, trying to make sense of something senseless? As Dr. Bilson advised, *Don't go looking for trouble.*

CHAPTER NINETEEN
PENELOPE

Penelope sat across from Suzanne, her "therapist," hugging her knees to her chest, hating Mom for dragging her here. What was the point? What could Suzanne say that would make everything better? That would tilt the axis in Penelope's world so that Micah didn't get drunk, didn't ignore her pleas to stop, didn't have sex with her, didn't get arrested, didn't give her the kiss of death socially?

"I'm really proud of you for coming today," Suzanne said after Mom left. "It must've been difficult."

"My mom made me." Penelope rested her head against her knees and closed her eyes. She was so tired. She couldn't sleep. Friday night haunted her; it felt so unreal, unimaginable, that she lived it anew each time. Always horrifying. Always relentless. She wanted to change the outcome, lock the door, push him off, yell, put on some damn clothes. But like when it happened, she was paralyzed, required to meet her fate.

"Give yourself some credit," Suzanne said. "You showed up. That's huge."

"You obviously don't know my mom well. Ignoring her is, like, not an option."

Suzanne smiled. "Can you tell me what happened Friday night?"

"My mom told you."

"I'd like to hear it from you."

Penelope's stomach growled; the hunger pains were indistinguishable from the all-encompassing pain weighing her down. She couldn't remember the last time she ate. Normally, she was on a strict diet devised by her sports nutritionist. Now, her muscles were likely wasting away. And she didn't care.

"Micah was hanging out with my brother—" She stopped, wondering if she should mention the drinking. Suzanne said she'd keep their meetings confidential, but Penelope knew a warning wouldn't stop Mom. Best to be safe. She didn't want to get Micah in more trouble. "He was waiting for me after my shower. He kissed me and followed me into my room. He, I don't know, got too excited or something, and I was just in a towel, so..." She turned and looked out the window, pressing a hand to her stomach, thankful the sunglasses blocked her tears. Was she pregnant? Mom said the pill should've prevented it, but they wouldn't know until she got her period. Pregnant. At fourteen. Unthinkable. And yet, this was her new reality. "I don't understand. Micah's not a jerk...he usually listens."

"Tell me about him."

Penelope closed her eyes. Imagined Micah's lips brushing hers. The warmth of his palm clasped inside her hand. His whispered words. His eyes widening when he saw her. The weight of his head resting against hers. The smiles. Oh, his smiles! Different for every occasion.

"He's my best friend," she said. "Obv, I have other friends, but Micah—" She shook her head. "I can't imagine life without him. But now..."

"What?"

Seeing him would gut her. Enduring his hate. "He'll never forgive me."

"Forgive you for what?"

Micah blamed her for getting arrested. She didn't stop Mom. Didn't tell the truth—whatever that meant. Penelope pulled the tassels of her hoodie tight, forced herself to breathe. "I don't want to think about this anymore. I just want to be me again. The real me."

Last Friday, she was killin' it during her match. Being aggressive, stepping inside the baseline. She could still feel the crack of the racquet as it pounded the ball, taste sweat on her lips. How could a few days, an hour, a moment, change someone so thoroughly? Take away her strength, drive, her very essence?

"You're still in there, Penelope." Suzanne's words joined the late-afternoon dust buds floating through the sunlight. "The way you're feeling right now, I promise, it won't be forever."

Such false hope. "Can we be done? I need to be done." Penelope stood up and walked out. That was enough for one day. For one lifetime.

CHAPTER TWENTY
ZOE

Stepping out of the elevator and onto the thirty-fifth floor of the U.S. Bank Tower, Zoe was struck by the opulence of the reception room for the law firm of Wilson & Wright, LLP. Gleaming wood furniture, a spiral staircase, twenty-foot floor-to-ceiling windows with a pristine view of Lake Michigan. Everything screamed money. Exclusiveness. Whiteness.

She looked at Micah, curious to see if he was awed, but his eyes were cast down, his hands tucked rigidly inside his jean pockets. Rage emanated from his pores like steam from hot tea. When she picked him up at the police station two days ago, he was terrified. Shaky. Desperate. But once home, a switch flipped, and he became angry. Started ranting about being discriminated against because he was Black. Blamed her for letting him grow up in this white, suburban community, letting him assimilate, think he wasn't any different. It turned into a huge argument when she saw that he posted these ideas on Instagram. She made him take down the post about Penelope, talked to him about posting about the case, but she feared the damage was already done.

As a mom, she tried to strike a balance, be real about the inequities of the world, but optimistic he could overcome any prejudices he encountered. *The world has never met Micah Gray*, she always told him.

She understood his anger; remembered the first time she realized having Black skin othered her—and not in a good way. A white girl refused to hold Zoe's hand while playing red rover during kindergarten, saying she didn't want to get Black cooties. Like Zoe, Micah needed to learn how to use that anger to work within the system to make changes.

"Let's check in," she said to Micah.

"You do it." He walked across the lobby, taking a seat by the windows. A power play. He defied her because he could. She was safe. But being a punching bag grew old fast.

Zoe gave the secretary a stiff smile and explained they had an eleven o'clock appointment with Attorney Sarah Levine. When Zoe learned of Micah's arrest, she called her client, Layla, the only lawyer she knew. Unfortunately, Layla was a divorce attorney. *Sarah Levine,* Layla said after Zoe explained the situation. *She's the best. Passionate. Fearless. You can trust her.*

And expensive, Zoe thought as she sat next to Micah. This meeting alone cost two-hundred and twenty-five dollars. A five-thousand-dollar retainer if they wanted to move forward. How would Zoe pay? Dip into her retirement account? A high-interest loan? She rolled her shoulders, stretched her neck from side to side, trying to relax her muscles, her mind.

"Ms. Gray?" A svelte woman with a platinum blonde pixie haircut approached. She wore a charcoal suit, immaculately pressed, and had icy blue eyes. "I'm Sarah Levine."

Zoe stood and shook her hand. "Zoe. And this is Micah." Micah merely nodded.

Sarah led them to a meeting room with a large oval conference table and impressionist art on the walls. Sarah sat across from them, her back to the blanket of Lake Michigan, pen hovering over her yellow legal pad.

"I've reviewed the arrest report," Sarah said, diving right in. "Charge of third-degree sexual assault. But I'd like to hear from you, Micah, about what happened."

Micah recited the familiar story. A mother should not know how and when her son loses his virginity, but, thanks to Amelia, she'd never forget.

"No more talking to the police without me," Sarah said when he finished. "Don't be swayed by false promises about telling the truth. Silence is golden."

Zoe underwent a swift dizzy spell, overwhelmed by her mistake in letting the police question Micah. Telling him to be truthful. She'd been raised to fear the cops, not defy them. She didn't know she had the right to tell the cops no. "What happens now?" Zoe asked. "Can they really prosecute him for sexual assault?"

"They can and they will," Sarah said, shuffling papers. "First things first. You'll be contacted by a social worker to discuss Micah's background; Judith Kenley—"

"She called yesterday..." Zoe hesitated, registering Sarah's surprise. "Is that bad?"

"That's prompt," Sarah said eventually. "But irrelevant. Regardless of what she recommends, the DA *will* charge you." Micah slumped in his chair as the news settled in. "We'll have a preliminary hearing in a couple weeks, you'll enter a denial, and the DA will make an offer. Essentially, a reduced penalty to admit responsibility. Or we can go to trial and argue for a finding of non-delinquency."

"What happens if he's found delinquent?" Zoe asked, each word an ice pick to her brain. "Could he...go to prison?"

"A juvenile detention center, not prison," Sarah said. "Thankfully, most Wisconsin judges have gotten their heads out of their asses and stopped moving kids to adult court, except for the most heinous cases." She smiled at Zoe and Micah, who didn't share her cheer. "If he's adjudicated delinquent, it could be anything from therapy to house arrest to juvenile detention. It's his first arrest, so that's a plus."

"But I'm innocent." Micah looked boyishly worried with big dark eyes and a pouty bottom lip. "Doesn't that matter?"

"I will make it matter," Sarah said with a steely toughness Zoe respected. "There's no jury in juvenile court. We only have to convince the judge she consented."

Micah's head fell against the table with a bang.

"What? What is it, baby?" Zoe asked, resting her hand on the back of his neck.

"You really think a judge is going to give me a break?" he asked.

"It's not a break. You're innocent," Sarah reminded him.

Micah sat up, eyes bleary and derisive. "Yeah, but I don't look innocent. You catch my drift?" He turned to Zoe. "Xavier says none of this would've happened if I was white."

"I've won with Black clients before," Sarah said.

"The judge wants to find the truth, Micah," Zoe added. "Remember that." Being Black didn't help. But Zoe didn't want him viewing this as a self-fulfilling prophecy. His skin as a liability. That was a feeling he wouldn't easily shake.

"What about that paper they gave me?" Micah dug in his pocket and unfolded the Temporary Physical Custody Order. "These conditions—no R-rated movies, curfew. They're lookin' to trip me up."

"That's a standard TPCO for sexual assault," Sarah said. "The social worker will ensure compliance, but the court will also look to you, Zoe, to monitor him, when deciding whether he can stay at home."

Zoe nodded slowly. Enforcing these conditions would create a parent-child relationship she never wanted. Growing up in a strict Christian house, where her parents all but strapped a chastity belt on her, locked up the alcohol, cough syrup and nail polish, Zoe vowed to trust her son. She didn't supervise his movie choices or demand passwords to his social media sites, like Amelia did. Patrol his comings and goings. And they talked. Really talked. But privacy, apparently, was something he relinquished in the arrest. What happened to innocent until proven guilty?

"What does 'no sexual contact mean?'" Micah asked.

"Don't have sex," Sarah said flatly. "Under Wisconsin law, it's a crime for teenagers to have sex anyway. It's usually not charged if both kids are consenting, or 'cooperative' as it's termed, but don't do it." Sarah narrowed her eyes at Micah. "And stay off social media. I know your generation likes to broadcast every whimsical thought, but your posts are giving the prosecution material."

Zoe narrowed her eyes at Micah. "I told him the same thing."

"Talk to your mom. Find a priest. Hell, call me," Sarah said, before turning to Zoe. "Teens are impulsive. You need to save him from himself."

"I will." How would she supervise his every move with a full-time job? She had no choice but to set rules, become a helicopter parent. He'd hate her—a price she was willing to pay to keep him out of juvie.

"Now," Sarah said, turning to a fresh page in her notepad. "Tell me about the girl."

The girl. While Penelope wasn't Zoe's daughter by blood, she was Zoe's daughter through love. Penelope confided in Zoe. Talked about her dreams of winning a grand slam or the unrelenting pressure to be perfect.

"She's my best friend." Micah bit down on his lip. "I don't understand why she's saying this stuff. And she won't talk to me—"

"You can't talk to her, Micah," Sarah interrupted. "No texts, no calls, *nothing*. Understand?"

Micah rested his elbows on his knees, hanging his head.

"She's driven. Passionate," Zoe said. "But that passion also makes her emotional. I think she wanted to have sex and then freaked out afterwards." Zoe stopped short of blaming Penelope. *But Penelope's not a victim*, she reminded herself. If anything, Micah was the victim. Arrested for a normal rite of passage.

"Emotional." Sarah wrote. "Perhaps unstable—"

Micah's head snapped up. "She's not unstable! The police must've twisted her words; they did it with me."

"Penelope told her doctor and the police you forced her to have sex," Sarah said. "Apparently, she was bleeding from lacerations to the vaginal wall."

"It wasn't—" He rubbed his eyes, his voice guttural. "I thought girls bled the first time."

"They do," Zoe said. If they didn't use a condom, they likely didn't use lube. And Penelope was probably nervous, it being her first time. So, no, while she wished Penelope never experienced this pain, the tears weren't evidence that Micah forced her.

"Until I get the medical reports, I can't tell you the extent of her injuries," Sarah said.

"She wasn't hurt." Micah's words were barely audible. "I would've noticed. I would've stopped."

"This must be difficult," Sarah said. "To have your life flipped upside down. But you're not alone, Micah. You have to trust me. Work with me, not against me."

"He would never do this," Zoe said, needing Sarah to believe in him.

Sarah nodded. "Don't talk to the police. Stay off social media. School. Practice. Home. Lay low."

Zoe looked out at the lake, watching the metallic waves bob across the surface. Instead of calming her, it suggested a storm was brewing. "What happens now?"

"We wait," Sarah said simply. "No news is good news."

No news is good news, Zoe repeated to herself as the meeting ended. Somehow, that didn't reassure her.

CHAPTER TWENTY-ONE
AMELIA

Amelia pushed her cart halfway down the cereal aisle before she saw Zoe, studying the ingredients on an oatmeal box. Heart pounding, fight or flight instinct told Amelia to retreat. But Amelia couldn't avoid her forever. Correction. Amelia didn't want to avoid Zoe. Austin was right. There had to be a way to connect among the wreckage.

Ever since Micah's arrest a few days ago, Amelia thought about calling Zoe. But the part that blamed Zoe stopped her. Micah's action were the dividends of Zoe's free-range, friend rather than enforcer, honesty-at-all-costs, parenting. Zoe described herself as sex-positive, a philosophy she shared with Micah, whereas Amelia's conversations with the kids about sex were usually an awkward comment to something on TV. As in, *Being a virgin in high school is not social suicide*, when watching *Booksmart*.

Her hands were slick against the cart handle as she pushed it toward Zoe. "Hey," Amelia said. When Zoe didn't respond, she nearly turned around. Then she saw earbuds in Zoe's ears. She reached over and touched Zoe's arm.

Zoe's face registered shock, then confusion and finally landed on anger. She yanked out her earbuds and said nothing.

"I saw you." Amelia gestured behind her, down the aisle, as if that explained everything. Up close, Zoe looked tired. Her normally glowing skin looked dull, the bags beneath her eyes caked with concealer. Her red lipstick bled into the creases of her lips. "How are you holding up?"

Zoe's nostrils flared as she inhaled. "Not good, Amelia."

"This is a nightmare," Amelia agreed. "For everyone. Penelope won't talk. Doesn't sleep—"

"She's obviously talking some." Zoe chucked the oatmeal into her cart. "Enough to get Micah arrested."

Amelia swallowed her apprehension. She dealt with angry vendors, distraught brides, clients that thought money bought indentured servitude. But dealing with Zoe's anger cut right to Amelia's core. While they had disagreements, they never argued. Not like this. With so much at stake.

And what right did Zoe have to be angry? She was across the street while Micah took advantage of Penelope, never once thinking he might be up to no good. Why didn't she check on the kids? "Honestly?" Amelia said. "Micah's arrest traumatized her further. She just wants to forget, pretend it never happened."

Zoe shrugged. "So, let her."

Amelia flinched, surprised at Zoe's callousness. "I think that would be the worst thing, don't you? Having her bury something so traumatic?"

"No." Zoe laughed softly. "Actually, I think the worst thing is having cops interrogate Micah. Arrest him. Going bankrupt to hire a lawyer so he won't end up in juvie for a crime he didn't commit."

"Crime he didn't commit?" Amelia took a step toward Zoe, her voice hushed, but seething. "You really think Penelope made this up?"

"You *really* think Micah assaulted her?"

"You didn't see her—"

"I don't have to see her," Zoe snapped. "I know my son. I thought you did too."

Zoe expected Amelia to give Micah a pass because she knew him, loved him. But what about Zoe's relationship with Penelope? Didn't Zoe have compassion for P? "This was a mistake," Amelia muttered and grabbed her cart, swerving it in the opposite direction.

"Is there a chance she's pregnant?" Zoe called. "Micah says they didn't use a condom."

Amelia turned around and marched back toward Zoe, annoyed that she would shout such a private issue in the middle of the grocery store. Furious by her use of the word, "they." *Micah* didn't use a condom. Penelope had no choice. "She took the morning after pill."

If she expected gratitude from Zoe, once again, she misjudged their friendship. "Why did you call the cops?" Zoe asked. "This is Micah's life. A Black boy charged with raping a white girl." A tremor went through Zoe's voice. "How do you think that's going to turn out?"

Amelia froze, stunned by the accusation. "It's not about race, Zoe. It's about protecting my daughter. If anyone else did this to Penelope, you'd tell me to do the same. You're blinded by your love. Fine. But don't discount my love."

"Do you think the cops see Micah as we do? A boy that loves Marvel movies, still lets me cuddle him, bakes a cake for my birthday each year." Zoe let the question breathe before continuing. "I didn't think so."

Amelia briefly closed her eyes. "I never thought—"

"What a privilege, not having to think about it."

Amelia's frustration bubbled over. "Penelope's suffering. She doesn't understand how Micah could've done this. She needs an advocate, not someone to downplay it."

"Has it occurred to you that Penelope's suffering, isn't talking to you, because she lied? Every day, the lie gets bigger and bigger." Zoe used her hands to mimic a growing balloon. "Telling you. The doctor. The police. Then Micah gets arrested. She must be terrified, knowing she has to double-down...unless you remind her that it's okay to tell the truth."

Amelia couldn't stand here and listen to Zoe call Penelope a liar. Before leaving, though, she needed to correct Zoe on one matter. "Just so you know," Amelia said, "I didn't call the cops. I took her to the hospital because she was bleeding. The doctor reported it after examining Penelope." She pounded her hand against her heart. "Not me."

Amelia watched as Zoe's mouth gaped like a fish. Not wanting to hear another word, Amelia headed for the exit, leaving her cart for some poor employee to unpack. Fuck this! Fuck my life! She yelled at her kids for using that language, but the feeling was never more apt. She tried to be a good friend, the bigger person, just as Austin suggested, and what did she get? Accusations of raising a liar? Being racist for letting the police investigate her daughter's sexual assault? FML. That's right.

Once inside her car, Amelia batted away tears of frustration. Loneliness. Loss. Unlike marriage, friendship can be dissolved in a moment. There was no document, child, law, binding them together. And yet, it held the same power to gut her soul.

CHAPTER TWENTY-TWO
PENELOPE

On Tuesday morning, a week after everyone else started school, Penelope and Mom sat in the guidance office, listening to Ms. DuPree reiterate that Penelope had the school's complete support. Penelope half-listened, more concerned about how the other kids would treat her, while Mom pegged Ms. DuPree with questions.

"We've modified your schedule to ensure you don't have any classes or study periods with Micah," Ms. DuPree said. "We'll also have you hang back after class and a chaperone will escort you once the bell has rung to avoid him in the halls."

Mom turned to Penelope. "That sounds good, right?"

Penelope cringed. Could she be more conspicuous? Perhaps they could strap a sandwich board to her shoulders, liar on one side and slut on the other. Time-saver.

She didn't want to be here. Wanted to be at home, where she felt safe. But over the last week, Mom insisted that Penelope get up, get dressed, go for walks, eat. Develop a normal routine again. Penelope finally relented on school just to shut Mom up—*Are you okay? What can I do? Do you want to talk?* Endless. Fucking. Pestering. But, sitting here now, inhaling the chemical smell of cleaner and gym shoes that somehow all schools smelled like, she regretted giving in. Was it too late to change her mind? Would Mom let her leave?

"Here's your hall pass," Ms. DuPree said as the door opened. A pale, redheaded girl with freckles walked in. "Penelope, this is Mia. She's your chaperone this week."

Mom stood up and shook Mia's hand, but Penelope stayed in her seat. They all turned to her with expectant eyes, as if awaiting a hat trick.

Mia smiled, breaking the silence. "You have English with Ms. Drake first. She's fantastic."

Mom plastered on a smile too. "English! You love reading," she said, using the fake voice she used to use to convince Penelope to eat her broccoli. "Do you want me to walk with you guys?"

That offer was enough to get Penelope moving. "No. I'm ready."

"Stop by if you need anything," Ms. DuPree said. "I'm always here."

Penelope would rather take a nail file to her eye. Without looking at Mom—she wanted Mom to hurt as bad as Penelope did being forced to come to school today—she followed Mia out the door. Penelope wasn't tough, but she could still act the part.

As Mia and Penelope walked to the fourth floor, Mia played twenty questions, only stopping when they reached the classroom door. "Here's my number," Mia said, handing Penelope a folded piece of paper. "Text whenever. The girls and I—we've got your back."

Penelope received several similar DM's, girls she didn't know telling her she was brave, to reach out if they could help. Brave? About what? And how could they help?

"Thanks." Penelope took the paper and opened the classroom door. The teacher fell silent and dozens of faces turned to look at Penelope. *I'm dead*, Penelope thought. *Officially. Disintegrating into ashes.*

She took a seat next to the window, keeping her head down the entire period. When the bell rang, Cleo Watters approached. Penelope and Cleo hung out in the same clique, but never alone. Cleo, like the rest of her "friends," texted about Micah. Pushed for details. Penelope ghosted everyone.

Cleo bent down and threw her arms around Penelope. "I've been so worried. How *are* you?"

"I'm okay." Cleo's sidekick, Sophie Ferguson joined, while the rest of the class watched, packing up at a murderously slow rate.

"Did Micah really, like, force you to have sex?" Cleo stage whispered the word "sex," the scent of her cinnamon gum fanning Penelope's face.

"Or did you want to?" Sophie asked, voice like a foghorn. "There's so many rumors."

Penelope swallowed the first threat of tears. "I'm not supposed to talk about it..."

"That's cool," Cleo said, at the same moment Sophie said, "That's a choice." Ice cold, perpetually bitchy. That was Sophie.

"Girls." The teacher walked over. "Get to class."

Cleo gave a sympathetic smile. "Text me."

"You okay?" Ms. Drake asked, resting a hand on Penelope's shoulder.

OMFG. Even the teachers knew. "Fine."

Penelope went to wait by the door for Mia, where she was treated to whispers, insults, and accusations—*Is that her? Slut. Liar. I feel bad for her*—as kids filtered inside. It felt horrible, standing there. Worse than horrible. Agonizing. She often felt on the periphery socially, different because she'd rather play tennis than watch makeup tutorials on YouTube, but she'd never been an outcast. Ollie and Micah always had her back. But she was alone now.

Periods two and three were a repeat of English class. Kids gawking, others throwing low key shade, a few pitiful smiles. When she got to the library for fourth period study hall, she chose a table in a secluded corner with no windows, surrounded by towering stacks of books. She wanted to be alone, invisible, vanish from everyone's sightline.

She pulled out a copy of her earth science textbook, pretending to read about coal production. Penelope froze as a boy, scratch that, *man*, sat across from her. He was Black, at least two-hundred pounds, with biceps that size of grapefruits.

"You know what gets me?" he asked, his voice low. "You're all up on my boy, Micah, all summer long, can't get enough, and then once you have sex, you start tweakin.' Running to the police. All because sex isn't part of your good-girl rep."

Two girls Penelope didn't know joined, one sitting next to the guy and one next to Penelope. She felt trapped, her exits blocked, the high bookshelves ensuring no help would come. The secluded corner now menacing.

"Have you seen her play tennis?" the girl across from Penelope asked. Long dark hair. Eyelash extensions. Pink pouty lips. "She tries to be a thirst trap, wearing skirts that show *everything*." She frowned. "Epic fail, doll."

"It's always the quiet ones," her friend agreed. "All horned up from lack of attention."

"Listen," the guy said, leaning across the table. "You're going to say whatever you need to say to get these charges dropped. Okay?"

"How about telling the truth?" the first girl taunted. "Admit you're a slut and end it."

Penelope stood up on shaky legs. She walked toward the entrance of the library, feeling the heat of eyes on her back. Despite every instinct telling her to flee, she would not run. She would not give these people her tears. Somehow, the fighter inside willed her on.

She pushed open the library doors. Why did she come to school today? Give in to Mom's idea of reclaiming normalcy? She saw the Insta comments. Knew people supported Micah. Hated her. Nothing would be normal again. Stupid, stupid, stupid.

Eventually, she found an outside door. She pushed through, not caring whether it set off an alarm. She had to get out. Leave—and never come back.

Once outside, she ran home. Fear coated her lungs, feeding her muscles with each breath. Panic held her brain hostage, refusing to let the nothingness seep through.

By the time she reached her front porch, she was a sweaty, shaky, blubbering mess. Why were people so mean? Why did they assume the worst about her? Were they right? There were dozens of ways she could've stopped Micah. And yet, she lay there, letting Micah have his way. Had she wanted it? Did curiosity take over? The need to do something reckless? Not be perfect for one second?

Her keys! She left everything at school when she ran out. She fell to her knees, tugging her hair, screaming in frustration. She couldn't take any more! This was too much!

And then, perhaps because God knew she hit her limit, she felt a familiar trickle leak into her underwear. Her period. It came. The morning-after pill worked.

She rested her head against the porch, crying. How was this her life? Instead of celebrating another tennis victory, she was celebrating her period?

She felt a hand on her shoulder and turned to see Zoe crouching next to her, looking beautiful in a blood-orange sundress. Without thinking, she flung herself into Zoe's arms.

"Shh." Zoe rocked her back and forth. As Penelope's cries dwindled to whimpers, Zoe loosened her grip. "What's wrong?"

Penelope sat back on her heels, swatting away tears. She found it easier to talk to Zoe than Mom. Zoe exuded chill, while Mom defined extra. Mom kept raising the bar, expecting Penelope to work harder, accomplish more, be perfect. Penelope knew she'd fall short eventually, but she never expected it to happen this way. Watching Mom treat her with kid gloves confirmed Penelope's fears that she was now damaged.

But she wasn't pregnant. Imagine Mom's disappointment if she was.

"Everyone hates me," Penelope said. "They think I'm lying...about Micah." When Zoe didn't say anything, Penelope realized that Zoe agreed. "You must hate me too." Penelope scrambled to her feet. But she had nowhere to go. She was still locked out. And she needed a pad. Before she bled through her underwear. "Can you let me in? I don't have my key."

Zoe patted the porch. "Sit down, P. Whatever's going on with you and Micah, I'm always here for you, okay?"

Penelope lowered herself to the ground. "I never meant for this to happen."

"You can still stop it," Zoe said.

Penelope looked at Zoe. Her eyes soft with concern. It confused Penelope. Was she telling Penelope to lie? "What?"

"You don't have to go forward with this case. Not if you don't want to."

Penelope shook her head, too hurt to ask Zoe whether she believed her. "It doesn't matter. As soon as Micah posted that message on Insta, he branded me. No matter where I go, I'll always be a slut. The white girl that ratted out her Black boyfriend to the police."

"I've made him scrub his Instagram," Zoe said. "He's not allowed to post anything without showing me first. Definitely nothing about you."

Zoe was too late. Nothing could be scrubbed. Not completely. With one post, Micah stole not only her trust, but destroyed her reputation. Her identity. Her future.

"I'm so tired," Penelope sobbed. Pathetic. Why couldn't she stop crying? Where did her mental toughness go? "I can't sleep. And all I want to do is forget. Move on, you know?"

Zoe cupped Penelope's chin, kissing her forehead. "You're the strongest girl I know. You'll get through this." She pulled out her phone from her purse. "I'm calling your mom."

Penelope listened as Zoe explained to Mom that Penelope was upset and left school early. Her voice was overly polite. None of the warmth she had when speaking to Penelope. And from the sounds of it, Mom was all business too. "I don't feel comfortable leaving her home alone," Zoe said.

If Zoe was concerned, why didn't she stay with Penelope?

Zoe passed her the phone. "She wants to talk to you."

"Hey." Penelope debated whether she should tell Mom about getting her period. No. Too many people already knew private details about her body. Mom could find out like everyone else, when she didn't pop out a baby in nine months.

"What happened? Are you okay? Do you see Micah?" Mom fired questions machine-gun style. A subtle reminder that she was at work and Penelope had roughly thirty seconds to spit it out.

"The kids—" Penelope cut herself off. Today went beyond mean. They stalked Penelope into that library like prey, feasting on her pain. "Mom, I'm done. Seriously. I'm not going back."

"Do you want me to come home?" Mom asked, apparently willing to do anything to fix Penelope. Even skip work. If only Mom could fix her.

"No. God, stop."

"Tell me what you need."

"Just...just tell Zoe to let me in the house."

"I'm calling Austin," Mom said. "He'll come over and stay with you."

As if she was five and needed a babysitter. "Fine."

Penelope ended the call and pressed her head between her knees. Zoe didn't want to stay with her. Blamed her for getting Micah arrested, whether she'd admit it or not. Each day Penelope's world got smaller and smaller, the people she could count on being swept away like ball marks on a clay court.

At least she had Ollie; as long as he was by her side, she'd be okay. They'd find a way to survive together. They always did.

CHAPTER TWENTY-THREE
AUSTIN

Austin just finished teaching his Tuesday morning ladies group—four stay-at-home moms that were as competitive about their tennis game as they were their dress size—when he received Amelia's phone call.

"It's Penelope," Amelia said, breathless. "She left school. Zoe found her melting down on the porch. Obviously, Zoe can't stay, and I'm at this event downtown—it would be difficult—she doesn't want me—Ahh!" Amelia took an audible breath. "I need to know she's okay."

"I'm on it." When Derek died six years ago, Austin was floundering on the professional tennis tour, having enough talent to make it to the top three-hundred in the world, play in ITF's and challengers, but not enough to make a good living. He moved back to Wisconsin to help Amelia with the kids. They needed him then and they needed him now.

"Thank you." She sighed. "I hope you don't have to cancel much."

"Don't worry about it." Austin owned a private, sixteen-court indoor/outdoor tennis club with one of his college teammates. He had more flexibility to cancel a lesson than she could bail on a party.

He ended the call and walked through the curtain that divided the tennis courts from the lobby doors. After grabbing his keys from his office and jogging to the parking lot, he leadfooted it to Amelia's house. Penelope, much like Amelia, was born operating at an intensity that led to greatness. And sudden downward spirals.

Five minutes later, he parked in Amelia's driveway. Penelope sat on the porch with Zoe, resting her head between her knees. A hiss of air escaped his mouth, a breath he didn't know he was holding.

Penelope looked up as he approached. Her eyes were shot with crimson, lips chapped and chewed. Her collarbone created an unhealthy valley to her neck, as if an unkind word would snap the bone. "Can you let me in?" Penelope asked. "I want to lay down."

"Sure." He turned to Zoe. "Wait here, okay?" She nodded.

He unlocked the door, following Penelope inside, watching as she filled a glass of water in the kitchen. "Did someone say something?"

"Just that I'm a liar, a slut—" She gulped the water. "Never mind."

"Who said this?" he asked, daring to come closer. She hadn't let anyone close, including him, since that night. "Which kids?"

She barked a laugh, her eyelashes shiny with tears. "What're you going to do? Track 'em down? You can't stop the rumors. They're everywhere."

There was nothing he hated more than not being able to take away the pain of someone he loved. She was too young to feel this hopeless. "What would you do right now, if you could do anything?" he asked. Amelia accused him of spoiling the kids, bending the rules without good reason. Well, so what. Given his relationship rap sheet, Penelope and Ollie were the closest he'd probably ever get to having kids. And if now wasn't a reason to buy Penelope's happiness, a smile, hell, anything to stop her tears, he didn't know what was. "Great America? Let's go. Want to try every dessert at Kopp's? I'm game. Netflix binge? I'll sit through all seven Harry Potters."

"There's eight," she said.

He grinned. "Fine, eight. You strike a hard bargain."

Just as he thought she was about to cave, she turned toward the stairs. "I'm tired."

"P...come on."

"Maybe later." She disappeared upstairs, her footfalls soft.

He'd give Penelope some time, then try again.

Walking back outside, he saw Zoe sitting on the top step. In a bright orange sundress and hair in shoulder-length dreads, she looked feminine, yet badass.

"Thanks for calling Amelia," he said, sitting next to her. A lawnmower revved a few houses down, the breeze bringing the scent of cut grass. "I know she appreciated it."

"I still care about the kids." Zoe looked across the street at her house while she spoke. "I care about Amelia. I'm just...really angry with her."

Her toes were polished a bright orange to match her dress. A toe ring on the second toe. It amazed him how women paid attention to the smallest details. "Is it weird? Being here?"

"It reminds me of being excluded as a kid, whether because I was Black or not cool enough or just because kids are mean. I see you guys coming and going and it's a constant reminder that we're not welcome anymore." She turned to look at him. "And it hurts, to know we were never really family. That we're forgotten so easily. Penelope and Ollie have each other. Amelia has you. But, Micah and I, we're floundering in this new space."

He rested his hand gently against her wrist, his fingertips feeling the steady brush of her pulse. "I'm still your friend."

She nodded, trying to smile, landing in a grimace. "Thanks."

Everyone was falling apart on him today. "Are you okay? Really?"

Her chin started to tremble. Her jaw locked, trying to keep the emotion inside, but, all at once, tears fell, a backlog she'd probably been holding onto since Micah was arrested. He rubbed her back, wondering if she had anyone to confide in. He didn't know much about her family, a brother that lived in Cleveland, parents she kept a cordial, but distant relationship. But Zoe was right. They abandoned her. He never thought to check in, too consumed with calming Amelia, supporting Penelope, distracting Ollie.

"I'm worried," she said, blotting tears with her index finger. "All the time."

"I'm a good listener." He sat back, resting his palms against the wood porch and tilting his head up to enjoy the warmth of the bright sun, giving her time to recover. She'd talk if she wanted, or not, but maybe sitting next to her would help. With women, he learned

114

saying less sometimes meant more. That was his plan, anyway, one he would use on Penelope as soon as he was done here.

"I'm worried Micah will go to juvie," Zoe eventually said. "And even if he avoids juvie, he'll forever be changed. The confidence, the playfulness I love will disappear. He's already talking about how this happened because he's Black. I just—I never wanted him to walk around, feeling like there's a target on his back." She shuddered, struggling to breathe through her fears. "I worry I'll go broke paying for his defense. That I didn't hire the right lawyer. That I made a mistake, letting him talk to the cops. I worry I'm a bad mother." She took a deep breath. "I was home that night. I could've hung out over here, but I never wanted to be all up in his business, like my parents were. And now he's paying for my mistakes."

"You're an amazing mom, Zoe," Austin said. "And he's a good kid. Yes, he makes mistakes, tests limits, but he's a teenage boy. And here's the inside scoop, we're all idiots at that age. But he's learning, and, frankly, he's lucky to have you." Austin pulled off his ball cap, running his hands through his sweaty hair. He still didn't know what happened between the kids. He believed Penelope felt unheard, hurt, but Micah forcing her? None of it added up. "Will you make all the right decisions with this? Hell, I don't know. Amelia thinks she's doing a horrible job too. The only thing I know for sure is that everything you guys do for those kids comes from love. Micah knows you're there for him. Always. And, well, that's everything."

Zoe stared at her hands, twisting the ring on her pinky finger. "I hope you're right."

"It has to happen at least once, right?"

This earned a smile. "You sell yourself short."

"Better than overselling myself," Austin said, relieved to be bantering. That was his and Zoe's sweet spot. "My goal is to keep women pleasantly surprised."

Now, she laughed. Mission accomplished. They both stood up. "Call me if you need to talk," he said. Amelia probably wouldn't like it, but Austin wanted to help everyone heal. Besides, anger clouded

Amelia's judgment, made her lash out at the wrong person. Zoe wasn't the enemy.

Not that he'd tell Amelia. He knew her well enough to steer clear of that storm.

"Thanks." Zoe met his eyes. They lingered on the porch, standing an inch too close, the air thick with uncertainty of how to leave such an intimate conversation.

"No problem." Austin retreated inside the house with a quick wave. He rested against the door, his fingers touching the knob, confused. He felt vibrant, an almost queasy excitement. Because of Zoe?

He laughed, finding the thought absurd. Zoe was Amelia's best friend. Austin teased her. She gave it back just as good. But there was something about her today—her vulnerability? Her openness?—that shook him. Changed the way he saw her.

He dismissed the thought, ignored the feeling, knowing it would complicate an already complicated situation, and went in search of Penelope. Perhaps he could bat a thousand in the cheer-up department.

CHAPTER TWENTY-FOUR
AMELIA

Amelia drove through I-94 traffic, cursing the late hour. She spent the last twelve hours at a brewery downtown, where she organized Milwaukee Magazine's Forty Under Forty annual event. It was nice paycheck, even better networking. But it came at a cost, as everything did lately. When she received Zoe's call that Penelope left school, Amelia offered to come home. Despite being in the middle of perfecting lighting, double-checking nametags against the guest list, tracking food deliveries, she wanted Penelope to know she came first. Always. Maybe P read through her offer, knew she couldn't leave, because Penelope told her to stay.

Amelia cut across two lanes to exit the freeway, feeling the sting of rejection afresh. The more she tried to be Penelope's rock, the further she pulled away. She should be glad that Austin jetted over, but why didn't Penelope want her mom?

Turning onto her street, Amelia kept her eyes on the deciduous trees lining the curb. The leaves were already starting to change hues—burnt-orange, crisp-yellow, Mars-red. At the last second, she snuck a glance at Zoe's house, but all was dark. Emblematic of their friendship. Zoe's call today was a courtesy. No affection, no apology. The facts and nothing more.

Which was fine. With Austin's support, Amelia didn't need Zoe.

Amelia parked in the garage and walked inside the house. Halsey played on the Wi-Fi speakers, expressing the anger Penelope kept bottled inside. Austin stood at the sink, his back to her, scouring a pan. She pulled up beside him, gazing out over the living room where Penelope lay on one couch and Ollie sat in the chair opposite. "How are they?" she asked, thankful that the loud music would mask their conversation.

Austin pursed his lips. "Quiet," he finally said.

"She didn't give you any details?"

"Nope."

She took the pan from him and gave him a small smile. "Let me do the rest. You've already gone beyond today."

Amelia turned down the music and walked Austin to the front door. As she passed the couch, she noticed Penelope's eyes were closed, her phone resting on her stomach. Ollie waved goodbye to Austin, or perhaps hello to Amelia. After letting Austin out, she ran a hand through Ollie's fohawk, relishing how he didn't shy from her touch. "Whatcha doing?" she asked.

Ollie held up his dogeared copy of *Almost, Maine*. "Memorizing."

"How's play practice?" Landing this role was a lifesaver. Ollie could shine, make new friends, explore his passion for once, instead of living vicariously through Penelope's and Micah's. And get away from this mess.

"Good."

"How's P? I heard she had a rough day."

"Kids are..." His hesitation told Amelia she'd get a sanitized, parent-friendly version. "Saying she wanted it. That she's trying to trip him up—"

"Stop!" Penelope yelled.

Amelia flinched. She thought Penelope was sleeping. Amelia sat on the edge of the couch, squeezing Penelope's foot. "Come on, let's get some hot chocolate and talk."

Penelope rolled away. "I'm not five. You can't bribe me with hot chocolate."

"I'm sorry I couldn't leave work," Amelia said, targeting what she hoped was the root of Penelope's anger. "But I'm here now. Tell me what happened." Nothing. No response. Not even a grunt. "How about I take tomorrow off and we spend time together? Come up with a plan for school?"

Again, nothing.

"I heard some kids ganged up on her in the library," Ollie said. "Like, some of Micah's football friends? Some cheerleaders—"

Penelope narrowed her eyes. "Can you not, Ollie?"

"What?" Ollie asked. "Am I wrong?"

She blinked away tears. "It doesn't matter."

"How was it with Zoe?" Amelia asked, trying another tactic to get Penelope talking. "Was she...nice?"

Penelope flipped onto her back. "She told me I could stop this. She doesn't believe me either. No one does."

Amelia smoothed her hands over her dress, trying to remove the tremor. That was why Zoe ran across the street this afternoon. Not to help P, but rather seize an opportunity to talk to her alone. "I believe you. Austin and Ollie believe you—"

"Everyone hates me," Penelope said, her face scrunching up as tears fell. "They blame me for getting Micah arrested. They called me a slut! A liar! A spaz!"

Penelope spat each word, wanting Amelia to swallow the poison. If only Amelia could. Guilt burned her tongue like hot coals. Her one job was to protect Penelope and she sent her into battle with flimsy assurances from the school that they would pick up where Amelia left off.

"This is all *your* fault." Penelope jabbed her finger at Amelia. "*You* called the police. *You* got Micah arrested. You ruined my life."

"Penelope," Amelia whispered, stunned by the accusation. It was one thing to hear it from Zoe, but another to hear it from her daughter. Didn't Penelope understand, everything Amelia did was to protect her? Help her heal?

"Don't." Penelope tucked her knees to her chest, hugging her legs. "I don't want to hear it."

"But you need to hear it." Amelia spoke firmly but not loudly. Penelope was emotional, on the brink of losing it, and Amelia had to be the voice of reason. "Micah did this. He's responsible for his actions. Not you. Not me. Not anyone else."

"You couldn't just leave it alone, could you?" she asked, almost pleading, her blue eyes wrought with tears. "I told you I wanted to forget it. And you kept pushing." She slapped her knee. "You always keep pushing."

"I don't get it," Ollie said. "If he hurt you, why wouldn't you want him to get in trouble?"

The scathing look Penelope gave Ollie rivaled Medusa. Amelia witnessed the splinters in their bond since the assault, fractures that grew with silence. Ollie was depressed, Penelope grieving. At a time when they should band together, create a circle of support, her family transformed into a triangle with acute edges. Never had Amelia felt so surplus. Neither would let her help. This sudden vulnerability unnerved her.

"If you want to blame me, fine," Amelia said. "But you should know Dr. Bilson called the cops." Penelope's gaze, which was fixed on Ollie, slowly turned toward Amelia. "The police decided a crime had been committed after talking to you both. I didn't tell them to do anything." Amelia softened her voice, dared to touch Penelope's hair. "It probably feels like everyone hates you, but your real friends will stand by you."

Penelope ducked her touch. "I don't have any friends, Mother. You took care of that."

Amelia couldn't break through. "I think we should see your therapist tomorrow."

Penelope stood up and screamed, her chest heaving as if running at a dead sprint. "You. Never. Listen." Then left the room, a tantrum reminiscent of her toddlerhood.

"Are you okay?" Amelia asked Ollie, desperate to be of use. "At school?"

Ollie shrugged, not looking up from his script.

"I know it must be hard, everyone talking about Penelope—"

"It's hard without Micah," Ollie cut in. "I know I should hate him, but...I can't."

"Missing him is normal—"

"I just can't hang out with him." The chill in Ollie's eyes, the pain he sought to cover with anger, took away Amelia's breath. Ollie was her sensitive, kind, intuitive child.

"Ollie," she said. "How do you think that would make Penelope feel? She already thinks no one believes her."

"Right." He grabbed his script and followed in Penelope's wake. "Gotta do what's best for P."

Amelia couldn't tell whether it was sarcastic. Under no circumstances could he hang out with Micah. Didn't he get that?

Needing to be proactive, she walked to the kitchen island and grabbed her phone, leaving two messages. The first with Suzanne, asking for an emergency appointment tomorrow. The second with Ms. DuPree, the school guidance counselor, requesting a meeting to discuss how Penelope could safely attend. Obviously, a chaperone didn't cut it.

Not quite finished, she pulled up Zoe name, finger hovering. How sweet it would feel to call Zoe, unleash her anger. How dare Zoe come over here today, pretending to care for Penelope. Manipulating the situation. Manipulating a child! But she was determined not to waste any more mental energy on Zoe. That was energy she needed to help Penelope.

Instead, she poured a glass of wine, drinking it standing up in front of the sink. Each mouthful medicinal. She replayed the argument with Penelope, wondering what she could've done differently. She tried to see Penelope's display of emotions as progress, but it was hard to feel good when she directed her venom toward Amelia. She doubted Penelope lashed out at Zoe, despite Zoe accusing Penelope of lying, encouraging her to change her story.

Amelia felt torn. Should she call the police? Beg them not to press charges? Amelia spent hours reading through blogs, both survivors and their loved ones, looking for guidance. She didn't know exactly how to help Penelope, but she knew what *not* to do. Silencing Penelope, letting her internalize shame or guilt, letting her sweep it under the rug, forget without ever really forgetting, would have devastating consequences on her mental health. Amelia had to see this case through, even if it damaged their relationship in the short-term.

CHAPTER TWENTY-FIVE
ZOE

Zoe climbed the home bleachers at the high school football stadium, worried she looked unsupportive in her ombre blue maxi dress and jean jacket in the sea of maroon and white bulldog paraphernalia. The bleachers were packed with parents and students, all eager to watch Friday night football under the lights. Not a single person looked familiar. She took a seat halfway up, at the thirty-yard line, missing Amelia. If things were different, she'd be next to Zoe, cheering on Micah.

Someone nudged Zoe from behind. She turned around. "You missed it!" a woman said. "Micah got a touchdown!"

Zoe worked late, missing the first half to help pay attorneys' fees. "That's awesome," she said, not remembering this woman's face from football orientation, but appreciating her enthusiasm.

"Caught the ball on the twenty and slipped two tackles to run it in," the man next to her added, eyes never leaving the game.

"Give me your number," she said. "I'll text you the video."

Optimism blossomed in Zoe as she exchanged names and numbers. Maybe she'd make friends with the other team parents. Put Amelia in her mental rearview mirror.

Turning back to the game, Zoe's eyes tracked Micah. Disappointed when they didn't throw him the ball, anxious when they did. He moved fluidly, looking strong and lean, nothing like the boy that feasted on Lucky Charms while playing Madden in his boxers.

A time out was called midway through the quarter. Bent over her phone, texting appointment reminders to her clients, Zoe's neck tingled. Some sixth sense signaled danger.

Zoe looked up, watching as a group of girls walked across the football field, wearing #MeToo shirts. They carried neon posterboard signs above their heads. "Only yes means yes! Ask first!" "Boys will be boys held accountable for their actions." "#MeToo #SilenceBreaker" They stopped at the Bulldogs bench, chanting something Zoe couldn't make out.

Zoe's stomach plummeted. She stood, weaving her way down the bleachers, terrified at how quickly the situation could escalate. Too many stories like this ended in tragedy. She had to get Micah out of there.

As Zoe moved, tensions intensified. The football players started yelling at the girls. Getting in their faces. Pointing fingers. Still, she couldn't see Micah. Some of the crowd booed; others cheered. Kids held up phones. A local television crew battled to get footage. Zoe pushed past people, frantic. Could they identify Micah on the news? He was a minor, but also the accused.

She ran to an opening in the fence, guarded by security. They wouldn't let her through, but she was able make out Micah, number twenty-seven, safely standing among football players. Escorted by school officials, the girls walked backwards across the field, yelling amidst the chaos, before disappearing through the fence opposite.

A few minutes later, the game resumed, but Micah remained on the sidelines. He cheered, clapping and high-fiving, the movements forced, painful only to her trained eye. Zoe's frustration grew as the coach kept Micah on the bench. It wasn't his fault the girls held a demonstration. Yet on the bench, he remained.

When the game ended, Zoe followed the football team to the school. The scent of chlorine and floor polish led to the boys' locker room, where students and parents waited outside. She stood at the end of the hall, wanting to avoid the gossip. It echoed anyway. Micah's and Penelope's names on everyone's lips. *She's lying. He forced her. Thirsty slut. He's so cocky.*

Empathy rose inside Zoe—for both kids. Enduring the gossip, everyone's snap judgments. No wonder Penelope ditched school!

How did Micah make it through each day? Zoe wanted to tell everyone to shut up, but she stayed quiet, refusing to fuel the fire.

Nearly an hour later, Micah emerged from the locker room. The last kid out. He wore navy joggers, riding low on his hips, and a white Bulldogs shirt. His jaw was tense, his lips zipped. "Micah," she called down the empty hallway.

She tried to hug him, but his spine stiffened. "Not here."

They walked to the car in silence, ignoring the few remaining kids in the parking lot. Once home, Micah went to the fridge and pulled out a bottle of Gatorade, chugging half of it before speaking. "Coach kicked me off the team."

Oh no they didn't. "They can't do that."

He shrugged. "Guess they can. Coach wants me to focus on taking care of myself. Whatever that means."

"I'll call Sarah." Zoe grabbed her phone. "There must be something—"

"Let it go." Micah appeared resigned. Football was over. Probably basketball season too. He lost his best friends and now his teammates too.

"Baby, are things okay at school?" Zoe asked. "Are those girls calling you out?"

"The football guys have my back. Some of the girls, though? It's like they're scared of me." He looked down, scuffing his shoe on the hardwood. "They stare at me, but won't talk to me. Teachers, too. They don't want anything to do with me."

"They shouldn't ignore you—"

"I think we're well past what should happen." He looked at her, his beautiful dark eyes in mourning. He tossed the Gatorade bottle in the recyclables. "I'm going to bed."

She grabbed his hand. "Micah, promise me you won't post anything—"

"Damn!" he snapped, pulling his hand away. "I just..." He rubbed his jaw. "I know. Okay? You don't have to always be on me."

Yes, she did. It was her job to be on him twenty-four-seven. "Leave your phone charging by your bed. I'll be checking it before I go to sleep."

He groaned, but went upstairs without furthering the argument. She was helping him, she told herself. Doing what was necessary. And to that end, she searched the kitchen for the papers listing his coach's number. Naturally, her call went to voicemail. Coward. She left a message, her voice like spun sugar, requesting a conversation to discuss Micah's dismissal.

After eating leftover spaghetti, she navigated to the local news station's site, holding the phone at a distance, as if that would cushion the blow. The protest wasn't the top story, which was a relief, but the fourth headline down. She pressed play. The reporter said tensions were high after a student was arrested last week for allegedly sexually assaulting another student away from school property. They included shots of the girls' protesting, the team yelling, the crowd reacting. Nothing singled out Micah. A small blessing. The reporter interviewed a couple students; a girl talked about the importance of believing girls, while a boy said it was scary, that anyone could make up these allegations and ruin someone's life.

In the middle of her third replay, her phone chimed. A text. Austin! She startled and the phone slipped through her fingers. She sat on the floor, resting her back against the peninsula, and picked up the phone. *Are you okay?* Austin texted. *Worried about u.* A simple question, but it meant everything. She felt indescribably lonely outside the locker room tonight. And here was Austin, reaching out.

I'm scared, Zoe admitted. *Coach kicked him off the team.*

I'm sorry. How's Micah dealing?

Unlike Amelia, Austin still made room for Micah, remembered the boy he was instead of the nasty allegation attached to his name. *Disappointed,* she texted.

She watched as the bubbles appeared and then disappeared. Her body deflated, her back forming a question mark as she slumped. It was stupid, getting worked up. Austin was being kind. Nothing more. Even so, she missed him. Missed how his fingertips touching her wrist the other day felt like an electrical storm running through her veins. Missed his gritty voice. Kind chocolate eyes... One conversation and her crush hit back hard, a thousand memories of lazy Sundays talking and laughing, toeing the line between friendship and flirtation.

Sorry, he texted. *Always here if u need to talk.*

She almost asked whether she could call now. But it was Friday night. Austin would be out, meeting women with a tenth of her baggage. *Thx. Sorry ur caught in the middle.*

In a way, they were all caught in the middle. Zoe and Amelia, defending their kids. Penelope and Micah caught between warring groups at school. This police investigation. Ollie and Austin, collateral damage. After talking to Penelope, witnessing her confusion, Zoe felt sure this—police, protests, the families estranged—wasn't what she wanted. But the situation had spiraled out of control. The past wasn't recoverable and the future looked bleak.

CHAPTER TWENTY-SIX
MICAH

By Sunday afternoon, not even two full days since he was kicked off the football team, Micah was going stir-crazy. He wasn't used to having Ma creepin' on him, tracking his movements on social media, editing his Netflix options, telling him no to kicking back with his friends. He decided to get out, go for a bike ride—a ride past Austin's tennis club. It was a beautiful day—sunny, mid-seventies. Penelope would for sure be playing outside.

He hadn't seen her since leaving her bed two weeks ago. Damn. As angry as he was with her for staying silent, he missed her. Still loved her. Somehow, his mind was able to juggle both emotions, so that if he saw Penelope, he wasn't sure whether he would scream at her or kiss her.

He pedaled slowly on the bike path that ran behind the chain-linked, fenced-in courts, searching out her long, strawberry-blond braid. Recognizing only Austin on court, Micah pulled his hat lower and walked his bike to a nearby tree, set back twenty-five yards or so. He sat down, content to wait. One glimpse. That's all. Then he'd be on his way. No one said looking broke the rules.

He took off his socks and shoes, the soft grass tickling his feet, enjoying the contrast between the warm sun peeking through the trees and the damp soil, the methodic crack of the racquet hitting balls. Still, he wasn't able to relax, his thoughts taking a familiar frustrating turn. No football practice tomorrow. Unbelievable. In the locker room Friday night, he sat dazed, as Coach told him his season was over. Before leaving, he snapped out of it, arguing he'd been arrested, not convicted. Penelope would come around. She *had* to. But it fell on deaf ears. Coach didn't want his name tied to this controversy.

Friday night, Micah scrolled through Insta before bed. #metoo blew up after the protest, as if their suburb was littered with girls being sexually assaulted. *My boyfriend pushed his way inside me, saying he had to feel me... Boys don't understand no... Guys want to get laid. Straight up.* Some posters tagged him, others Penelope, crucifying him for some other dude's sins.

So messed up. All of it. And Micah was powerless to do a damn thing. He couldn't afford to get into a war of words. His attorney wanted him to keep a low profile. And Ma was pounding *that* Kool-Aid. Xavier and the guys posted some responses, but Micah was losing the popularity contest. If that was what this was. With Penelope disappearing from school, he became a bullseye everyone wanted to hit.

A familiar face walked across the grass toward him now, but it wasn't Penelope. It was Ollie. With his hands shoved in his pockets, loopy gait and hunched shoulders, all that was missing was his smile. And Ollie always smiled around Micah.

"Haven't seen you for a minute," Micah said, tugging on his socks and shoes, thinking about all the calls, DM's that went unanswered. He considered Ollie a brother. As good as blood. But the way Ollie ghosted Micah made him realize their bond was as fragile as sand. A weak current of lies washed it away.

Ollie stood over him. "Dude, you messed with my sister."

Micah stood up, shaking his head. "Messed with your sister? Are you for real, bruh? She's my girlfriend. You'd know that if you bothered to hear my side of the story."

Ollie crossed his arms. "One kiss doesn't make her your girlfriend."

The shock of Ollie's words stole Micah's breath. Why was Penelope still lying? To Ollie of all people? "That what she said?" Micah asked. He ached to know Penelope's thoughts.

Ollie stepped closer. Micah could smell Ollie's minty breath, which was coming in short bursts. "She said she kissed you because she was curious. She doesn't like you like that."

Micah laughed, even as the words struck a nerve. If he didn't laugh, he might cry. And that was a no go. "We messed around all summer. She wanted this, man. Wanted me."

"Shut up!" Ollie kicked the grass. "You're lying. She would've told me."

"She's the one lying."

Ollie cleared his throat. "If she was your girlfriend, why didn't you tell me?"

"I wanted to," Micah said, finally feeling like he was getting through to Ollie. "But she got pissed whenever I brought it up. Why don't you ask her? Tell her what I said."

"I—I can't. You have no idea what she's been like." Ollie sniffled and wiped his nose. He was so sensitive, but did Micah drag him for it? Hell no; wouldn't let anyone else do it either. And what did Ollie give in return? Silence. "Penelope's freakin.' One second, she's crying, the next, she's raging. She won't even go in her room—not since that night with you."

If Penelope was upset, could it be true? Could she really feel their night together was a horrible mistake? That he forced her—

No. No fucking way. He couldn't believe it. He *wouldn't* believe it. It was the police. Her mom. The mob of girls online. Messing with Penelope's head. Twisting their night into something toxic.

"Why'd you go up to Penelope's room anyway?" Ollie asked, curbing Micah's spiraling thoughts. "You were drunk. You said you were going home."

"I wasn't drunk," Micah said. "A bit turnt up, maybe."

"See, you're lying!" Ollie's hand smacked his forehead. "You drank way more than me. And I was destroyed."

"Not way more," Micah mumbled, defiant.

"You should've stayed with me." Ollie's voice softened. "Made sure I was okay."

"I'm not your ma."

Ollie flinched, his eyes tearing up before hardening over. "Tell me the truth, did you rape her? Or were you too drunk to notice that she didn't want it?"

"Rape her?" Micah froze, shocked at how such a violent, ugly word rolled so easily off Ollie's tongue. If he couldn't convince Ollie of his innocence, what hope did he have of convincing a judge? "I love her—"

Ollie threw the first punch. A clean hit to Micah's cheek that caught him off-guard. He fell back on his heels before pouncing on Ollie, pushing him onto the grass. They rolled on top of one another, grasping, hitting, kneeing, swearing. A dirty fight. No rules. It didn't take long for Micah to gain the edge. He was bigger, stronger, quicker. Getting knocked around during football prepared him to meet this moment, whereas Ollie groaned, unaccustomed to pain. Micah's adrenaline egged him on. Each hit a valve releasing pressure. Ollie would be the last person to accuse him of raping Penelope.

"Stop!" someone yelled, yanking Micah off Ollie.

Micah fell back on his butt, breathing heavily, watching as Austin pulled Ollie from the ground. Blood dripped from Ollie's nose onto his T-shirt. "Go home, Micah," Austin said.

"Tell P to tell the truth," Micah said between breaths.

"Maybe she already did." Austin wrapped an arm around Ollie's back, supporting his body as they walked toward the tennis courts.

"I can't take this anymore," Micah said to himself. He shivered, suddenly cold. A cold that originated inside him. What just happened? Did he really beat up his best friend? What was wrong with him? What was wrong with everyone else? How could everyone he thought loved him—Ollie, Amelia, Austin—be so quick to believe the worst?

CHAPTER TWENTY-SEVEN
OLLIE

Ollie pulled away from Uncle Austin as they walked past the tennis courts, frustrated and embarrassed that he was holding onto Ollie like a child that ran into the street without looking both ways. People stopped their tennis games, watching with undisguised interest. And why wouldn't they? He probably looked ridiculous with a bloody nose and fat lip.

Why did Uncle Austin step in? Why couldn't he let Ollie fight 'til the end? Let him at least pretend to be a man.

In the parking lot, Uncle Austin held open the passenger side door of his Audi TT for Ollie. Ollie lifted his shirt, wiping blood from his nose, not wanting to stain the leather seats. Uncle Austin treated this car like his baby, not letting them eat or drink inside of it.

"You two solve anything?" Uncle Austin asked, lowering himself into the driver's seat.

"He's an asshole." Ollie enjoyed the way the curse tasted on his lips. Asshole. Fuckhead. Cocksucker. But words weren't enough. He hated Micah. Hated him for hurting Ollie. Caring about Penelope more. Ruining everything.

"He's your best friend," Uncle Austin said, pulling out of the parking lot. "Take some time—"

"He's dead to me." Ollie rested his pounding head against the headrest and closed his eyes, trying to decide who he hated more, Micah or Penelope. Both lied. Snuck around. Kept secrets.

What happened between Penelope and Micah? Who should he trust? Penelope was his twin, but Micah's explanation made more sense than Penelope's sudden curiosity to kiss him. And there were times when Ollie got home from drama camp that he couldn't find either Penelope or Micah. Both their phones mysteriously switched off.

"Did you know Micah and Penelope were together?" Ollie watched as Uncle Austin slowly nodded. "So, I'm the only one. Awesome." Ollie laughed manically. Was that the only reason Micah was still friends with him? To get close to P?

He was done with Micah. Check that. Done with both of them. They could have each other. Or not. Either way, he was done feeling guilty that he got drunk that night. Didn't protect P. Obviously, if she was sneaking around, she didn't want his protection.

He was also done feeling bad for Penelope. She was emotional all week, crying at times and others deathly quiet, finally confiding in Ollie that one of Micah's football friends threatened her to get the charges dropped. To think, he walked over to Micah today, ready to tell Micah to keep his football friends away from her. Good thing he didn't waste his breath.

"Micah told me the night it happened," Uncle Austin said as they stopped at a red light. "He said the sex was consensual. That they'd been together all summer."

"He lied to me."

"He wasn't doing it to hurt you. All he could see was Penelope." Uncle Austin smiled as they accelerated through the green light. "Just wait until you first fall, Ol. Nothing else matters. Not even your best friend."

Ollie looked out the window. "You don't get it."

"Explain."

From the moment Ollie met Micah in preschool, Ollie always wanted to be around him. Micah was born cool. This last year, though, wanting to be around him took on an urgency and fevered excitement. Became an obsession. Could he tell Uncle Austin the words he hardly dared to say to himself, that he was gay?

No. Not Uncle Austin. The guy who filled his calendar with hot girls. He'd think Ollie was a freak. Act all awkward and overly polite.

He had thought about telling Penelope, but not anymore. It wasn't safe to tell anyone.

By the time Uncle Austin pulled into their driveway, Ollie still hadn't said anything. He moved to open the door when Uncle Austin tugged on his sleeve.

"Hey," Uncle Austin said. "I'm here, if you want to talk. Whatever. Whenever."

Ollie averted his eyes. Did Uncle Austin know something? But how could he? No. He was just being nice.

When they walked in the house, Mom was standing at the kitchen island, chopping vegetables. She dropped the knife when she saw him. "What happened?" She rushed toward Ollie, cupping his chin with her fingers. "Who did this?"

Mom was beautiful, blond hair, blue eyes, the kindest smile. But now she looked, well...worn down in a wrinkled T-shirt, gym shorts, a limp ponytail, and no makeup.

"He got into a fight with Micah," Uncle Austin said, pulling out his phone.

"Ollie!" Mom said. "I told you not to hang out with him—"

"Last time I checked, he assaulted Penelope, not me," Ollie cut in, relishing the surprise on her face. He was the "good" child. Never made waves. When Penelope had a match or wanted a certain food or movie, he always gave in.

No more. He was done. D-O-N-fucking-E. It felt good to curse. Fuck!

"Sit down," Mom said, grabbing the first aid kit from beneath the sink. "Let's get you cleaned up."

Ollie pulled out a stool at the kitchen island and sat. Mom took a warm wash cloth and wiped away the blood. Even though she was gentle, it felt like she was touching a raw nerve, the pain pulsating from his nose up to his skull and down the back of his neck.

"Why did he hit you?" Mom asked.

"I hit him."

"Okay," she soothed, placating, disbelieving. "Why did you hit him?"

Ollie bit down on his tongue. "Does it matter? We're not friends anymore. You got what you wanted."

"Ollie," Uncle Austin said, looking up from his phone. "Don't—"

"Don't what?" Ollie's voice cracked.

"Go easy on your mom," Uncle Austin said. "This is hard for everyone."

"I know you miss him," Mom said, "but imagine how Penelope would feel if she knew you were spending time with him."

Penelope. Every thought, word, and action of Mom's was about Penelope. What about Ollie? His feelings? Did anyone care? "I need to lie down. My head hurts."

"Wait. Take these." She placed two ibuprofens in his hand. Then she went into the freezer, handing him Penelope's ice therapy packs. He almost said no, not wanting to touch anything of Penelope's, but the pain won out. "Ice. Twenty minutes on, twenty minutes off."

Ollie trudged up the stairs, pausing at the top when Penelope emerged from her room. She stopped short when she saw him. "What happened?" she asked, eyes wide. "Are you okay?"

"Fine." He brushed her shoulder as he walked past. "Not that you care."

Silence, then, "What does that mean?"

He didn't have words. Or he had too many words. Too many feelings. Nothing coherent. Nothing piercing that would wound, let her know how deeply she hurt him. He wasn't like Penelope. Her outbursts sounded like scripted Netflix dramas. Ollie? He'd frustrate the viewer with how he ended up apologizing for his feelings because he hated hurting others.

He wasn't going to do this now. Eventually, yes. He'd write out his thoughts if he had to. She wasn't going to get off easy this time.

Ollie walked to his room, slamming the door. Oh, but how the slam hurt his head.

For a minute, he stood by the door, expecting P to come barging in, demanding answers. He was ready to tell her to go away, almost looking forward to making her feel second to his problems for once, but she didn't come. Well, fuck her too, then.

He fell onto the bed, closing his eyes, pressing the ice packs against his face. It felt like an amoeba was growing under his skin, pressing the flesh out, making it bubble and contort. He didn't dare look in the mirror. How would he go to school tomorrow? Maybe he should skip.

No. No way. He wouldn't be a coward like Penelope.

Would Micah have any bruises? He flashed back to Micah being on top of him. Hitting him.

Oh God. Oh. My. Fucking. God.

Ollie turned over, pressing his face against the pillow, wishing he could erase the memory. Ollie got excited before around Micah, but he could always hide it. Today, they were too close to hide anything. Hands. Legs. Chests. Everything touching. Having Micah on top, even as he was beating on Ollie, felt euphoric. Every dream, thought, fantasy mixed together in the best and worst way.

Did Micah notice? Or was he too distracted? But how could he *not* notice? The only thing worse than Micah knowing was if he outed Ollie before he was ready. The slutty sister and gay brother. The rumors would never end. They'd both have to quit school.

And what did it mean that he got turned on while getting pummeled? He might not only be gay, but possibly an S&M freak?

Who would ever love him?

CHAPTER TWENTY-EIGHT
ZOE

Zoe reserved Sundays for chores. She cleaned the kitchen and bathrooms, put fresh sheets on the beds, and cooked a crock-pot meal for the week so Micah had dinner when she worked late. She just set the crock-pot timer when he burst through the back door, banging it hard enough to dent the wall.

His cheek looked swollen, the blood vessels in his right eye on blast. "Are you okay?" she asked. "What happened to your face?"

He froze, startled. Then flexed his hand, the knuckles bloody. "I got in a fight," he mumbled.

Micah didn't get in fights. "With who?"

"Ollie."

She closed her eyes, gripping the counter behind her for balance. She could no more imagine Ollie getting into a fistfight than she could imagine Penelope having sex. Was something in the water? Had everyone lost their goddamn mind?

"He asked me if—" Micah's jaw tightened. "If I raped P. Like I'm some fucking monster."

She didn't often shout, but right now, she felt like yelling. Even with the threat of juvie, Micah was still going rogue, as if none of his actions had consequences. As if the world was out to dog him. "So, you hit him? Jesus, did you not hear Sarah—"

"He hit me first!" Micah yelled.

"Lay low. Don't get into trouble!"

"I was chillin'—"

"Where?" Zoe demanded. "Where did this happen?"

A long pause. "The tennis club."

A fresh dose of frustration soared through Zoe's blood as she realized he went to see Penelope. "The police could pick you up if you get caught with P." She slapped her thighs. "Come on, Micah! Think!"

"I am thinking! I'm thinking if my best friend thinks I'm a rapist, what are the chances any judge believes me?"

She heard the pain in his voice, how close he was to breaking. "I know this is tough—"

"No, you don't." He put his hands on his hips. "You have no idea what this is like. You've never been arrested. Have people think you're a criminal. Spew hate online. Start protests."

Her heartrate accelerated with each accusation. She felt impulsive with anger, terrified of what she might say or do. "I need—I need—" What did she need? A friend. A stiff drink. A break from Micah. Someone to tell her she was doing okay. *Breathe*, she reminded herself. "I need an hour. Away. Time to think. Calm down. Then we'll talk. Can I trust you to stay home?"

"Yeah," he grumbled.

"Put some ice on your face." She grabbed her keys, ready to leave, before turning around. She held out her palm. "Give me your phone."

His lip curled up in disgust. "You serious?"

"Deadly." She already had his passwords, but after getting in a fight, she'd confiscate the phone. Stop him from making this worse with a stupid post or text.

He pulled it out of his pocket and slapped it into her palm, before storming away. She closed her eyes, waiting for the inevitable bedroom door slam. Hearing the bang, she put on flipflops and left.

Outside, her hands trembled as she gripped the steering wheel. She was too keyed up to drive. Instead, she walked along her tree-lined street, letting fresh air be a balm to her soul. The pale blue sky a reminder that she was but a speck in this universe, that her problems, while stressful, were insignificant.

A half-mile later, she arrived "downtown"—a four block strip in their suburb filled with restaurants, shops, and small businesses. She took a seat on the patio of The Fine Pair, ordering a glass of Pinot from a college-aged girl with cellulite-free legs that went on for days. Then Zoe pulled out her phone, surprised to find a text from Austin.

Bad news. Caught Ollie and Micah fighting, he wrote.

He told me, Zoe texted back. *Did u c what happened?*

At Amelia's. Call u after?

Did Amelia know he was texting her? *At Fine Pair. Needed a drink to calm down.*

Alone?

She hesitated. Was he asking to join her? *Yes.*

B there in twenty.

A nervous ball of anticipation played Ping-Pong with the stress in her stomach. The server delivered her wine and Zoe took a big gulp, letting the cool, crisp liquid settle her nerves. This stress wasn't good for her. She wasn't used to it. Wasn't built for it. She prided herself on being Zen, riding out the waves in the face of calamity.

But Micah getting arrested? Facing sexual assault charges? Possibly going to juvie? She aged years in the matter of weeks. *You can't make someone care,* her father told her when, at twenty-one, having just graduated cosmetology school, she found herself pregnant and heartbroken. When Duante refused to meet Micah, become even a cursory father figure, she decided her dad was right. Surely this logic didn't apply to Micah? She *had* to care enough for both of them, make this sordid mess go away.

"I come in peace." Austin approached, clad in a pair of navy-blue tennis shorts, a tight white shirt that showed off the curves of his biceps, and a white Nike cap. He opened his arms and she, against her better judgment, stood up and let him envelop her, inhaling a mixture of sweat and soap. A delicious, intimate smell that stirred parts deep inside her. Parts she hid, ignored, resisted. No more. Every cell, every nerve, every breath, screamed as if on fire.

Sitting down, she smiled nervously, too aware of her body. Their proximity. Her desire.

Before either said anything, the server swung by, and he ordered a Spotted Cow.

"Listen," he said. His long, dark eyelashes framed his brown eyes. Flecks of gold shone in the irises, hidden treasures. "I need to ask you something. It's important." He exhaled. "Whatever happens between the kids, you and Amelia, can you promise you'll always be my hairstylist?"

She closed her eyes, shoulders shaking as she laughed. This felt good. Familiar. Easy.

"You think it's funny, but you're a magician with my hair. Look!" He pulled off his hat. Sweat flattened his brown hair into a bowl, while the humidity curled the ends like Farah Fawcett. "It becomes unmanageable if someone else so much as looks at it."

The server dropped off his beer. Zoe took advantage of the interruption and grabbed the hat and tossed it at him. "It's the hat that makes it unmanageable!"

He rapped his knuckles against the table, then pointed at her. "See? That's the type of advice I can't live without."

Can't live without. She luxuriated in those words, wondering if there was a hidden double meaning. She was too old to act this way. But sitting close to Austin, the freedom of late-afternoon drinks, the subtle flirtation, the break from Micah—

Micah. She steered herself back on track. "What happened with the boys?" Zoe asked, her voice sounding stiff, even to herself.

"I'm teaching on court and look over to see them talking by the trees. I thought, great!" Austin threw his hands up. "Ollie's been depressed, missing Micah, and I'm sure Micah feels the same. Anyway, things got physical and I ran over. By the time I got there, Micah was on top of Ollie, hitting him." Austin paused for a drink. "Ollie threw the first punch, if that helps."

A small blessing. "What did Amelia say?"

He laughed. "Oh...I'd put her reaction at DEFCON one."

Zoe nodded, expecting no less. "Will she make trouble?"

"Trouble?"

She squeezed the stem of her wine glass, at risk of snapping it. "Is she going to call the police? Report Micah for assault?"

Austin frowned. "No—I mean—" He flipped his hand, filling in the gap. "She'd be reporting Ollie for assault too."

Zoe's shoulders relaxed a fraction. "I don't know what to do." Micah resented her for enforcing the terms of the TPCO, but hearing the consequences from their attorney, his social worker—that didn't resonate either.

"Exactly what you're doing now," Austin said as clouds shaded the patio. "Support him, be there for him on the off chance he wants to talk. That's what I'm trying to do with Penelope. She used to always tell me things, but now?" He rubbed his scruffy chin with the palm of his hand. "She's so quiet. Fragile."

Zoe flashed back to Penelope on the porch, her eyes darting back and forth, panicked, as if she was trapped. "I think both Micah and P are scared right now."

"For different reasons, yes, but I'd agree with that. As for you, your sanity, I think you need to give yourself a break every once and awhile. Space to come to terms with what's happened."

"It's hard." She sipped her wine, searching for a word to describe how nice it was to talk to someone who made her feelings a priority. Safe, she decided. That's how she felt right now. Like she could say anything and Austin would try to understand. Without judgment. "Everyone's being split down the middle, forced to take sides, when there's so many nuances, so many moving parts. I mean, for you to show up today, when you're obviously team Amelia, it's—" She nodded, waiting for the emotion to pass. "It means a lot."

He squinted into his beer bottle. "I'm not 'team Amelia.' It's more complicated than that. Watching Penelope fall apart. Amelia trying to fix something that might be unfixable. Ollie fighting. Micah arrested. You?" He winced. "I can see stress weighing you down, when I'm used to you being so...light." The clouds parted, the sun embracing them. "I want the best for everyone. A solution. And yet, I'm helpless to do a damn thing."

"You're helping me." Right then and there, Zoe decided she no longer had any reason to steer clear of Austin. Amelia might not have called the police herself, but she betrayed Zoe, not warning her. "Your texts, coming here, just knowing someone cares."

"Talking to you helps me too." Time stretched as they held each other's eyes. Then he smiled, tapping his beer against her wine glass. "And then there's always drinking."

Zoe's stress was still there. Her worries. Frustrations. But beneath it, like the first bud of a flower appearing in spring, there was promise. Hope. A feeling that perhaps all was not lost.

CHAPTER TWENTY-NINE
AMELIA

Amelia exited the high school late Monday morning, looking to the sky. While the thunderstorms abated, the bulbous gunmetal clouds threatened an encore. She hurried down the stairs, taking the path toward the visitors' parking lot, mentally rehashing her meeting with the guidance counselor, Olivia DuPree. Olivia suggested Penelope continue to work from home, but come into school one morning each week to get questions answered and turn in her work. Meeting with Olivia in the guidance office would eliminate the threat of bullying, while Penelope grew comfortable being at school. A start. From there they would work up to half-days and eventually full-days.

Amelia was walking past the fieldhouse, when, out of nowhere, she nearly crashed into someone coming out the doors. Amelia stuttered an apology before recognizing Zoe. "What are you doing here?" Amelia asked. The wind carried a familiar whiff of Zoe's perfume. Crisp oranges and grapefruit, a hint of vanilla, sunshine after a spring shower. Memories of countless hugs, sweatshirts borrowed, shared hotel rooms.

"Talking to Micah's football coach," Zoe said, jerking her thumb at the fieldhouse behind her. "They kicked him off the team after Friday night's protest."

"That must be difficult." Amelia saw video of the protest. It was everywhere; parents and kids alike sharing it faster than germs in a sneeze. She watched it with conflicted feelings, happy the girls were supporting Penelope, but also angry on behalf of both kids. While minors were protected from identification on the news, it was the wild west online, with Penelope's and Micah's names attached to gossip that kids traded like bullets.

"It's a 'provisional suspension.' Apparently, getting arrested violated the student-athlete code of conduct." Zoe's tone suggested this was Amelia's fault, even though Amelia already told her she didn't call the police. "Depending on the outcome of the case, he'll be able to rejoin."

Amelia said nothing. An "I'm sorry" would be disingenuous. And asking how Zoe was holding up was too much after she manipulated Penelope last week. Everything about this situation was unimaginable and heartbreaking, but this, right here, experiencing the gulf between her and Zoe, opened a fresh wound. It couldn't be any different, but that didn't blunt Amelia's pain.

"Did Micah tell you why he and Ollie fought yesterday?" Amelia asked instead. Ollie and Penelope used to always spill the truth, whether out of guilt or genuine closeness or because Amelia threatened them within an inch of their lives. But not anymore. Both her children shut her out at a time when she needed encyclopedic knowledge of their minds.

"Ollie called him a rapist." Zoe's eyes flashed murderously, while her voice stayed dangerously low. "A rapist, Amelia. For having sex with his girlfriend."

"They didn't have 'sex.'" Amelia gritted her teeth. The words felt like splinters inserted into her gums. "Micah *assaulted* her. There's a difference."

"How long are you going to keep pushing that storyline? Until he goes to juvie? What price is high enough in your mind for stealing Penelope's virginity?"

"Her virginity!" Amelia repeated, incredulous. "Penelope's traumatized—"

"Amelia." Zoe pressed her fingers to her temple, as if Penelope's audacity to not want to have sex with Micah was giving her headache. "I understand she's upset. Confused. And I feel for her, I truly do. But because of her accusation, *her words*, Micah's been judged and convicted by the police, his coach, the girls at school—no one wants to listen to his side. Even Ollie thinks he's guilty."

144

"He is guilty!" Amelia yelled, having lost her patience. First Zoe tried to convince Penelope to retract her statement. Now, she downplayed Penelope's struggles. "You don't care about her. About what she's going through. About how Micah hurt her. You just care about getting him off."

"And what would you do? If someone accused Ollie?" Zoe stepped closer to Amelia. "Believe the girl? Over your son?"

"Ollie would never—"

"But Micah would." Zoe let out a long breath. "Jesus, you're unbelievable."

There was no compromise here. Both felt their child suffered, was still suffering, a grave injustice. "I'm done," Amelia said, walking off.

"Is Ollie okay?" Zoe called after her. "I, for one, actually do still care about your kids."

Amelia knew what she was asking, but instead, she turned around and said, "I worry that none of them are okay. That what happened is going to haunt them for the rest of their lives."

Zoe fixed Amelia with a stare, her whisper as chilling as a cold-blooded scream. "Well, at least your kids won't be dealing with it in juvie."

Amelia strode to her car, her heart beating like a heavyweight fighter. Unlike the boys, they weren't fighting with their fists, but both of them were going for the knock-out punch, using every weapon in the arsenal to protect their children. Damn the costs.

CHAPTER THIRTY
PENELOPE

Without the pressure of school hanging over her head, Penelope experienced a new sensation. Energy. Energy that synthesized itself as anger. She was sick of being afraid to leave home. Sick of being as fragile as a snow globe. Letting words crush her. Memories dictate her day. Her therapist, Suzanne, applauded her anger. Wanted to delve into why she chose anger to masquerade her pain.

Penelope wasn't here for it. She wanted to feel like herself again. And the only path back was tennis. Tuesday morning, after Ollie and Mom left, Penelope walked to the tennis club. As an owner, Uncle Austin let her and Ollie have free court time. He didn't even make Mom pay for private lessons with him or group lessons—a fact P knew helped after Dad died. A fact which bolstered Penelope's confidence. Uncle Austin believed in her talent.

She took the long way, through the residential streets, wanting to avoid the high school, already dreading her Thursday morning "meeting" with Ms. DuPree. Going to school would suck even more, since Ollie wasn't talking to her. Nothing less than she deserved, really.

Twenty minutes later, she scanned her membership card at the front desk, checked out a ball machine, and pushed it outside to court six. Tucked in the back corner with overhanging trees that created shadows everyone else hated, it was her own tennis oasis. No one would bother her.

She waved at Uncle Austin as she passed his court. He waved back, but didn't jog over. Unlike Mom, who'd attack her with questions—she could never let it *be*. How could twins be so different? Mom and Uncle Austin. Penelope and Ollie. She was convinced life in utero was survival of the fittest, each twin sucking up the best DNA available. Uncle Austin stole the chill straight under Mom.

When she stepped onto court six, she closed her eyes and inhaled—rubber, sunscreen, sweat. Home. She was finally home.

She warmed up with jumping rope and some footwork drills. Her feet sluggish, quads screaming, lungs burning. Her body shedding rust in equal amounts to sweat. She squatted, sucking air, terrified she ruined everything. What if her fight was gone? What if her tennis dreams were just that, dreams? There was no room for weakness on court, yet she was riddled with anxiety.

When in doubt, don't think, she reminded herself. *Do.* She set up the ball machine and started with some side T's at the service line, searching for a rhythm. As she inched back toward the baseline, her muscles loosened and her steps grew confident. It hurt, but a good hurt, one derived from hard work. Not failure. Not guilt. Regret. Emotions that held her under water these past couple weeks.

She went through basket after basket of balls, stopping only to pick them up and hydrate. Hitting didn't allow for thinking. Remembering. It was an emotional nerve block.

A couple hours later, as she packed up, she found herself smiling, overcome with another rare emotion, pride. For leaving the house. Playing tennis. And not going through the motions, but improving.

Uncle Austin caught up with her as she left and offered a ride home. "Your backhand looked good," he said in the car, discussing it as if today was any other practice. "You're really driving through the ball."

"I didn't have the strength to put enough spin on the ball. My legs were lead."

"What'd you have the machine set at? Level eight? Sideline to sideline? Serena would lose her legs after two hours, too."

Penelope doubted it, but took the compliment, basking in the normalcy of tennis talk. Endorphins zapped through her, giving her such a high that when they passed the hardware store, she yelled at

Uncle Austin to stop. Inspiration hit and she had to act. Fix the bad juju in her room.

In aisle three, she found a sea blue paint. She told Uncle Austin how she wanted to change the vibe in her room. Imbue calmness. "Maybe then I'll be strong enough to move back in."

"Smart move." Uncle Austin held out his fist for a bump. "Change what you see, change what you think, change how you feel."

"Change your perspective," Penelope intoned, feeding back his oft-used coaching tip.

They laughed as she brought the paint card to the front, waiting as the clerk mixed the color. Uncle Austin paid for the paint—perk of inviting him along. After Uncle Austin dropped her home, she felt wracked with another unfamiliar feeling. Hunger. She made a ham, kale, tomato, and mustard sandwich on whole grain and shoved it in her mouth.

Taking a deep breath, she opened her bedroom door, bracing for that panicky feeling that sent her running to Mom's bed. Before it could set in, she threw the windows open. Tore posters from the wall—Serena Williams, Novak Djokovic—ripped the curtains off the rods, the sheets from the bed, pulled the furniture away from the walls.

She started painting. With Marin Morris giving a private concert on Spotify, she felt not happy, but productive. Time passed without any deep thoughts. She reveled in the simplicity of it.

Abruptly, the music cut off. She turned around to find Ollie holding her phone. "What're you doing?" he asked. The bruises on his face looked like an impressionist painting of pain.

"Painting," she said. "What does it look like?"

"Why?"

She looked around the room. Two walls done, two to go. She already felt better. Stronger. "This room had a bad vibe. Just walking by—" A flutter of panic squeezed her lungs. "How can I forget that night if I'm reminded of it every day?"

Ollie sat on her bed. "What *did* happen that night?"

She started painting again, her back to Ollie. "You know what happened."

"Do I? I don't think so."

"You know enough."

"Nothing to add? You're not leaving anything important out?"

She turned around, gave him a death stare, before painting again. "I told you I don't want to talk about it."

Silence. Then, "Micah told me you're his girlfriend. That you guys messed around all summer. That you wanted to have sex that night."

The paintbrush fell from her hand, splattering blue paint across the sheets she lay on the ground.

"You lied to me," Ollie continued. "Over and over and over."

Again, Micah's behavior caught her off guard. How could he betray her trust? Was he trying to hurt her? Get revenge because Mom forced her to talk to the police? "I lied—and I'm sorry. But not about what happened that night."

"Right," Ollie said, all sarcasm.

Penelope slid to the ground, resting her head against the wall, realizing, too late, that her hair and shirt were now sticky with paint. "I lied because I didn't want you to feel excluded. Like Micah chose to hang out with me over you."

Ollie idolized Micah. Emulated, defended, listened to him, always, without question. Got bummed when Micah hung out with other friends—even Penelope. Possessive wasn't the right word—that sounded stalkerish. But Ollie was sensitive. Somehow, he ended up hurt without Micah doing anything wrong. She knew spending time with Micah would wound.

"You guys think I'm a freak, don't you?" Ollie's cheeks flushed. "Never even kissed a girl—"

"No, no. I'm the freak." She spoke quickly, choking on her tears, knowing her protest was worthless. "Not you. I assumed Micah would get sick of me. And it scared me, how much he could hurt me. I tried to stop, but—" *But I fell in love.* No more. She would never give, speak, *think*, that feeling about Micah again.

"I don't believe you. Do you know how much that sucks?" Ollie scrunched up his face, so as to not cry. "You're my sister and he's—I don't have anyone anymore!"

She cried harder, knowing exactly how alone he felt. "I'm sorry, I never thought—"

"You never thought I'd find out," he said, standing up.

"You believe me about that night though, right? About what Micah did?"

He rested his head against the frame of the doorway, tears making his bruises shine. "I believe you regret it."

The blow of his words felt physical, a shattering of her heart. "You're taking his side?" Penelope swiped away tears, anger getting the better of her. "You really think I'd lie about something this big?"

"I can't deal with this," he mumbled.

"You?" She gasped. "You can't deal with this? Are you kidding me?"

"You're not the only one with problems." He left and she threw the paint brush at the door, enjoying the way paint splattered across the floor.

Tears clouded her vision, but even with the obstruction, it was clear she was a desperate girl in a desperate struggle to pretend she was fine. That she could forge a new way. Sitting there all alone with her thoughts, she realized there was no new way. No one believed her. Not even Ollie. Her world just dwindled to nothing.

CHAPTER THIRTY-ONE
AMELIA

Amelia and Penelope stood in the reception area of the district attorneys' office next to a tall plant. Or a small tree. Horticulture wasn't Amelia's thing. "Are you nervous?" Amelia asked, referring to their meeting with Jack Kelly, the attorney assigned to Penelope's case.

Penelope shrugged, her favorite method of communication. It felt like she had a per diem on words, refusing to waste any on Amelia. And now, Penelope and Ollie weren't speaking either. *She lied to me,* Ollie said when Amelia asked. About what remained a mystery. When she pressed him for answers, he said nothing. Never had the tension been higher in Amelia's house.

Amelia heard her name and turned around. A man in his forties with close-cut, blonde hair walked toward them with a bouncy gait, as if his joints were lined with silly putty. He held out his hand. "Jack Kelly."

"Amelia Swanson." She shook his hand. "And this is my daughter, Penelope." Penelope nodded and looked away.

"Thanks for coming." He led them down a hallway, which lined the perimeter of the architecturally unique, cylinder-shaped courthouse. Sunlight beamed along their path through the floor-to-ceiling windows. Amelia would've enjoyed the view above the trees, if not for being there to discuss her daughter's assault.

They settled in a conference room, Jack sitting across from Amelia and Penelope, his fingers interwoven, resting on the table. "A little background first," Jack said. "I'm one of two prosecutors for the county that deal with juvenile sexual assault. I've tried hundreds of cases, but, having said that, I still can't imagine how hard these past couple of weeks must have been for you. I'm so very sorry,

Penelope. It's a testament to you, your strength, that you're willing to share your story, trust me to help make this situation fractionally easier."

Amelia reached for Penelope's hand, which was cold and lay against her lap like a dead fish.

"I want to hear from you what happened," Jack continued, his voice soft, but upbeat, a coach that knew his star player was as delicate as a dried dandelion in the wind. "And what you'd like to have happen going forward. Okay?"

Penelope nodded.

"Whenever you're ready."

Penelope detailed finding Micah outside the bathroom, kissing, falling into bed, working her way to the assault. She spoke quietly, with none of her usual confidence or emotion. Perhaps it was a protective mechanism; if she didn't connect the words to herself, they couldn't hurt her.

"Was there any romantic relationship before that night?" Jack asked.

Penelope hesitated, drew in a breath. "Kissing...since the beginning of the summer."

Amelia looked at Penelope closely, uncertain she heard correctly. "But you said that night was the first time."

"I was scared." Penelope squeezed her hands between her thighs. "I thought if you knew the truth, you'd think it was my fault. That maybe I wanted this. But I swear to you, Mom—" Her lower lip trembled. Amelia saw her at one, five, ten years old...always tough, refusing to show weakness. "I never wanted this. I never thought..."

Amelia spun her chair toward Penelope and opened her arms, relishing the weight of Penelope's head against her shoulder. Their hearts beating in tandem once again. Her daughter safe. "I never would've blamed you," she said in Penelope's ear. How could she not have noticed a change between the kids? Were these the lies Ollie was upset about? He hated when they excluded him. But then why didn't he tell Amelia the truth? She pulled back, cupping

Penelope's chin. "I believe you. Remember that. This changes nothing." She turned to Jack and said, "Penelope told the police they didn't have a relationship. Will that hurt her case?"

He sat back in his chair, crossing his leg at the knee. "It's not uncommon. Victims tend to think if they had a previous relationship, no one will believe they didn't want it this time. It's explainable, but yes, somewhat damaging."

"I wish I knew why he did it," Penelope said, her voice ravaged.

"And I wish I had an answer," Jack said. "Sometimes good people make horrible choices. Particularly teenagers. Brain development takes roughly twenty-five years. Did you know that?"

Penelope shrugged.

"The prefrontal cortex—" Jack pointed at his forehead. "—which helps with making decisions, thinking through consequences, isn't fully developed at your age. Instead, you rely on your amygdala, the part of your brain that registers anger, desire, fear. And when those decisions are made in the heat of the moment? Bad things can happen." Jack scribbled something on his notepad that Amelia couldn't read upside down. "Have you talked to Micah since the assault? Text? Phone?"

"He's texted and DMed." Penelope looked away. "I haven't responded."

Amelia bit her tongue, physically having to stop herself from grilling Penelope. She felt like both her children lived double lives, purposefully deceiving her.

"What do the messages say?" Jack asked.

Penelope shrugged. It was a wonder she hadn't thrown out her shoulder. "He's angry. Wants me to tell the truth. Stuff like that."

"Can you pull up the texts on your phone?" he asked.

Penelope flinched. "What? Now?"

"Yeah. Per court order, he's not allowed to contact you, digital or otherwise. Depending on what they say, we can bring additional charges for witness intimidation."

Penelope visibly paled. "No. I don't—we shouldn't do that. He hasn't done it lately."

Jack reached across the table, holding out his hand. "I'd still like to read them."

Penelope slowly reached into her pocket and pulled out her phone. Amelia watched as she clicked on Instagram, navigating to her DMs. Only then did she hand the phone over.

"I'll take screen shots and email them to myself. But don't delete them, we might need the raw data," he said, wincing. "I'm not exactly what you call tech savvy."

When he finished, Penelope took back her phone and stood. "Can I go to the bathroom?"

Jack gave her directions. "You know you shouldn't contact him either, right?"

Penelope froze. "I wasn't going to." Then she left.

"Can I see the texts?" Amelia asked.

Jack turned his computer to face her. Most of the messages were Micah asking Penelope to call him, explain what happened, tell the truth. One message stood out to Amelia, *Quit playing and tell the TRUTH. Ur Mom is fucking with my life.* She was fucking with his life? Micah was a teenager, scared and lashing out, but it still pissed her off. She opened her home to him, loved him like a son, and he took advantage of that kindness. Took advantage of her daughter. "Unbelievable." She sighed. "Micah blames me for getting arrested."

"They always blame someone," Jack said. "Usually, several someones. It's never them, their behavior, that landed them in this situation. Tell me, how's Penelope coping?"

"I think she's confused and hurt. They were close—closer than I knew obviously. And she's..." Amelia hesitated, unsure of how to describe Penelope's intensity. Passion. Determination. She wasn't your usual teenager, obsessed with Instagram and TikTok. Until a couple weeks ago, Amelia would've bet her life that Penelope never kissed a boy. The consequences of her naivety burrowed further into her heart. "Penelope's unique. She's a top tennis player, spends

154

hours training, travels with my brother to junior tournaments. She won't let anything get in the way of going pro...until now." Amelia laughed sadly. "Yesterday was the first day she played since it happened. The lack of tennis is more concerning than her silence. Tennis is her oxygen. Her life. Her—"

Penelope came back and plopped in her chair. Amelia wondered if Penelope was telling the whole truth now. Somehow, Amelia doubted it. She didn't doubt the assault, but there was more. Details missing. Call it women's intuition, mother's instinct—whatever. She knew.

Jack said, "Next week is the preliminary hearing. Micah will be charged with third degree sexual assault. It's possible he'll plead delinquent—"

"He won't," Amelia said. "He believes Penelope consented."

"What?" Penelope bolted upright in her chair. "When did you talk to him?"

"I didn't," Amelia said quickly, startled by her reaction. "I ran into Zoe."

Jack pulled off his glasses, cleaning them with a handkerchief from his breast pocket. "If that's the case, Penelope, you would have to testify at trial."

Penelope's eyes thickened with tears. "Meaning what?"

"It won't be like the movies. There's no jury. No one in the gallery. But Micah will be there. He has a right to question you as part of his defense." He paused. "Is this something you'd be willing to do?"

"I—" Penelope's head dropped to her chest. "I don't know."

Amelia believed Penelope's fighting spirit was still alive. While Micah hurt Penelope in an unimaginable way, she was down, not out. Amelia remembered a match from the Orange Bowl last spring. Penelope's opponent cheated, calling lines wrong, muttering insults to Penelope during changeovers. Penelope mixed up her game, gave spin instead of speed, her consistency driving the other girl crazy. Amelia was astounded by Penelope's maturity, her ability to keep cool in face of chaos. *She played mind games because she wasn't good enough,* Penelope told Amelia afterwards. *I wasn't going to let her get away with treating me like that.* Amelia wanted Penelope to get inspiration from that girl, the girl that wouldn't take crap from anyone. Amelia vowed to get her there.

"You'll be ready," Amelia said, squeezing her shoulder. "Therapy will help. I will too."

"You don't lis—" Penelope tightened her ponytail and stood up. "Can we be done?"

"Do you have any questions?" Jack asked.

"No." Penelope's voice was curt. She walked out.

Amelia stood and grabbed her purse. "Sorry, she's..."

"Just keep being there for her," he said, walking with her. At the elevator, they caught up with Penelope, but she kept her back to them. Jack handed Amelia his card. "Call me, email me, anytime. While I can't change what happened, I can help you get to the other side."

The elevator dinged and Amelia and Penelope stepped inside. They plummeted to the ground floor, both staring silently ahead. Penelope didn't talk the entire car ride home. But as they pulled into the garage, Penelope turned to Amelia, scowling. "Do you ever listen to me? Or is it always about you? What you want?"

"I don't understand," Amelia said slowly.

"A trial, Mom? Are you kidding?"

"We don't know if there'll be a trial. That's why we went today. To find out the next steps."

"I don't want any more steps." The late-afternoon light was dim through the garage window, but Amelia could make out pain through the shadows crossing Penelope's face. "I want this over," Penelope said. "You know that. Why would you tell him I'd testify?"

"I just think—" The slam of Penelope's car door cut Amelia off.

Amelia gripped the steering wheel, resting her head against it, the adrenaline that pushed her through the meeting leaving her body in a single, emphatic swoop. Amelia didn't want a trial either, but the

156

thought of Micah getting off, not understanding how he hurt Penelope, how many lines he crossed, kept her up at night. If he wouldn't accept responsibility, then they would go to trial.

Wearily, she opened her car door and stood, shaking out her legs, trying to energize her body for the next battle. She would go inside, promise Penelope she *was* listening, understood Penelope was scared, but that standing up for herself, telling Micah that what happened wasn't okay, would help her recover. Amelia didn't have time to fall apart. Penelope needed her, now more than ever.

CHAPTER THIRTY-TWO
MICAH

Micah sat at his desk in algebra class, staring at the clock, unable to focus on anything except for the minutes ticking by at a dismal pace. All morning, he'd been hyped up, his stomach spinning nerves like a cotton candy machine, as he waited for ten-thirty. Wondering what, if anything, was going to happen. Whether it would work.

Three more minutes and he'd find out.

After Ma's meeting with Coach went nowhere, the captains of the football team—Xavier, Bentley, Cole—demanded that Coach let Micah play. Xavier argued the suspension was premature—innocent until proven guilty. But Coach claimed the decision came from above.

Two minutes.

Not one to give up, Xavier decided they would stage a walkout. Last night, the football team started a low-key campaign to recruit students—skip class, help the football team win, support Micah— through DM's and Snapchat. Micah stayed awake most of the night, worried what his attorney would say if she knew about the walkout. She wanted him to keep a low profile. But she also wasn't living his life. He had too much time and anger. No outlet. He need normalcy. Sports. Friends. Parties.

One minute.

Micah wiped his palms on his jeans. What if some kid ratted them out? Or worse, the school called the police? After his fight with Ollie, Micah couldn't afford any more trouble with the police. Or Ma.

Go time.

Micah grabbed his books and bolted from the room. Not his finest moment, but damn, the nerves hit hard! Out in the hall, a dozen or so other kids also left their classrooms. Micah let out a breath he'd been holding since last night. He wasn't alone. The boys had his back. He couldn't forget that.

He took the stairs down to the second floor, walking through the hallway toward the outer door. Something fiery caught his eye. He backtracked, pushing past kids.

Penelope.

She sat at a table in the guidance office, reading a textbook, her fingers twirling the ends of her long braid. She wore dark leggings and a blue hoodie. Typical P, looking like a dime in something casual. Twenty days passed since he saw her. Twenty days filled with questions, frustration, agony, anger. Yet, he was speechless, immobile; all he could do was drink her in.

As if sensing his presence, she looked up, her blue eyes widening to the size of a Disney princess. Despite the hell her lies caused, he smiled. He missed her. Her beautiful face. Her laugh. How she smelled like apples. Tasted like sunscreen. The way she moved like a ballerina on court, every muscle in concert. Used his last name as a nickname. G-*ray*.

Penelope bit her lip, a move she knew drove him nuts. Was it intentional? A catcher's signal? Yes, he decided. She missed him too! His heart flooded with relief. She was a puppet, her mom, the cops, pulling the strings, looking to take him down. He needed to talk to her. Tell her he understood she was scared of getting in trouble, but she had to tell her mom the truth. That she wanted to have sex too. Only she could fix this.

He stepped toward her, she his sun, pulling him closer, blinding him to the conditions in his TPCO, Ma's warnings, the walkout. All gone. To hug her. Hell, to kiss her. Run his lips—

A hand jerked him back. Xavier. "Let's go."

"I can't. Penelope—" Before Micah could explain, Penelope stood, her face flushed, movements hurried, as she fled to the back office. "I need to talk to her."

"That girl is trouble," Xavier said, as they walked down the now empty hallway. "See how she ran from you?"

Why had she freaked? P wasn't scared of anything, certainly not him. "She's just..." Micah searched for a way to defend her. A task that grew increasingly difficult the longer she stayed silent. "Confused."

"She's fire, that's for sure." Xavier pushed through the outside doors. "Keep chasing her and you'll get burned."

Micah stopped up short when he got outside. A hundred or so kids crowded the courtyard. Not what he hoped. Not in a school of a thousand.

Cheers rang out as Xavier stepped up on the cement ledge circling the flagpole, jiving like Rocky before a fight. Bentley handed Xavier a megaphone. Kids held up their phones, recording it like a concert. He saw Principal Weinstein, followed by a few teachers, exit the school on the other side of the courtyard.

"Can I get a hell yeah?" Xavier yelled, putting a hand to his ear, feeling an invisible beat.

"Hell yeah!" the crowd chanted back.

"Can I get a hell, yeah, yeah?"

"Hell, yeah, yeah!"

"Micah. Get on up here!" Xavier grabbed Micah's shoulder, tugging him up. Micah looked out at the crowd, light-headed, transfixed. "I'm gonna be one-hundred with y'all. Micah, my man, he loves his girl. But the po-lice? They fixed on him. Arrested him for having sex. *Sex!*" The word echoed and Micah cringed inside. "How many of y'all are hookin' up?" The crowd cheered. "I don't see any of y'all getting arrested! Tell me, what are the cops playing at? Why's the school draggin' him, not letting him play football? Why's his girl acting sus, lying about—"

Principal Weinstein stepped up on the cement ledge and snatched the megaphone from Xavier's hands. Instead of cowering, Xavier cupped his hands around his mouth and shouted, "Let Micah play! Let Micah play!"

The crowd took up the chant, and for a moment, Micah felt warm. Optimistic. Supported.

"Anyone not back in class in five minutes will be immediately suspended," Principal Weinstein announced. "Let's move, people!"

Boos exploded, but kids walked toward the school.

"You two, stay here," Principal Weinstein said, watching the kids with his arms crossed.

When Xavier planned the walkout, when Micah saw the kids outside, heard their cheers, he thought...maybe. Maybe his luck would turn. Maybe someone would step up. Do the right thing. Stupid! Beside Ma, every adult he knew turned their backs. He wanted to hold onto the lightness he felt when he saw Penelope, but his life was a rollercoaster flying downhill. Today would not be the day for an upswing.

After the courtyard emptied, Principal Weinstein asked, "Do you understand the safety issues you've created here? It's my job to ensure each student is cared for during school hours. That means in your seat, in class, learning. That's what your parents expect. It's what I expect."

"We were—" Xavier started.

"No. My turn to talk," Principal Weinstein said. "How can I do my job when kids are running outside, possibly leaving campus, standing in the parking lot where they could be hit?"

"How is it fair to kick Micah off the team?" Xavier asked. "You're deciding he's guilty off some girl's—"

Principal Weinstein held up his hand. "Micah was suspended indefinitely. Pending the outcome of the case, he can rejoin sports. That's the best I can do."

Micah strained his neck to keep his head held high, fighting off the weight of another disappointment. If everyone kept doing their best by him, he'd end up in juvie. He was so over this. Unfortunately, it wasn't over him.

"In the meantime, you both have a week's detention. Let's get you back to class."

Micah dragged his feet. He didn't want to deal with everyone. Not that he wanted to go home either. Ma watched over him, enforcing those insane court conditions as if it was her life on the line.

With no choice, he walked back inside the school, conjuring the image of Penelope's sweet face, the current of love pulsating in the air between them—until she ran. She gave him life. It terrified him to think that if she stayed scared, she could take it away too.

CHAPTER THIRTY-THREE
PENELOPE

Penelope tucked her hands underneath her thighs, trying to stop the shaking, as Ms. DuPree looked over her schoolwork in the guidance office. Instead of suppressing the tremble, it rumbled up her arms, pushing her to the brink of convulsive sobs.

She closed her eyes, trying to calm down, but snapshots of Micah filled her mind. *Micah.* The look of bliss that softened his face when he saw her just now. The smile that crept across his cheeks, the secret one he flashed while eating ice cream or making an inside joke. Then that football guy appeared, the one from the library—

Her teeth started chattering. Micah was friends with this guy? Did Micah send him to threaten Penelope? Could Micah be that angry? His smile today told her no, but seeing the two of them talking left her shook.

"Penelope?" Penelope opened her eyes. Ms. DuPree looked worried. "Are you okay?"

Leave. Leave! LEAVE! Penelope nodded, clenching her jaw, not trusting her voice.

The phone rang and Ms. DuPree answered, speaking in a hushed voice. After hanging up, she handed Penelope a stapled pack of papers. "Here's your work for next week."

"Thanks." Penelope shoved the papers in her backpack. She stood to leave but Ms. DuPree asked her to hang back.

"Some students held a walkout in support of Micah's rejoining the football team," Ms. DuPree said, speaking in the soothing tones one would use to calm a baby. "Everyone has been sent back to class, but until the hallways are clear, I'd like you to wait here."

Penelope closed her eyes. A walkout. The only surprising part was how much Micah still had the ability to wound her. He seemed intent on doing and saying anything to keep the spotlight on her. Make everyone hate her. Ensure she didn't have a single friend left in the world. Including Ollie.

Ollie. Was he at the walkout? Would he go that far to betray her?

"This isn't a judgement of you, or the case..." Penelope blocked out Ms. DuPree's voice. Because, really, what did her thoughts matter? What did anything matter? Even when Penelope did nothing, somehow this situation got worse. She was at a loss as to how to do less, avoid attention, get the other kids to stop undressing her with their eyes, assaulting her with their posts, using her pain to feed the gossip mill.

Eventually, Ms. DuPree stopped talking altogether and they sat in awkward silence. Many minutes later, Ms. DuPree escorted Penelope outside. Walking home, Penelope pulled out her iPhone, watching the Insta stories her "friends" posted about the walkout. Videos of kids cheering and dancing. Micah's friend giving a speech. She couldn't make out all his words above the noise, but she got the gist. Micah got arrested for having sex because he was Black—not because he did anything wrong. Like the school, she flipped on him.

She wanted to chuck the iPhone in the street, let a car run over it. She could never go back to school. Not after that public berating. How could Micah smile at her one second and stand by the next as that guy called her a liar? Why was it so easy for all her friends to believe Micah over her?

She unlocked the front door of her house, threw down her backpack, and ran upstairs. She felt dirty, disgusting, filled with an oozing blackness that coated her insides like tar. After starting the bath, she ripped off her clothes, keeping her back to the mirror. She couldn't stand the sight of her body. Hated looking into her own eyes. Hated the cowardice she saw.

Lowering herself into the scalding water, she plunged her head underneath. Heat clawed at her skin, a punishing sensation she enjoyed. Perhaps she should let go, end it all. No one would miss her. Micah was telling anyone who would listen that she was a liar.

Ollie hadn't talked to her for two days—a record. Mom, a raging workaholic, would probably be relieved not to have to worry about P. Today's walkout served as a reminder that none of her friends cared about her. Out of school, out of mind.

Why continue fighting this? What was there for her?

Nothing. Nothing. Nothing.

Her lungs burned, her muscles shook, but her brain refused to turn off. Give in. She rose out of the water, gasping. Coughing.

"What's wrong with me?" she cried, digging her nails into her scalp, needing the pain. "What the fuck is wrong with me?"

She pressed her head between her knees, sobbing. She wasn't suicidal. And yet the thought felt instinctual, like the gnawing of hunger or the tug of sleep. It terrified her.

She was alone. Losing control. Waiting for someone else to step in, save her. But no one would. Mom, Ollie, Micah, Uncle Austin, Zoe—they all abandoned her one way or another.

And with that thought, came a memory. After Dad died, she started acting out on court, pouting when a point didn't go her way, slamming her racquet, talking back. One day, Uncle Austin had enough, cutting practice short. *I'm always here for you,* he said. *But once you're in a match, I can't help you. You have to figure out how to win by yourself. Some people thrive under that pressure, some crack.* She accepted the challenge, coming to love tennis because it required mental strength. Independence. She alone won or lost. No one else to blame. No one else to take the glory.

She needed to adopt that mindset now, accept she was alone—and find a way to thrive. Pushing herself out of the tub, she grabbed a towel and wrapped it around her body. Her hair dripped water on the hardwood floor as she walked to her bedroom. She froze. A flashback of that night hit her brain like a mallet to a lever. Micah following her. Pushing open her door.

"Stop it!" she yelled. She threw on leggings and a sweatshirt. Covering up. Ridding herself of the nakedness that led to this awful mess.

Once dressed, she called Mom. "Come home."

"What's wrong?" Mom sounded panicked.

Penelope steeled her voice. She would not tell her what happened in the bathroom. She wouldn't tell anyone. "You said if I needed you, you'd be there."

"Yes—"

"Then come home." Penelope ended the call.

Now, the hardest part. Penelope closed her eyes, took a deep breath, knowing she had to cancel Micah. To save herself. Accomplish her dreams. She pressed the screen of her iPhone, making the apps shake. One by one, she deleted them. Instagram. TikTok. WhatsApp. Snapchat. Twitter. She kept YouTube to watch tennis. Mom kept calling, but Penelope hit decline. If she didn't do this now, with the suicide attempt fresh in her mind, she would lose courage.

Fingers trembling, she pulled up Micah's number. She forced herself to remember how he pushed inside her without asking. Sent angry DM's. Told his squad to threaten her. Organized a walkout. Stayed silent while she was bullied online.

There was no going back.

As she heard the garage open, she blocked Micah's number. Then deleted it from her contacts. A stupid precaution, given she knew his number by heart. Still.

The back door slammed. "Penelope!" Mom's feet pounded up the stairs. She appeared, red-faced, breathing hard, inside Penelope's doorway. "You're okay!" She pressed one hand to her heart, the other gripping the doorknob. "Jesus! Answer your phone! Do you have any idea how worried I was?"

"Worried about what?" Penelope asked, curious if Mom actually had been listening. Watching Penelope's downward slide, waiting in the rafters to swoop in and save her.

"You. I saw Micah held a walkout."

Disappointment crushed Penelope, momentarily stealing her voice. Mom might track them on social media, hover over their

166

homework, viewing habits, friends, but she wasn't in tune with her. She didn't care that Penelope wanted to stop the case, stop therapy, stop thinking about that night. Move on.

"I want to home-school," Penelope said, looking Mom in the eyes. After finishing runner-up at the Orange Bowl last spring, the USTA invited Penelope to train in Orlando. Mom said no, promising Penelope that when she needed more court time, they'd switch to home-schooling. She'd cash that promise in now. "Start training more. Get back on track."

Mom sat on Penelope's bed and patted the spot next to her. Penelope sat. "Tell me what happened. Did you see Micah?"

Penelope rolled her eyes. "This isn't about Micah. It's about me. I've wasted too much time being sad. I'm done. I'm putting my energy back into turning pro."

"Sweetie." Mom pulled Penelope close, pressing her lips against Penelope's damp hair. Much as she tried to resist, she felt herself leaning into Mom, accepting the comfort. "It doesn't work that way. You can't just decide you're over it. Not something like this."

Penelope shrugged her off, standing up. Mom always did this. Told Penelope she could talk to her about anything. Then completely dismissed her. "I can and I will. I'm not going back to school."

"Well...there'd be some conditions if we did this."

"Like what?" Penelope asked.

Mom's fingertips strummed her lips. "You'd have to up your therapy from once to twice a week. Join that Marquette training group so you're around other kids, not just with Austin. Obviously, do the schoolwork—"

"But you agree," Penelope said, relieved.

Mom grabbed the hairbrush off Penelope's dresser, tapping Penelope's shoulder with it. She turned around, letting Mom brush her hair. "I like seeing you excited again. I feel like I'm driving blind, trying to get us safely through—"

Penelope turned around. "This is how I'll feel safe. Playing tennis. Home-schooling."

Penelope hated the thought of a double dose of therapy, but could live with it. She could live with almost anything if she didn't have to go to school again, endure the stares, the gossip. She could finally put the assault behind her. All the memories, all the heartache.

Goodbye. Good riddance. GTFO.

CHAPTER THIRTY-FOUR
AUSTIN

Austin finished preparing the burgers and put them in the fridge, wondering what else he needed to do before Zoe arrived. It wasn't until he got out the mop and started sweeping microscopic dust from the floor that he realized he was nervous. Saturday night, cooking Zoe dinner at his condo, held a constellation of connotations and risks he only realized now.

I'm not doing anything wrong, he told himself as he buzzed Zoe in. *Just being a good friend.* Yet, he could track Amelia's thoughts as easily as an incoming storm. She'd flip if she found out he and Zoe were texting. Meeting for drinks. Having dinner together. She expected tribal allegiance to Penelope. But his heart beat for both sides.

Would Penelope be upset that he was spending time with Zoe? Impossible to tell anything with her lately, but Penelope loved Zoe. Austin's gut told him that Penelope understood the nuance; it was Micah that hurt her, not Zoe.

All thoughts of Amelia and Penelope disappeared when he opened the door to find Zoe, smiling wide, looking beautiful. Not the frazzled woman from yesterday who, while cutting his hair, talked about sending Micah to her parents for the weekend because she needed to recharge after he organized a walkout. Austin always thought Zoe beautiful, but her relationship with Amelia put her squarely in the friend zone. Spending time together without Amelia these past few weeks, however, he noticed her beauty afresh. Try as he might, unable to *not* notice her now.

Hence, his guilt. And nerves.

"Wow," Zoe said, handing him a bottle of wine as she walked inside his condo. "Your place is amazing!"

He smiled. "Let me give you the grand tour."

He lived in lofted condo in a converted warehouse. As they walked through, Zoe enjoyed details that made most people's eyes glaze over: original brick walls, floating staircase, exposed piping and intricate woodwork in the ceilings. Her enthusiasm reminded him of snowy Sunday afternoons watching HGTV together, while the kids were downstairs and Amelia worked on her laptop.

They ended the tour in the kitchen, where he opened the wine, pouring her a glass. He grabbed an Octoberfest Lager for himself and the burgers from the fridge.

"Come on." Austin opened the balcony door, stepping outside, and put the burgers on the grill. The sun was setting over the buildings to the west, a paint-worthy collage of oranges, reds, and yellows. The temperature balmy for early October. "How'd it go last night? Dropping off Micah?"

She tapped her fingernails against the steel railing, looking at the downtown skyline. "Well, if my goal was to make him hate me, then I won." She explained how Micah spent the hour driving to Fond du Lac alternatively yelling and giving her the silent treatment. "I vowed to never be strict like my parents, but maybe that's what he needs. A stern hand." She drank her wine. "Maybe it's what we both need. I woke up this morning, and—" Her shoulders relaxed. "—I felt lighter. I wasn't stressing, wondering what mood Micah was in or what he'd get up to or what we'd argue about."

"I'm glad you took time for yourself," he said, turning back to the burgers. "The last few weeks have been rough on you."

"Amelia said something that stuck with me. That none of the kids will leave this unscathed." Zoe turned to look at him. "But I don't think the adults will either."

The thought hung between them, as poisonous and heavy as cigarette smoke. Not wanting to think about it, he put the burgers onto the buns and served her first. He sat across from her, salivating over the aroma of charred meat and melted cheese. Nothing beat a burger. To his delight, she dove right in, none of this dainty shit his dates displayed, chucking the bread or claiming to be full after three bites.

Over dinner, the conversation flowed easily. They talked about his favorite places to travel while on tour. She spoke of wanting to visit South Africa, Australia, Costa Rica.

"Won't happen anytime soon, though," Zoe said. "I had to take out a line of credit on the house to pay for Micah's attorney."

"It's that expensive?"

"If we go to trial, it'll cost ten thousand or more." It was dark now, but he could make out the sobering line of her mouth through the yellow glow of the streetlights. "Don't have that lying around. And they—" She swallowed audibly, giving a slight nod, before gaining control of her emotions. He reached over, squeezing her hand. "They made me feel like trash, asking for the loan. Like it was expected that my son would be arrested."

He didn't know what to say. Settled on, "I'm sorry."

"Money comes and goes. But Micah—I can't lose him. And I'm terrified that he doesn't get it, that he'll keep acting out, posting on social or organizing another protest. Something that will make the DA or the judge double down..." She looked up at the moon, blinking away tears. "Amelia could stop all this. End it with one phone call. Here I am, paying emotionally, but also financially, and she's..."

They tiptoed around Amelia all night, but now she pulled up a seat at the table. Whispered in Austin's ear. Reminded him that, come hell or high water, he'd better be by her side. As she would be by his. "Amelia's hurting too. More than you know," he said quietly. Dinner might not have been a betrayal, but he wouldn't, he *couldn't*, sit here and let her minimize Amelia's pain. "She's doing the best she can to protect Penelope."

"Protect her against Micah." She matched his soft tone, her eyes boring into his. "*Micah.*"

Somehow, they were still holding hands, their faces close enough that he couldn't tell whether it was the breeze or her breath against his cheeks. "Listen, I want to be your friend." Was friendship still the prevailing thought here? Because he didn't hold hands with friends, didn't lean in close enough to kiss. "But Amelia's my sister. Penelope's like a daughter to me."

"I'm sorry." She let out a long breath. "I shouldn't have put you in the middle."

"I'm sorry, too." He sat back, pulling his hand away and running it through his hair. He needed to think without the current of electricity that sparked when he touched her. "You came here to relax and here we are, rehashing everything."

"Honestly, tonight was perfect. Good food, good company. Well," she retracted playfully, "almost perfect."

He rubbed his jaw to stop the smile that wanted to form. "Is that a hint?"

"Dessert?" She raised her eyebrows. "My sweet tooth is coming on strong."

"Let's look." They collected the dishes and walked inside, where, much to her disappointment, he only had fun-sized Snickers in the freezer. "There's a frozen yogurt bar down the street," he offered, rinsing the dishes.

"I can low-brow it with Snickers tonight." She caught him off guard when she grabbed the plates from him and loaded them in the dishwasher. In three plus years, Mady never lifted a finger. *This is what it's like to have a partner.*

"Low-brow?" He clutched his heart. "Snickers were my mid-match pick-me-up."

"You should've got a sponsorship."

"Unbelievably, they weren't interested."

She pressed her hip against the dishwasher, closing it. The silence in the room lengthened and they both laughed quietly.

Perhaps it was their years of friendship, a connection with a solid foundation, but this felt right. He ached to hold her, let down his guard and just be. All foreign emotions.

172

"Thank you, for tonight," she said, breaking the silence. "I needed this."

While weighing his next move, whether he should make *any* move, his hand reached out, seemingly on its own accord. His fingertips cupped Zoe's chin, tilting it up so they looked into each other's eyes. The attraction felt like white noise, drowning out all rational thought.

"You're incredible," he murmured, moving toward her at an agonizing pace, telling himself he could still pull the ripcord, quit acting selfish and insensitive. Stopping just before her lips, he rested his forehead against hers. He felt the flutter of her eyelashes against his skin, heard her breath hitch, smelled sweet wine on her breath.

She closed the infinitesimal gap, teasing his lips with her own, a soft brush that beckoned him to come and get it. He cupped the back of her neck, pulling her in, tasting her.

His heart sped up, passion leading the way as he stepped onto the path of duplicity.

CHAPTER THIRTY-FIVE
ZOE

Kissing Austin, Zoe felt an exhilarating mix of desire, ease, and release. She wasn't thinking about Micah. The trial. Money. Amelia. Everything departed her mind, a waterslide for her worries, leaving her with an aching, pulsating, raw need.

He pressed her against the dishwasher, while she explored his body, grasping, basking, and cataloguing muscles she previously appreciated from afar. All while kissing. Intense, spine-tingling kisses. Kissing with their whole bodies, like teenagers, where it wasn't a prelude, but the goddamn event.

His stubble scraped her chin, a mix of soft and hard that sent shockwaves of pleasure to her center. Wanting more of him, she ran her hand across the front of his jeans, teasing the cement block of his cock.

He groaned, an almost primal sound, before suddenly pulling away. "Wait, wait," he said. A wrinkle of worry creased his brow. The telltale—*What the fuck have I done?*—face men wore once blood started the voyage back to their brain.

"It's okay," Zoe said. It wasn't. "I get it." She didn't.

"I've thought about this. I *want* this. But, in all my fantasies, it didn't come with this sickening side of guilt." The beauty in his brown eyes made the pain of his words acute.

Zoe walked toward the door, unsteady on her feet, lips buzzing, dampness between her legs, determined not to feel guilty. For years, she ignored, downplayed, *suffered* her feelings for Austin, worried if they dated and broke up, her makeshift family with the Swanson's would end too. But there was no family anymore. No sisterhood with Amelia. Amelia cut her and Micah out of the picture and burned it like a vengeful woman on Valentine's Day.

174

Austin caught up with her at the door. "With you," Zoe said, "I feel..." Special. Beautiful. Myself. *Enough.* "Seen. I'm old enough to know how rare that is. To not give it up because it pisses someone off."

Austin stuffed his hands in his pockets, his gaze painting the floor. "It's not just anyone. It's Amelia, the kids. With my mom gone—we only have each other. Much as I wish it was just you and me in a bubble, their feelings matter."

"Figure it out." She pressed her lips softly against his. "You know where to find me."

Stepping outside, the air cooled her heart, hormones, and head. She refused to mourn this. Another time, another place. But there was no space to rent inside her head for new worries. Fireworks exploded and sparkled between her and Austin tonight. While she hoped they'd build on that kiss, she wasn't holding her breath.

CHAPTER THIRTY-SIX
AMELIA

It was past eleven on Saturday night and Amelia couldn't sleep, tossing and turning in bed. Penelope was taking baby steps—sleeping in her room, playing tennis—which should've comforted Amelia. Instead, new questions plagued her. Why weren't Penelope and Ollie talking? What happened to Penelope at school on Thursday? How could Amelia get Penelope to open up? To see therapy as a means of healing instead of prolonged torture?

Desperate for sleep, Amelia got out of bed, padding past both kids' closed bedroom doors. She noticed light under Ollie's door, but Penelope's was dark. In the kitchen, she opened the freezer, moving aside ice cream, pizzas, frozen meats, looking for an old bottle of vodka. She needed to knock herself out. Not much of a drinker, a couple shots would do the trick.

The bottle wasn't there.

She flipped on the lights and unloaded the entire freezer. It was gone. She stood there, dumbfounded, shivering from the cold air.

While she never caught her kids drinking, she wasn't naïve. One of them must have taken it. Perhaps Penelope drank to dull the pain? Or maybe Ollie's anxiety drove him to it? She didn't know who was the likely culprit. And this scared her. More evidence that she was out of touch.

Taking several deep breaths, she walked upstairs. Normally, she'd go in guns ablaze, but tonight, she would listen. Try to help. After all, she was struggling too. She could hardly blame them for seeking out something to numb their thoughts when she planned to do the same.

Seeing the light still on beneath Ollie's door, she knocked and stepped inside. He lay on his bed, a copy of *Almost, Maine* in his hands. He looked up, the yellow and green bruises on his cheeks reminding her of his preschool watercolor projects.

"How's rehearsal going?" Amelia asked.

"Good, actually."

"I can't wait to see the play." Amelia scanned the bedroom for the bottle, finding nothing. "Austin, P, and I will come, cheer you on."

He smirked. "P won't come."

Amelia considered this. Thought about asking him again what happened with Penelope, but let it go. She had bigger issues. "Did you take a bottle of vodka from the freezer?"

Several emotions flashed across his face—surprise, confusion, and, finally, guilt. "Yes."

She cleared her throat, overcome with emotion. She knew this situation hit him hard, but had no idea he started drinking to cope. "I know you're upset—"

"It's all my fault," he interrupted. "I should've told Micah no. I could've stopped them..."

"What do you mean?"

"The night P and Micah...whatever. Micah and I, uh, drank. I got sick..." Ollie pulled his knees to his chest, resting his head on top, looking away from her. She could hear tears clogging his throat. "That's why I had no idea what happened. I passed out."

The why of the assault suddenly became clear. Micah, a novice with alcohol, who likely had sex on the brain 24/7, didn't listen to Penelope, didn't stop, because his brain wasn't functioning correctly. He saw an opportunity and went for it. Amelia doubted he would've done the same sober. It didn't excuse him, but it also didn't make him a monster.

Amelia walked to the window, pulling back the curtain to look across the street at Zoe's house. It was dark. Looked abandoned on the cloudy, moonless night. Did Zoe know Micah was drunk that night? Probably. She and Micah discussed sex, drinking, and drugs with ease. Yet, Zoe didn't tell Amelia. Maybe it was retribution.

177

Maybe she was trying to save Micah. Whatever the reason, it hurt. Another fracture to their broken bond.

"I've been trying to figure out why Micah would act so-so-so horrific," she sputtered, finally landing on the right word. "And yet you knew, this entire time."

"I didn't want to make more trouble." Ollie wiped away tears, always the more sensitive of her kids. "I miss him, Mom. I miss the way things were. And I thought, maybe if I don't say anything, maybe him and P would work this out."

She sat on the bed and hugged him, remembering how he used to fit in her arms. Now, she fit in his. Another reminder that her kids were growing up. That they had secret lives. That they couldn't be trusted to accurately report that the sky was blue.

"Does Penelope know?" Amelia asked. "About the drinking?"

Ollie nodded.

"Is that why you two are fighting?"

"No, she's—" He abruptly shut his mouth. "They're both so stupid. They never should've—" He cut himself off again.

"This isn't your fault," she said. "Micah got drunk. He hurt Penelope. Not you."

"Whatever." He lay down, staring at the ceiling. "I don't care."

This was new too. Ollie shutting down. But, as she was learning with Penelope, pushing rarely helped. Amelia hoped in time he would adjust to this new normal without Micah.

She stood up. "Get some sleep."

Downstairs, she called Austin three times, getting voicemail. She slapped her phone down on the table, annoyed he was ignoring her calls, likely in favor of some girl he'd entertain for one night. She needed him, his levelheaded approach. His experience as a drunk, horny teenage boy wouldn't hurt either.

She rummaged inside her purse, looking for Jack Kelly's card. She wasn't sure if this information changed anything legally, but it shifted her perspective. She remembered getting drunk the first time, the way it unlocked her inhibitions. Adults learned to set limits, but teenagers didn't have that self-awareness.

She dialed Jack's number, expecting to leave a message, but he answered.

"It's Amelia Swanson," she said, flustered. "I—I wasn't expecting you to answer."

"On weekends, I transfer my office calls to my cell. What's up?"

"I found out something tonight..." She pressed a hand to her stomach, hating to admit weakness or failure. Especially as a parent. But she told him the truth. About being unable to sleep, the missing vodka, confronting Ollie. "Does this change anything? I mean, he was drunk."

"Drunk or not, he still had sex without her consent," Jack said. "If we absolve him, he'd do it again. Do you want another girl put in the same position as Penelope?"

Good point. "You're right."

Amelia settled on the couch, pulling a blanket over herself, listening as he explained how he'd introduce the drinking at trial. "That is, if we go to trial," he said. "Most consent-based cases end up settling out of court. I'll offer Micah a consent decree at the plea hearing this week and then—"

"What's a consent decree?" Although Jack wasn't talking fast, it felt like she was sprinting after a train, each new thought making it impossible to catch up.

"A list of conditions—sexual assault therapy, alcohol treatment, curfew, among others. If he successfully completes these programs, a year from now, I'd dismiss the charges. But it's up to him whether to accept this deal or ask for a trial."

Dismiss the charges? Amelia was aghast. Micah would get a fresh start, meanwhile the assault would stay with Penelope forever. "So, he'd just get off?"

"This is intensive therapy," Jack said. "It won't be easy. And you have to remember, the purpose of juvenile court is to rehabilitate, not punish. I'll fight for Penelope, I promise. But I also want to get

Micah help so I don't have another girl in my office, suffering because of him."

"Okay." She still didn't like the thought of Micah getting off easy. A little therapy and boom—done. But if she got caught up in punishing Micah, Penelope would suffer. She would leave the legal decisions to Jack. Her thoughts had to remain on helping Penelope work through the assault, get more of herself, her power, back each day.

CHAPTER THIRTY-SEVEN
ZOE

Zoe sat in the first row behind the defense table in The Honorable Judith Myer's courtroom on Monday morning for the preliminary hearing. The hearing hadn't started yet and Sarah was busy preparing Micah.

"The judge will ask how you plead and you'll say, 'I'm entering a denial,'" Sarah said to Micah. Their chairs were angled back to allow Zoe to hear better. "Say it for me."

"I'm entering a denial," Micah repeated dutifully, his expression grave.

"It's like a not-guilty plea, but the language is different in juvenile court. You're essentially saying the facts in the Petition are untrue. Then the Court will schedule a trial date. It's quick."

Zoe looked around the courtroom. It was tiny. Windowless. Stern. The judge's desk was at the front, raised a few feet, presumably to intimidate. A witness box and the clerk's desk flanked each side. An American flag and State of Wisconsin flag hung on the wall behind, with a seal posted between, further imposing authority. The State's attorney was at a table to Zoe's right.

The clerk announced, "State of Wisconsin versus Micah Gray. Case number 2022JV003281. All rise for the Honorable Judith Myers."

Everyone stood as the judge walked in. She was mid-forties with curly dark hair, rimless glasses, and pursed lips. Zoe feared having a woman judge worked against them, but Sarah said Judge Myers was a former public defender, known for fairness. *Here's hoping,* Zoe thought, sitting back down.

After reading the charge, third degree sexual assault, the judge said, "What evidence does the State have to support the Petition?"

"Your Honor, the State has the victim's statement wherein she reported she did not consent to having sex. This statement is consistent with what she told the emergency room doctor when seeking treatment for the assault. The victim sustained injury, which the State will provide testimony to show is inconsistent with consensual sex." The attorney flipped a page and then continued speaking. "While the accused contends the sex was consensual, the State possesses messages where he tries to intimidate the victim into changing her story..."

Zoe nearly bit off her tongue as anger drowned out his words. Much as she tried to monitor Micah's phone usage, it wasn't enough.

Micah had always been open with Zoe about girls—until Penelope. Why had he kept her a secret? Could the affection be one-sided? An unrequited crush? He would never hurt Penelope intentionally, but what if it was unintentional? She remembered the devastation on Penelope's face while crying on the porch—

No. Micah wouldn't lie to her. Not with what was at stake. And yet, wouldn't that be exactly why he would lie? Because he was afraid?

Zoe pushed away her doubts. Blood trumped truth. She had to start thinking like Amelia.

"Mr. Gray, do you understand the charge laid out in the Petition?"

Micah cleared his throat. "Yes, your Honor."

The judge peered down at Micah. "And how do you plead?"

He swallowed audibly. "I'm entering a denial."

"Ms. Gray," the judge said. Zoe started, caught off guard. "Do you feel you can supervise Micah properly? Ensure he complies with the Temporary Physical Custody Order?"

The saliva in Zoe's mouth dried up faster than dew in the desert. "Yes, your Honor."

"The Court shall enter a denial into the record and order that the TPCO stay in effect until trial or a consent decree is reached." She looked at her computer. "I'll set a final pre-trial date for October twenty-fourth, at ten a.m. Any pretrial motions should be filed no later than October fourteenth. Trial is set for Monday, November fourteenth, at nine a.m. Anything else?"

Both attorneys declined and the judge rammed her gavel, ending the hearing.

The State's attorney handed Sarah some papers before leaving.

"What's that?" Zoe asked, trying to read over Sarah's shoulder.

"The consent decree. The State's offer in lieu of trial. Come on," Sarah said, handing Zoe the papers. "Let's go talk."

Zoe's eyes flew across the pages as she followed Sarah and Micah out of the courtroom. One year at-home supervision with leave to attend school and court-mandated treatment...One year of therapeutic sex offender treatment...Absolute sobriety, including alcohol and drug treatment counseling...No new charges...Upon completion, the State would dismiss the Petition and the accused would not have to register as a sex offender.

Her hands shook. When would Zoe work if she was supposed to supervise him and drive him to therapy? How would she manage another year of his attitude? His anger? Depression?

Stop! she scolded herself. *Stop thinking about yourself!*

From the moment she first held Micah, slick with vernix, his mouth twisted in outrage at moving digs, it was the two of them against the world. She whispered promises, lips pressed against his velvet cheeks, fingers cupping his delicate head, to always be there for him. To protect him. These papers delivered a verdict of how she felt short of that promise. She acted headstrong, raising him in defiance of her parents' rules. Developed a friendship, instead of acting like a parent. A disciplinarian. But no more.

Accepting this deal would be a struggle. She hated the idea of having him admit to something he didn't do, but he'd be at home. With her. Not in juvie. No paper trail would follow him. The ordeal would end. For these reasons, she'd find a way to make him accept this.

CHAPTER THIRTY-EIGHT
MICAH

Micah paced inside the small, boxy courthouse conference room. All he saw and felt was red; hot, sticky anger, clotting his blood, stealing his breath, from listening to that prick attorney talk about him like he was a predator that needed to be neutered. Penelope a wilting flower that needed round-the-clock care to bloom again.

"You just sat there," Micah said to Sarah. "You didn't defend me at all."

Sarah said, "It's a plea hearing. We don't argue facts."

"Micah, sit down." Ma pulled out a chair. "Getting mad at Sarah won't help."

He looked at Ma. Her normally glowing skin looked wan, her mouth stretched in a frown. She sent him to his grandparents this past weekend, unable to stand being around him. A horrible weekend he spent outside, pulling weeds with Grandma or inside watching football with Pa. Ma took his phone too, further isolating him. When Ma picked him up yesterday afternoon, some of her vibrancy was back. They didn't even argue on the way home. But today's hearing put them back in the mud, clawing at each other to find a way out.

"This is the consent decree," Sarah said, holding up some papers. "An offer to avoid trial, provided you obey these conditions."

Micah sat down, his body rigid, adrenaline flashing like a lightning storm. "Okay."

"One year of extended supervision. You'd be allowed to go to school—"

"Are sports part of school?" Ma asked.

"Not necessarily," Sarah said. She looked at Micah, gauging his reaction, but he gave her nothing. The words lost all meaning as soon as she said one year. He struggled the last few weeks without football, his teammates, friends. A year was unthinkable. Impossible.

"Next," Sarah said. "Sex offender treatment. Twice a week. This would include group therapy where you'd learn about sexual assault laws and healthy boundaries. And individual therapy to work on accountability, acting on appropriate sexual feelings, and developing a safety plan for when you're feeling vulnerable."

"Oh, hell no," Micah whispered.

"Just listen," Ma said.

Micah dug his nails into the underside of the wooden table. "You really think I need this? That I don't understand 'healthy boundaries?' 'Appropriate sexual feelings?'"

"No, I—"

"If I can't even convince you I'm innocent, then fine." Micah slumped in his chair, breathing hard. "Put me in jail. I give up."

Ma squeezed his arm. "I believe you, I just...can't lose you."

"Alcohol and drug assessment and treatment," Sarah said, watching him closely. "Do you know why the DA included this?"

Micah thought back to that night. Could Penelope have tasted the vodka? Possibly, but P was as good as gold, she wouldn't be able to identify it. And she would've called him out if she did.

Ollie. That two-faced little bitch. Wasn't it bad enough he accused Micah of being a rapist? Threw a punch? Now, he had to hop on the betrayal bandwagon? Sell Micah out?

"Ollie and I drank that night," Micah said quietly, knowing his confession was a blow. To his case. To Ma. To any hope of having a life again.

"Why didn't you tell me?" Ma asked.

"Or me?" Sarah chimed in.

Technically, no one asked, so he hadn't lied. "I didn't think it mattered."

"Didn't think it mattered?" Ma's big eyes and fierce tone was enough to tell him he was in trouble. Again.

"Were you drunk?" Sarah asked.

He wasn't sober. Better to downplay it. "Nah, just...vibin'."

"You're sure?" Sarah asked. "You remember everything?"

"Yeah," he said. "Why?"

"Blacking out wouldn't be a defense, but it would give the judge a reason why you and Penelope had different interpretations. Why you might have misread her signals."

"I didn't misread anything." Penelope kissed him back. Touched him. She never said no.

Her quietness afterward was the only odd sign. P was never quiet. Bible, he thought they were basking in the glow together. But maybe if he wasn't flyin' so high, he would've asked if she was okay.

Shiiit. Did they have a point? Could he have missed something? But no. No! Penelope said being with him felt perfect. If she was upset, she wouldn't have said that. She always told him what's what.

"All right, last but not least," Sarah said, "no new charges and no violations of the TPCO, which will become a Permanent Physical Custody Order upon signing this."

"What if there's a smaller issue?" Ma said, giving him the side-eye. "Clearly, he's having trouble staying off social media."

"There'd be a hearing and he'd be given consequences, such as community service or house arrest." Sarah's mouth morphed into a stern line. "This isn't a joke, Micah. Think before you post. Better yet, don't post. Don't DM Penelope."

"They twisted my words," Micah said. "I was trying—"

"Intent doesn't matter. Only the act of contacting her." Sarah paused. "Let her go, Micah."

"Sarah's right," Ma said. "I know it's hard, baby, but you have to forget about her."

Micah shook his head. They didn't get it. He could no more forget Penelope than he could forget to eat.

"The plea is the safer option," Sarah said. "If we go to trial, the judge might impose more stringent conditions, such as placement in a juvenile hall."

"Or maybe she'll realize I didn't do anything wrong."

"Perhaps. Are you open to negotiating the terms of the consent decree? Maybe I can get sports added? Work with the DA and your school?"

Micah put his head down and bit his knuckle to stop a scream. "I. Did. Not. Assault. Penelope."

No one said anything. Did they think he was lying? Had everyone gone crazy? Even if they told him there would be no punishment, he wouldn't plead guilty. Because he wasn't guilty—not of sexual assault.

He hurt Penelope. Yes. It killed him to think of her bleeding. Going to the hospital. He wished she would've said something. He would've gone with her. But that's what happened to girls their first time—they bled! He never forced her. He wanted to be closer—he thought she felt the same. He *still* thought she felt the same.

Ma eventually broke the silence. "What are his chances of winning? At trial?"

"Experts will provide context, but, in most consent-based sexual assault cases, it comes down to who the judge finds more credible," Sarah said. "Penelope or Micah."

"Penelope might not testify," Ma said. "She's struggling. Amelia's the one pushing trial, not P."

"Wha—" Micah choked on his questions. When did Ma talk to P? Why didn't she tell him? *We don't lie to each other*, Ma always said. *You and me, baby, ride or die.*

"If she testifies that she didn't consent to having sex," Sarah said, bringing him back to the immediate problem, "I think you'll lose."

Micah shook his head. "P lied to her ma, the doctors, cops, whatever, but there's no way she'd be able to look into my eyes and lie." Their bond was too strong, built on too many years. He felt the rush of love last week when he saw her in the guidance office, the way the air shifted, drew them together. "On my life, she'll tell the truth."

"You're taking a huge risk," Sarah said, "assuming she holds the same truth as you."

The warning echoed in his head, *You're taking a huge risk.* It *was* a risk. What if Penelope didn't tell the truth? What if she was still afraid of getting in trouble? Would she lie, knowing he could go to juvie? Hard to believe, but what if? *What if?*

Then again, he was the one living this nightmare, bearing the consequences, dealing with the hate. Not Sarah. Not even Ma. He had to clear his name. He took a deep breath, holding Ma's eyes. "I want a trial."

Simple enough. When your back is pressed against the wall, you fight.

CHAPTER THIRTY-NINE
AMELIA

Standing at the baseline of Austin's indoor tennis club, watching Penelope run forward to hit drop shots, Amelia felt, if not peaceful, then normal. For over a decade, she watched Penelope practice, picking up balls with the hopper, clapping encouragement, shouting reminders to move her feet and be aggressive. Deferring to Austin as her tennis coach, but having her say. It was stressful, teetering that line between motivating and putting undue pressure on a child prodigy, but today, Amelia smiled. Soaked in the hunger on Penelope's face, the determination in every step and swing, the subtle fist pump when hitting a winner.

Penelope's energy reemerged with the switch to a state-accredited online school. She fit school in around her court time, gym training, and, of course, twice-weekly therapy visits. She still had an attitude with Amelia, didn't hang out with friends, and ignored Ollie, but Suzanne reminded Amelia that it was early days.

Amelia's smile abruptly vanished when her phone vibrated with a call from Jack Kelly. She'd been waiting over a week to hear whether Micah accepted the consent decree. Pushing past the curtain in the backcourt for privacy, Amelia exchanged greetings with him before asking, "Any update on the consent decree?"

"Yes," Jack said, drawing out the syllables. "Micah wants a trial."

Amelia rubbed a kink in her neck that would soon stretch across her skull, becoming a thunderous headache. "When will that be?"

"November fourteenth," Jack said. A month. "I kept the offer open, though."

"Meaning?"

"Kids often act tough until the eve of the trial. Then they can't sign a deal fast enough."

189

After answering his questions about Penelope, Amelia ended the call. She rested her forehead against the cool cement wall. She knew Micah wouldn't accept the deal. She objected to the consent decree on principal—why should Micah get off easily when Penelope was in the midst of hell? And yet his rejection weakened her knees. He could've ended this mess—legally, at least. Maybe not the best end, but one out of Amelia's hands. Now, she had decisions to make, questions of how far to push Penelope, whether she *should* push Penelope. And no easy answers.

Back on court, Penelope finished practice. She gave Austin a fist bump before grabbing her water bottle. Amelia walked over. "You looked amazing," Amelia said, smiling. It was nice to see Penelope sweaty again, the glow of hard work. "My baby's a fighter."

Penelope turned her back to Amelia to retie her shoe. Somehow, Amelia always got it wrong. She understood this was a normal parental complaint about teenagers, but with Penelope, it felt personal. A current of hostility ran through each interaction ever since their argument about the possibility of a trial. Amelia hoped agreeing to home-schooling would help, show she was listening, but, so far, no luck.

"Come on," Austin said, playfully snapping a towel against Penelope's back. He always made her laugh. "Let's go talk."

They walked down the back hallway to Austin's office. The rain was relentless today, sounding like thousands of hammers pounding the metal roof above. Every fall, when the weather turned cold, Penelope pointed out the benefits of moving to Florida for year-round training outside. This year, Penelope said nothing. Then again, that would've required her to actually speak to Amelia.

Austin flopped into his desk chair, talking about the goals for the week ahead. Penelope listened from the doorway, mopping her face with a towel. Amelia perched on the table opposite Austin, not wanting to move a pile of racquets from the only other chair.

When Austin finished, Amelia dove in. "Change of topic, you guys. I spoke with Attorney Kelly." Austin met her eyes, but

Penelope feigned a fixation with her water bottle. "Micah rejected the consent decree. Trial's set for mid-November." Penelope's face looked like a porcelain doll. She didn't so much as blink. This nothingness was the same reaction she gave when Amelia tried talking to her about Micah's drinking. Amelia bit the inside of her cheek so as to not verbally shake Penelope down. "Penelope? Thoughts?"

Penelope held up her empty water bottle. "I need more water."

Amelia got up and shut the door behind her. "She hates me," Amelia said.

"She hates what you're doing to her," Austin said.

Amelia knocked the racquets off the chair and sat down, crossing her arms. "What *I'm* doing to her? Are you kidding me? I'm bleeding myself dry, trying to help her. But here's the thing, I can't help her heal if I don't know exactly what I'm trying to fix. That's why I keep on her. Make her go to Suzanne. I can't watch her suffer and do nothing." Still, Austin said nothing. "And it's working. Five weeks ago, Penelope wouldn't leave bed. Two weeks ago, Penelope would've hit balls half-heartedly. Today, she cared! A win! A *huge* win."

"Yes, a win, but she's still not herself. I have an idea, which I know you won't like, but might help Penelope." Austin paused. "What if we let her talk to Micah?"

"Oh, hell no." Amelia jumped up, tension making her hamstrings stiff. "Absolutely not."

"Could you listen before flipping out? I meant with you and Zoe there, obviously."

Amelia sat back down, tapping her fingers on her thigh. "I'm listening."

"We're losing precious time here. Penelope's only fourteen, but these are formative years. She needs to start competing again, but it'll be worse if I send her out when she's not ready." He cleared his throat and said quietly, "I don't think she'll feel like herself again until she talks to Micah."

Amelia bit back a retort, finding patience somewhere deep within. "Why? Did she say something?"

"No, but—"

Amelia held out both hands, palms up. Case closed. "Well, there you go."

"Penelope's never quiet," he said. "Never backs down. But ever since that night, she's...fragile. Lost her confidence. But maybe if we give her the chance to let out her anger, get some answers from Micah, she'll feel emboldened."

"But she'll do that at trial."

"No, she won't." Austin pulled his hat down over his face before putting it back on. "The trial doesn't allow for a conversation, a give and take for them to work things out."

"Austin!" Amelia reached out with both hands, wanting to throttle him. How could he be so obtuse? "You can't work out a sexual assault! It's not something two people, certainly not two teenagers, can compromise on. 'Oops, sorry, shouldn't have forced you to have sex. My bad.'" She rolled her eyes. "You just can't."

"Maybe it's because I was a teenager boy, maybe because we know Micah, but I've said from the beginning, I think it's more complicated than you're allowing."

"You're right," Amelia said with faux patience. "He was drunk, not himself, but it doesn't release him of responsibility."

"It doesn't. But don't you think P would feel better, hearing him take responsibility? Don't you owe it to Zoe to see if there's a less contentious way to handle this?" Austin brushed a hand against his stubble. "Zoe's stressing—" Austin's hand froze. "I mean, I imagine she's freaking out. Micah could go to juvie. *Juvie.* What if Penelope or Ollie was in that position?"

Amelia turned away, not wanting to picture it. Losing Derek taught her how grief ate away at your soul. Then reassembled you, perfect parts imperfectly slotted together.

She knew Zoe was suffering; they both were. But she couldn't get on board with Penelope talking to Micah. While progressing,

Penelope wasn't strong enough to bat down his excuses. He was charming. And if he got Penelope on his side, what would happen to the case? Would he suffer any consequences? No. Amelia couldn't let that happen.

"I feel horrible for Zoe—"

He cut her off. "Then do something about it."

"—but she doesn't want to face facts."

"You asked me what you're doing wrong and I'm telling you. Forcing Penelope to testify will backfire." Austin swallowed. "She doesn't want this."

"And you're suddenly the expert?" Amelia snapped. "He'll walk if she doesn't testify. You think she'll feel good about that, not only being assaulted, but watching him get away with it? What if he does this to another girl?"

"Amelia, come on."

"Come on. You come on!" She reared on him. "All along, you've been downplaying this. Is this some bro code? Penelope's your niece—"

"And I'm trying to help her. Fuck, Amelia, there's not one way to handle this. No one's going to give you a gold star at the end." He was breathing hard. They both were. "Listen, I just want what's best for her. Whatever will make her feel okay again." Austin shrugged. "I thought that might be talking to Micah, but you're her mom. What do I know?"

"I'm in over my head, Austin." Amelia's shoulders unhinged. Watching him back down gave her courage to admit the truth. "Part of me thinks it will empower her to testify, but the other part? The one that hears her say she wants to move on, thinks I should let it go. But the one thing I know? Talking to Micah can't happen. What if it sends her back into that black hole? I can't—I can't go there. I can't let *her* go back there." Amelia rubbed her eyes, rubbing away the tears.

"Okay." Austin leaned over, sitting with his elbows on his thighs, staring at his hands. "Forget I said anything."

The door opened. "Can we go already?" Penelope asked, her attitude as toxic as ever.

"Not your Lyft driver," Amelia joked, trying to diffuse the tension. She stood up and said goodbye to Austin. Then she rested her hands on Penelope's shoulders, steering her down the hall and out of the tennis club. A thought hit her. How did Austin know Zoe's feelings? He talked intimately about her struggles—had he called Zoe to check in?

No. No way. Yes, they were friends, but through Amelia. Under these circumstances, she doubted he'd make the overture. It reeked of betrayal, and Austin was the last person that would betray her.

Her closeness with Austin made her think of Penelope and Ollie, who were still on the outs. A divide she tried to reconcile, understand, without success. Ollie, like Penelope, was moody, distant, and depressed, seemingly living at school for play practice. Neither would open up, but Amelia wouldn't stop trying.

Less than two minutes into the drive home and Amelia was unable to suffer the silence. "How do you feel about Micah rejecting the consent decree? That he won't admit what he did?"

Nothing.

Amelia tried again. "Are you worried about having a trial? Testifying?"

"Stop." Penelope held up her hand. "Just stop talking about the stupid trial for one second."

Amelia opened her mouth, ready to remind Penelope that there were no wrong or right feelings about this. But watching Penelope slip on her headphones, put another barrier between them, she got mad. Why was all of Penelope's hate directed Amelia's way when Micah was the one that brought on this disaster? She was just trying to love her, help her heal.

Amelia swerved, pulling over on the side of the road in front of a house. She turned and stared at Penelope until she took out the headphones. "Listen," Amelia said, "I get that you're upset. And I'm here whenever you're ready to talk. But you don't get to treat me like

194

a bug you want to crush. I'm your mom and this is difficult for me too. Understand?"

After several seconds, Penelope nodded. Amelia swore she saw tears in her blue eyes, but Penelope closed them before she could be sure.

Satisfied, Amelia pulled back into traffic and said a small prayer. That the trial would bring relief, healing, a fresh start that they all desperately needed. That she was doing right by her daughter. That, one day, she and Penelope would be back on friendly terms.

CHAPTER FORTY
PENELOPE

After putting on her helmet, Penelope rode her bike out of the garage and toward the street, experiencing a pang, like the pluck of a guitar string, deep in her gut. The air was brisk. The sky overcast. Leaves on the trees already shifted to reds and golds. Many fell to the ground, crackling as she biked over them on her way to therapy. A phantom scent of burning in the air. Fall. The season of back to school. Classes to ace. New friendships. Crushes.

Never again.

Penelope took classes online from the comfort of her couch. Watched Netflix for company. Trained until she was tired enough to not think. Went to therapy twice a week where it felt like Suzanne used a verbal pliers to try and crack open Penelope's head, get to the core of her fears. But a deep dive wasn't possible. Penelope refused to go there, not when she was regaining control of her life.

A short bus rode past her, screeching to a stop at the red light. Penelope braked too, her eyes drawn up to the rectangular windows of the bus. A little girl with pigtails waved. The boy next to her blew farts against the window. Another boy from the seat behind gave the girl bunny ears. It could've been Ollie, Micah, and her—ten years ago.

How was it possible to feel old at fourteen?

She sped through the green light, glad to put the kids and the memories behind her. When she got to Suzanne's office, she locked her bike and took the stairs to the third floor, disappointed to find Suzanne waiting. Penelope savored when the person before her ran long, cutting her session short. Sharing is caring and she'd happily share her therapy time.

Penelope settled on the couch, taking the reins, recounting the story of the kids on the bus. Talking first, at length, but little depth, was Penelope's newest strategy.

But today, Suzanne wasn't having it. After trying, and failing, to pry something substantive from the bus experience, Suzanne said, "I heard Micah rejected the consent decree."

Penelope tore the rubber band from her ponytail, combing her fingers through the long strands. Even though Suzanne supposedly didn't share anything Penelope said with Mom, Mom had no problem sharing her concerns with Suzanne. "Naturally, my mom called you."

"She's worried by your lack of reaction," Suzanne said.

"Should I be happy? Excited to send him to jail? Because I'm not." TBH, sometimes she *did* want Micah to suffer. Not like die or anything, but she wasn't too good for a nice revenge fantasy where he was publicly humiliated at school like she was or sprained his ankle, busting a tackle. Then she felt shitty. She wasn't a good person.

"How are you feeling?" Suzanne asked.

Penelope twisted her hair into a bun before letting her hands drop to her thighs. The thought of discussing that night with anyone, let alone in front of a judge, lawyers, family—Micah!—filled her with so much anger, fear, regret, and nerves that she felt like she might explode. A piñata of emotions.

"I'm trying to move on," Penelope said, downplaying her reality. Nightmares still came. After showering, she felt like an extra in *The Purge* as she ran from the bathroom to her bedroom. She panicked around strangers, worried about what they might say. Fearful of being touched. Would she ever be normal again? Have a body that felt like her own? "Mom knows this and still she..."

"What?" Suzanne pressed.

"Won't let me be. She's decided that I need to talk. With you. With her. In front of a judge, apparently. So, is she listening?" Penelope gave that question airtime. "Or does she only want to hear what I think if I agree with her?"

197

"You've told her this?"

"More or less."

"Why do you think your mom wants you to talk to me?"

Penelope shrugged, pulling her hoodie around her ears, purposefully being difficult.

"Can you acknowledge that she's coming at this from a place of love?" Suzanne rested her elbows on her knees, palms cradling her chin. "That she's experienced loss and hardship and learned that refusing to talk about it could have devastating consequences."

"I know she loves me, obvi. But does that matter? Micah said he loved me and look what he did." Penelope squeezed her eyes shut, annoyed she engaged.

"Penelope," Suzanne said softly. "The way Micah hurt you, that's not love. That's abuse. Your mom wanting to protect you, help you heal, that's love. Maybe there are better ways she could go about it, but her concern comes from love. Real love."

Penelope pressed her fingers into the corner of her eyes, trying to stop tears from blossoming. Why didn't Mom and Suzanne understand that dragging her back to that night over and over again, picking at her memories like a scab, kept her trapped in a house of horrors?

When she no longer thought she was going to cry, she looked at Suzanne. "You saying Micah didn't love me pisses me off."

"Why's that?"

"Because he does. Did—at least, he used to."

Suzanne raised her eyebrows. "How do you explain why he hurt you?"

If she knew the answer to that question, she could finally move on. For real. "Silver lining," Penelope said. "If we go to trial, he'll have to tell me why." Penelope swallowed, trying to suppress the emotion. But it wanted out. "Why'd he do it? Like, why? I really want to know. He was drunk. I get it. Whatever. Still, it doesn't make sense..."

"I'm sure he'll give all sorts of reasons, but the answers you're looking for probably don't exist. Because there is no good reason why someone would do this."

Then what's the point? Penelope wanted to scream. *If he doesn't have answers, if you don't, then why am I here? Why have a trial?* Instead, she said, "I'm going to be late for tennis."

Suzanne stood, grabbing something off her desk. Then she sat on the couch next to Penelope. "Here." Suzanne handed her a leather-bound journal. "I'd like you to write down how you're feeling each day. Even just a few sentences. Phrases. Words. This isn't an English assignment. I won't check it. While I'm happy you're playing tennis again, building up your confidence, you need a safe place to let this out. As Sun Tzu said, 'If you know neither the enemy nor yourself, you will succumb in every battle.'" Suzanne held Penelope's eyes. "Work through your feelings, Penelope. Challenge yourself. You'll emerge stronger, smarter, more at peace, if, *if*, you take the time to fight the battle now."

Penelope took the journal, paging through. Her clammy hands left fingerprints on the heavy stock beige pages. What if writing the truth sent her reeling backwards? To the bathroom, holding her head under water? But what if this was a path out of limbo?

Penelope trusted Uncle Austin on the tennis court, her nutritionist on what to eat, her trainer on how to build muscle. Perhaps she could try trusting Suzanne on how to heal her mind. Her heart.

A few thoughts each day. Just for herself. She could endure that. Endure and prosper, perhaps.

CHAPTER FORTY-ONE
AUSTIN

Austin parked in the lot at Veterans Park, maneuvering to get out of the car without spilling the coffee he held in one hand and hot chocolate in the other. He set both drinks on the hood of his car while he fastened his jacket. The late October wind had bite, while the gunmetal sky foreshadowed a punishing winter. Relishing the warmth from the beverages, Austin started down the cement path toward the tennis courts to meet Zoe.

Three weeks passed since Zoe came for dinner. Three weeks filled with restless sleep, delusional pep talks to find someone else, and mediocre distractions. He felt like a fuck-boy for kissing her, starting this. For once, he couldn't blame his usual hang-ups with intimacy; he wanted to talk until dawn, uncover every secret her body held, build a relationship.

But each time he thought about telling Amelia the truth, he faltered. What would be enough for Amelia to forgive him? Love? Marriage? A baby? Nope. Nothing would help. Amelia would argue the betrayal came the moment he kissed Zoe. Maybe even further back, the night he talked to Zoe and Micah while Penelope's wounds still bled.

And Amelia would be right. During a crisis, families closed ranks, supporting, listening—anything to facilitate healing. Dating Zoe would be as lethal as detonating a bomb. Amelia might ice him out, as she did Zoe. The risks were too great; he had to listen to his head, not his heart. Tell Zoe they couldn't spend time together now. Maybe not ever.

Sitting on the bench outside the tennis courts, Austin remembered teaching tennis here for the rec department during high school. Back then, he dreamed of going pro, meeting a beautiful woman in Greece or Brazil or Thailand, and retiring rich. He usually laughed at his delusions of grandeur, but today, the blade nicked an artery. Zoe was the first woman since Mady, maybe the first woman *ever*, that he could see a future. A wedding, kids—everything. And he had to end it.

"Fuck me." He tilted his head back and closed his eyes, sniffling because the cold made his nose run.

He heard Zoe approach, her boots crushing the fallen leaves. Standing up, he hugged her, holding his breath so as to not inhale her sweet scent. A pitiful attempt to trick his hormones into dormancy. Going for a walk was both pragmatic and strategic. Micah was at school, and being outside, cold, with people around, suppressed Austin's desire to undress her with his mouth.

Austin handed Zoe her cup. "Thought hot chocolate might warm you up."

"Thanks." Her closed-lip smile didn't reach her eyes. He'd been around enough pissed-off women to know that three weeks of silence after a mind-bending kiss fell short. By miles.

"Let's walk," he said, his feet weighed down by the words he had to say, the pause that would likely become permanent. "It'll keep us warm."

The conversation started with easy topics—weather, work, Netflix binges—before ramping up to the trial. She talked about her battles with Micah, how he accused her of punishing him for rejecting the consent decree by taking away his phone at night. His anger wore her down, made her feel like she was sleepwalking, a fog shadowing her each day.

Austin listened. It was all he could offer. His efforts to help everyone heal failed.

By the time they reached the pond, the words he rehearsed refused to come. Just walking and talking, breathing the same air as her, made him happy. Not surface happy, but deep in his muscles, laced in the blood his heart pumped—she switched him on. Was it fair to sacrifice his happiness? Especially when he already gave up playing tennis to move home and help after Derek died? He'd been around the world, literally and figuratively, hook-ups, friends with benefits, girlfriends. Zoe was the real deal. A gamechanger.

He chucked his coffee into a garbage bin and watched as Zoe carried on for a few steps. Realizing he wasn't next to her, she turned around. "Come here." He beckoned her with his hand. She walked slowly, as if to ward off what was to come. When she got close, he took the hot chocolate out of her hands, tossed it, then interlaced his fingers with her. "These last few weeks have been hell. All I've wanted is to see you, talk to you, touch you."

"Well," she said lightly, "here I am."

Austin wrapped his arms around her, needing to be closer. Wanting to reassure her he wouldn't pull a disappearing act again. Be clear about his feelings. "I. Want. You," he said. "This might sound stupid, but when I'm with you, I feel the same as I do stepping onto a tennis court. At home. At ease. Exactly where I'm supposed to be."

A brilliant smile stretched across Zoe's face. Compared with the slate sky, the wind cutting through their clothes, Zoe's brown eyes radiated warmth. "I want you too."

He kissed her. Again. And again. And again. Dizzying kisses that made him forget where they were, the problems inherent in kissing her.

Zoe pulled back, resting her forehead against his heart. "What about Amelia?"

"She'll be upset. And she has a point," he said, talking fast. "The timing is horrible. But I also know she loves you. There's not room for that love right now, but, in time, she'll accept you. Accept us." She would have to. Closing the door on Zoe was no longer an option. Austin wanted to believe his bond with Amelia was too strong to break. It bent with each argument and eased back into place. But this, this would be the ultimate test.

"That's a very optimistic view," Zoe said, not hiding her skepticism. "Some might consider it delusional."

"Amelia wants me to be happy." A projection of confidence he didn't feel. It wasn't just telling Amelia that worried him. Penelope's silence put him on edge, too. Coaching her, telling her he'd be there to support her at trial, proved he was in her corner, right? She'd understand that his feelings for Zoe didn't change his belief in her, right? Under normal circumstances, yes, but nothing about P was normal right now. "Are you worried about Micah? What he'd think?"

"I..." she faltered, squinting up at the sky. "I have no idea how he'd react. But I'm not planning to find out—at least not now. Trial starts in two weeks and he has enough on his mind."

"Should we—" Austin stopped. He saw an opening, a way of delaying the inevitable, but a delay was better than nothing. A delay might give Amelia time to calm down, gain perspective, depending on the outcome of the trial. And, honestly, she didn't need any more stress right now either. "Maybe we should hold off on telling anyone until after the trial? See how things play out? Give us time to figure this out too?"

"I like that." She pressed a light kiss against his lips. "Let's keep it low-key."

Even that, the smallest of touches, left him aching for more. As wrong as this might be—But was it wrong? If this happened at any other time in the past seven years Amelia would've been ecstatic—it felt natural, right, inevitable, when he was with her.

They finished their lap around the pond, stopping every few feet to make out, both gluttonous for affection, intent on getting their fill.

The good feelings lasted only as long as he was with her. After saying goodbye, he drove to his tennis club. A heavy, cloying fear filled his lungs, spreading through his body with each breath. What if Amelia made Penelope switch coaches? Stopped him from hanging with Ollie? Took away his house key? Issued an ultimatum? Either way, he was screwed, but if he quit Zoe, he was miserable. But the price of happiness was high, possibly too high if Amelia and the kids never forgave him.

CHAPTER FORTY-TWO
MICAH

When Micah got home from school on Thursday afternoon, he walked through the back door with a smile. Ready to flex. Ma might think he was indifferent, but he recognized the last couple months had been a strain. She logged extra hours at the salon. Parenting podcasts replaced music. Instead of bringing home trouble, starting another argument, he had good news to share. A nearly perfect report card for the first quarter. All A's except for a B in geography, but really, with an iPhone, that class was dead.

Ma sat at the peninsula in the kitchen, gazing at her phone with a smile, a smile his arrival killed. "Ready to go?" she asked.

"Where?"

"Trial prep with Sarah." She sighed. "Micah, I told you about this."

He forgot. It happens, but she'd take it as evidence that he wasn't taking this seriously. "I have good news. Got my report card." He opened the school app on his phone, handed it over, and busted a little "Renegade" dance, celebrating a rare victory.

"We should show Sarah." Ma rubbed her chin. "Maybe good grades would sweeten the deal."

He stopped dancing. "For real? That's all you have to say?"

She stood up, handed him his phone, and kissed his cheek. "Proud of you, baby, but you always get good grades. It shows how strong you are that you didn't use this as an excuse."

"An excuse?" he sputtered. That shit hurt. This quarter was hell. He started high school. Lost his two best friends. Got arrested for sexual assault. Kicked off the football team. Faced the possibility of going to juvie. Had teachers looking to fail him. And *still*, he made honor roll. "When did you stop having my back?"

"I always have your back." She reached for him. He stepped backwards. "You may not like the changes around here, but I'm trying to protect you."

"Maybe I don't want your protection," Micah yelled, before walking back out the door. "Not if it means dealing with this shit."

He got in the car and waited, his foot tapping up a storm. She used to celebrate his wins, big and small. Now, when he stumbled, she lashed out. And when he persevered? She took it for granted. Found something new to stress about. And the more she stressed about being supermom, the more it blew back on him.

When Ma got into the car, Micah turned his body toward the window. "Don't."

For once, she backed down. They drove in silence. But no sooner had they entered the elevator of Sarah's building, she started in again. "Please listen to Sarah. Be open-minded."

His ears popped as they flew up the thirty-five flights. Open-minded was code for not questioning Sarah. But he read history, knew exactly where blind loyalty got Black people. Hell, Ma was the first one to teach him that lesson.

Inside the conference room, Sarah started with the prosecution's witness list. No surprises there. Amelia. Ollie. Penelope. A couple doctors. The shock came when Sarah told him he was their only witness. "Just me?" Micah asked. "Won't that look bad, when they're parading all these people?"

"We don't *want* anyone else to testify," Sarah said. "It was a private, intimate encounter between you and Penelope. No one else. We want to show the judge you're confident Penelope consented to sex. Anyone else's testimony is irrelevant because they weren't there."

"I guess..." He understood the strategy, but was it smart? Would the judge understand? Or would it look like he couldn't get a single person to vouch for him?

"And you won't be without support," Sarah said. "I've asked some of your teachers and coaches to submit character references."

Micah slouched in his chair. He doubted any would actually do it. The arrest followed him around school like a never-ending fart, silent but deadly. Outside of his football crew, no one got close. Definitely not the teachers. None of the girls. He dreamed of being famous, but maybe God got confused, because Micah was now infamous.

"Micah got an amazing report card today." Ma nudged his arm. "Show her."

Micah pulled out his phone, sliding it across the conference table.

Sarah looked over his grades. "Nice work!"

Micah's face warmed. He couldn't remember the last compliment he got. From anyone.

"Do you think it'll help?" Ma asked.

"Academic achievement always helps, but more at sentencing." Sarah's eyes held Micah's. "I'm hoping we don't get there. Now," she said, turning back to her laptop. "Our defense strategy on cross is two-pronged to create reasonable doubt. First, there's no evidence a sexual assault took place. Yes, the doctor concluded Penelope had vaginal fissures, yes, she was bleeding, but this happens during consensual sex, too. She was nervous and no lubrication was used."

But there was lubrication. He went down on her. Even though she asked him to stop, he could feel her getting excited. At least, he thought she was excited. Suddenly, he couldn't remember exactly what made him think that. The details were blurry. Sweat trickled from his armpits, dampening his shirt. How could he forget? Could it be the alcohol? Making him think one thing in the moment?

Fuck. What if he panicked like this on the stand? Second-guessed himself? Said the wrong thing? Forgot something important? Blew his case?

"Second," Sarah said, "Penelope is a proven liar—it was her idea to keep your relationship a secret. Then she lied to the police, again denying the relationship. Fact: her word alone cannot be trusted."

Bees swarmed Micah's stomach as he imagined the state attorney taking a fine-tooth comb to his story. Trapping him like lawyers did on TV.

Whenever he tried to picture the trial, his mind cut out. A blockage. He could only picture after. Being free. Vindicated. Sarah pushing these details, going over his testimony, giving him tips on what not to do—namely, don't lose his shit—jacked up his nerves.

He stood up, walking around the table. Sarah's silvery eyes followed him. "Nervous?" she asked.

"It's a lot." Micah stopped and rested his hands against the window, the setting sun blanketing his body.

"Attorney Kelly left the deal open," Sarah reminded him, as if Ma didn't do that every freakin' day. "One year at home, going to school, treatment—"

"And everyone would think I forced her," Micah whispered.

"But you'd be home," Ma said.

He wanted to be home too. But not if home was another prison. Not if Ma went all Big Brother on him, surveilling his phone, TV, and friends. Not if every girl looked at him with fear in her eyes.

"I can't say I'm guilty of something I didn't do." He might not have remembered every single detail, but he knew he didn't force Penelope to do anything she didn't want. They were in it together, start to finish. "Can't believe you'd want me to, Ma. You're always telling me to stand up for myself, speak the truth. By going to trial, I'm doing that."

"You're right," she said. Two words filled with agony.

Later that night, Ma was at work and Micah lay on the couch, watching Netflix, bored and lonely and horny, but too afraid to watch porn for fear that Ma or his social worker was creepin' on his phone. He got up and closed the drapes, blocking the sightline to P and Ollie's house. Buttery light shone through their windows, reminding him of laughter, love, safety. A year ago, he was there. Did they miss him? Was his ghost haunting their house like Penelope and Ollie haunted his?

He turned off the TV and went upstairs. Grabbing his Beats by Dre headphones, he put on Khalid, needing something lowkey to numb his thoughts, fade to sleep. But sleep wouldn't come. He might have talked a big game about truth and innocence, but in his room, all alone, he squeezed his pillow tight. Should he settle? Suck it up, do the time?

If he did that, for the rest of his life, everyone would think he was guilty of sexual assault. People might not believe he was innocent if he went to trial and lost. But *he'd* have peace of mind. He'd know that he fought. He'd know it was the corrupt police, the lawyers, the judge. Not him. That had to matter, right? Martin Luther King, Jr., Rosa Parks, Malcolm X—they all took a stance, gained and lost, some bigger than others. But it helped everyone. If Black kids just kept taking deals, accepting punishments for crimes they didn't commit, would it ever stop?

Laying in his bed, wondering if his nights sleeping there were numbered, he thought about Penelope. Her innate goodness. Their years of friendship. Love. He understood why she lied. Kept quiet. At least, he tried to understand. He knew how small he felt when cornered by the police. And Amelia wasn't one to mess with.

But at trial, he had to believe Penelope would tell the truth. That she would do the right thing. Save him.

Please, he repeated over and over, a prayer, until sleep came. *Please.*

CHAPTER FORTY-THREE
OLLIE

By the time Ollie left school after play practice, it was dark and cold outside. Sleet transformed into a fluttering of snowflakes right before his eyes. Ollie stuck out his tongue, tasting the flakes as they skirted and twirled in the golden glow of the streetlights.

Play practice always invigorated Ollie, made him optimistic that his world wouldn't always be this small. Other than reciting his lines, he never talked much, instead watching the ease with which the upperclassmen carried themselves. Gay. Bi. Pansexual. Words and identities he'd never heard spoken without apology, distain or laughter. A reminder that perhaps Penelope and Micah weren't his people. That his people were waiting, shifting to make room for him, a reservation to cash in—just as soon as he felt comfortable in his own skin to take the leap.

While the play opened up a new world for Ollie, going home locked him inside his old one. Everything was about Penelope. Always. Before it was tennis, now it was the assault *and* tennis. Lawyers and therapists headlined dinner conversation, with Mom distractedly asking Ollie about his day. Uncle Austin was suddenly too busy for Ollie, too.

Turning onto his street, Ollie heard a repetitive banging, a slap-pound-slap, he immediately recognized. Protected by darkness, Ollie rested his head against a tree and watched Micah play basketball in his driveway. Ollie's heart matched the pounding of the ball as Micah dribbled out to the perimeter, jumping gracefully into the air, releasing the ball, and following through with his right hand. A perfect arc that ended with a swish—*Kobe!*

Micah missed the next shot, the ball ricocheting off the front of the rim and rolling down the driveway. Without thinking, Ollie ran across the street and stopped the ball with his foot. Micah pulled up short. Not surprising, considering their last conversation ended in blows.

Ollie turned around to look at his house. The windows, outlined in soft yellow rectangles, looked inviting until he remembered what his night held once he stepped through the door. Deciding he didn't care if Mom saw him out here playing, he chucked his backpack on the wet grass, grabbed the ball, and dribbled down the driveway toward the hoop. Sports bored Ollie, but an unwritten code existed among boys. You needed to play to fit in. A code Ollie hadn't questioned until he auditioned for the play. Met other boys that didn't want to sit around, sweating and swearing, using a ball to prove their toughness.

Micah got Ollie's rebound, taking his shot. Swish. Swish. Bank. Ollie's turn. This pattern continued, making Ollie wonder whether, just for tonight, they would pretend nothing changed. That they hadn't got drunk together. That Ollie hadn't almost kissed Micah. That Micah hadn't lied to Ollie. Chosen Penelope over him.

"So, what're you doing here?" Micah asked, getting Ollie's rebound and tucking the ball between his hip and his arm.

"Playing ball."

"Who asked you?"

Ollie took the hit, stepping into the shadow of the garage. "We're never going to be friends again?" Ollie's voice rose. He sounded pathetic. His emotions transparent. A plus when acting, toxic when trying to play off a broken heart as a lost friendship.

"Dude, you're testifying against me."

After their fight, Ollie was certain Micah suspected his secret. But Micah's ego saved Ollie. Micah was too worried about himself to notice Ollie's excitement. Let alone expose him. "Not *against* you," Ollie said. "I'm gonna say we drank."

Micah spun the ball on his index finger. "That's all?"

"Don't know anything else—you and P made sure of it."

"That's P's fault, not mine," Micah said. "I wanted to tell you everything."

Ollie's heart skidded to a stop. Did Micah miss him? "Whatever." Ollie tucked his hands in his pockets, his skin raw from the cold. He was stupid. Getting excited over nothing. Again. He was like a lab rat. Micah gave him a crumb and he came running. Even knowing Micah would never, ever love him back.

Micah tsked, shook his head. "Why did P quit school?"

The abrupt turn caught Ollie off guard. And stung. Had it always been this way? Micah fishing for information about Penelope and Ollie too stupid to notice? Even now, when Penelope was taking him to trial, he still loved her. "That football guy you're always with," Ollie said, stepping into the floodlight, "threatened her."

Micah dropped the basketball, the bounces echoing through the silent, cold air. "Threatened her?"

Ollie looked away, hating how much he wanted to kiss Micah. Hating that he still felt this way. "I don't know the details. But whatever happened with you guys—it messed her up bad."

Micah's eyebrows furrowed. "What do you mean?"

Penelope wasn't right. Her quietness. The way tears welled in her eyes without prompting. But Ollie didn't know if she was heartbroken, regretful, or if Micah forced her. He'd probably never know. "I gotta go."

"Whoa!" Micah grabbed Ollie's jacket. "You can't say that and leave. Messed up how?"

"She's not talking," Ollie said, jerking away. Different day, same result. He was caught in the middle. Invisible to both of them. "Not to me. Not to anyone."

Ollie walked down the driveway, suddenly exhausted. It was too much. Being this close to Micah. It wasn't Micah's fault, not really. Ollie was the freak. A masochist, showing up here, hoping for the impossible.

"Tell Penelope—"

"Tell her yourself," Ollie shouted back. "I'm done."

The bounce of the ball against the pavement was the soundtrack to his tears as he crossed the street. He wiped his nose. Then his eyes. Crying over Micah. Again.

It was good they weren't friends anymore. He didn't fit in Micah's world. If only Ollie had the courage to jump headfirst inside his new world. Be himself, without hating himself, for having to live that life.

CHAPTER FORTY-FOUR
ZOE

As the clock ticked past midnight, Zoe was wide awake, lying in bed, reading articles on the racial disparities in the Wisconsin juvenile justice system on her iPad. The glass of wine did little to mask her growing anxiety, and Austin, whom she'd come to rely on for comfort, was late. The trial started in less than a week. With Micah refusing to accept the consent decree, refusing, really, to consider anything but a finding of non-delinquency, Zoe's anxiety turned her into an insomniac.

The more she read, the more Zoe believed the deck was stacked against Micah at trial. While overall numbers in the Wisconsin juvenile system had gone down, Black incarceration rates increased nearly one-hundred percent compared with white kids. One reason for this, cops penalizing Black kids for crimes just as likely to occur among white kids, hit home. She kept going back to the fact that they had sex. Sex! Sex that left Micah glowing and Penelope devastated. Zoe believed in her heart they got caught up in the moment. Would Penelope admit as much? Zoe didn't know. But she sure as hell doubted the State would be prosecuting this case if two white kids were involved.

Making matters worse, according to several articles, the victim and judge were both white, while the defendant was Black. Zoe laughed. You didn't need a Ph.D. to know that spelled disaster. Zoe experienced enough microaggressions to know that white people were still considered more truthful. And Black boys? Please. An entire prison system perpetuated and profited from the myth that Black boys were inherently dangerous and dishonest.

Which begged the question of how to advise Micah. If she told him to go forward with the trial, she would be supporting him, but she wouldn't be protecting him. She talked to him about the racial issues at play. How the judge might see another Black boy in trouble, not Micah the individual. These conversations were a delicate balancing act. While she wanted him to understand the realities of the world, she didn't want these racist ideas to infect his soul, his outlook on every person he met or place he visited. But, for reasons she didn't understand, he believed the truth of his testimony would outweigh any prejudice. And, if she kept on him to accept the consent decree? He would think she didn't believe him. Either way, their relationship would suffer.

Her phone buzzed. Austin. *Here*, he texted. Zoe quickly reapplied some lipstick and mascara to distract from the bags under her eyes, and went downstairs to let him in. While they mostly talked on the phone and texted, Micah slept like the dead, allowing Austin to sneak over for a few late nights. Micah had always been cool with Austin, but the arrest changed everything. Secrecy was best until the trial was over. And until she knew Austin was for real. Doubts lingered that he would really choose her, choose a relationship, once Amelia found out.

Zoe opened her back door, stepping into Austin's arms, his warmth taking away the sting of the cold November night. She buried her face in his neck, feeling her heart slow as she inhaled his crisp, earthy scent. Every time she saw him felt like taking a freebase jump—she fell faster and harder. Years of holding back gave her little restraint now. Reluctantly, she pulled away and closed the door.

"How goes it?" he asked with a smile, his curly hair falling into his eyes. The tight jeans, fitted shirt, and blue trucker jacket—*Sex! Now!* her body screamed. But her head won out, knowing they needed to talk.

"I'm okay," she said, lightening her voice, aware that she was a ball of stress.

"No, you're not." He pressed a hand to the small of her back and led her through the kitchen to the couch in the living room. "Come. Sit. Spill."

After dinner at Austin's condo, Zoe vowed never to put him in the middle again. That brief glimpse of panic when she pressed him about Amelia served as a warning. But Micah's future was on the line. Zoe already suffered—her savings gone to hire Sarah, her once smooth relationship with Micah filled with speed bumps, her friendship with Amelia a memory—to keep Micah out of juvie. Now, she'd risk losing Austin too.

"How's Penelope?" Zoe asked, snuggling her feet between his thighs, warming her toes.

"She's okay." He rubbed his scruff with the heel of his palm. "Playing better. But...the fire in her eyes—it's not back."

Austin's concern echoed what Micah told her the other day. That he heard Penelope wasn't doing well. Micah wouldn't say how he knew, but promised Zoe he hadn't contacted her. With Sarah mentioning that some "victims" declined to testify to prevent further trauma, Zoe needed to find out whether this was a real possibility. "Do you think she'll testify?" Zoe held her breath.

"I think so," Austin said eventually. "Amelia feels it will be healing, to tell Micah how he hurt her."

Healing! Penelope wouldn't heal by putting Micah away. Living with that guilt would tear her apart. "Can you find out?" Zoe lightly massaged the back of Austin's neck. "With Micah pushing for a trial, I could give him better advice if I knew."

"I can't get in the middle of this, Zoe." He reached up, squeezing her hand. "I'll listen for as long and as often as you need, but I can't...I can't be strategizing with you."

Were her expectations too high? She loved Austin, which only made the fall that much more painful. He would never truly commit to her, be an ally, with Amelia in the shadows. "Why didn't I see it before? You think he's guilty, don't you?" Zoe lashed out, hoping Austin would deny it. "That he forced Penelope."

"I believe Penelope got hurt." He shifted forward, resting his elbows on his knees. "If you want to take that as an indictment that he's guilty, fine. You're in good company. Amelia accused me of downplaying—"

Zoe smoothed out the anger in her voice. "It's one question, Austin."

"I'm already lying to her." He briefly closed his eyes. "I can't take on anything more."

While he always let her vent, she saw now that he was worn down too. And she was making it worse. If she continued, she'd end up pushing him away. She wanted to empathize—Amelia was his sister. Penelope his niece. Naturally, he was torn. But she couldn't. Because empathizing, for Zoe, was too close to admitting Micah crossed a line.

"So, you'll just let Micah go to juvie?" Zoe's tears materialized as quickly as eyedrops. "Because you don't want to upset Amelia?"

Austin caught a tear with his thumb. "Zoe, even if Penelope decided not to testify, I don't think they'd let him walk."

"I'm worried," she whispered, sickened by the truth. Because Austin was right. Sarah said it would be better if P didn't testify, but it wouldn't guarantee a finding of non-delinquency. They could prosecute him, using the testimony of the police and doctor. "I don't know what to tell Micah. Should he plead? Accept responsibility for something he didn't do to avoid juvie? Or take his chances at trial, where the judge will likely believe Penelope?"

"If it was me—"

"That analogy doesn't work." She sat up on her knees, cupping his face. If they were going to be together, he needed to be willing to listen, learn, understand that while Zoe and Micah shared Austin's world, they lived under a different set of rules. "Micah's Black, Austin. I wonder whether this would even be going to trial if he was white."

Austin shook his head. "Amelia wasn't thinking of it like that. Penelope was hurt and she wanted to help."

"But the cops made assumptions, knowing he was Black. The DA sure did. The judge will. Maybe Amelia should challenge herself to understand that while her intentions weren't racist, Micah is now caught up in a racist system."

Austin took her hand. "You're right. That—that, I'll talk to her about."

A small concession, but it was something. "I try to remind myself that Amelia hasn't changed, the circumstances have, but it's hard."

"Focus on taking care of Micah," Austin said, using his thumb to trace small circles on the insides of her palm. She looked down at their intertwined hands. Black and White. A study of contrasts. And yet, their hearts beat with the same love. "Taking care of yourself. That's what matters now."

He brushed kisses on the inside of her wrist, the pulse point waking her nerves like an agonizingly delicious alarm clock. Giving in to the moment, letting Austin love her, wouldn't solve anything. Nothing, in terms of Micah. But with stress and insomnia eating her alive, she *needed* this, minutes of bliss to carry her through the coming days.

CHAPTER FORTY-FIVE
PENELOPE

After spending all Sunday morning at the gym, Penelope's aching muscles welcomed a warm shower. She rubbed shampoo into her hair, mentally cataloguing her workout. She started with yoga, followed by circuits of tens, three times—weighted squats; weighted lunges; pull-ups; push-ups; dumbbell flyes; bicep curls; calf raises; leg extensions; box jumps—then finished with sprinting intervals on the treadmill. Dressed in black, with her Nike cap pulled low, Penelope felt both invisible and invincible. At the gym, like the tennis court, she was capable. Strong. Nobody's victim.

Stepping out of the shower, Penelope wrapped a towel around her body and raced to her bedroom, trying to outrun the memories. What if she'd dressed before Micah came up? What if she'd skipped a shower? If she hadn't been naked, this never would've happened. One minor decision and her life was forever altered. So. F'n. Unfair.

"Let's go!" Mom yelled up the stairs, the decibel warning Penelope this was now a code red situation. Mom hunted her down at the gym, all but dragging her out for a meeting with Attorney Kelly.

Penelope threw on leggings and a sweatshirt, and twisted her long, wet hair into a braid. Then she walked downstairs and followed Mom into the garage, getting into the backseat of the car, Ollie having claimed the front. She wasn't sure why he was coming, but chalked it up to Mom's new psycho obsession with family QT. First order of business was reconciling Penelope and Ollie.

Twenty minutes later, sitting across from Attorney Kelly in a conference room at the courthouse, Penelope wished she would've hidden in the sauna at the gym. Risking heat stroke had to be better than preparing for trial. A trial she didn't want. Not that anyone, least of all Mom, cared what she wanted.

Attorney Kelly's words were gentle, but his gaze exacting, pinning Penelope with his grassy green eyes. She recognized a fellow competition junkie. Woke as he may be, he also wanted to win.

"As the disclosure witness, your mom will testify first," Attorney Kelly explained. "About finding you that night and taking you to the hospital. Dr. Bilson, who treated you in the emergency room, will testify next. Then Dr. Harris—"

"Who?" Mom interrupted, looking up from her notepad. Why she was taking notes was beyond Penelope.

"Our sexual assault trauma expert. She'll testify as to the stages of grief and recovery."

"Ah..." Mom jotted this information down.

"Officer Avery goes next, then Ollie—"

"What?" Penelope practically screeched. Ollie looked up from the end of the table where he was playing on his phone. She didn't want him to know the details of that night. He already knew enough. And hated her for it. "Why does Ollie have to be there?"

"He'll lay the foundation for Micah being drunk during the assault," Attorney Kelly said.

Penelope dropped her head onto her arms, burying her face in the table.

"What's wrong?" Mom asked, resting a hand on Penelope's back.

What's wrong? Was Mom for real? They were turning the worst night of her life into a parade of horribles and couldn't understand why she was upset? "Ollie's testifying and nobody thought to tell me?"

"Every time I talk to you about the assault, the trial, your therapy, you play music, close the door, yell at me to go away," Mom said. "What should I have done? Text you?"

"Micah posted about the trial on Insta," Ollie said. He handed Mom the phone. Penelope peeked at the picture. Micah stared directly into the camera, a close-up. His lips slightly parted, his dark

219

eyes soulful, holding her gaze. "Tomorrow," he posted. "The truth will out. #truth #BlackLivesMatter #juvenilejustice"

Penelope's heart pounded as she studied the picture, marking her fear in beats. Micah looked intense. Confident. The confidence reminded her of that night, how he looked at her like he knew exactly what she wanted, knew her body better than she knew herself. Nothing like the smiling, sweet-talking boy she grew up with.

"He still doesn't get it," Mom said, passing the phone to Attorney Kelly. "This isn't about race, it's about consent."

"He'll understand tomorrow," Attorney Kelly said.

"Some kids are saying you're targeting him because he's Black," Ollie said as two pink blotches rose across his cheeks.

Penelope sat up. "Is that true?" Was this about justice? Or was Attorney Kelly not allowing her to move on, forget, because of some racist agenda?

"I'm prosecuting this case because he assaulted you," Attorney Kelly said. "End of story. He could be Black, white, purple, for all I care. I don't give passes to anyone, nor do I target anyone. His actions brought him to trial, nothing else."

Instinct told Penelope it was more complicated, but she couldn't say how.

"Micah posts this stuff because he's struggling with what he did," Mom said. "It's not easy to take accountability, especially when an act, like getting drunk and committing sexual assault, is wholly out of character."

"By going to trial, we'll make sure he gets the help he needs," Attorney Kelly said. Then he turned to Ollie and started running through his testimony.

Penelope's mind stayed glued to Micah. She hadn't seen him since that day in the guidance office. Was he still DMing her? Late at night, she ached to download the apps. But, so far, she resisted.

"Okay," Attorney Kelly said, standing up. "Field trip." Reluctantly, Penelope followed. They took the elevator down to the third floor, through the sunlit hallway, ending at a locked door.

Attorney Kelly flashed his keycard. "This is Judge Myers' courtroom." The bolt clicked and he opened the door, letting Penelope pass through. Penelope looked around the courtroom, underwhelmed. No windows, lots of wood, a couple tables, two rows for seating. Sparse. Utilitarian. Boring.

"It'll be a small group," Attorney Kelly said. "The judge, court reporter, defense attorney, Micah and his mom, the three of you, plus your uncle."

Penelope rolled her eyes. Micah already broke the internet, hollering her name. A closed courtroom couldn't fix that.

"Come up to the witness stand, Penelope." Attorney Kelly unlatched the Dutch door, holding it open for her. "I figured you'd be more comfortable tomorrow if we practiced here today."

When Penelope sat, her opinion of the room shifted. An optical illusion. It no longer looked quaint, but rather stifling, intimidating, nausea-inducing. She looked up at the judge's desk, imagining some old woman towering over her, eyes accusing Penelope of being a slut. Wasting everyone's time. Good girls didn't parade around in towels. Tease boys. Expect them to be satisfied with a hand job. Complain afterwards that they never wanted to have sex.

"I'll start with tennis, school, your friendship with Micah and Ollie," Attorney Kelly said.

Remembering how close the three of them used to be brought tears to her eyes. She glanced at Ollie, who sat in the first row with his head down, thinking he might intuit her need. But no. She pinched her thigh, refusing to cry.

"Then the assault. Let's practice now, going step-by-step," he continued, "starting from when you got home."

Penelope looked past his shoulder, repeating the story, trying to detach from the words, but clips appeared in her head. Certain events triggered these reels. Wearing a towel. Seeing people kiss. The taste of lemonade. She never thought about it willingly.

"It's important to emphasize the different ways you told him no," Attorney Kelly said when she finished. "You told him to leave. Said you had to change. Closed your bedroom door. Told him you'd meet him downstairs. Said you shouldn't be messing around. Told him you didn't like it." He counted off the instances on his fingers, his words smooth, nothing like the jagged pieces of glass she felt in her throat when speaking about that night. "You have to be consistent."

She imagined Micah sitting at the table across from her as she spoke, maybe ten feet away, his anger a wall of fire. She put the end of her braid in her mouth, sucking the damp hair. "What if I forget?"

"I'll ask a question to help you remember."

She found it difficult to swallow. *What if I black out? What if I puke? What if I look at Micah and my love comes rushing back? What if my fear comes rushing back?*

"Now, the defense attorney will grill you," he said. "Try and get you to admit that you wanted to have sex. That afterwards, you regretted it. Changed your story. Use short, deliberate sentences. You said you didn't want this. He didn't listen. He didn't stop." Attorney Kelly slashed his hand through the air. "Nothing extra."

Walking out, Penelope took one last look around the courtroom, trying to regain her initial impression, but it was gone. She didn't want to do this. She *couldn't* do this.

"One last thing," Attorney Kelly said when they got to the elevator. "Micah will listen to the whole trial, because, as the defendant, he gets to confront all the witnesses against him. But the rest of the witnesses, including you, have to be sequestered until it's their turn to testify. This ensures no one tailors their testimony to another witness. Once you testify, you can either listen to the rest of the proceedings or return to the conference room. Up to you."

"I want..." Penelope hesitated. There was only one question that mattered, one answer she needed. Why? Why didn't Micah stop? "I'd like to hear Micah's testimony."

"That's your choice, but understand—"

Penelope nodded. "He thinks I'm lying."

"It might hit you hard, hearing him downplay what happened," Attorney Kelly said.

"Or hearing him blame you," Mom said.

"He's not going to apologize," Ollie added.

"Whatever," she mumbled. They all thought she was an idiot. But she knew Micah best. She'd be able to pick a single truth from a thousand lies he might spin. She knew, *knew*, he'd have a coded message only she could understand. And she wasn't going to miss it.

Walking to the car, Mom wrapped her arm around Penelope. "You're really brave," Mom said, kissing her cheek. "I'm proud of you."

Despite the warmth and comfort of Mom's touch, Penelope pulled away. She wasn't brave. Being brave would've been pushing Micah away. Yelling her desire to stop. Fighting her own battles instead of involving Mom, the police, the law. Her cowardice led to her punishment, having to testify against her best friend. Her first love.

She had one night to gain courage. Or get away.

CHAPTER FORTY-SIX
MICAH

The morning the trial began was also the first snowfall of the year. Micah sat on his bed with his forehead pressed against the cold window, watching the flakes fall from the steely sky, listening to the skid of wheels against the slickened pavement. He remembered lying here after he and Penelope had sex, thinking life couldn't get any better. What would've happened if P hadn't told her mom? If they entered high school as boyfriend and girlfriend?

That thought was so far from his reality, it belonged in a fantasy with witches and dragons and magic spells. Nope, his life, the uncut version, belonged on Netflix—another docuseries highlighting the ways the police, courts, *society*, dimmed the light inside Black boys. A one-way ticket aboard the school-to-prison pipeline. Would his ticket get stamped today?

With the trial finally here, his beliefs about justice and truth took a backseat to his fears. He didn't want to be found guilty. Yeah, yeah, his record would be sealed, but the conviction would stalk him. Kids would talk. The internet, the cloud, NSA, whatever was storing each keystroke, would never forget.

The only option was winning. He *had* to make the judge see the truth.

Adrenaline pushed him out of bed and into the shower. He put on some vintage Kanye, dancing along, but his vibe was off, either too fast for the beat or a second behind. Breathing hard, Micah toweled off and put on his suit. It was too baggy—he preferred clothes tight, cut to flatter—but Ma refused to shell out money tailoring a suit he'd outgrow by year's end. And he was the reason money was tight, so he took the suit, but added a touch of class, a blush-pink tie. Glancing in the mirror, he smiled. Ignored the tremble at the corners. With the suit jacket swung over his shoulder, he looked on fleek, like Steph Curry after a game.

Downstairs, he found Ma sipping tea, staring out the kitchen window. Her eyes were puffy. Cheeks shiny. She'd been crying. Again.

His phone sat on the peninsula in front of her. Ever since the walkout, she kept it at night and handed it back in the morning. He made to grab it, but she put her hand on top of his. "Micah. You've been posting about the trial again." She opened up the screen on his phone. "What's this? 'Tomorrow. The truth will out.' Do you realize that the DA, the judge, *everyone*, is reading your posts?"

He stepped back, too weary to stomach any more of her worries. "I hope they are. How else am I supposed to get my truth out? Let people know I didn't do this."

"It looks bad, Micah. Can't you see that?"

He took a deep breath. "You told me not to contact Penelope and I haven't." It nearly killed him, especially after Ollie said she was hurting, but he didn't. "This doesn't violate any of my release conditions. It's just a statement."

She put her face in her hands. "You're being antagonistic, giving the judge a reason not to like you. I've told you from the beginning, appearances matter and yet you..."

Her disappointment weighed heavily on his already burdened shoulders. "I'm trying to help."

"Micah." She stepped forward, pressing both palms against his chest. "I know you'd never hurt Penelope, but the consent decree—"

He tsked. "Not again."

"It's about protecting yourself. Doing what's best for your future."

If he accepted the consent decree, the next year would kill them both. "Believe in me, Ma."

"I do—"

He forced a smile. Tried to lighten the mood. "Then stop naggin' me."

She sniffled, pressing her fingers to her mouth, muzzling herself. "Give us a twirl," she said, her voice strained. He danced in a circle, tugging at his shirt collar. "Um-hmm. Dress the part."

"You look good too, Mama." If he was being one-hundred, her black pants and white turtleneck sweater made Ma look old. He preferred her prints and costume jewelry, the eyeliner that flicked up in the corners, her bright red lipstick. But Sarah had them dressing for church. And Sarah's word was gospel, according to Ma—like Jesus, Sarah would grant him salvation.

"I got you Lucky Charms," she said, pulling the box out of the pantry and setting it on the peninsula. "Eat up. We gotta leave in ten."

He grabbed a baking bowl and poured in half the box. Ma had her doubts, but she was standing by him, starting him off right with his favorite cereal. He took a large bite, savoring the sugar rush. Savoring the thought that today might just be the day his luck turned.

Let it be true, he thought. Let. It. Be. True.

CHAPTER FORTY-SEVEN
PENELOPE

Penelope sat in the backseat next to Ollie, while Mom drove and Uncle Austin rode shotgun. While in no hurry to get the courthouse, Penelope needed out of the stuffy car. Now. Her lungs struggled to grab a full breath, as if she was wearing a corset, one that cinched tighter with each block they passed.

How would she get through today? Confess the most embarrassing, confusing, and horrifying details of her life? She lay awake in bed last night, trying, for the first time, to remember. The memories came, one after another. Explicit. Raw. Punishing. A horror movie that had her balling her fists, screaming at herself. Do something! Fight back! She could feel Micah's handprints on her body, burning her skin, a poisonous fear coating her insides, silencing her. When Mom asked her this morning if she was ready, instead of saying, *I can't do this,* she let Mom hug her. Tried to absorb Mom's confidence, be the old Penelope, the girl that never backed down from a challenge, never disappointed.

After Mom parked at the courthouse, Penelope flung open her door and stood, inhaling the crisp air. Snowflakes dusted her face and jacket. She closed her eyes, wanting to stay here, let the cold numb her thoughts. But Uncle Austin wrapped his arm around her shoulder, gave it a squeeze, and led her inside. And having him take the lead helped. Loosened the corset.

Once inside, they took the elevator to the third floor. Attorney Kelly waited in the hallway, directing them toward a conference room. A small round table, four chairs. Mom insisted Penelope sit, but she remained standing, needing the option of running away. Ollie, in a rare showing of solidarity, stood next to her while the adults sat.

"How do you feel?" Attorney Kelly asked Penelope.

Like someone took a cleaver to my heart and force-fed me the pieces. "Okay."

Attorney Kelly went over the witness order again and then asked if she had any questions. She shook her head, her eyes skidding away.

Mom hugged her on the way out, resting both hands on Penelope's shoulders, holding her at arm's length, her identical blue eyes asking the question—*Are you okay?* Why did Mom need words? There was a time when Mom looked into Penelope's eyes and knew what was wrong and how to fix it without Penelope pausing her whimpers. When had that changed?

"You are *everything* to me," Mom said, her voice cracking on the word everything.

Embarrassment paused the chaos inside Penelope's head. "You're such a spaz."

Mom gave a wan smile. "I'll never be basic."

"Please," Penelope said, "don't ever use that word again."

"Second that," Ollie said, but they all smiled now. Relaxed a fraction. And maybe that was Mom's intention.

Then it was just her and Ollie, with nothing to say. The wall clock ticked down the seconds until her testimony.

After a few minutes, Ollie said, "I'm getting food." He left, apparently unable to stand being alone with her.

Which was fine. Perfect, really. She didn't need a babysitter. What she did need? Air. She took the elevator to the lobby, stepped outside, sat down on the cement ledge by the steps, and waited for the numbness to take hold.

CHAPTER FORTY-EIGHT
AMELIA

Amelia's hand shook when she held it against the Bible, taking an oath to tell the truth. It wasn't religious retribution that had her on edge. It was Zoe. She sat in the row behind the defense table, directly in front of Amelia, maybe fifteen feet away, her body unnaturally still. Anger crackled like electricity in the air between them. Today, this moment, Amelia's testimony, would lower their eleven-year friendship into a coffin.

From Zoe, Amelia's eyes slipped to Micah. He scanned the room, as if trying to make sense of how he ended up here. Or possibly, just avoiding her eyes.

Needing support, a fist-pump, a nod, something, she looked at Austin. He sat in the row behind the prosecution table. But she couldn't get his attention. He looked dazed. Bluish half-moons resided beneath his eyes. She hadn't given enough thought to how this was affecting Austin. Ollie too. All her energy was focused on helping Penelope.

Jack cleared his throat, snapping Amelia's attention to the lectern, positioned between the prosecution and defense tables. He started by asking her name, occupation, relation to Penelope, before addressing the Incident.

"What happened after you got home?" Jack asked.

"I found Ollie downstairs, sleeping on the couch. He felt sick and I helped him to bed."

"Sick?"

"Nauseous. Dizzy." Amelia shrugged. "I assumed he ate something off."

"Did you come to find out differently?"

"Yes, Ollie later admitted he and Micah drank vodka that night."

"How did you react?" Jack asked.

"I was upset, obviously, that the boys abused my trust. But it also explained..." She looked at Micah, feeling conflicted. The ceremony of the room, the stakes of the trial, made him look younger, like the boy she helped raise. Not the perpetrator her mind conjured. "Look, I've known Micah since he was three. He's—" She stopped herself from saying a "good kid." Because good kids didn't commit assault. "I think the alcohol loosened his inhibitions and he took advantage of Penelope's innocence."

Amelia saw Zoe's eyes widen. Perhaps it was too much to hope that a light came on, that a middle ground appeared, one that didn't vilify Micah, but still required him to accept responsibility.

"What happened after you got Ollie in bed?" Jack asked.

"I knocked on Penelope's door. When she didn't answer, I went inside." In a blink, Amelia was opening the bedroom door, confused that her half-naked daughter lay immobile on the bed. An image that would haunt her forever. "She was lying on her bed with a towel—" Amelia gestured toward her hips.

"You have to use words," Jack reminded her. "The court reporter can't note movements."

"The towel was pushed up around her waist. Her breasts were exposed, most of her thighs too. She was staring at the ceiling—not even blinking. I—I thought she was dead." Amelia glanced at Zoe, curious to see if her steely defense of Micah was weakening. But Zoe was looking at the ground. Was she tuning Amelia out? Had to be. Zoe couldn't listen to this and still think Micah did nothing wrong.

"What did you do?"

"I ran to her. Called her name. Felt for a pulse. She was alive, but she wouldn't speak."

"Then what happened?" Jack asked.

"I grabbed some clothes. When I pulled on her underwear, the towel flapped open. I noticed blood around her vaginal area. There was also a shiny substance that I realized was sperm. I begged her to tell me what happened."

"Did she answer?"

"No. I finished dressing her and then held her. Eventually, she said Micah was waiting after her shower. That he followed her into her room and wouldn't leave. She squeezed her thighs together as she spoke, which confirmed my suspicion that they had sex. I asked her if she wanted to have sex—her whole body shook. She shut her eyes, shaking her head."

"Was she in pain?" Jack asked.

"She said she hurt everywhere." Amelia paused. "Given the blood and sperm and how upset she was, I took her to the hospital."

"How was Penelope's demeanor at the hospital?"

"She was mumbling to herself, shaky, crying off and on."

"And you chose not to have a Sexual Assault Nurses Examination done on Penelope?"

"Right."

"Why?"

"A couple reasons." Amelia took a deep breath, knowing she had to nail this part, explain why she declined this extra step. "We already knew Micah assaulted her—we didn't need DNA. And Penelope was upset—I didn't want to traumatize her more with an arduous physical exam."

"That's all," Jack said, taking a seat.

Attorney Levine replaced him at the lectern, dressed in a sharp navy pantsuit, silk ivory shirt. Diamond studs. Amelia had clients like her. Confident, smart, successful women; women she admired.

"Penelope never verbally told you Micah forced her to have sex, right?" Attorney Levine asked.

Amelia raised her chin. "I asked her if she wanted to have sex and she cried and shook her head."

"And during this conversation, she never said that she told Micah she didn't want to have sex, correct?"

"She was obviously traumatized—"

"I'm not disagreeing. I'm asking if she said any variation of the words, 'I told him no.'"

Amelia wracked her brain. "No."

"So, isn't it possible, that this 'trauma' was a result of regret?"

"No."

"Or perhaps she was afraid of how you might react to her having sex?"

"No."

"No?" Attorney Levine's smile was condescending. "The only possibility, in your mind, is that Micah forced her?"

"If you knew my daughter—"

"Your daughter has a history of lying, doesn't she?"

Amelia gritted her teeth. "All kids lie at times. But she wasn't lying about this."

"You had no idea she was meeting up with Micah this summer while you were at work, correct?" Attorney Levine asked.

"No."

"You had no idea they were dating, correct?"

"She didn't lie," Amelia said, taking the fall for Penelope. "I never asked. That was my fault for being too busy to notice."

"Now, you were present when the police questioned Penelope, correct?" Attorney Levine asked, pivoting topics like a veteran interviewer.

"Yes."

"And when she met with Attorney Kelly for trial prep?"

"Yes."

"Did Penelope want to attend these meetings?"

Amelia scratched her cheek. "Penelope hasn't wanted to do much of anything since the assault."

"Alleged assault." Attorney Levine smiled patiently. "Let me be clearer. Did Penelope ever tell you she didn't want a case brought against Micah?"

Penelope said she wanted it all to go away, but Amelia assumed she meant the assault. "Not in those exact words," Amelia said slowly, wondering if she just committed perjury.

"No further questions."

232

Amelia stepped down, sweaty and lightheaded. It happened too fast; the last hour passing in the blink of a sneeze. Jack gave her a closed-mouth smile as she walked past him. Taking her seat next to Austin, she panicked; it was a smile you gave someone when they bombed on stage.

CHAPTER FORTY-NINE
ZOE

Zoe sat in the row behind Micah and Sarah, listening to Dr. Bilson, the emergency room doctor, testify about treating Penelope. She tried to concentrate on Dr. Bilson's words, but found herself studying Judge Myers, trying to determine how she was interpreting the information. A waste of time! The judge's expression never changed—eyes that flitted to her computer screen, mouth as straight as a country road, a black robe that conferred a godly aura.

Look alive! Zoe wanted to shout. Did she see the real Micah? His kindness? His fears? His innocence?

"Permission to approach the witness, your Honor?" Sarah asked, jarring Zoe out of her mental diatribe.

"Granted."

Sarah walked to the stand and handed Dr. Bilson a paper. "Is this a true and correct copy of your medical report of Penelope Swanson, dated September 4, 2022?"

Dr. Bilson pulled on her reading glasses. "Yes."

"Will you read the highlighted section?"

"'Patient presented with injuries from a suspected sexual assault. Patient appeared emotionally distraught. When questioned, patient said Micah kissed her in her room. She asked him to leave, but he wouldn't. Stated he did some 'stuff' to her that she didn't like, but would not explain what. Physical exam confirms penetration.'"

"Thank you." Sarah took the sheet and walked back to the lectern. "Based on this report, Penelope never said she was sexually assaulted, correct?"

"Unfortunately, I've dealt with hundreds of sexual assault victims and have become familiar with what we call 'Rape Trauma Syndrome.' While the intensity of reactions vary, shock is common.

They often act stunned and dazed, preoccupied as they go in and out of the memory, as they try to process it. They resist talking about the assault or can only talk about certain parts of it." The doctor pushed her glasses up the bridge of her nose. "This was the case with Penelope. She needed a lot of encouragement to talk, reminders that she was safe, and, yes, there were parts she couldn't verbalize without breaking down."

"You didn't answer my question. Penelope never told you Micah forced her to have sex, right?"

The doctor opened and closed her mouth before saying, "No, but that's not uncommon."

She didn't tell anyone because it didn't happen, thought Zoe. The kids didn't communicate. But lack of communication isn't a crime. It's just stupid. Teenage stupidity the State was attempting to criminalize.

"Dr. Bilson, you testified Penelope had vaginal fissures, tears, which also led you to believe she was sexually assaulted, correct?"

"Correct."

"In fact, vaginal fissures are quite common, aren't they?"

"The skin in the vagina is delicate and thus susceptible to splits and tears," Dr. Bilson said.

"And these tears can come about for a variety of reasons, including a bacterial infection, certain medications, unhealthy eating habits, consensual sex?"

"True, although when you have a patient pinpointing sexual assault..."

Sarah smiled. "But Penelope didn't pinpoint sexual assault. She never said those words. So, let's review. You were presented with an emotional teenage patient with vaginal lacerations. Lacerations that have many causes, including consensual sex. Yet you took her mother's word that she was sexually assaulted. Is it your practice to make such leaps in your diagnoses?" Sarah sat down. "Don't answer that. No further questions."

Zoe had to sit on her hands to stop herself from visibly celebrating. Sarah was calculating, yet graceful. A legal dynamo. Exactly what Zoe paid for, leveraged her house for. To save Micah.

"Any redirect, Attorney Kelly?" the judge asked.

"Yes," Attorney Kelly said, standing. "Based on your education, training, and experience as an ER doctor the past twenty years, was the fact that Penelope did not explicitly state Micah forced her to have sex important in your assessment?"

"No," Dr. Bilson said, louder than necessary. "My job isn't to investigate the alleged crime, but to treat the patient. Penelope's emotional disposition, combined with her injuries, furthered my belief that she was, in fact, assaulted. Thus, I treated her for sexual assault."

"No further questions."

Zoe sat back, deflated. The testimony was a gut check. Without a single word on Penelope's part that Micah assaulted her, they would put her baby away.

Zoe turned her scathing eyes to Amelia, wanting an answer for how she could so blithely destroy Micah's life. But Amelia and Austin had their heads tented together, talking. In that moment, Zoe hated them something fierce. She knew Austin would be here today, supporting Penelope. He was her uncle. She understood. But watching him console Amelia was too much. She faced forward, looking at Judge Myers, who sat expressionless in her tower.

Damn her. Damn them all.

CHAPTER FIFTY
MICAH

Micah squeezed a small exercise ball in the palm of his hand as he listened to Doctor Rebecca Harris, an "expert" on sexual assault trauma, testify. Sarah stressed that nothing would damage his case more than if he was sighing, rolling his eyes, chirping—no emotions, please! So, he squeezed, while inside, he burned. The ball would be a pancake by lunch.

He snuck a look behind him, at the courtroom door, anxious to see Penelope. Sarah said she wasn't allowed in until she testified, allegedly to ensure she didn't change her testimony to match the evidence. But he knew they didn't want her listening because she'd be forced to correct the evidence. Tell the truth. Stop this. And the way the state's attorney lined up his witnesses like a firework display, he wouldn't stop until the grand finale.

"Dr. Harris," Attorney Kelly continued. "In your expert opinion, is it unusual that Penelope would have a hard time admitting she was sexually assaulted?"

"Absolutely not," Dr. Harris said. She was a tall woman with frizzy brown hair. The pitch of her voice reminded Micah of a bird squawking for food. "Most victims are exhausted from surviving the assault. They don't have language, particularly young victims, or where the victim is close to the attacker, to put their feelings into words. Many times, victims blame themselves or feel shame, which makes them withdraw. They're trying to convince themselves it didn't happen, or it wasn't that bad, so they can forget it."

"Forget it happened?" Attorney Kelly repeated, feigning surprise. Micah wanted to chuck the ball at his head.

"Yes." Dr. Harris nodded. "It's a common reaction. Victims are often uncomfortable being vulnerable. They don't want to live in fear any longer, and therefore try to reclaim their power by moving on quickly."

"Turning to the hospital visit," Attorney Kelly said, "Penelope's mother declined to have a Sexual Assault Nurses Exam. In your experience dealing with juvenile sexual assault victims, is this unusual?"

"No. Parents want to protect their children, not prolong the suffering. Particularly where it's an acquaintance-rape."

"Objection," Sarah said, sounding a mixture of bored and annoyed. "Speculation. She doesn't know why Ms. Swanson denied the exam."

"Sustained," the judge said.

"No further questions."

Sarah stood up and buttoned her suit jacket. "You never met with Penelope, correct?" Sarah asked.

"That's correct."

"And so, these 'opinions,'—" Sarah used air quotes. "—are not based on this case, correct?"

"I haven't treated Penelope, personally. But I understand she's in therapy—"

"The truth is," Sarah said, talking over her, "you have no idea how Penelope feels, whether she's struggling with the issues you've detailed, correct?"

Dr. Harris took a breath. "Seeking out therapy suggests she's struggling."

Therapy? Micah couldn't imagine Penelope sitting still long enough. Let alone indulging her emotions. Penelope didn't indulge. She moved. She conquered.

"Dr. Harris, can you ballpark the percentage of sexual assault accusations filed that turn out to be false?" Sarah asked.

"Somewhere between two and ten percent. It's rare, considering most sexual assault cases are never reported in the first place."

Micah looked up at Sarah, unsure how those numbers helped. Was she trying to make out that he was one of the unlucky few?

"I'm not an expert like you," Sarah said with a smile, her praise landing on the right side of shade. "But in my research, most false accusations come from teenage girls that want to avoid getting into trouble, correct?"

"I've read that, yes," Dr. Harris said. "The false accuser is lying to serve a goal—to get out of trouble, establish an alibi, or to get revenge. But false accusations usually involve claims of aggravated assault—not scenarios where consent is at issue. As in this case."

"These same studies also concluded that up to half of all false complaints are lodged by someone other than the alleged victim, usually the parent, correct?"

Dr. Harris nodded. "I believe so."

"In reviewing the case notes, you presumably read that Ms. Swanson took Penelope to the hospital, correct?" Sarah asked.

"Yes."

"And you also read that Ms. Swanson sat in on meetings with the police and the prosecutor, ensuring Penelope participated, correct?"

"I know she sat in on the meetings, but the reason is more likely to support Penelope."

"Again, you don't know."

"I don't know."

"In your opinion, who's accusing Micah of assault? Penelope or her mother?"

"I have no idea."

Micah bit the inside of his cheek, palpating the ball at a frenzied pace.

"No idea," Sarah repeated. "I think that sums up your opinion perfectly on this case. You have no idea."

"Is that a question?" Attorney Kelly asked, flinging his hand up in the air.

"I'll withdraw. No further questions." Sarah sat down and Micah smiled at her. "Stop smiling," she said without moving her lips.

Micah wiped his face clean, but his heart soared. For months, he shouted his truth to deaf ears. Forced himself to turn down the consent decree, go to trial, even knowing his chances of walking away in this rigged system were small. Because if he didn't fight for himself, no one else would. Because when you see an injustice, you don't bend over and take it, you stand taller.

Seeing Sarah go to bat for him, take big swings at witnesses, gave him one thing he sorely lacked, hope. Not pie-in-the-sky hope, but this-could-really-happen hope.

If Penelope told the truth, this could all end. He could get his life back.

CHAPTER FIFTY-ONE
PENELOPE

Penelope was sitting on a cement ledge outside the courthouse, watching the snow cast a wet, sludgy blanket on the parking lot, when Ollie found her. He handed her a bottle of Mountain Dew—their favorite soda—keeping one for himself. Then he opened his jacket, pulling out a Snickers bar and a bag of Cheetos, letting her choose. She took the Snickers.

"You weren't supposed to leave the room," Ollie said, sitting next to her and opening the Cheetos. He tilted his head back, inhaling the snack as if it was a beverage.

"You left first."

Ollie actually smiled. "Real mature."

Penelope let the cool sweetness of Mountain Dew wash down her throat. She unwrapped the Snickers and chewed bite after tasteless bite. Mom didn't let them eat junk food and it didn't take long to remember why. Penelope's stomach roiled in protest of the artificial flavors, high fructose corn syrup, and whatever else they snuck in. Back training full time, nothing passed her lips that didn't serve a purpose. Fuel, muscle-building, muscle-recovery. Nothing tasty.

Or maybe her stomach felt like she swallowed nails because she would testify soon. Either way, she felt ill. She pressed the soda to her forehead, trying, literally, to freeze her thoughts into submission.

"You okay?" Ollie asked, surprising her again. Was this a truce?

Penelope shook her head, shutting her eyes before tears could appear.

"Just tell the truth," Ollie said. "No one can be mad at you for that—not even Micah."

She laughed. His advice absurd. Micah didn't work like that. And Ollie knew it. "He'll be mad."

"Do you care?"

"If I didn't care, do you think I'd be freaking out?" Penelope snapped. "Every minute, of every day, I wish for the moment I'll stop caring."

"Me too," Ollie said quietly, his lips tugged in a frown, cheeks flushed. The same look he wore when talking about Dad. Except Micah wasn't dead. She took away Ollie's best friend. And she never apologized. Never thought about it. Like a selfish bitch, she blamed Ollie for deserting her, even though his reasons were justified.

Ollie always made sure everyone else was happy—at his own expense. She needed to fix this. "It's okay to be friends with him." With each word, the promise extracted a fee from her heart. "He didn't hurt you."

Ollie ran his hands along his thighs. Unlike her, he could feel the cold. He could *feel*. "It's not—it's more than that."

"I get it," she said. "You wanna have my back—"

"No. You don't understand." He closed his eyes, his long, dark eyelashes curling like parentheses. When he didn't say anything, she feared he was angry. That he'd iced her out again.

"I want to understand," she said.

Minutes passed. The howling wind, traffic, the screech of the courthouse doors the only noise. A whisper, a mumble—she couldn't decipher it. Still, she said nothing. Waited him out.

"I love him," he said, looking up at the sky, blinking rapidly, eyes the color of fresh blueberries, glistening with dew.

"So, go, hang out with him. I'll deal—"

"Penelope." His looked at her. The quiver of his lower lip cut right through her. "Listen to me. I *love* him. I wanted him to choose me." He splayed his hand against his heart, then pointed at her. "Not you."

Penelope sat back, stunned. *I love him*, she repeated in her head, trying it on for size. Weirdly, it fit. Slotted puzzle pieces together she didn't know were on the board. Reasons she felt guilty for being with Micah, reasons she lied to Ollie. It explained why Ollie flipped out about their relationship, grew depressed. Explained Micah's power over Ollie. "Have you always felt this way?"

Ollie inhaled. "I'm not, like, labeling it. I just—I know how Micah makes me feel."

She betrayed Ollie. Let someone come between them. Put herself first because being with Micah felt so damn good. "I'm sorry. I should've told you."

"Yeah, you should've." The muscles in his jaw flexed. "He asked me how you were doing."

Penelope's stomach lurched, an unexpected dip in a rollercoaster. When did Ollie talk to Micah? Did it mean Micah still loved her? Did it matter? "Tell me exactly what he said."

"I'm such an idiot. The way you two light up when talking about each other." He smiled tightly. "Then again, you never noticed how I felt. So, apparently, we're all self-absorbed."

Ollie wasn't going to tell her what Micah said. He hadn't forgiven her. Not completely. Bitterness remained. Bitterness she now understood derived from jealousy.

But talking was better than not. And Ollie trusted her again. Told her his truth.

She asked, "How are you so calm? Aren't you worried he's going to hate you for testifying?"

Ollie crossed his arms. "Don't you get it? It doesn't matter."

"You never know. Maybe, eventually, you could be friends again." Penelope didn't know if she was saying it for her benefit or his.

"Last year, I had this low-key fear that Micah was going to ditch me, that I'd become too sensitive or weird or clingy. And then it finally happened—" He tugged at his ear. "Some days, it's horrible, but others...I like not feeling strung up all the time, wondering if he'd find out the truth, if he could ever love me, if he'd out me. It was...exhausting. I'd rather be alone and depressed—at least I can just be."

"I thought he loved me. That he wouldn't hurt me."

"And then he did." Ollie looked at her, seeking confirmation.

"Yes." She lied to Ollie, but never about that night.

"Guys!" They turned to find Austin, charging toward them, talking into his phone. She rarely saw him angry. Even at tennis, his patience ran eternal.

Ollie stood. "We needed some air."

"Damnit, then tell someone." Austin ran both hands through his hair. "Let's go." Austin gestured toward the stairs, all but pushing them inside.

They rode the elevator in silence. When the doors opened, Mom stood, waiting. "Ollie, they're ready for you," Mom said, her voice clipped. "Penelope, you're next. Austin? Stay with her."

Penelope's heart thudded as Ollie and Mom disappeared inside the courtroom. She wasn't ready. But she couldn't speak. The words got caught in her throat—a panicked feeling she could only compare to the night with Micah. When he lay on top of her. Pulled down his shorts. Pushed inside her. She wanted to say stop, move, but her body was no longer hers. He held the power.

She bolted across the hallway, through the bathroom doors, making it just in time to puke a neon stream into the toilet. She couldn't leave—not with Uncle Austin guarding the door. But she also couldn't go in that courtroom, speak about what happened that night.

She was trapped.

CHAPTER FIFTY-TWO
OLLIE

Ollie's eyes flitted over the top of everyone's head—a trick he learned to combat stage fright—as he scanned the courtroom from the witness stand. Attorney Kelly stood at the podium, Mom sat to his right, in the first row behind the prosecution table. Micah's lawyer and Micah sat at a table directly in front of Ollie, Zoe in the row behind, all three ramrod straight, shoulders back, staring at him, like three bowling pins. Ollie gulped. The twin fears of wanting to be seen and stay closeted forever battled it out as he testified.

"On the night of the September second," Attorney Kelly asked, "you hung out with Micah?"

"Yeah," Ollie said. "We ate pizza and played Madden."

"Whose idea was it to drink alcohol?"

"Micah found half a bottle of vodka in the freezer. He suggested mixing it with lemonade."

"How much did you drink?" Attorney Kelly asked.

"Two glasses."

"How much did Micah drink?"

"I wasn't watching him, like super close—" Why did Ollie say "super close?" It sounded weird. Or was he paranoid after telling Penelope? He took a deep breath, reminding himself that he wasn't on trial. No one cared about his feelings. What he lost. Everyone was too busy stressing about Penelope and Micah. "Micah finished the pitcher, so he definitely had more than me."

"Then what happened?"

"I got sick in the bathroom."

Ollie still didn't know whether it was the alcohol or the proximity to Micah that made him sick. Sick with longing. Sick with fear that he would slip up, kiss Micah, causing the metaphorical gun pressed to

Ollie's head to fire. Sick with regret that he fell in love with someone he could never have.

"Where was Micah?"

Ollie shifted in his seat, letting his eyes drift toward Micah. Micah met his gaze without emotion. Ollie's heart propelled with that toxic mix of excitement and anxiousness, the feeling of standing atop a bridge, not knowing whether he would fall or fly. Short of never laying eyes on Micah again, he doubted his feelings would ever go away. "He left. Said he was going home."

"No further questions."

To think, as Ollie was bent over the toilet, puking, Micah was making his move on Penelope. Not worried about Ollie at all. What if Ollie had alcohol poisoning? Hit his head? It didn't matter. Because Micah did what Micah wanted. And Micah didn't want Ollie.

Penelope gave Ollie permission to be friends with Micah, but ever since joining the play, seeing other kids that were unabashedly themselves, Ollie no longer wanted to pretend. Hide in plain sight. He just wanted out. Out of this love triangle that never had room for him. Out of Micah's life. Most days, out of his own head. His heart. Skip ahead to this promised land where everything "gets better."

"You didn't speak to Penelope the night of the Incident, correct?" Micah's attorney asked when she got to the podium.

Ollie coughed. "No. I got sick and passed out before she got home from tennis."

"And you didn't hear any strange noises? Screams? Thumps? Yells for help?"

"No."

"You didn't go upstairs at all, correct?"

"Not until my mom woke me up."

"So, you have no idea what went on between Penelope and Micah?"

"No."

246

She pulled off her glasses and assessed him. What did she see? Ollie looked down, not wanting to know. "That's all," she said.

Ollie felt like he let Penelope down. But what was he supposed to say? He didn't know anything. A few minutes ago, he told P he loved Micah. Three words he swore to take to his grave. And what did she give in return? An assurance she wasn't lying. But no details. No confession. Nothing.

At least Penelope apologized. Micah didn't think him worthy. Better yet, Micah thought he did nothing wrong.

Micah's eyes tracked him as he stepped off the witness stand and walked toward Mom. It's funny. Laughable, really. For months, all Ollie wanted was for Micah to look at him. But now that Micah was looking, Ollie turned away. He told Penelope the truth today, but Micah wasn't worth it.

Ollie was getting out of the triangle.

CHAPTER FIFTY-THREE
AMELIA

After Ollie finished testifying, court recessed for lunch. Amelia and Ollie emerged from the courtroom to find Austin standing outside the ladies' bathroom. Evidently, Penelope was hibernating. Or just plain hiding. Amelia told the guys to head the cafeteria without them. With the clock ticking down an hour, Amelia needed every minute to calm Penelope.

She pushed open the bathroom door to find three stalls, but Penelope's whimpers made her easy to locate—a cry Amelia could pick out among thousands.

"Penelope." Amelia knocked on the handicap stall. "You okay?"

She moaned. "I'm sick."

"Take your time. Court doesn't start for an hour."

After a couple of dry heaves, Penelope said, "I can't testify, Mom. I'm sorry. I know you're disappointed, but I just can't."

Amelia silently absorbed this news. She'd been worried all along that Penelope wouldn't discuss the assault. That she truly believed, with determination, she could forget it. That she isolated herself from Ollie and her friends. Amelia knew this would catch up with her, become too much to handle. And now here Penelope was, confirming as much.

Amelia pressed her hand against the door, wishing she could cradle Penelope's face. "I'm not disappointed. Not at all. What you've gone through—" Amelia pressed her fist to her mouth and cleared her throat. "I've never been more in awe of your strength. You're fourteen. Fourteen! I'm thirty-eight and I don't understand any of this. And yet you've carved a path forward, decided you aren't going to let this stop you from achieving your dreams." It was rare for Penelope to listen. But maybe Amelia was the one that should've been listening. Penelope said she didn't want this. Yet Amelia pushed ahead, adamant that seeking justice, standing up to Micah, would aid her recovery. But not if it made Penelope sick. "I don't know where you get it, but there's a fighter in you that refuses to give up. And choosing not to testify today, that's not giving up, P. Not at all. That's strength—it's fighting for yourself, taking care of yourself emotionally. Most adults I know aren't strong enough to do that."

"Mom?"

"Yeah?"

"I get it from you," Penelope whispered. "You always fight. I'm trying really hard to live up to your expectations—God, I hate disappointing you."

"You could never—" Amelia spread her arms wide, practically hugging the door. "Can you let me in, sweetie?"

"I'm, uh, too dizzy to stand."

Amelia grimaced as she looked down at the dark blue tile disguising dirt and germs and other unknowns. But she needed to get to Penelope. Now. This wasn't a moment she'd get back. She had to make this right.

She hitched up the hem of her dress, bunching it around her hips, said a quick prayer of thanks for choosing tights this morning, and squatted. The opening was roughly three feet. She'd have to get on her stomach. She lay on the cool tile, using the palms of her hands to push herself forward, as if swimming through sand.

"Oh. My. God." Penelope sat on the ground next to the toilet, a few feet from the stall door, her mouth parted in horror as she watched Amelia. The paleness of her face made her red-rimmed eyes glow. "Mom! This floor is disgusting! Puke just, like, splashed on it!"

Amelia bumped her butt on the bottom of the door as she attempted to sit up. A self-esteem boost. "Yeah, well, you're sitting on it too. Besides, I needed to hug you."

She maneuvered next to Penelope, wrapping her arm around Penelope's shoulder, pulling Penelope's head to her chest.

"You'll probably give me an eye infection," Penelope said.

"We have insurance."

Penelope looked up at her. "Who are you and what have you done with my mother?"

Amelia kissed her forehead. "I forget you're not my baby anymore. That you can make your own decisions. You don't need me as much." Amelia rested her head against the tile wall, vowing to shower the moment she got home. "Sometimes I wonder what kind of mom I would've been if your dad lived, whether I'd be more relaxed."

"Mom, you have, like, no chill." Penelope sat up. "Sorry, not sorry. Even if Dad was here, you'd still be you—bossy, all up in our business, pushing us to succeed."

But Derek would've provided balance. Fun. Silliness. "Don't hold back."

Penelope looked away. "I still need you..."

"But?"

"I just need you to love me even when I do something you don't agree with. Even when I disappoint you. I mean, what if I get up there today and you hear some stuff you don't like?"

She rested her hand atop Penelope's. "If you don't believe that I love you no matter what, then I've failed as a mother."

"No, I mean..." Penelope rolled her eyes. "Obviously, you'll love me, like you won't turn me out on the streets, but you'll be disappointed."

"You keep saying that."

"Because I always feel this pressure to be perfect for you." Penelope's haggard voice echoed in the small bathroom. "Ever since you found me that night, it's like, you think I'm damaged. And I can't—I wish you'd look at me like you used to, like I'm on the brink of greatness, instead of treating me like a mental patient."

Amelia tried to parse through Penelope's emotion to find the truth. "There's no part of me that blames you for what happened. You liked Micah. Being with him was exciting. I get it—a million years ago, I was a teenager, too. But that doesn't mean you asked for any of this." Amelia ran her fingers through Penelope's hair, combing the long strands. "If I'm treating you different, it's because I can't stand seeing you hurt."

"Come on."

"I'm serious. You haven't experienced this yet, P, but when you become a mother, you give your baby your heart. You feel their pain or disappointment or happiness acutely. You can't protect against the hundreds of ways the world will let your baby down. And let me tell you, there's no worse feeling than not being able to take away your baby's pain. I'd do anything to fix this for you and perhaps that's where I went wrong. Pushing you to testify. Thinking I could fix it." Amelia inhaled—urine, puke, but also apples. Pure Penelope. "But you're not damaged. Or better yet, we're all damaged. We all have scars. But I'm confident you'll take those scars and make something beautiful."

"See, there you go, putting pressure on me."

Amelia bit her tongue. "I'm sorry—"

"Joke." Penelope smiled, a bit of color coming back to her face.

"Can you stand?" Amelia pressed her hands on the ground, pushing herself up to standing. "I should tell Attorney Kelly you won't be testifying."

Penelope fixed her stare on the toilet paper dispenser. "Maybe you're right. Maybe I should testify. Get it all out there. Purge and be done."

Amelia looked down at her beautiful daughter, utterly confused. Perhaps this was about power. Being able to make her own decisions. As Penelope said, her fighting instinct came from Amelia. Or maybe she needed Amelia's reassurance that she'd love her either way.

Whatever the reason, Penelope stood, her mouth a fine line, the same look of determination she had when returning serve. Amelia grabbed her hand and they walked out of the stall together. The best part? Penelope held on tight.

CHAPTER FIFTY-FOUR
MICAH

Micah sat at the defense table, squeezing his exercise ball, counting reps of ten, trying to keep both his mind and hands busy while waiting for court to resume. Any minute now, Penelope would testify. He hoped she'd tell the truth. But doubt lingered. The Penelope he knew never would've let this charade continue. And yet, she had. Were they lying to her? Did she understand what could happen to him? Or did she feel he did something wrong?

"All rise," the bailiff said.

The judge, draped in black, walked up the steps to her seat. "The State may call its next witness."

"The State calls Penelope Swanson." Micah heard the door creak open, the tap of heels across the wood floor, and turned to look. But Penelope's attorney blocked Micah's view with his body, as if he didn't trust Micah's eyes not to assault her. Micah thought he detected the scent of apples as she passed, but that could've been his mind playing tricks. Penelope sat in the witness chair, angling her face away from him, her long hair a curtain.

Attorney Kelly started by asking Penelope her name, age, height, weight. Then he said, "Can you tell the Court what happened on the night of Friday, September second?"

"I got home from tennis and went upstairs to shower. Afterwards, Micah was waiting for me in the hall."

"Do you see Micah here today?"

"Yes." Penelope turned and looked at him. Micah leaned forward, as if getting an inch closer would tell him something. But her eyes gave him nothing.

"Can you point to him and describe what he's wearing?"

She pointed her index finger at Micah. "A black suit, blue shirt, and a pink tie." She turned away, swimming back under her waterfall of hair.

"Let the record reflect that the victim identified the juvenile as Micah Gray," Attorney Kelly said. "What happened when you saw Micah in the hall?"

"He said he wanted to congratulate me on my match. Then he kissed me."

"How did that make you feel?"

Penelope shifted in her seat, and Micah, a mimic, did the same. He'd been so focused on the truth ringing out that he hadn't considered how uncomfortable it was to share details of their private world. He was glad Ma was sitting in the row behind him. Made it impossible to see her reactions.

"I liked it," she said. Micah's heart banged an applause. Relief. Oh, sweet relief! "But I felt weird too, wearing only a towel. My mom was out. And Ollie...I was worried he'd find us. He didn't know Micah and I were together. It's—it's complicated, with the three of us being friends."

Micah remembered that Sarah said this secrecy worked for him. Showed Penelope had a pattern of lying, manipulating situations to her benefit. Micah never thought about it like that, but here he sat, accused of sexual assault. Allegedly, based on her word. So, maybe there was some truth to it.

"Did you tell Micah you felt weird?"

"I told him that he shouldn't be up there. That we'd get caught."

"Did he leave?"

"No."

Micah didn't leave because he knew Ollie was too sick to come upstairs. Not because he wasn't listening.

"Then what happened?" Attorney Kelly asked.

"I needed to change. I said I'd meet him downstairs."

"Did he go downstairs?"

"No. He caught my bedroom door as I closed it and came inside. Then he kissed me again."

Micah massaged the ball with both hands, twisting it like he was going to throw a knuckle ball. She was laughing, joking around. Why wouldn't he think she wanted him to stay?

"How did this make you feel?"

"Uncomfortable. Kissing in my room, wearing just a towel, it was..." She released a deep breath that sounded like a strong gust of wind in the microphone. "Too much. Too fast or whatever."

Penelope still wouldn't look at him. Was she coached to ignore him?

"Then what happened?"

"We were kissing and he tripped. We fell onto the bed." Penelope hesitated. "That's when I started to panic for real because he was lying on top of me. The towel—it wasn't covering me enough."

Yes, Micah was buzzed, but he wasn't oblivious. He knew she was nervous. He was too! But it was nervous excitement. They were alone. In bed. Getting naked. Doubt trickled into his belly, an icy fear that he read her wrong.

"Did you say anything?" Attorney Kelly asked.

"I said we should stop 'cause I was worried that Ollie might find us. And he told me not to worry."

He thought she was worried about getting caught. Not about what they might do. He wasn't a mind reader!

"And then?"

"He guided my hand to the front of his shorts and helped me, like, rub him, over his clothes." She looked down; her face flushed a cherry-red that reminded Micah of watching her play tennis. "Then he pulled down his shorts and boxers and put my hand back."

"To his penis?"

"Yes." She swatted away a tear. "I said his name, trying to get his attention." She shook her head. "It's like the Micah I knew wasn't there."

Micah heard Ma sigh behind him, but didn't know what it meant. Was she disappointed in him? Losing faith in him? His innocence?

"I know this is difficult, Penelope, but I need you tell us what happened next."

"He-pulled-apart-the-towel-and-went-down-on-me." She blurted it as one, long word. Supercalifragilisticexpialidocious. "I freaked out. I was squirming, trying to get away. I told him I didn't like it."

Or squirming because she liked it. Girls squirmed in porn. Had he read her wrong on this too? He just wanted to make her feel good, as good as she made him feel.

"What did he do?"

"He told me to relax and tried again for a sec, but I said I needed to pee. And he stopped. Then he came back up by me, said he loved me, and—" Penelope covered her face with her hands, muffling her words. "He pushed inside of me."

"Did you have the ability to leave?"

"No. His was on top of me, but it's more I wasn't sure what was happening at first. And then I realized, like, OMG, I'm having sex. And I froze. I couldn't move. Couldn't speak. I didn't understand why this was happening. Then, he finished. And the pain came. Bam!" Penelope clapped her hands once. Micah jumped, every nerve on alert. "I felt like dying."

Attorney Kelly let that thought simmer.

Micah bit his lip. Hard. Refusing to let the tears fall. He had no idea she felt that way. Why didn't she tell him? They talked about everything. Then again, why didn't he ask? Maybe that was where the alcohol came in. He was flying too high to look down, see Penelope clearly. He assumed the moment meant the same to her as it did him.

"What happened after?"

Penelope wrapped her arms around herself. "Micah held me."

At least she remembered that. The judge couldn't believe that he'd want to hurt her and then hold her afterwards, could she?

"Did you talk?"

"Maybe. I kind of blacked out."

But they did talk! Micah remembered telling her that being together felt perfect. And she agreed! Did she really not remember? Was that possible?

"The pain was... horrible," she continued. "It started deep inside and spread until my whole body was on fire."

Micah grimaced, remembering the blood. The blood he assumed was normal.

Attorney Kelly continued asking questions about the hospital, police, and Penelope's life now. Micah tried to listen, but, truthfully, he was back in her room, reliving that night. Yes, he got too excited. He should've asked if she wanted to have sex. But wasn't she equally to blame for not telling him to stop? Saying no? Why didn't the communication work both ways? Why was it all on him? Because he had the dick?

Now, more than ever, he was certain they could work this out if given the opportunity to talk. He wanted to stand up, tell Penelope that he fucked up, apologize for hurting her. Tell her he still loved her.

But it was too late. He sunk down in his seat as Sarah began her cross-examination, afraid of what Penelope would say next. What else he might learn about himself.

CHAPTER FIFTY-FIVE
PENELOPE

Penelope felt both lightheaded and hyperaware as Micah's attorney took the podium. Despite puking, the Mountain Dew ran havoc through her bloodstream, zapping her fingers and toes while her head stayed woozy. An extra layer of protection, perhaps, seeing that night with Micah through a faded lens. One she desperately needed.

"Officer Avery testified that when interviewing you, you said there was no prior romantic relationship with Micah. Is that true?" Micah's attorney asked, her icy blue eyes making Penelope shiver.

"No, I mean, yeah, yes, I said that." Penelope made herself slow down. "But no, it's not true. We were together all summer."

"You lied to the police?"

"I was worried—"

"Yes or no."

"Yes."

"One of the places you and Micah secretly spent time together was his bedroom, when his mother was at work, correct?"

Penelope looked down, avoiding Mom's eyes. This was one reason she feared testifying. That Mom might change her mind, agree Penelope was at fault. That she led Micah on. "A few times."

"And yet you're asking this Court to believe you were terrified to be alone with him in *your* bedroom?"

"That night was different." Like police lights flashing on the side of the road, Penelope felt her eyes being pulled in Micah's direction. *No.* She wouldn't look. "I wasn't wearing clothes, for one. But also, his attitude. He wasn't listening to me."

"You willingly kissed him, right?"

"Yes."

"You willingly got into bed with him?"

"Ye..." Penelope caught herself. "No, we tripped."

"You willingly stroked his penis, right?"

Your fault, your fault, your fault. "I never thought he'd want to have sex." Sex was as farfetched as drinking or getting high. She'd try it one day, but not for a long, long time.

"You refer to it as sex." Micah's attorney cocked her head to the side. "Tell me, Penelope, do you think he assaulted you?"

"Uh..." It was a trick; a verbal Rubik's cube Penelope couldn't solve. "He just did it. I mean, he didn't ask me to have sex, right? And I didn't want it, so—"

"How did you let him know you didn't want to have sex?"

"When he went down on me, I told him I didn't like it."

"You told him you didn't like oral sex, but when you two started having penetrative sex, you never said no or stop, correct?"

Attorney Kelly's advice—stick to your story, give short answers, don't elaborate—suddenly felt impossible. "When I said I didn't like it, I meant that I wanted to stop everything."

"Perhaps that's what you meant, but not what you said. So, I'll ask you again." The attorney pounded every word. "How was Micah supposed to know you didn't want to have sex?"

Penelope squeezed her hands into fists. "Because we never talked about having sex. We'd never seen each other naked. I mean, there's an order to stuff, and he jumped, like, several steps." Getting angry invigorated her. Flushed out some of the embarrassment, made her focus.

"While having sex, did you hit or push him away?" Micah's attorney asked.

"No."

"Did you scream?"

"No."

"And just to confirm, you gave him no verbal cue that you wanted to stop, correct?"

"No." Penelope bit her cheek so as to not cry. "It happened so fast." How could she convince everyone that talking was beyond her?

258

That shock stole not only her words, but her breath, her fight? How do you verbalize that? The feeling of being trapped and confused?

"Now, you testified that you cuddled and talked afterwards. Do you remember agreeing that having sex with Micah felt perfect?"

Penelope remembered trying to act normal, trying not to scream. "I was scared."

"He was no longer on top of you, correct?"

"Correct."

"You could've left the room? Gone downstairs to ask your brother for help? Called your mom?"

"Yes."

"But you did none of those things, correct?"

"No, I was—"

Micah's attorney talked over her. "You were overwhelmed, understandably. Losing your virginity is a big moment, but you weren't scared of Micah. He never threatened you."

"Objection," Attorney Kelly said. "If there's a question, I'd love to hear it."

"I'll rephrase. Did Micah ever threaten you?"

Penelope answered without hesitation. "No."

"The truth is, Penelope, you regret losing your virginity and you're blaming Micah, aren't you?"

Penelope's body tightened, the intensity of her anger making her ache. "The truth? God, what does that even mean? The truth! The truth! That's all I've heard since this started. Who's telling the truth? Guess what? I'm sure Micah has his truth, but this is *my* truth. Micah came into my room, we messed around, and he had sex with me." Penelope rolled her eyes, hearing the word sex again. "Assaulted me, whatever. He didn't ask. I didn't want it. I never wanted this!" She gestured around the courtroom, losing control, but unable to stop. "Any of this! He broke my trust—he broke me..." Penelope batted tears away. She was sobbing now. She turned and looked at Micah through what felt like a rain-splattered window. He was biting his lower lip, his eyes wide. *Say something! Anything! Show me you understand!* "I will never be the same, Micah. Do you get that? Never. I can't imagine ever being alone with a boy again. I can't go to school because I'm treated like a freak. I have no friends. I'm scared all the time. You took everything..."

Penelope's sniffles echoed in the courtroom. She couldn't take it anymore. This search for "the truth." As if it would solve everything. As if it could actually be uncovered. The truth was her experience. Who were they to question it?

The judge offered a box of tissue and Penelope took one, wiping her runny nose.

"Your Honor, may I approach the witness?"

"Granted."

Micah's attorney pointed at something on a sheet of paper. "Is this your phone number?"

Penelope glanced it over. "Yes."

"And this is Micah's?"

"Yes."

She pointed again. "What's the date here?"

"September first."

"Your Honor, I'd like to introduce a text Penelope sent Micah as defense exhibit one."

"So entered," the judge said.

"Please read the text."

Penelope scanned the words, unsurprised. Micah already posted them on Instagram. "We need to stop. But I can't. Can't say no to you."

"The day before the Incident, you texted him that you couldn't say no to him. Tell me, were you frozen or panicked or overwhelmed when you texted those words?"

"Objection!"

"No further questions."

"Attorney Kelly, any redirect?" the judge asked.

"Yes." Attorney Kelly gazed at his laptop, before standing up and going to the podium. "Penelope, can you explain why you didn't leave after the assault? Get help?"

"I was in shock. How could anyone help me? It was over."

"And when you sent that text to Micah, were you referring to sex?"

"No. I was talking about us. Hanging out. We were lying to everyone and I knew it was wrong, but I lo—" Penelope stopped, unwilling to give him that part of her. "I liked him too much to stop. That's what I meant."

"Prosecution rests," Attorney Kelly said.

"Any re-cross?" the judge asked.

"No."

The judge banged her gavel. "Let's recess for a half-hour. Then the defense can present its case."

Penelope stepped out of the witness box with her head down, the tendons in her neck as tight as cords. She was afraid of what she might see if she looked around. Micah's anger? Ollie's jealousy? Mom's disappointment? Frustration from Attorney Kelly?

But when she reached the first row, she felt, rather than saw, Mom's arms around her. "I'm so proud of you."

Penelope melted into Mom, letting the stress and tension drain from her body. If the goal was to feel whole again, she failed. She felt just as confused, angry, frustrated, and depressed. But it was over. There was that. And now, she'd get to hear Micah's response. The elusive why. His truth.

CHAPTER FIFTY-SIX
ZOE

Zoe sat in the conference room, listening to Sarah give Micah a pep talk, while her mind rehashed Penelope's emotional testimony. Zoe believed Micah—no question. But as she witnessed Penelope, a girl she loved, helped raise, struggle to make sense of her first sexual experience, Zoe felt a deep sense of empathy. That push and pull girls experienced between what they want and what they're told is appropriate, the fear of being found out, the inability to speak up, was far too familiar a battle for Zoe to dismiss.

"The judge is going to believe Penelope," Micah said. He stood against the wall, his shoulders slumped, head down, voice quiet. Defeated.

"I'll grant you she was persuasive," Sarah said, "in what she *believed* happened, but you're going to be just as persuasive that she was into it."

He ran a hand over his face, covering his eyes. Was he crying? Zoe couldn't tell. "It's my fault. Maybe I would've noticed she was upset, not been as selfish, if I was sober."

Sarah got up and stood in front of Micah. While several inches shorter, her rigid posture and firm words commanded attention. "Now is not the time to have a crisis of consciousness. You've said from day one that you didn't force her. That she wanted this as much as you. That you loved her. Do not let her testimony, which she prepared and recited like an actress, change what you know to be true."

"But what if I'm wrong?" He addressed this question to Zoe. "What if I didn't listen?"

Sarah turned to Zoe. "Five minutes. Talk some sense into him." She left, the door clicking shut behind her.

"Micah, sit down, baby." Micah reluctantly sat. Zoe grabbed his sweaty hands, squeezing them. It might be noble for Micah to sacrifice himself, admit fault, but Zoe couldn't let him do it. "I know you're overwhelmed. You've waited months to hear what Penelope's thinking—"

"I no longer think I'm blameless." His lips twisted in anguish. "I can't."

"You don't know what you think."

He jerked away. "Don't talk down to me."

"I'm not." Zoe reached over, pulling his hands back inside hers. "I'm saying that because it's confusing for me too. It's confusing for everyone. That's why the judge will take a few days before deciding the case. She's not going to make a snap decision and I don't want you to make that mistake either. Please, *please...*" Zoe rested her forehead on his wrists. She couldn't bear to lose Micah, even for a day. "Don't be impulsive. Stick with the testimony we discussed."

Several seconds passed before he asked, "What are you confused about?"

She sat up. "What?"

"You said P's testimony left you confused. Do you not believe me anymore?"

Belief. Like the truth, it blew in the wind, changing directions, shifting with each new bit of information. Believing Penelope didn't necessarily mean Zoe disbelieved Micah. It was clear Penelope felt wronged, regretful...but she also didn't speak up. She didn't give Micah a chance to do the right thing. He had no idea she was freaking out. Was this victim-blaming? Convenient thinking? Parenting run amuck? If so, fine. Zoe refused to delve deeper. These were two teenagers who didn't communicate and therefore left the encounter with diametrically opposed feelings. End of.

"I believe what I've always believed. That you two got in over your heads," Zoe said. "Maybe it was the secrecy. Maybe it was hormones. Alcohol. Fear. Fear to speak up. Fear to back down.

Bottom line, I think you both would do things differently if you could go back."

Micah looked down, nodding slowly.

"Does it make you guilty of sexual assault? Absolutely not." She cupped his chin, looking into his dark, soulful eyes. Eyes she fell in love with at first sight. Eyes she promised to protect. Eyes that now pleaded for support. "Nothing she said made me change my mind about that."

"But I hurt her, Ma." A tear trickled from Micah's eye. "That's why I have to accept responsibility."

"No," Zoe said sharply. She took a deep breath, evening out her voice. "Now is not the right time. There's too much at stake."

"Do you think she'll ever talk to me? Hear me out? Be friends again?"

Did he really think they could go back? That the trial would end today and, tomorrow, they would go to Amelia's for dinner? His naivety reminded her of how young he was. That, despite every injustice he endured, he believed in happy endings.

Then again, was she any wiser, thinking she could have a relationship with Austin? That Amelia would be an obstacle instead of a roadblock? That Austin would suddenly put Zoe first?

"Technically, if the judge finds you not delinquent, you could talk to her, but baby, as far as being friends, too many things have been said and done. Eventually, there might be forgiveness..." Zoe thought of Amelia. No apology could atone for the emotional, physical, and financial hell Amelia put her through. "But, no, it can't be like before."

Sarah ducked her head back inside the room. "Court's about to start."

Micah and Zoe stood. Before they left the room, Zoe tugged his sleeve. "I know you. I know your heart. You are a kind, loving boy. You would never intentionally hurt her." She kissed his cheek. "Remember that up there."

264

As they walked back into the courtroom, Zoe worried she hadn't gotten through to him. Micah was passionate; wore his heart like a badge of honor. She loved it about him, but, right now, she hoped he'd toe the line. Not voice every last feeling.

CHAPTER FIFTY-SEVEN
PENELOPE

Penelope watched from the row behind the prosecutor's table as Micah testified. Mom sat next to her, Ollie on the other side of Mom, then Uncle Austin. Penelope wished it was just her and Micah in the room. No distractions. Nobody listening in. They started it and now they needed to finish it.

Micah's attorney, speaking in a tone much friendlier than she used with Penelope, asked, "When did your friendship with Penelope become romantic?"

"June sixth at roughly nine-fifteen. A group of us were playing hide-n-seek and Penelope and I hid together in one of those plastic toy houses. I looked at her and everything changed. I realized my best friend in the world was also the most beautiful girl in the world. We ended up talking and eventually, many minutes later..." He laughed softly and Penelope's stomach summersaulted. She felt like she was watching a movie, like *Titanic*, where you can enjoy the beginning of the love story despite knowing everything went to hell. "I kissed her."

"How did the relationship proceed from there?"

"We met up whenever our moms were working and Ollie was busy."

"Why so secretive?"

"Penelope was afraid. Her mom is really strict. And Ollie? She thought he'd be upset, too. She made me promise not to tell."

Penelope felt Ollie's eyes on her. Did he feel jealous? Angry with her lies? Guilt wrapped around Penelope's heart like a rope, Micah and Ollie tugging on the ends. Like before, Micah won her attention—she waited too long to hear his explanation.

"How did you feel about keeping that secret?"

"It was hard." Micah splayed a hand against his chest. "I'd do anything for P. But I hated lying to Ollie. He's my boy. And lying to Ma? It felt...wrong."

"Was Penelope struggling with keeping this secret?"

"Objection," Attorney Kelly said. "Speculation."

"Micah was spending every day with Penelope last summer," Micah's attorney argued. "I think he's equipped to speak to her state of mind."

"I'll allow it," the judge said.

"She'd get angry whenever I brought it up," Micah said. "I didn't understand how she was okay with lying, but when P makes up her mind, there's no changing it."

She was stubborn. Played every point like it was her last. Never gave in. But WTF? Micah made her sound diabolical.

"What happened on the night of September second?" Micah's attorney asked.

"I was kicking back with Ollie. We went looking for food and found vodka." Micah shook his head. "Not the best idea, but we'd never drank before and wanted to try it."

"How much did you drink?"

"A couple vodka-lemonades."

"How did you feel?"

"Happy. A little loopy."

"What happened next?"

"Ollie got sick, so I went to find Penelope. She was in the shower. I waited for her outside, in the hallway. When she finished, we talked about her match and kissed and stuff."

"Did she ever ask you to leave?"

"No."

Penelope lurched forward. How dare he lie? Mom rested a hand on her knee, but P brushed her away.

"She wanted to get dressed," Micah said, "but she said it playfully, like she was inviting me to stay."

"Then what happened?"

"We started kissing and sort of fell onto the bed. It got intense. Fast. We were feelin' on each other. She—" Here, his eyes dug into hers, scratching, clawing, pleading, with an intensity that overwhelmed her. *Please*, his look said. Please what? What did he want from her? "She started rubbing my penis. I wanted to make her feel good too, so I went down on her."

Penelope sat back, slouching low, wishing the ground would swallow her whole. Sitting with her family, listening to Micah discuss going down on her, had to be one of Dante's circles of hell.

"Had you ever done this before?"

"No. But I thought she would like it and I wanted to make her happy."

He wanted to make her happy. A misguided attempt. But the Micah she knew, she loved, was there that night.

"How'd she react?"

"She moved away. Told me she didn't like it." He held up his hands, two stop signs. "So, I stopped."

Was she to blame for not specifying every sexual act? Maybe. But even accepting fault for not speaking clearly, one question nagged. If she didn't want to have oral sex, why would he think she'd be okay having sex? She grabbed the notepad Attorney Kelly gave her and wrote the question.

"What's wrong?" Mom whispered.

Penelope shielded the paper from Mom's prying eyes. "Nothing." She tapped Attorney Kelly on the shoulder and handed it to him. She wasn't trying to trip up Micah—she needed an answer.

"Were you upset when Penelope told you she didn't like it?" Micah's attorney asked.

"Not at all. We started kissing again and it got emotional. We pulled back, staring into each other's eyes. I thought she wanted to be together. I told her I loved her—it was the first time I said that..." His voice trailed off, eyes hanging heavy. "Then—then we had sex."

"Had you ever had sex before that night?"

"No. I was—" He ran a hand over his face, softening his voice. "I was a virgin."

"Did she push you away?"

"No," he said.

"Did she tell you to stop?"

"No." More forceful now.

"Did you have any idea she wasn't enjoying it?"

"No. I thought—I thought she felt the same as me."

"And how did you feel?"

"In love. It was the best night of my life." He looked at Penelope. "She said she felt the same."

Penelope kept her eyes locked on Micah, searching for the truth. His best night was her worst. His dream was her nightmare. How? How could two people who knew each other inside and out, loved each other, be so disconnected?

Listening to him, she was filled with more questions. And no answers.

269

CHAPTER FIFTY-EIGHT
AMELIA

Amelia watched Penelope out of the corner of her eye as Micah testified, reassured that Penelope wasn't crumbling under his gaze. Because he was gazing. Every word, sentence, explanation was directed to Penelope. No one else existed. The emotion between them was palpable—regret, angst, sadness. Possibly love. Amelia felt like a voyeur. How had she failed to notice their connection?

"What's life been like since the arrest?" Attorney Levine asked.

"I've lost everything," Micah said. "My girlfriend. My best friend. I got kicked off the football team. Teachers either talk down to me or ignore me. Kids—they're mean. Everybody thinks they know what happened, know me." He looked at Penelope. "Worthless. Everyone decided I'm worthless."

"What's your biggest concern going forward?"

"What am I *not* worried about?" Micah laughed incredulously. "My name will always be tied to this. What college football program will look at me? What girl will want to date me when she Googles my name? When I go for a job, they'll search too, right? I'll be explaining this forever."

Amelia was more worried about Penelope's future; her ability to trust, be intimate. He took away Penelope's sense of safety, her innocence. Drunk or not, Amelia wouldn't forget it.

"Y'all can deny it," Micah continued, "act like this is a fair trial, but I've already been tried, whether or not I end up 'adjudicated delinquent.'"

Amelia saw Zoe's shoulders drop ever so slightly, perhaps only detectable by Amelia because she knew her best. Had Zoe reached her limit with Micah too?

"How have you gotten out your side of the story?"

"Through social media, mainly. I've spoken up, because, I believe, if I was white, I wouldn't have been arrested. I would've been given the benefit of the doubt that Penelope and I were in love. That this was a miscommunication. But that didn't happen. The cops didn't listen to me. They saw a Black boy and pegged me as guilty."

Amelia looked down at her hands while the questioning continued. Taking Penelope to the hospital, encouraging her to talk to the police, see a therapist, testify—Amelia made these decisions with Penelope's health and recovery in mind. Micah's race was irrelevant.

But just because Amelia's intentions were honorable didn't mean the rest of the process was handled that way. Were the police overzealous in their investigation because Penelope was a white girl accusing a Black boy of sexually assaulting her? Did they have to arrest Micah at school? Brand the image inside his teachers' and classmates' minds that he was dangerous. Would the judge's implicit bias weigh on her ruling? And Jack. Whenever she wavered, expressed doubt, he told her to focus on the fact that Micah was drunk and Penelope never consented.

Taking the facts in a vacuum, then yes, she agreed. Prosecute. But what in life happened in a vacuum? Nothing. The vacuum didn't account for the decade-plus relationship between Penelope and Micah. Amelia's negligence in leaving vodka in the freezer. Zoe's negligence for not checking on the kids.

There was plenty of blame to go around. She believed Micah bore most of the responsibility, that the alcohol diluted his common sense, that he pushed things too far with Penelope. But he wasn't cruel. He was selfish, immature, reckless. But also in love. She believed it now, watching the gentle way he spoke to Penelope.

Having all the facts before her like a Thanksgiving feast, Amelia still didn't know what, if anything, she should've done differently. Not stand up for her daughter? Not seek out justice? Let Penelope internalize that she wasn't worth being heard? Somehow, these thoughts made her feel guiltier—that she could absolve herself with the defense of motherhood. That she could fall back on that privilege of saying her hands were clean.

CHAPTER FIFTY-NINE
MICAH

Attorney Kelly tapped his pen against the lectern three times, a rapping sound that hit Micah's ears like the last few warning beeps of an impending bomb. Micah sat up taller, his spine straight as a needle, reviewing Sarah's advice for cross-examination. Be likeable, but not smooth. Empathetic, but not apologetic. Listen carefully to each question. Do not volunteer information. If you make a mistake, correct it. Most importantly, stay calm.

"The night of September second," Attorney Kelly said. "You testified you felt loopy; is that another word for drunk?"

"I wasn't one-hundred percent with it," Micah said.

"Ms. Swanson had a rule prohibiting you from entering Penelope's bedroom, correct?"

"Right."

"Yet you followed Penelope into her room after her shower, right?"

Micah hesitated. "Yes."

"Even though Penelope told you that you weren't supposed to be there, right?"

"I thought she meant because of Ollie. That he might find us."

"Once inside the bedroom, she *again* asked you to leave so she could change, correct?"

"She was laughing. I thought she was joking."

"She asked you to leave a third time once you started kissing on the bed, right?"

Put together, it sounded terrible, but there were good moments between. Moments that made Micah believe Penelope wanted him there. "She was kissing me back. And, again, she said she wanted to stop because of Ollie and I knew he was sick. That he wouldn't interrupt us."

"You'd never seen Penelope naked before that night, correct?"

Micah cleared his throat, embarrassed. "I saw parts."

"Parts. But her naked, you being naked, that never happened before, right?"

"Right."

"That's a pretty big step, physically?"

"I guess."

"You guess," Attorney Kelly repeated loudly into the microphone, making Micah sound like a jackass for being flippant. "You were the one that pulled down your shorts and underwear, correct?"

"I think so."

"And you put her hands on your penis?"

Micah tried to remember. "No—I don't know. Either way, she kept her hands there."

"You don't think it matters, if you put her hands there or if she chose to do it?"

"Yeah, it matters." Micah laughed, exasperated, before abruptly cutting himself off. "But if she didn't like it, she would've moved away."

"You were on top of her, correct?"

"Yes."

"And how tall are you?"

"Six-foot-one."

"What do you weight?"

"One-fifty."

"You're thirty pounds heavier, four inches taller, and you think she could've moved away if she didn't like it?"

"The fact that I'm bigger didn't stop her from speaking. Like when I went down on her, she had no problem telling me she didn't like it."

"Here's what I don't understand." Micah detected something in Attorney Kelly's tone, something like glee, that made Micah grind his teeth hard enough to crack a molar. Attorney Kelly enjoyed tearing Micah's life apart. "Knowing she didn't want to have oral sex, what made you believe she wanted to have penetrative sex?"

Micah's head swirled with thoughts. What did one have to do with the other? And how could he explain the moment? The love he felt for Penelope? Saw reflected in her eyes? Even if he had words, could he still say them? Knowing now that Penelope didn't feel love, but was frozen with terror? "I felt this connection between us when I looked at her. I thought she wanted to be closer."

"Exactly. *You* felt. *You* thought. But you're not sure anymore, are you?"

Micah looked at Penelope, her blue eyes glowing from across the room. "How can I be, considering what she said? Despite the way you're trying to paint me, I do listen. She says she didn't want it. I didn't get that feeling that night, but I can't ignore what she's saying now."

"Yet you ignored her on three different occasions when she asked you to leave or stop that night. Could your ability to listen today be due to your sobriety?"

"Objection," Sarah said. "Badgering. He's admitted to being under the influence."

"Sustained. Move on, counsel."

"After the assault, you didn't stay long, did you?"

"After we had sex," Micah corrected, "I had to leave before her mom came home."

"Because you knew you weren't supposed to be there, correct?"

"Objection," Sarah said. "Asked and answered."

"Sustained."

"After being arrested, you were given a Temporary Physical Custody Order, laying out the conditions of your release." Attorney Kelly held a sheet of paper. "May I approach?"

"You may," the judge said.

275

"Is this a fair and accurate representation of the TPCO you were given?"

"Yes."

"Your Honor, I'd like to include the TPCO as Exhibit Three."

"So entered."

Attorney Kelly turned back to Micah. "Did you comply with those conditions?"

Micah nodded. "Yes."

"You didn't have any contact with Penelope?"

"I mean—" Micah's voice cracked. "I saw her in school. Once."

Attorney Kelly held up another sheet of paper. "Is this your Instagram handle?"

Sweat dampened Micah's armpits. "Yes."

"And this is Penelope's?"

"Yes."

"Can you read the date at the top?"

"September sixth of this year."

"Your Honor, the State would like to introduce this direct message via Instagram into evidence as Exhibit Four."

"So entered."

"Please read."

"R you hurt???" Micah read quietly, trying to soften the angry message. "That's the line the police r feeding me. What happened after I left? Quit playing and tell the TRUTH. Ur Mom is fucking with my life."

Attorney Kelly walked back to the lectern. "Once again, you were aware of a rule—do not contact Penelope—and you ignored it, right?"

He should've listened to Ma. Lay low after the arrest. "I was confused. When I left her house, things were perfect—"

"Perfect for you, right?" Attorney Kelly said. "Not Penelope."

"I wanted to understand what happened."

"Time and again, you do what you want, regardless of whether it hurts the girl you claim to love." Attorney Kelly waved his hand, dismissing Micah. "No further questions."

"Any redirect, Attorney Levine?"

"Yes." Sarah stood up. "How soon did you send this DM after you were released from police custody?"

"An hour."

"Did the police explain the TPCO to you?"

"Officer Avery told me to ask my lawyer any questions."

"Had you meet with me yet?"

"No."

"Do you feel you understood the TPCO and consequences of violating it when you sent this DM?"

"No."

"No further questions."

"Any recross?" the judge asked.

"Just one question," Attorney Kelly said. "Permission to approach the witness?"

"Granted."

"Read paragraph four," Attorney Kelly said, handing him the TPCO.

Micah sighed. "The juvenile must refrain from contacting Penelope Mae Swanson. 'Contact' includes that which could occur via written correspondence (letters, emails, instant messages, text messages), phone calls, and/or indirect interaction."

Attorney Kelly put his hands in his pockets. "What confused you about that paragraph that you thought contacting Penelope was permissible?"

"I just got arrested. I was scared. Not thinking properly, okay? It looks obvious now—" Micah stopped, pressed his lips together. He. Would. Not. Cry. "But it was a hard day."

"No further questions."

As Micah stepped off the stand, reality crushed what little hope he had left. Even sticking with the plan, not taking responsibility, apologizing, he knew he lost. How long he'd be going away for was the only question left.

CHAPTER SIXTY
ZOE

Zoe exited the bathroom and walked toward the courtroom with her head down, her thoughts jumbled from Micah's testimony. Heels clacking against the tile floor made her look up. Amelia, Austin, Penelope, and Ollie approached opposite. The whole gang. Austin held Zoe's eyes. His lips—lips she loved—parted. What? she wanted to ask him. What is left to say? How can you fix this?

"I don't want to listen to closings," Penelope said as everyone got congested at the courtroom door. Zoe could either weave her way through them or wait. Awkward. Annoying.

"Go to the conference room," Amelia said.

"I'll go with her," Ollie said, trailing after Penelope.

Amelia opened the outer door to the courtroom, holding it for Austin, eyes skirting past Zoe as if she was wallpaper. Austin stepped through the outer doors, but didn't follow Amelia inside the courtroom. Stuck inside the vestibule, Austin squeezed Zoe's hand, the lower half of their bodies blocked by the door. The warmth of his hand, so familiar and yet newly hers to touch, liquified her heart. Why did they come together now? Why not last year? Five years ago? Such perfectly imperfect timing.

"You're not alone," he said. "I'm here for both of you, okay?"

It wasn't enough. But what else could Zoe ask for? He was in an impossible situation—they all were. "Okay."

She let go of his hand and they walked through the doors, parting to take seats on separate sides of the aisle. The judge entered shortly thereafter and invited the State to begin its closing argument.

Attorney Kelly stood up and buttoned his suit jacket before moving behind the podium. "Your Honor, for you to adjudicate the juvenile delinquent, the State was required to prove, beyond a

278

reasonable doubt, that the juvenile had sexual intercourse with Penelope and that Penelope did not consent. The first element is not at issue. Both parties agree sexual intercourse took place. In deciding whether Penelope consented to sex, you should look at the facts and circumstances, what Penelope and Micah said and did both before and during the alleged assault. As this Court knows, Micah's belief that Penelope consented is no defense, if the facts support a lack of consent. The facts here show that Micah does what Micah wants, rules be damned. He got drunk." He held up a finger, counting off each point. "Went into Penelope's room, despite her mother's rules. Refused to leave, even after Penelope asked him to do so on three separate occasions. Forced her to have penetrative sex after she asked him to stop performing oral sex. After being arrested, he violated the TPCO and harassed Penelope."

Zoe smoothed her hands over her thighs. One word, one sentence, even several, she reminded herself, would not decide the case. The judge would take the facts as a whole.

"Penelope did not resist the assault," Attorney Kelly continued, "but, as this Court knows, physical resistance is not required to prove sexual assault. This is because everyone reacts to trauma differently. For Penelope, being sexually assaulted, not only by her boyfriend, but by her best friend of eleven years, sent her into shock. Unable to speak, move, or fight back."

Zoe took a deep breath, inhaling the truth. Penelope didn't want to have sex. That didn't mean Micah assaulted her. But he read Penelope's signals wrong. Intuited interest from silence, read fear as nerves, glossed over her polite rebuffs. If they got out of this unscathed, and that was a big if, she'd find a way to guide him, set limits, ensure he understood that consent could never be assumed.

They just needed to get out of this.

"The evidence bolsters Penelope's account of the assault," Attorney Kelly said. "Dr. Bilson testified that Penelope presented with bleeding due to vaginal lacerations. Tears consistent with nonconsensual sex. Dr. Harris, an expert psychologist who studies

PTSD in sexual assault victims, testified that Penelope's demeanor—quiet, tearful, regretful—was common among sexual assault victims. Officer Avery verified that Penelope's account of the assault has remained unchanged.

"Given the evidence, the State asks this Court to find the juvenile delinquent. The State believes, with the proper treatment, Micah can be fully rehabilitated. Toward that end, the State recommends one-year probation, placement at home, compliance with both alternatives to sexual assault treatment and alcohol and drug treatment programs. A Permanent Physical Custody Order, conditions mirroring the TPCO. Upon successful completion, the State would recommend dismissal. Thank you."

Zoe swallowed back tears. Micah would not go to a juvenile detention center. He would live at home. Yes, he had to attend therapy, which he would hate, but he could go to school, have friends, play sports. Nothing would be noted on college applications. Worst case scenario, he still had a path forward.

"Your closing, Attorney Levine," the judge said, inscrutable, as always. If she was weighing one side more favorable than the other, Zoe couldn't tell.

"Attorney Kelly is right." Sarah's voice boomed through the small courtroom. "Consent is based on words and actions. Penelope's words and actions show she consented to having sex with Micah. She willingly kissed him. Willingly touched his penis. The one time she was unwilling, when Micah performed oral sex on her, she told him to stop and he did.

"She felt comfortable speaking up, because Penelope and Micah have been best friends and neighbors since they were three. They spend holidays and vacations together. They keep each other's secrets. There is no overt evidence, through words or actions, to show she didn't consent to penetrative sex.

"Moreover, this Court should question Penelope's credibility. Penelope kept her relationship with Micah a secret from both family and friends. Lies upon lies over a three-month period. Then she lied to the police about having a relationship with Micah. These lies caution this Court against finding Micah delinquent based solely on her word."

Zoe nodded along. Perhaps the judge, who had yet to blink, would agree too.

"Finally," Sarah said, "as Micah testified, his life has been severely damaged by this charge. He lost his best friends, got kicked off the football team, treated poorly by teachers, teased by his peers. I ask this Court to right one of the many wrongs he has endured and find him not delinquent."

Zoe noticed that Sarah said nothing about Micah being Black. Perhaps, as a white woman, she didn't feel comfortable addressing it. Or, maybe she really didn't believe it was relevant. Whatever the reason, Micah would be proud that he stood up for himself. Despite knowing it might hurt him, that Zoe told him to tone it down, part of her was proud. She was raising a strong man. An independent thinker. Growth was necessary, but the building blocks were there.

"Thank you, counsel," the judge said, squinting at her computer. "We'll reconvene Wednesday afternoon at one for my decision."

Zoe wished the judge would end their misery and issue her ruling today. She didn't want to obsess about the verdict for the next two days.

"Court is adjourned." The judge banged her gavel and left. Everyone talked at once, the noise bouncing off the walls. The pent-up energy of a last day of school.

Zoe hugged Micah, squeezing him tight, not letting him intuit her concern. As she hugged Sarah, she felt heat on her back, a magnetic pull. She turned around, fearing Amelia. Instead, Austin stood at the door, holding it open halfway, waiting for her eyes. He nodded toward the hallway.

An invitation. An apology? A reconciliation? A goodbye?

"Can you take Micah down to the cafeteria?" Zoe asked Sarah as they walked out of the courtroom. "Explain what will happen Wednesday? I need a minute."

Zoe waited until the elevator doors closed behind Sarah and Micah before approaching Austin.

"Let's walk," he said.

Proximity made her heart soar. Despite everything, she loved him.

CHAPTER SIXTY-ONE
AMELIA

After closing arguments, Amelia stayed in her seat as the adrenaline drained from her body. She heard voices, the skid of chairs against wood, the dull pounding of the door closing. But it was all background noise to her thoughts, a TV with the volume set low. Penelope and Ollie skipped closing arguments and were probably eager to leave.

Still, she sat. Utterly drained.

They fought a battle today, but there were no winners. From the weariness on the children's faces, Zoe's hunched shoulders, Austin's silence, to the punishing crick in Amelia's neck from absorbing the testimonial blows, no one left unscathed. In two days, the judge would rule, but emotionally, the sentence was already laid down.

The sentence in Amelia's case being negligence as a mother. She thought she knew her kids' lives inside and out, trusted that they would come to her if something was wrong. But she wasn't paying enough attention, or perhaps paying attention to the wrong things. One question haunted Amelia today. What if she hadn't walked into Penelope's room that night? Would Penelope have said something the next morning? Or would she have shut Amelia out, lied, thinking she had no other choice? Listening to today's testimony, Amelia guessed the latter.

Penelope opened up today, but that took months of pleading and prodding. What if Amelia didn't notice the next time something was wrong? How could she protect her?

Her only option was to keep asking the kids questions, be available, listen, amendable to changing her opinion. It didn't feel like enough right now, but maybe it would pay dividends later.

"Ready?" Jack asked, ushering his laptop inside his briefcase.

Amelia looked around. The courtroom was empty. "Yes."

As they walked to the elevators, Jack explained that the judge would issue her decision Wednesday. If she adjudicated Micah delinquent, she would sentence him immediately. "Sentencing in juvenile court is more about rehabilitation than punishment," Jack said, pushing the up-elevator button. He was going to his office, while she needed to get the kids from the conference room. "We have a great recidivism rate; with the proper treatment, roughly three-quarters of kids sentenced for sexual assault don't offend again."

"That's...promising." She wasn't sure where her feelings stood for Micah after today. She couldn't forgive what he did to Penelope, but she also couldn't forget how vulnerable he looked on the stand. The love he still exhibited for Penelope.

After saying goodbye to Jack, she went across the hall. Pushing the conference room door open, she found it empty. Then she checked the bathroom. Nothing. She walked the perimeter hallway, thinking maybe they got bored and decided to wander. Darkness seeped through the floor-to-ceiling windows. Her eyes traced the street lamps as they faded in the distance, like tracks of a roller coaster, showing the grid of the city.

Her phone buzzed. Ollie. *Outside. Front stoop.* Relief was short lived. As she rounded the curve, making the oval loop back to the elevators, her feet ground to a halt.

Roughly twenty yards away, Zoe leaned against the wall. Austin stood in front of her, close enough that they shared the same air. The intimacy was palpable, the rumbles of their words drifting down the hall, too soft to decipher.

And then Austin reached out, ever so gently, linking his fingers inside Zoe's.

Amelia blinked back her surprise, blinked back tears, betrayal like a sucker punch. There was no mistaking the gesture for friendship, not with the unwavering eye contact. Micah stole Penelope's innocence and now it felt like Zoe was stealing Austin from her.

284

Amelia should've turned around, gone outside to find the kids. Instead, she walked toward them. She needed to know what else was going on without her knowledge.

Both turned, hearing Amelia approach. Their hands darted apart. Guilt strung up their faces, shock freezing the small-motor functions.

"Amelia," Austin said.

Amelia took in Austin's brown eyes, trying to gauge the truth. She remembered their conversation where he suggested letting Penelope and Micah talk. Instinct told her he seemed overly familiar with Zoe's thoughts, but she dismissed it, too preoccupied with helping Penelope. Now, she wished she would've questioned him, just for peace of mind. To know whether he would've lied to her face, or, like her kids, was guilty of omission.

"How long has this been going on?" Amelia asked.

Austin reached up, scratching his cheek with his index finger, buying time. It was only two or three seconds, but a warning to tread lightly. Amelia turned to Zoe. But Zoe looked past her, down the hall.

Today highlighted how the bonds they sowed could unravel in an instant. That, if put to the test, Austin might choose Zoe over her. Their family. Right or wrong wasn't up for grabs—Austin clearly crossed the line—but was it worth testing him? Possibly losing him? She waited for his answer, wanting to forgive him, but forgiveness was hard, nearly impossible, when neither offered an apology.

CHAPTER SIXTY-TWO
AUSTIN

How long has this been going on? A reasonable question. But how to respond? When he started talking to Zoe? Met her for a drink? Their first kiss?

"I was planning to tell you when the trial ended." Austin glanced at Zoe. She bit her lip, seemingly having to restrain herself from speaking. "I didn't want to stress you out more."

"How long, Austin?" Amelia's voice was low, steely, as if white-knuckling her voice box.

"When Penelope left school early that day, Zoe and I got to talking and she—she needed someone to listen. She doesn't have what we have." He spoke about his relationship with Amelia in the present tense, as if he could replenish the strength of their bond like gas in a car. "It started with making sure she was okay and spiraled into texting, then hanging out—"

"Did it occur to you during all your *texts* and *hangs* that we needed your support?" She laced her words with sarcasm. "That maybe Penelope would've opened up sooner if you tried harder? That maybe Ollie could've used a friend?"

Austin shoved his hands in his pockets, teetering back on his heels, anger making his muscles taut. "I've been there for them. Every day. You too. To say that I've failed or somehow short-changed—" Zoe reached over, resting her hand on his arm. One touch, but it said more. *Calm down. I've got you.*

"I tried to keep my distance," Austin continued. "I knew how much this would hurt you, and you know, *you know,* I'd do anything to protect you. But staying away from Zoe? It was killing me." He cleared his throat, surprised to find emotion getting the better of him. "I love her, Amelia."

286

Amelia stared back, her jaw rigid. The words tumbled out of his mouth naturally. As he learned from Penelope today, all he had was his truth. His lone regret? The first time he said these words to Zoe, the first time he'd say them to any woman, not out of fear or obligation or apology, but because it was the truth, was in the middle of an argument. With his sister.

"I didn't do this to hurt you," Zoe said. "Neither of us did. He showed up, Amelia." She looked at Austin, eyes beaming—perhaps because she loved him too? "Showed up for me, like no man has ever done."

"And I didn't push this case to hurt you, Zoe. Yet you've taken every opportunity to silence Penelope." Amelia tossed a hand in Austin's direction. "Apparently, hooking up with Austin so he'd convince me to drop the case."

Austin stepped between them. "That's not fair—"

"I was protecting Micah," Zoe said.

"And now?" Amelia's eyes widened. "After hearing all the evidence? You still think *he's* the one that needs protecting?"

Austin read the truth on Zoe's face, the truth they all digested today. Micah hurt Penelope. He pushed limits. Confused her. Abused her trust. Whether it was alcohol or hormones or misguided love, Micah misread Penelope. The blame lay at his feet.

Much as Austin wanted to hate Micah, watching him in the courtroom, listening to his testimony, Austin was struck time and again that he was just a kid. One who regretted his actions. Was overwhelmed by his mistakes. Who wanted to do better.

"He's my son," Zoe said, thankfully not needing Austin's support. Support he wouldn't have been able to give, a silence that would cause an impassable rift between them. "I'll always protect him."

He wasn't so lucky with Amelia. Her eyes demanded Austin take a side, blood before love. "Penelope was brave today," he said. "The strength it took to get up there, speak about this; I think this will be a big step forward."

Amelia looked down, shaking her head. "Get a ride home with Zoe." She walked away, disappearing around the bend of the hallway.

Once again, in not making a decision, he made a decision.

Zoe rested her head against his chest. "I'm sorry."

He pressed his nose to the crown of her head, inhaling her scent—jasmine, oranges, citrus—waiting for the rush of dopamine that usually calmed him when around her. But not this time.

Panic muzzled his senses. He couldn't give up Amelia and the kids. But the thought of losing Zoe—

Fuck. "I need to make this right," he finally said.

Zoe stepped back, sinking her top two teeth into her bottom lip. "What would be right?"

Zoe needed assurances, but he couldn't give them. He saw now that there would be no reconciliation between the women. Hope for a future with Zoe was slipping through his fingers. He had to tug it back, find a way. "I'll talk to her."

Austin watched helplessly as the shades closed over Zoe's face. "We should get going," she said.

They walked down the hall without speaking. Despite leaving together, they both knew his promise to talk to Amelia was a non-answer. A promise of nothing. Like Amelia, Zoe saw right through him.

CHAPTER SIXTY-THREE
PENELOPE

Penelope sat next to Ollie on the second-floor landing of their house late Monday night, listening to Mom and Uncle Austin arguing in the kitchen below. They used to eavesdrop on their parents this way, but obviously hadn't done that since Dad died. Tonight, it felt right. With the trial over, they wanted comfort, reassurance that life might go back to normal. Somehow, Uncle Austin and Mom fighting about his relationship with Zoe—WTF???—filled that need.

Penelope didn't know what to think about Uncle Austin and Zoe. Bad timing, for sure. Point for Mom. But also, cool? They always laughed together. And Penelope did miss Zoe. Unlike Mom, Penelope didn't blame Zoe. The complication was Micah. Would Penelope have to see him if Zoe and Uncle Austin dated? She wasn't ready for that. She started feeling better after deleting her social media, his number, avoiding contact with him. Seeing him today felt like the removal of a lung, her breath short, her brain lax.

"Out of all the women in Milwaukee, you had to fall in love with Zoe," Mom said, sounding worn out.

"It's not like I chose to," Uncle Austin said. "It just happened."

"You chose to do something about it."

"You've been on me for years to commit, stop fucking with twenty-somethings. I was just listening to you."

Silence. Then laughter. As usual, Uncle Austin's humor eased the tension. Whatever happened with Zoe, Uncle Austin would be around. Mom couldn't stay mad at him for long.

"Let's go," Penelope said to Ollie. She stood and tiptoed back to her room. It was dim inside, lit only by the warm light of her bedside lamp. She got into bed, pulling the covers over her hips, her head hitting the pillow like a bowling ball. Amazing how one day, a day where she didn't play tennis or do cardio, could leave her so depleted.

Ollie flopped down on the end of her bed. He lay on his back, one hand curled behind his head, the other resting on his heart. "This'll suck. Having Uncle Austin divide his time between our house and Zoe's."

"We should move. It'd solve everything," Penelope said.

Ollie raised up on his elbows. "Move? Where? Are you serious?"

"Florida. I could train full-time. Still live with you guys." Leaving. Starting over. Not having Micah across the street. Kids knowing personal details of her life. "It'd be perfect."

"Ha! Mom would never leave her job." He lay back down, facing away from her. Murmurs from Mom's and Uncle Austin's conversation filtered up through the vent. "Was today as bad as you thought? Answering questions?"

Worse—in a way she hadn't imagined. "When his attorney started pointing out my mistakes, all the ways I could've stopped him, it's like she took the darkest thoughts from my mind, the ones that keep me up at night, and exposed them. And, she might be right." She didn't want to keep having these thoughts. Today was supposed to fix her heart, her mind—at least apply a goddamn Band-Aid. "I could've—I should've spoken up."

"Do you think he should be punished? I mean, if you could decide?"

"I don't know." She ran her hands over her face. "Maybe having him listen is enough."

"He still doesn't get it. Why he was wrong." Ollie's voice was quiet. "It's all about how his life is ruined. Not yours."

"I know, right?" Penelope dug her fingernails into the bed. "Why won't he apologize? I mean, just say you're sorry, you know? How hard is that?" She splayed her hands flat, forced out a breath. "I was hoping he would today, but..."

"He didn't."

"Nope." Staying up late, talking like this, reminded her of when they were younger. Sleepovers. As always, her brain tagged Micah, the third member of their trio. When would it stop? Let her off the hook?

"I want to play tennis," she said. "All day, every day. Whenever I hit the ball, I feel better. Like, I can be someone other than the girl that got..." She rolled her eyes and made air quotes, still not sure how to identify with the phrase. "The girl who got 'sexually assaulted.'"

He grinned at her. "So, play tennis. Become the girl that got 'sexually assaulted' *and* wins majors. It makes for a hell of a platform. You'll be rich, anointed as a Queen, in this woke life we live."

She kicked him. "That sounds opportunistic."

He rubbed his hip, pretending it hurt. "I thought it sounded like a survivor."

A survivor. She had survived. *Was* surviving. Ongoing. TBD. But, what if? What if one day, she felt okay enough to talk about it? Share her story? Help other girls find the courage to speak up? It was a lofty goal, but, then again, so was becoming a professional tennis player and she wouldn't back down from that.

CHAPTER SIXTY-FOUR
MICAH

On Wednesday afternoon, Micah sat next to Sarah in the courtroom, awaiting the judge's decision. His foot tapped a steady beat as the clerk called the case to order. Ma sat in the row behind him, anxiety coming off her body like heat on the pavement, making Micah sweat. Penelope wasn't here. Amelia showed up alone, which Micah took as a bad sign. Penelope wanted nothing to do with him, even after hearing his explanation.

The judge cleared her throat and Micah sat up taller. "After listening to the testimony and going over the evidence..." Here, the judge paused, looking at Micah above her glasses. "I conclude the juvenile is guilty of third-degree sexual assault under Wisconsin law and I thereby adjudicate him delinquent."

Everything became white noise, a whirling rush of thoughts. Guilty. Sexual assault. Delinquent. Sarah rested a hand on his wrist, snapping him back to reality.

"While I believe both juveniles were credible in their testimony," the judge said, "it's not a defense that Micah believed Penelope consented. Several factors led me to conclude Penelope did not freely consent. Penelope asked Micah to leave several times. She told him she wanted to stop when he performed oral sex. Her lack of physical and verbal resistance when Micah penetrated her is not indicative of consent either. As discussed by Dr. Harris, there's no correct way to act when the body is under assault.

"Turning to rehabilitating Micah, I'm encouraged by the letters I received in support from his football coach, two teachers, and several teammates. Read these letters, Micah. Many people believe in you and want you to succeed. I am among them. I believe you have a good heart. I believe you loved Penelope. I also believe you made some very poor choices that night."

Micah bit down on his lip, fighting tears. He had people in his corner? Was it true? Coach? What teachers? The judge's kindness struck a chord, made him think she might leave him with a warning, a second chance—stupid, right? Still, hope burned.

"I'm going to follow the State's recommendations. One year probation, placement at home," the judge said, reading from her computer. "Completion of one year of alternatives to sexual assault treatment. Alcohol and drug abuse assessment to determine treatment needs and thereafter compliance with those requirements. Compliance with the conditions in the Permanent Physical Custody Order." She turned to Micah. "If you follow the rules and complete your treatment, I'll dismiss your case and seal your records. If you violate any of the conditions, including contacting Penelope—letters, emails, DM's, texts, phone calls, or speaking with her directly—you'll receive a sanction. We'll hold a dispositional hearing where I'll decide the consequence: thirty days house arrest, twenty hours community service, or ten days in secure detention. If you continue to violate the conditions, your placement at home will be reviewed. You could have to register as a sex offender." She paused. "Please don't let it come to that."

Micah nodded, sensing she wanted an acknowledgment. Meanwhile, the punishments echoed inside his head. The "pass" he was being given, if he could call it that with all the work required, held danger at every turn. One mistake and he'd be out of his house.

He had to do better this time around.

"I cannot control social media and certain comments might live forever in cyber-space, but you are young," the judge said. "And what you do going forward is more important than a decision you made one night when you were fourteen. Anything further, Attorney Kelly?"

"No, your Honor."

"Attorney Levine?"

293

"No."

"Good luck, Micah." She banged her gavel and left.

He rested his face in his shaky hands. It happened so fast. Hope a mirage, there one second, gone the next.

Ma squeezed his shoulders, her head resting against his. "Do the work, follow the rules," she said. "It's a year, not forever."

"Think of treatment as an opportunity," Sarah said.

He felt overwhelmed, their support suffocating. Too much perfume and false optimism. But it also filled him up, reminded him, as the judge said, that he had people rooting for him.

"Yes," Sarah continued, "there will be discussions about appropriate sexual behaviors and building healthy relationships, but you'll also learn coping mechanisms, recognize triggers that lead to bad decisions, how to communicate your emotions. You'll gain a level of self-awareness that'll help you succeed in life."

Based on Penelope's testimony, he needed some help listening. Reading signals. Not being so impulsive. Intentions can be one thing, but actions can lead to something altogether different. Something damaging.

"Here's the permanent physical custody order," Sarah said, sliding the paper in front of him that the clerk just delivered. Ma peered over his shoulder to read. "Same conditions as before, but one new. You'll have to write Penelope a letter at the end of treatment, wherein you accept responsibility and apologize."

While he hurt Penelope, he had a hard time accepting he assaulted her. Assault. He hated that word. The violence it implied. The implication that *he* was violent. Uh-uh. No way. That was a step too far. But Sarah bringing this up now, months in advance, served as a warning to wrap his mind around the idea. All it took was swallowing his ego, making himself vulnerable, admitting he did wrong. No easy task.

After saying goodbye to Sarah, Micah and Ma took the elevator to the lobby and walked out to the parking lot. He shoved his hands in his pockets, shivering in the cold. Neither talked. But the surprises weren't done. Amelia stood next to their car. Had she come to gloat?

"Micah, get in the car." Ma handed him the keys. "Amelia and I are going for a walk."

He got in the passenger seat, turned on the car, and jacked the heat. He watched Ma and Amelia take the path down to the courtyard. Whatever. Micah didn't care about Amelia. The damage was done. They'd share the same street until he left for college. End of.

He closed his eyes, picturing the next year. Would any girl date him? Would he spend high school an outcast? Would the teachers see the verdict as proof he wasn't worth their time? One thing he knew for sure, getting pissed off wouldn't change anything. Listening to Penelope's testimony, he realized his anger—at Penelope, Ma, Amelia, Ollie, the cops, *everyone*—was his way of avoiding looking at himself. Taking himself to task. That stopped now. Penelope had both nothing and everything to do with the next year. Nothing because he wouldn't see her. He'd follow the conditions, no cap. Everything because she was his impetus for change, for life, for love.

There was light. Three-hundred-and-sixty-five days from now. It was up to him to walk toward it. Today was day one. He grabbed his phone, pulled up Instagram, choosing a black background with block white letters. Ready to start fresh. For inspiration, he turned to the King. Martin Luther King, Jr. *I have decided to stick with love. Hate is too great a burden to bear.*

He hit post.

CHAPTER SIXTY-FIVE
ZOE

Zoe saw Amelia first. Her fire-engine red peacoat served as a lighthouse among the cars in the parking lot. Panic and dread, curiosity and nostalgia, hit Zoe, one punch after another, so that by the time she and Micah reached their car, she felt battered and beaten. She considered driving away, not giving Amelia time. Too much happened—Zoe needed time to process Micah's conviction. The permanent restrictions. But another part of her wanted to have it out, once and for all.

Zoe handed Micah the car keys. "Let's walk," Zoe said to Amelia. Zoe stepped over the curb, walked through the soggy, snowy grass, and onto the path, taking it down toward the courtyard. The water fountain was off, the benches fluffy with snow. Zoe brushed off the seat and sat.

Amelia stood by the fountain, her back to Zoe. "Do you love him?" Amelia asked, her words faint in the wind.

Zoe assessed her coolly. Micah just got sentenced and she wanted to have it out about Austin? "Why? What difference does it make?"

Amelia turned around, the tip of her nose bright red from the cold. "It's everything."

Zoe stayed up late Monday night, waiting for Austin to return from Amelia's, but he never showed. She spent twenty-four agonizing hours stressing about the potential verdict, wondering how she would adapt her work schedule to shuffle Micah to a myriad of therapy appointments, whether Austin chose his family over Zoe. Late last night, he showed up. His conclusion, take things slow. Let everyone adjust. Logically, it made sense. She had yet to tell Micah and that wouldn't be an easy conversation. But emotionally, Austin cut her off at the knees. How could he profess his love in one breath and tell her to slow down in the next?

She didn't want to share these uncertainties with Amelia. "What do you want? I mean, to talk about?" Zoe gestured behind her, toward the courthouse. "Obviously, you already got what you want."

"This isn't what..." Amelia walked over, wiping the snow off the bench next to Zoe with her bare hand before sitting down. "I wanted to tell you I'm sorry, for not talking to you that night. I panicked when I saw Penelope. The panic turned to helplessness. Which turned to anger. And as the weeks passed, as Penelope got worse, as you continued to defend Micah, wouldn't acknowledge *any* wrongdoing, it became easy to blame you." She looked at Zoe. "But you deserved that conversation. Not only because you were my friend, but because we promised, when it came to the kids, to always be there for each other."

Zoe let out a slow breath, remembering how betrayed she felt when the cops showed up. For years, Zoe and Amelia operated under a tacit understanding that they were both doing their best to raise kind, spirited, smart humans. Going about it different ways? Yes. But always supportive. Would Zoe have been able to acknowledge wrongdoing if Amelia came to her first? If Amelia approached the situation as a problem with the kids collectively instead of pointing fingers? Her instinct would have always been to protect Micah, but perhaps, if they had a conversation, an ongoing dialogue, she would've encouraged Micah to take some responsibility.

"I. Believe. Penelope," Zoe said, the words emerging from her mouth disfigured and disjointed—the best she could do. "That she didn't want to have sex. But I also believe Micah didn't know that." A gust of wind had both Zoe and Amelia burrowing inside their jackets. Zoe actively strained her jaw, trying not to chatter. "I wish you would've come over—I wish—" Zoe stopped. It happened. Nothing could change the past. She didn't want to rehash what ifs. What if Micah didn't drink? What if Zoe checked on the boys?

What if Penelope said no? What if, what if, what if. Micah would get treatment. He'd learn a tough lesson, emerge a better man. Zoe would make sure of it. "I genuinely hope Penelope will be okay. That she finds a way to move on."

"Honestly, I don't know if testifying helped or hurt. There's no easy answers. No clear path forward." Amelia looked up. The overcast sky bounced off her blue eyes, making them gleam like sapphires. "For any of us."

The words hung in the freezing air, a rope for Zoe to grab. She could listen to Amelia, commiserate with her struggles. Zoe could share her fears too. Both were mothers, plopped in an unfathomable situation, trying to do best by their kids. The comfort of a thousand memories of their friendship drew Zoe in, but too much scar tissue formed for her to let go.

"I appreciate the apology, but I can't be the one you vent to anymore," Zoe said. "I'm sorry if that sounds cold—"

Amelia held up her hand. "I get it. I wasn't asking for your friendship."

"Then what are you asking for?"

"Do you love him?" Amelia repeated with urgency. "Because Penelope needs Austin. I need Austin. Ollie—our family needs him. And if this is anything other than love, I'm asking you to stop. To let us heal."

"I love him," Zoe said, a slight stomachache appearing as she catalogued the pain in Amelia's eyes. Too much hurt had been volleyed back and forth. "I really do."

Zoe stood up and walked back to the car. She did love Austin. Whether love would be enough to build a future together, she didn't know. Many uncertainties lay in their path. But her friendship with Amelia was over. All the years Zoe spent concealing her feelings for Austin, playing down the attraction, dating other men—never again. She deserved to find happiness too.

As she approached the car, she noticed the desolate look on Micah's face. She blinked away her tears, reminding herself that he was her priority, guiding him through this next year. If Austin fit in, great, but Micah would never come second, in her heart or in her mind.

CHAPTER SIXTY-SIX
AMELIA

When Amelia pulled out of the courthouse parking lot, her first instinct was to call Austin. Tell him what happened at the hearing. But things were awkward at best and damaged at worst. Let him hear it from Zoe. Amelia needed to focus on Penelope. Would she be happy to hear that Micah was found delinquent? Relieved he couldn't contact her for another year? Amelia remembered the electricity between Penelope and Micah, the way it stripped the air from the courtroom. Did seeing Micah make her miss him?

Amelia drove with one hand and held her fingers up to the vent with the other, letting the heat thaw them. One year of sexual assault treatment. Was it a fair sentence? While she'd never go as far as Zoe and say it was a miscommunication, she didn't feel comfortable with Micah going to a juvenile detention center. There were few absolutes in her mind about that night, but she knew, down to her marrow, that Micah wouldn't have hurt Penelope, taken those risks, unless he was drunk. It wasn't a legal defense, but in Amelia's mind, it was a mitigating factor. The sentence ensured he learned his choices had consequences, gave him an avenue to grow, stopped him from hurting anyone else. Amelia could live with that. Would Penelope feel the same?

She parked in the garage and let herself inside the house, listening to determine Penelope's location. Hearing nothing, she hung up her coat, set down her purse on the kitchen island, and went upstairs. Penelope's door was closed. She knocked twice before opening it, as always, feeling a palpitation of fear as she flashed back to opening the door that night.

Penelope lay on her stomach, holding a highlighter, head bent over a textbook, earbuds tucked inside her ears. She didn't look up until she felt Amelia's weight on the bed.

"Well?" Penelope pulled out the earbuds. She hadn't wanted to attend the hearing and Amelia didn't push her.

"They found him delinquent."

Penelope gnawed on her lower lip, looking past Amelia. "What does that mean?"

"He'll get treatment for sexual assault and alcohol." Amelia tucked Penelope's hair behind her ear. "He'll have restrictions, meaning he can't contact you, but he'll be living at home and going to school."

Penelope sat up, pulling her knees to her chest. "So, his life will go back to normal."

"Not normal, no. Treatment will be difficult, school won't be easy either..." Amelia didn't have a good answer. "Were you hoping for more?"

Penelope didn't say anything for a long time. Then, "I was hoping he'd say sorry."

Amelia wrapped her arms around Penelope, holding her while she cried. These weren't the uncontrolled sobs of the past few months, but rather the final drain of pain that she was drawn into this situation, that this was an experience she would carry forever.

Penelope pulled away, wiping her nose with the back of her hand. "What if...what if I forgave him anyway? Suzanne's been talking about how forgiving him is something I can do for myself. To move on." She looked at Amelia. "Eventually, I mean."

It would be a good while before Amelia could forgive Micah, but if Penelope needed to do it, Amelia wasn't going to stop her. "That's definitely something to think about."

Penelope started in on her lower lip again. "You're mad. I can tell, you don't like it."

"It's not for me to be anything. Every step of your recovery has to be about what you need." Penelope gave a small nod, but Amelia sensed reluctance. Even after their conversation in the courthouse bathroom, it was clear Penelope internalized a deep-seated fear of disappointing Amelia. One that would take several conversations, deliberate actions on Amelia's part, to show Penelope that *she* set the expectations. Not Amelia. "And I messed up at the beginning, trying to direct too much of it. But going forward, I'll help you in any way I can. And if you want to forgive Micah, well, I'll support that. I won't support you spending time with him, but I'll support that gesture."

Penelope looked away. "I'd like to be alone now."

"Okay." The dismissal stung. Amelia reminded herself that nothing changes overnight, that it was normal for Penelope to want space, privacy. Penelope told her how she felt instead of shutting her out. Progress. But as a mom, you never stop wanting more. Wanting the exquisite closeness of when they arrived in this world, when you were their whole world. Everything afterwards feels like the gradual chipping away at your soul. "I'll be downstairs if you need me."

Amelia left the bedroom, but instead of going immediately downstairs she walked over to Ollie's room and stepped inside. The room was empty, his bed made, clothes all put away. She missed him. He was in school, but the end of the trial made her realize how much she had been neglecting him to help Penelope. She pulled her phone from her pants pocket and texted him. *Micah found delinquent. One year sentence, at home, with treatment.* She clicked out of the messenger app before opening it back up. *Dinner tonight, just you and me? You choose the place.*

She walked downstairs, greeted by an empty kitchen. On automation, she pulled out her laptop and sat down to start working. The kids might not need her, her presence might cramp their style, but she wanted to work from home more, be around when she didn't have events. Just in case she caught them on an off day and they wanted to open up, talk about whatever was wrong in their lives. Or right. Amelia wasn't picky. She just wanted more of them while they were still around.

ONE YEAR LATER
PENELOPE

Penelope sat on a swing at Veterans Park, the waning afternoon sun giving the dead, corn on the cob-colored grass a golden glow. She twisted in a circle, twirling the chain with her mittened hands as tight as it would go, and then let go. The spinning distracted her body from the sub-freezing temperature, and her mind from Micah's imminent arrival.

Last week, Micah's sentence ended and Penelope received a hand-written letter from him. She didn't read it at first. Hid it in an old tennis bag. Yesterday, buoyed by a great practice, Penelope felt strong. Ready.

> Dear P,
> I'm sorry. When I think about what I put you through that night and every day since, I feel sick. I was drunk. Stupid. Curious. Above all, I was in love. But those are excuses—there are no excuses. I doubt you'll ever forgive me, but just know I'm trying to do better. Be worthy of a girl like you.
> Micah

It was so short! A paragraph! A few thoughts! After a year, that's all he had to say? She wanted more. Still had questions. Yesterday, she ran the idea of talking to Micah by Suzanne first and then Mom, who, amazingly, reacted with a reasonable amount of chill. All part of her new listening first, opining second, parenting. With permission, Penelope texted Micah, asking to talk. She wanted a conversation without adults, without legal consequences. Although she knew the consequences for her heart could be severe.

Micah rode up to the playground on his bike. She tugged down her beanie, covertly watching him as he parked his bike, tracing the lines of his lean body for changes. Living across the street, she occasionally saw him, but they never talked. They couldn't. But now, he was free.

And still, that night fastened its grip on her.

He walked with his head down, hands shoved in his jacket pockets. He stopped at the edge of the swings, where the grass met the black rubber mat.

"I got your letter," she said.

He nodded. "Good."

"Did you mean it?" Her voice shook. Hard to tell whether it was due to the cold or nerves. "Or was it just to get your case closed?"

He took a step toward her and then stopped. "Can I sit on the swing next to you?"

She gestured at the swing. *Be my guest.*

"You have to say yes or no."

Was he teasing her? But nothing in his face showed amusement. "Yes."

The swing screeched when he sat down, like nails on a chalkboard. Micah looked up, squinting at the hinges. "I meant everything," he said. "A year ago, I struggled to understand where I went wrong. But now? Yeah."

"What changed?"

"Therapy, therapy and more therapy."

She huffed a laugh, her breath a puff of smoke in the frigid air. "It's the worst, isn't it?"

He looked at her. The beauty in his brown eyes made her heart weep. "You too?"

"Twice a week," she said. "Only way Mom would let me homeschool and train full-time."

It took months of working with Suzanne for Penelope to believe the words sexual assault applied to her. That Micah could be her best friend, boyfriend, and also her attacker.

Forgiving herself remained an unanswered question. She wasn't there yet, possibly never. Penelope still thought she shouldered some blame for not saying no, for not pushing Micah off her, for just lying there. Suzanne encouraged Penelope to see that she set unrealistic expectations, that she did her best under the circumstances. That she wasn't responsible for his illegal actions. They did a lot of cognitive behavioral therapy, allowing for compassion as her first thought instead of criticism. Penelope resisted this. Competing at the highest levels of tennis required stringent levels of self-discipline. She feared having compassion off the court would bleed onto the court.

But if she could forgive Micah, shouldn't she be able to forgive herself? The question made her head spin.

"How's the training going?" Micah asked. "Ready to turn pro yet?"

"I'm playing more tournaments." Truthfully, it was harder than she imagined. Being away from Mom and Ollie. Watching her ranking make a slow climb. Figuring out how to learn from the losses and not get down. "I'll have to see what the next year holds. Whether I keep progressing." She shrugged. "I'm surprised Uncle Austin hasn't told you."

"Nah, he won't talk about you. If I ask, he just gives me a look. Like death on wheels."

The thought lit her up inside, knowing that Uncle Austin had her back, not only on the court, but also with Micah. He would always be there for her, regardless of how much time he spent with Zoe and Micah, becoming part of their family.

"Is it strange, having him date your mom?" Penelope asked.

Micah laughed. "No stranger than anything else this past year." His voice got quieter. "She's real happy, though. So, that's good."

Silence fell between them, awkward where it once would've passed without thought. She forced herself to breathe, in and out, organize her thoughts. She didn't want emotion or nerves rushing this. Suzanne told Penelope to be clear about what she needed from the conversation. "Why did you do it?" she asked.

He looked across the park, toward a footbridge with a stream running beneath. A couple walked over it, wearing winter jackets and ski hats. "I thought we were in love. That we both wanted it. It felt natural—to me."

She gripped the metal chains of the swing. "Love is what made everything so difficult to understand. I loved you and you hurt me. I trusted you—"

"I never meant—"

"You didn't even look at me," she said, twisting the swing to face him. "I was screaming inside, watching you, unable to move. Speak. You never opened your eyes. Not once. I felt like I was nothing. That I could've been anyone to you. So, no. I'm sorry. But no." Her voice was firm. The one Suzanne had her practice when setting boundaries. "You talk about love, but none of it felt like love to me."

He looked stunned, and she felt a desire to apologize for coming at him so hard. She squeezed her eyes shut, not wanting to see his sadness. She didn't come here to apologize.

"I know that now," he eventually said.

"What? What do you know?"

"That you not wanting to have sex isn't a sign that you didn't love me. That you weren't rejecting me, you were rejecting the act. That I should've accepted your limits, not pressured you." He ran a hand over his face. The words sounded textbook, but his angst was palpable. "You're so strong, P. It never occurred to me that you could be scared. Least of all, scared of me."

She laughed, finding the statement absurd. "I was scared of everything with you. Every day, I had to convince myself that even if you destroyed my heart, I'd be okay." She watched the sun plummet over the horizon, leaving them in the dusky, purple light. She didn't feel scared now. It was never that type of fear with Micah. "I knew I'd end up heartbroken, but I never imagined it would happen like that."

"You could've told me."

"I should've told you a lot of things. I hate thinking about that girl, how..." Penelope rolled her eyes, refusing to censor herself. "Thinking about how stupid she was. Naïve. Weak. Worried that if I told you to leave, pushed you away, called you on your shit, that you'd end it. I was so stupid. We were *both* stupid."

Her legs were bouncing as if she was on a stair stepper, nervous energy fizzing, needing a release. Micah reached out a hand, but snatched it back when his fingers were inches away from her thigh. She felt the phantom heat of his skin. Why did part of her still crave his touch?

"I do miss you," she said. Immediately, she wished she could snatch the words back. But that was her insecurities talking. She should be able to state her truth, how she felt, without needing his approval, needing anything, in return. In theory, of course. Suzanne's theory. Penelope's emotions didn't follow such a straight trajectory.

Slowly, he turned and looked at her. "I miss you too."

"But I can't, we can't be—it's too late." The thought of touching a boy, kissing, *more*, filled her with intense nausea. Would that change? Time would tell. If she never had a boyfriend again, so be it. As long as she had tennis, she'd be okay. "Maybe one day, maybe we could be friends, but right now..."

"I understand."

She stood and left, taking control, ending the conversation on her terms. Mental toughness wasn't about making herself untouchable, siphoning off all emotion, not needing anyone, but rather knowing how much she could handle, what answers would help her move forward, meeting that point, and then stopping. She got what she wanted. An answer. An audience. The truth.

For today, that was enough.

CPSIA information can be obtained
at www.ICGtesting.com
Printed in the USA
LVHW102137091122
732799LV00024B/732

9 781952 439445